INTERPLANETARY EDITION

BY EMILY MARTHA SORENSEN

LEGACY OF THE CORRIDOR

INTERPLANETARY EDITION

AND OTHER TALES OF TOMORROW

EMILY MARTHA SORENSEN

EDITED BY
JOE MONSON

HEMELEIN PUBLICATIONS

Interplanetary Edition and Other Tales of Tomorrow

Legacy of the Corridor, volume 7.

Cover artist: grandfailure (Tithi Luadthong). Used under license.
Cover and interior layout and design: Joe Monson

Stylized circuit background by vladystock. Used under license.
Rocket ornamental break icon by Fabián Alexis and used under CC-by-SA 3.0 Unported. Rocket removed from background and overlaid with black.
See commons.wikimedia.org/wiki/File:Antu_vstudio.svg

Edited by Joe Monson

Managing Editor: Joe Monson
Publisher: Heather B. Monson
Published by Hemelein Publications, LLC.
http://hemelein.com/

First Edition
First Hemelein printing, December 2022
10 9 8 7 6 5 4 3 2 1

ISBN:
978-1-64278-031-4 (trade paperback)
978-1-64278-032-1 (ebook)

Library of Congress Control Number: 2022946869

To Ben:
The best husband ever. And a half!

TABLE OF CONTENTS

LEGACY OF THE CORRIDOR

Way back in 1994, M. Shayne Bell put together *Washed by a Wave of Wind*, an anthology of short works by authors from "The Corridor", an area that covers Utah, most of Idaho, parts of Wyoming and Nevada, and stretches into Arizona and parts of northern Mexico. Sometimes, the area around Cardston, Alberta, Canada, is included, too. For those unfamiliar with this area, it was settled by Mormon pioneers, members of the Church of Jesus Christ of Latter-day Saints.

Shayne's anthology highlighted science fiction and fantasy works by authors from the area, as The Corridor contained an unusually high number of successful authors—for the population in the area—both genre and non-genre, both members and non-members of the predominant religion. That legacy continues today with an impressive list of authors such as:

Jennifer Adams • D. J. Butler
Orson Scott Card • Michael R. Collings
Michaelbrent Collings • Ally Condie
Larry Correia • Kristyn Crow
James Dashner • Brian Lee Durfee
Sarah M. Eden • Richard Paul Evans
David Farland • Diana Gabaldon
Jessica Day George • Shannon Hale
Mettie Ivie Harrison • Tracy Hickman
Laura Hickman • Charlie N. Holmberg
Christopher Husberg • Raymond F. Jones
Matthew J. Kirby • Gama Ray Martinez
Brian McClellan • Stephenie Meyer
L. E. Modesitt, Jr. • Brandon Mull
Jennifer A. Nielsen • Wendy Nikel

James A. Owen • Ken Rand
Brandon Sanderson • Caitlin Sangster
J. Scott Savage • D. William Shunn
Jess Smart Smiley • Eric James Stone
May Swenson • Howard Tayler
Brad R. Torgersen • Nym Wales
Dan Wells • Robison Wells
David J. West • Carol Lynch Williams
Dan Willis • Julie Wright

That's a big list of names, and it only *barely* scratches the surface. Hemelein Publications created this publication series to highlight authors from The Corridor, both well-known and lesser-known. We think Shayne did a wonderful job drawing attention to these amazing writers back then, and we want to continue what he started.

You can learn more about the series at:

http://hemelein.com/go/legacy-of-the-corridor/

Joe Monson
Managing Editor
Hemelein Publications

DOKI DOKI, WAKU WAKU

JOE MONSON

This is the second collected works volume for Emily Martha Sorensen on which I've worked. The first was released a year ago: *Dragon Soup for the Soul,* the second volume in the Legacy of the Corridor publication series. At that point, I'd read a few of Emily's stories here and there (and even published a couple or three of them), but I hadn't read a lot of them. Now, I've got a much better grasp on how she approaches her stories. And I like it.

Sometimes, an author's stories are somewhat hit or miss when it comes to satisfying the reader. However, with Emily's stories, I find myself liking a lot more of them than not, and really enjoying a big percentage of them. There are a few reasons for that.

She includes a lot of humor in her stories. I love humorous stories, stories that make me chuckle or laugh out loud, even stories that make me think, "Heh." as I grin. Her stories cover a wide range of humor, too, from goofy situations to deadpan zingers, from wordplay to puns, humor abounds in her works. Emily is very talented in that area, and almost all of her stories have something funny going on in some way or another. It's as if she's a writer or something.

Even with all the humor, a number of her stories deal with real situations with which most people can identify, and they are dealt with in a way that doesn't leave you depressed at the end of the tale. Some of the topics are pretty heavy at times, but presented in a way to shows the seriousness and also lifts the considera-tion of those topics up into the light.

Emily make her characters believable. They tend to be everyday people with just a little (okay, sometimes a lot of) quirkiness that makes the story more fun to read. You'll find all sorts of different characters here, including dragon riders, couples trying to settle into an unexpected marriage while trying to raise their baby dragons, tiny aliens, interstellar traders, a weredodo, and more.

She also has a penchant for romance in many of her works, and who doesn't love a little *doki doki*[1] moment now and then? I know romance is not for everyone, but—when applied judiciously in a story—it can increase tension and give the protagonist a goal. At least for me, romance can be exciting and fun to read. Yes, I'm weird that way.

While this volume contains less romance than *Dragon Soup for the Soul*, there's still a little bit here and there. Just enough to add a little seasoning to the collection. You'll find three or four more examples of Emily's fun and interesting poetry. There's plenty of *waku waku*,[2] too!

This collection was great fun to put together, especially because I got to read a bunch more of Emily's stories. I hope you enjoy it as much as I did.

Joe Monson
Editor

---

1. "Doki doki" (どきどき or ドキドキ) is a Japanese word that roughly translates as the sound of a beating heart and is often used in a moment of romantic thrill or excitement. For example, that moment when you see your soulmate, causing your heart to skip a beat and your cheeks to flush. Or when your romantic interest does something that makes you fall in love with them all over again. You can learn more here: https://www.alexrockinjapanese.com/the-meaning-of-doki-doki-in-japanese-english-how-to-use/.
2. "Waku waku" (わくわく or ワクワク) is a Japanese word that roughly translates to an appearance or attitude of excitement or thrill. One of the most recent examples I can think of is the character Anya from the manga series *Spy Family*. Though it's played more for laughs than seriousness, she will often say "Waku waku" when she's excited about something. You should go read and/or watch that series. It's hilarious! You can learn more here: https://www.alexrockinjapanese.com/how-to-express-excitement-in-japanese-10-words-and-phrases/.

THE ONCE AND FUTURE
TIME TRAVELER

I've always been weird.

My childhood was spent in many different places: Virginia, Massachusetts, Sweden, Mexico, Georgia, New Hampshire, and Hong Kong. When I tell people that, they usually say, "Oh, was your dad in the military?" I usually respond, "No, we just liked to move."

And I did enjoy it. A new location was a new adventure, a fresh start with people I'd never met before. I'm an outgoing extravert, so I kept hoping that in the new place we were moving, I'd find a friend. Maybe I'd even be popular.

It kept not happening.

In Sweden and Mexico, I spoke only English. In Georgia, I was nastily bullied. In New Hampshire, I was told I was the second most unpopular girl in the school. Naturally, I asked who the first most unpopular girl in the school was, and promptly went to make friends with her. That sort of worked out, but we had little in common, so the friendship wasn't much more than theoretical.

Shortly after I turned eleven, my family moved to Hong Kong. There, I got the worst of all worlds. I was an American among British and Hong Kongese, I was a Christian among atheists, and I was a confident nerd among a bunch of conformists. When I did things like, oh, yell at the principal for showing pornographic material on campus and making it mandatory attendance, my peers despised me and hated me. I wasn't that fond of them, either.

My teachers mostly loved me. I always found it easy to make friends with adults. But you can't exactly hang out with your teachers. My only classmate friend was Cheng, probably the smartest boy in the school. He was awesome, but we didn't spend much time together, because he preferred to spend all his time studying.

So I spent most of my childhood very lonely. Fortunately, I had books.

Plots were the adventures I craved, themes the sources of pondering I grew from, characters the friends I needed. I picked up realistic fiction from American authors because I craved a connection to the home I missed. I picked up historical fiction to experience cultures that weren't mine. I picked up nonfiction because I enjoy learning. I ravenously devoured fantasy because, well, *duh*.

And then there was science fiction.

My dad often handed me a science fiction book he had just finished and told me to read it. His idea of "appropriate for an eight-year-old" tended to involve 450 pages of small print, with lots of scientific jargon. Hard to get through, and I whined at first. He was unsympathetic. Eventually, I noticed that high-level concepts that were mind-pretzely were fun.

It didn't take me long to figure out that a) my father didn't seem to notice when a book he handed me was full of swear words (Daaaaaad!), b) I love optimism, and c) time travel *totally rules*.

About a third of what I write these days is science fiction. The rest is fantasy, or falls somewhere in between. For this short story collection, I suggested it be themed around science fiction, plus a bit of urban fantasy and I-can't-really-pigeonhole-this. The rest is history.

Or perhaps it's the future.

I'm a time travel nerd, after all. Who even knows?

—Emily Martha Sorensen
December 2022

FUTURE COP

THERE WAS a flash of light in the middle of the quad, and two high-pitched alternating notes blared.

Startled, I looked up from my laptop, where I'd been trying to type the first draft of a paper that was due in two weeks.

Other college students milling around in the crowd were turning towards the source of the noise. Some looked nervous, some excited, some kind of annoyed.

"Don't be alarmed," an amplified voice said. It was calm and soothing. "I'm a Future Cop, and I'm here to distribute warning balls. Please stay where you are until you've received one. Do not leave the area. Leaving the area without receiving one will result in a fine from the police in your own time."

My heart raced in excitement. I'd never seen a Future Cop before. Not in person, anyway. Of course everybody saw them on TV and in movies, but that wasn't the same. I'd heard that college campuses got a lot of Future Cop visits because people in college had lives that were highly in flux, but wow. This was only my first semester. I hadn't expected to see one this soon.

"Do not open your warning ball in public," the Future Cop went on, his amplified voice carrying across murmurs of the crowd. "Do not ask to see what others have received. Do not show the contents of your warning ball to others."

Around me, people were nodding. I did, too. I knew that. Everyone knew that. Warning balls were private. Violating that was a major faux pas. You didn't walk around naked in public, and you didn't ask what somebody else had gotten as a warning from the future, either.

The Future Cop started at the center of the quad, distributing warning balls to the ones nearest him. The crowd started to thin a little as most of those who had received theirs left.

Nobody seemed to be walking onto the quad, which was odd. This was one of the busiest places on campus, a thoroughfare for quite a few buildings, and it was right around lunch.

"Why isn't anyone coming?" I said in a low voice to the girl next to me, who looked several years older and was finishing off a microwaved fettuccine alfredo frozen dinner with a plastic spork.

"Time bubble," she said, waving her finger around. "Everything's frozen outside us. Watch your phone when you walk out. You'll know you've crossed the edge because the time will change as it updates from the satellite."

"Wow," I whispered. That was pretty cool. I hadn't seen that detail in any of the police procedural shows I'd seen, not that I watched that many.

It took more than twenty minutes before the Future Cop headed in our direction, so I went back to my laptop, trying to write more of the rough draft of my paper. It was hard to organize my scattered thoughts, though. I felt nervous and jumpy. What if, what if, what if —?

No, no, no, no. I'd be fine. I wasn't the one he was here for. Surely not.

The Future Cop reached the girl standing next to me. She held out her hand, he read it with a portable scanner, and the light flicked from yellow to green as it registered her identity. Instantly, a white ball rolled out of the hole at the bottom, and he pulled it out and handed it to her.

No one knew how that technology worked, since time travel hadn't been invented yet, but I assumed that the scanner sent data to the future, where some team of analysts put together the appropriate ball and sent it down through a time-travely chute, where it appeared right where it belonged and rolled out.

The Future Cop turned to me. I held out my hand, and he scanned it. While he was doing that, I took the time to examine him closely.

He wore a mask, like all Future Cops did, to shield his identity and prevent unnecessary wrinkles in the timeline. It couldn't disguise the fact that he was gorgeous, though.

His eyes were dark brown, almost black, rimmed with long eyelashes. His black hair was pulled back in a short ponytail that curled just a bit, my favorite hairstyle on guys. His skin was light brown, and he had muscular arms. I *loved* muscular arms.

Of course he had a wedding ring, blast it all. The cute ones always did.

A white ball rolled out of the machine, and he handed it to me. For an instant, our eyes met.

His eyes widened.

I jolted in horror. If he'd recognized me, that meant ... that meant ...

No! I was the future victim!

I shoved my laptop in my backpack and fled the scene, running towards the library. I didn't look back to see if the scene behind me had vanished as I hit the flow of normal time. I was no longer fascinated. I was too terrified.

Future Cops didn't come back for minor infractions, such as getting your laptop stolen or cheating on a test. They only came back to prevent major crimes like felonies, rapes, or murders.

Something really, really bad was going to happen to me.

I was supposed to open my warning ball in private, so I should have headed to my dorm room or at least to a bathroom stall, but I could not, absolutely could not, handle being alone right now.

I flopped onto one of the couches in the study area of the library, unzipped my backpack to shield my hands from sight of the other students, and tremblingly fumbled around my warning ball from within the deep recesses of my backpack.

Inside would be a piece of paper with the exact time and date and place and perpetrator.

For a criminal, there would only be the crime and a list of all the legal consequences that were going to befall unless they changed their mind about committing it.

My fingernails found the groove down the middle, and I cracked the ball open.

It fell in two halves.

It was empty.

I wanted to scream in terror.

Where's my warning?! How am I supposed to stay safe?!

But then my pulse slowed.

Oh.

Oh.

Ohhhhh.

It was a false flag.

I wasn't the victim. I wasn't the criminal.

It was just a false flag.

Ninety-nine percent of all the warning balls a Future Cop handed out were false flags, meant to obscure the identity of whoever in the crowd the warning ball was actually meant for. It was a policy to protect privacy. I'd always thought it was wise.

I'd never realized how terrifying it would be to be given one.

I stared at the empty halves of my white ball numbly.

I wasn't the future victim?

I was ... all right?

"You okay?" the boy sitting on the other end of the couch asked, looking up from his laptop and over at me.

"Y-yes," I stammered. I couldn't talk about why I was freaked out. I pulled my hands out of my backpack and moved to zip it up.

"Oh!" His eyes widened, and he quickly looked away, flinching. "Sorry."

So he'd seen the halves of my warning ball.

I breathed in and out. I finished zipping up my backpack. I really wanted to talk to someone about it, anyway. "It's okay. It's just—I've never been given a warning ball before. It scared me."

"I hear ya," he said. "I felt the same way the first time I got one."

"Shhh!" a guy on the couch across from us said, glaring at us as he looked up from his laptop.

He had a point. We were in a library.

As if reading my mind, the boy closed his laptop and put it away in his backpack. He got up. Relieved, I got up too, and we walked out together.

As we exited the library, he told me, "I was really freaked out I was the criminal. I was like, 'What am I going to *do* in the future?!'"

"I wasn't at all scared that I was the criminal," I said as we headed onto the quad. I was relieved to see that the Future Cop was nowhere in sight, and the flow of students heading to and from classes and lunch was now moving like normal. "But I was totally convinced I was the victim."

"I worried about that the second time. But you get used to it eventually," he assured me. "I've been given four now. Actually, I was too weirded out about the fourth one to even think to worry."

"Weirded out?" I asked, looking over at him.

"Well ..." He shrugged, and he looked a bit sheepish. "I could be wrong, of course, but I *swear* the Future Cop who gave me the fourth one was me."

I stopped abruptly. I stared at him.

He had a really ugly haircut, and his clothes were stained. His arms were skinny. He wasn't especially cute, except for the eyes.

Dark brown, almost black. Long eyelashes. He had light brown skin, too.

"Did that Future Cop have a ponytail?" I asked slowly. "And muscular arms?"

"That's the one, yeah."

"He was *really* hot."

The guy stopped abruptly. A smile slid up his face. "Yeah?"

"Yeah."

"I'm Brad."

"I'm Kelly."

"Do you want to go out for pizza?"

"I'd love to."

As we walked, his fingers touched mine.

I felt a bit giddy. I wondered who exactly that Future Cop was married to.

Author Note

(Steeples fingers.) I told you I'm a time travel nerd.

Now, you may also be wondering: Worldbuilding-wise, what kind of time travel is this?

The answer is: it's a time loop, but not all the time travel in this universe loops. Future Cops really can, and do, prevent serious crimes. There are some serious crimes they won't try to prevent—anything that would cause a Future Cop to never exist, or cause time travel to have never been invented, or cause the Future Cop organization to have never been founded—but they do their best to prevent the rest. Usually they succeed. Sometimes they fail. Nobody gives them credit for their successes, and everybody blames them for their failures. It's a thankless job.

They're constantly told to avoid starting time loops, because those can cause major problems, but, well … accidents happen.

Good thing this one has happy results.

MISS GALAXY

I NEARLY STEPPED into an oozing puddle.

"Excuuuuse me!" the alien beauty queen said.

My face flushed. "Sorry."

"Now, we brought you here because of humans' reputation for unbearable ugliness," my guide said, speaking cheerfully as if my presence here were a great honor instead of an involuntary abduction. "That will make you impartial in judging our Miss Galaxy competition. Come in!"

I followed him into the giant space dome, trying to feel flattered. After all, I had been chosen above all the humans on Earth. But it was pretty hard.

After all, back home, *I* had been Miss Galaxy.

Author Note

When I was a kid, I drew a set of paper dolls featuring a bunch of alien beauty queens in their various contestant outfits. One of them was a puddle with a bunch of interchangeable hair bows. I think in very strange ways.

INVOICE

TO THE UNITED NATIONS:

We have received your payment for the oil received from planet Zybxx. It is insufficient. We asked for 850 human children, and you only included 809. Please make up this deficiency before we eat our dinner next week.

Yours cordially,
    The Zybxx Corporation

🚀

AUTHOR NOTE

Believe it or not, this started out life as a really long short story! It was very dull. I fixed it.

THE MOST IMPORTANT JOB ON THE SHIP

"SO, what are you going to do for your Test Day?" Dad asked, prodding the spout in the middle of the table. A large bubble of water floated up, and he caught it in his cup. It splashed a little as he placed it on the table beside him.

"It's a secret," I said, taking a bite of my noodles. They were made from textured algae, like most of our food on this ship. We mostly only carried things like meat and spices for the alien passengers. It was a drag.

"Come on," Dad prodded, twirling his noodles around his fork to keep the sauce from dripping. It, at least, was not made from algae. It was made from powdered cream mixed with water when needed. On most noodles, it tasted pretty good.

"Nope," I said. "I wouldn't tell you even if you were the captain."

"I'm sure the secrecy doesn't apply to parents," he wheedled.

I snorted. "I'm sure it does."

Dad pouted while he shoveled a mouthful of noodles into his mouth. I scratched my left foot, which itched. Sometimes I wished both my feet were prosthetics. I never had to worry about my right foot itching, for one thing.

The door to our quarters opened, and Mom walked in. She looked haggard and tired, pulling off both of her gloves of office without saying a word.

"Would you tell the *actual* captain?" Dad asked hopefully.

"Nope," I said. "Hey, Mom, you're late for dinner."

"Status reports," she said shortly. "So many status reports. Tomorrow I'm going to talk to the chief engineer about the meaning of *urgent*. Also, *delegating*."

Dad hid a smirk. The chief engineer was his boss, and he loved it when Mom griped about him. He and his boss had never gotten along. Then an exaggerated pout showed up on his face. "Astrid won't tell me what she's doing for her Test Day!"

"Good," Mom said. "She's not supposed to. If rumors went around before the requestee had a chance to say yes or no, it would pressure them to agree."

Dad scowled.

I stared at Mom, my heart hammering. Did that mean she hadn't read the message I had sent this morning? She might have mistaken it for a personal message and put it off till later ...

Mom removed her captain's gloves and rolled them up. She unzipped the top of her shirt and tucked them into a hidden pocket, then zipped it back up again and clicked the top closed with a miniature fingerprint lock. She tapped the deflated ball by her place at the table with her foot, and it immediately inflated so that she could sit on it.

Mom ripped open the insulated cube sitting at her place on the table, and she pulled out her plate full of food and accompanying silverware. The cubes were edible and flavorless, and were fortified with vitamins and nutrients just in case, but they had a woolly, offputting texture, so most people just sent them back to the kitchens to be recycled into new cubes. Basically, they were meant to serve as a backup source of food to stave off hunger in case of emergencies.

We sat there in silence, eating.

I was starting to feel antsy. I surreptitiously used my free hand to pull out one of the gloves from my pocket, and summoned the display under the table. I tapped to pull up my messages and re-sent the one from this morning, now marking it "urgent."

"Astrid, are you checking something?" Mom asked suspiciously. "I've told you, no gloves at the table. Dinnertime is for conversation, not texting with your friends —"

A terribly annoying beep came from her interior breast pocket.

Mom put a hand to her forehead, then unzipped the front of her shirt to retrieve the gloves.

"Hypocrite," Dad teased.

"There's no choice," Mom sighed. "Someone sent me a message marked as urgent."

I held my breath as Mom pulled up her gloves and tapped her finger in midair to pull up her message display. It was invisible to everybody but her. Generally you could see other people's displays, just reversed as if it were shown in a mirror, but the captain's messages were always privacy protected.

"WHAT?!" Mom shouted.

She'd gotten my message.

Mom looked up sharply. "Astrid, you must be kidding."

I straightened. "I'm not kidding. I have the right to request any job on the ship."

"And I have the right to refuse it."

"Hang on," Dad said, looking from one of us to the other. "Am I to understand you requested the *captain's* job for your Test Day?"

"Yes," I said.

"No," Mom shot back. "You didn't. We'll pretend this never happened, and you can ask somebody else instead."

"That's not how it works," I said, tightening my fist under the table. "I only get one request, and I've made it. If I pass, I'll be assigned your job once I've finished the minimum training."

"And if you *fail*," Mom said sharply, "you'll be assigned a generalist!"

I knew that. Did she think I didn't know that? On a ship of specialists, a generalist was considered the bottom of the heap.

In theory, a generalist could be the equal of any given specialist, and possibly several. But in practice, that wasn't how it worked. The only people who worked as generalists were failures. Nobody requested that job on purpose.

Generalists were necessary, as they could substitute for any job they had completed the minimum training for. If somebody got sick or needed a vacation and they had no trainee, a generalist would fill in. But most generalists never bothered to complete the minimum training for the more prestigious jobs, since the training requirements for any of those would take years, and there was almost always a trainee to take over anyway.

So yes, I was taking a terrible risk.

"Why wouldn't you ask me before making an official request?" Mom exploded. "That's the usual protocol! What were you *thinking?*"

"I was thinking that you wouldn't give me a chance unless I backed you into it!" I shot back.

"Hey, hey!" Dad held up his hands. "No need to fight. Just refuse the request. Then she won't have a chance to fail, and she'll be assigned to some other job."

Mom eyed me. "*Why* do you want my job?"

That really ought to be obvious. I was the most qualified preteen on our city-ship, and I knew it. "Because it's the most important job on the ship."

There was silence that stretched between us.

"I don't think you'll pass it," Mom said. "It would be better if I deny your request. You're good enough at most fields that you'll definitely be assigned a good job."

"I don't want you to deny the request," I said, setting my jaw. "I want the chance to prove myself."

"Even knowing the risks?" she asked.

"Even knowing the risks."

"Even though I'm almost certain it'll end in you being assigned a generalist?"

That hurt. Why did she have so little faith in me?

"Even knowing the risks," I repeated firmly.

Mom drummed the table with her fingertips. The table was inflatable, like all furniture on the ship, so it made dull thumping noises as she tapped the thick rubbery surface.

I looked her in the eyes. The waiting was driving me crazy, but I didn't want to look away, so I shifted my leg with the prosthetic up onto my lap and started squeezing the sides to eject it and then slip it back on again. Over and over again.

"Fine," she said at last, breaking eye contact and swiping her finger through her invisible display. "On your own head be it."

I burst out a loud cheer. I had my Test Day!

"But," Mom said sharply, "if you fail, I never want to hear you whine one second about being a generalist."

That was an easy condition to agree to. I had no intention of failing.

"No problem," I said confidently.

On the morning of my Test Day, I was awakened by a sharp series of knocks on my door.

I rubbed my eyes blearily. I'd been so keyed up last night, I'd had an impossible time falling asleep. Apparently I'd managed it eventually, though.

Then I noticed the time display on my ceiling.

Holy heck! I slept through my alarm!

I scrambled out of bed and hopped the two steps to the doorway, not even bothering to shove on my prosthetic or turn the lights on or deflate the bed. I slammed my hand on the panel beside the door.

The door slid open smoothly, vanishing into the wall.

"Good morning," Mom said, holding her pair of captain's gloves out to me. "These will be yours for the next twelve hours. I assume you've studied all the relevant features and necessities."

"Y-yes," I stammered, grabbing them.

She made no comment about my still-inflated bed or sleepwear. "You can, at any time, cancel the test and ask me to take over again. Doing so will constitute an automatic failure. That would be wise to do if you feel the ship is in danger, however. Do you understand?"

"Y-yes." I squeezed the gloves in my hands. I had no intention of failing and giving up halfway through. If the ship wound up being in danger, I would handle it on my own.

"Good," Mom said. "I'll leave you to it."

She turned and walked the five steps from my bedroom door to the entrance of our quarters, tapping the panel lightly to open the door and step out through it. It closed behind her.

Cursing myself for sleeping through the alarm today of all days, I slammed the panel to shut my door and hopped the two steps across the room. I put on my prosthetic, careful to avoid the spots where squeezing would cause it to automatically eject, and used my real foot to stomp on the button to deflate the bed.

Once the bed was shrunk down and the room had more space, I stuffed it into the corner it belonged in and turned to my closet.

"Closet" was probably too generous a word, given that it was a wall covered in flexible loops that had an article of clothing stuffed through each one. But it was the closest thing to a closet anybody on the ship had.

I yanked down half a red shirt, half a grey shirt, and three sections of pants—red, black, and grey. Everybody on the ship wore modular clothes; it was the best way to have variety when your maximum weight capacity for personal items was so small. Most people wore a lot more than three colors in a given outfit, but I was in a hurry, and I didn't have time to mix and match much smaller pieces. Besides, I figured particolor would look less authoritative than just a few colors, anyway.

I unhooked the sealant from its spot in the corner, and laid out the pieces of clothing in the pattern I wanted. I gave them a quick spray, and the sealant hardened quickly, gluing them together in a seamless, flexible design. One of the seams over the bottom third of my pant legs wound up slightly lopsided, and I was tempted to grab the seal-remover from the hook beside the sealant so I could try again, but that would take precious minutes, and I couldn't afford any unnecessary delays.

Your pants always look lopsided on the right side, anyway, I reminded myself, pulling the pants on. *Thanks to the prosthetic.*

The reason I wore a prosthetic was that my right leg ended at the knee. It wasn't an injury; it was a birth defect. Warp jumps had a one-in-one-thousand chance of causing birth defects in first trimester fetuses. I was one of the lucky few.

Dirtside passengers were required to do a routine pregnancy scan before they could board a starship, and by law they weren't allowed to board if pregnant unless they signed a dozen liability waivers. When you belonged to a cityship, though, there was little else you could do but accept the risks. That was why most prosthetic limbs belonged to cityship citizens.

I didn't mind. There were a hundred other people on board with similar problems, and at least I wasn't missing an arm. Really, the only reason it mattered was that I thought I looked weird in skirts, so I avoided them.

I pulled on my clothes and glanced at the ceiling again. Nearly five minutes had passed. I was going to have to run to reach the ship's core in time.

"Hi, Astrid!" Dad called as I ran down the hallway past him. He was unsealing a panel in the hallway that looked like somebody had knocked it askew. "Are you heading off to start your —"

"No time!" I shouted. His job as a maintenance engineer started two hours earlier than Mom's job as captain, which was presumably why he hadn't been home to wake me up. Mom had no doubt been happy to let me sleep in, wanting to see me fail. "I'll see you later!"

"See you!" he called back, waving.

I glanced at the ceiling in the corridor, and saw that I had only two minutes left to reach the core. I panicked and sprinted desperately.

The morning of my Test Day was off to a roaring start.

When I got to the core of the ship and held up my captain's gloves in front of the red glowing panel, I thought for the moment that the locked door wouldn't accept me. But then the panel turned green, and the door opened.

I stepped in, panting heavily. I felt a thrill of pride that I had been the one the door had let in, not Mom.

An unfriendly-looking Gotharn stood in the middle of the room with his arms folded. Since Gotharns looked kind of like *Tyrannosaurus rex,* down to the white feathers, the gesture looked absurd with his spindly little arms. It was a mannerism he had no doubt picked up from the other citizens, who were mostly human.

A rumbling growl came from his mouth. "You're late," the translation box at his throat informed me.

I shook my head and doubled over, panting. "Not late. Ran all the way here. I —"

Rigel was already growling again.

"The captain is supposed to arrive ten minutes early," the box at his throat said in its usual monotone.

I stood up, indignant. "Well, that's not in the manual!"

The Gotharn rumbled. The box said, "That should be obvious."

I clenched my fists. I *had* planned to arrive early—and I was pretty mad at myself for sleeping in—but the fact of the matter was, I hadn't been late, and I refused to let him accuse me of it when I had, in fact, met the minimum.

Of course, fighting with your assistant had to be a definite no, even though that wasn't in the manual. So I kept from retorting, barely.

"Let's get started," I said briskly. I unbunched the gloves and tucked my hands into them. They had been molded after Mom's hands, and so were slightly larger than mine. The fit wasn't so bad that I couldn't get used to it, though.

I pulled up the new display I had as captain, which presumably was what Mom looked at every single day. I stood there, savoring the moment.

The settings were turned to only being contacted in emergencies for everything, but I presumed that was because Mom hadn't been on duty before. I quickly changed the settings to maximum authorizations required for everything.

Then I tapped my prosthetic foot down on the switch near the center of the room, and the ball for sitting on inflated.

I took a seat and settled down to go to work.

Every time I got rid of one item on my to-do list, another five popped up to replace it. The proliferation of messages was even worse.

"Is it like this *every* day?" I asked in exasperation.

Rigel rumbled. "You might be requiring too many authorizations."

"No," I said, setting my jaw. "I'm the captain. I need to know everything that's going on in the ship."

The Gotharn growled. "No, you don't," his translation box said.

Ignoring his unhelpful advice, I opted to pick up the pace. A lot of the messages I was getting were duplicates, so I only needed to skim them, tap, skim, tap, skim, tap—oops, that one hadn't been a duplicate. What had I just approved?

"Can I take back an approval if I did it accidentally?" I asked nervously, finger hovering in midair.

"No," Rigel said.

"Who designed this system?" I exploded.

"People who didn't expect captains to turn on 'all approvals required,'" Rigel said unsubtly.

I was starting to hate these messages. It was amazing just how many were generating. It seemed like there were two or three more every second.

Maybe Rigel was right. I hated to admit it, but this was too many for anyone to get through, even me.

"Fine," I said, and went back to my settings. I turned down the approval requirements by one notch in all categories. Now they were at nine, instead of ten. "Is that better?"

He growled. His translation box said, in its usual monotone, "If by 'better,' you mean, 'I just turned the settings to "no authorizations required except for emergencies,"' then yes."

"Mom only had it that way because she was off duty," I said huffily.

He rumbled. "No, she always keeps it that way."

I was annoyed, but I followed his advice with poor grace. I turned off all authorization requirements except for emergencies. By the time I finished, the number of messages that had proliferated thanks to the previous settings had more than doubled, but at least that stemmed the tide for now.

"Why is that setting even there if the captain never uses it?" I complained.

"Because, every so often, there's a good reason to use it in select places," Rigel growled, folding his puny arms again. He somehow managed to convey incredulity at my idiocy, despite the fact that his growls were unintelligible and the translation box spoke in a monotone. "In extreme emergencies, or in the case of someone who's brand new to the job, the captain might need to approve every little thing."

Fine, fine. It made logical sense. Mom was always talking about the importance of delegating. And of course, that was because the captain had more important things to do than approving things. I'd known that. The captain saved the ship on a regular basis.

I flicked my way through the pile of messages, approving everything, even the ones I didn't understand. By the time I got through all the hundreds of them, I was getting a headache. I stood up, stretched, tapped my non-prosthetic foot against the floor because it had fallen asleep, and then sat down again. I checked my to-do list, which should have populated automatically, but it was empty.

"Hey, Rigel?" I asked.

"Hmm?" He was fully absorbed in his own display and ignoring me.

"Why is my to-do list empty?"

"Mmm."

Neither he nor his translation box were being very helpful.

"Wanna hear a joke?" I asked.

He rumbled something so quiet that the box at this throat didn't even bother to translate it. No doubt because the Gotharn had no sense of humor whatsoever. The cityship had a betting pool on who could make him laugh first. It had been going for ten years, ever since he'd moved on board, and nobody had won yet.

"Two Gotharns boarded a cityship," I said. "The first one said, 'I think the temperature control is broken.' The second one said, 'Why is that?' The first one said, 'Because it's so cold.' The second one said, 'It isn't cold—you're molting, stupid!'"

I waited. Rigel made no response.

"Hello?" I hinted. "Molting?"

No reaction.

"Wanna pay some modicum of attention to me?" I asked.

He growled something soft that the box translated as, "Nnnn." He still didn't look up from his display.

So I hopped off the ball and stepped on his tail.

He let out a loud roar of fury, looking up from his display with fully-bared teeth and glowing eyes. The translation box helpfully translated this: "Don't do that again."

"You're my assistant," I said. "Do your job. Assist me. What am I supposed to be doing?"

He growled, swishing his tail across the floor away from my reach. He went on growling and letting out quiet-but-threatening roars for awhile. The translation box waited patiently until he was finished, and then repeated what he'd said in an intelligible language for me.

"You are supposed to do what captains are always supposed to do. You are supposed to wait for emergencies. A good captain is not needed for day-to-day operations. A good captain trains everyone so well that the captain is superfluous ninety-nine percent of the time. That is what good leadership means."

I stared at him in horror. "You can't mean that I'm supposed to sit here and do *nothing!*"

He growled and waved his flimsy little arms, the ones that looked so weak, they were almost vestigial. "You can entertain yourself, if you wish. I'm in the middle of a novel."

I was absolutely appalled. Here were two of the most capable, educated people on the entire ship, qualified to do almost any job, and their jobs were to do *nothing?*

I'd seen Rigel personally attack space pirates. I'd seen Mom stay awake for four days straight to argue for the lives of two of our citizens who'd been accused of murder while they were on vacation on a hostile dirtside world. I'd seen both of them yell (or in Rigel's case, roar) at high-ranking people who had failed to do their jobs properly.

That was what they'd done when I could see them. I had assumed that was what their jobs were like all the time. But the times when I didn't see them, it was ... *this?*

It was this *boring?*

I sat there, feeling increasingly twitchy, as I flipped through training manuals. I checked the ship's systems every few minutes, reread every status report and authorization message I'd gotten while I'd required them, and carefully researched each one I hadn't understood. Nothing had gone awry. Nothing was amiss. I desperately wished something had, so that that I could fix it.

By the end of the day, I realized in horror, *I'll end up with nothing at all to prove that I can be a captain. I'm going to fail unless there's an emergency.*

This explained what Mom had meant when she'd thought I would fail. She'd figured this would happen. My blood boiled to think of it. She'd risked me being assigned a generalist just because she wanted her job security!

Well, I wasn't going to let her win. If an emergency wasn't forthcoming, I would *make* an emergency.

I summoned up one of the miniature repair robots, the kind that were meant to crawl through ducts to replace small parts or reweld microfractures, and I ordered it to drill through the outer hull in a place right near the second storage bay. The safety precautions came up, of course, but that was the nice thing about being the captain—I could override everything. I sent it to that spot, I rechecked the emergency protocols for that kind of problem, and then sat back to wait for the messages to pour in for emergency instructions.

They weren't long in coming.

Eight hours later, two hull breaches repaired, the rogue robot that had begun drilling a third hole captured, and the robot destroyed, my shift ended. I had been pacing and furiously barking orders for hours, and my throat was raw, and I was exhausted. In a good way, as I had accomplished something terribly important. I felt exhausted and satisfied.

I was concluding the last of my debriefs. An engineer was praising me for all my decisiveness and leadership, which was impressive given that it was my first day —

My display vanished.

"Hey!" I complained. "What happened?"

Rigel glanced over at me. He hadn't budged from his position all day. He had, apparently, been so engrossed in his novel that he had not considered it worth his time to offer his expertise. Or perhaps he'd just been waiting for me to ask for his aid. Well, it was just as well. I'd been enjoying the glory too much to want to share it.

"I was being complimented," I snapped. "By the chief engineer! He said I handled the situation admirably, with decisiveness and aplomb, especially given that it was my first day. Why did the display disappear?"

Rigel said nothing, but he made his display visible and had it show the time in large numbers.

Oh. My Test Day was over. The gloves were no longer responding to me.

"I guess my shift is done," I said with disappointment.

Rigel growled softly. "So it is," his box said.

"Are you going to leave, too?" I asked.

He rumbled for awhile. His box said, "No, I'm usually on duty during the hours your mother sleeps. I took a booster shot to stay awake through the hours I usually sleep so that I could be here to advise you on your Test Day."

Ouch. I almost felt bad that I'd ignored him so much. Still, his advice had been valuable near the beginning.

"Thank you," I said.

He growled softly. "You're welcome," the translation box said.

"Hey," I said brightly, "what do you get when you cross a Gotharn with a lightning bolt? Give up? It's fried chicken!"

Nothing.

"Fried chicken?" I said. "Get it? Because you kind of look like giant plucked chickens?"

He said nothing.

I sighed. It had been worth a try. I headed toward the door, and it opened to show Mom's angry face glaring at me.

Uh oh.

I moved to step out of the core, but instead, Mom stepped into it and held out her hand. I placed the gloves in it. The door swished shut behind her.

"Um, so how did I do?" I asked.

Mom glared at me.

My heart raced. "How did I do?" I repeated, in a rather higher-pitch.

She said nothing. She pulled on the gloves and pulled up her invisible display. She tapped through several things and nodded sharply, then twisted her wrists to make it disappear.

"I was on the team that caught the robot," she said. "I told them to hold off the investigation until tomorrow. Thankfully, they listened to me. What were you *thinking?*"

I swallowed. "I was just thinking that —"

"Oh, I know what you were thinking," Mom broke in. "You were thinking that you wanted to play the hero. Is that it?"

Feeling a little ashamed, I nodded.

Mom let out a long, explosive sigh. "Astrid, what were you *thinking?* You put every citizen on board in danger! You punched a hole in the helm!"

"Only a little one," I said.

"Two and a half," she snarled.

"The second and third weren't my idea!" I defended. "Those were the robot's! It must have gone off the rails after I altered its programming —"

"Which makes what you did even *worse!*" Mom shouted.

I gulped. Okay, yeah, she had a point.

"The funny thing is," Mom said in a tight voice, "if you had been willing to just sit there and wait patiently in case anyone needed you, you probably would have passed. You have the educational qualifications to handle emergencies, and goodness knows you have no problem giving orders. But I knew you didn't have the patience, the humility, or the discipline to wait until needed. You said the captain is the most important job on the ship, right?"

I nodded, feeling a huge lump in my throat. Was she saying I'd ... failed?

"Well, that's exactly the wrong attitude," Mom said. "A good captain trains everyone else so well that their job is the *least* important one on the ship."

The least important job on the ship ... I felt faint.

"Not only that," Mom said in a clipped voice, "a captain's job is not just to save the ship from emergencies. It's also to prevent emergencies from happening in the first place."

Which ... I can now see is a thing I may have slightly misunderstood. I swallowed.

Rigel rumbled and growled for awhile.

His box translated, "Overall, her temperament seems unsuitable to being a captain, and I agree that her manufacturing of an emergency was unwise in the extreme. Still, her potential is so high in most fields. It would be a shame to waste her as a generalist."

So Rigel knew all along that I'd manufactured that emergency? I wanted to die. No wonder he hadn't bothered to step in and help. He'd been politely allowing me to play the hero.

"I agree," Mom said in a clipped voice, "but this was the path she chose. I warned her of the risks. She chose to take them anyway. I'm not going to bend the rules for her. I don't believe in nepotism."

Tears stung at my eyes. So I'd failed. I had failed, hadn't I?

Come to think of it, Mom hadn't actually said it.

"Did I ... pass?" I ventured in a small voice.

"*No,* you didn't pass!" Mom roared. "I can't believe you even asked that! You failed!"

I shrank down into myself.

I'd failed. Me. I'd be a generalist. *Me!*

Suddenly, I was angry. I was so angry that I wanted to hurt somebody. I needed something to throw, but there was nothing on hand, so I reached down to squeeze the spots on my prosthetic and wrenched it off. I launched it through the air, and it thudded really loudly into the wall.

"Honestly —" Mom began indignantly.

Then it bounced and konked Rigel hard on the head.

Rigel let out blood-curdling roar unlike anything else I'd ever heard before. It went on forever and ever and ever, each scream more terrifying than the last.

"HA HA HA HA HA," the translation box at his throat informed us.

Wait.

"Were you *laughing?*" I burst out.

Rigel's tail swished back and forth. He growled with great dignity.

"Of course not. Don't be silly," his translation box said.

"You *were!*" I accused. "You were laughing!"

Rigel rumbled quickly. "I would never do any such thing."

Mom's lips trembled. She was looking amused.

Rigel growled. "I fail to see what's so funny," the translation box said.

I hopped over and held out my hand, mimicking his great dignity. "May I have my half-leg back, please?"

Mom burst out in a long snort of laughter.

With an air of feeling very put-upon, the Gotharn kicked my prosthetic half-leg over to me. I scooped it up from the floor and reattached it to my knee.

Mom and I caught each other's eye, and we burst out laughing, doubled over. It had been a long time since we'd laughed together. It felt like years.

"Go home," Mom said at last, sobering. "You'll start as a generalist tomorrow."

I nodded. There was no point in arguing. I had said I wouldn't complain, so now I had to live up to it.

I adjusted my prosthetic to fit comfortably, went to the door, walked out, and headed down the hallway.

The worst thing possible had happened. I was a generalist.

And yet, it didn't seem like a complete and total defeat. After all, I'd made a Gotharn laugh. A person who could do that could do anything.

Maybe they could even make an overqualified generalist the most important job on the ship.

AUTHOR NOTE

I may ever-so-slightly relate to overconfident, misunderstood child geniuses. When I was a kid, I had a crush on Wesley Crusher.

... What? He was *cute!* I think we would've been friends.

TIME SWITCH

"CORDIE! CORDIE!"

Saylie heard the voice behind her, but ignored it.

"Cordie!"

I'm home. Saylie's eyes ran hungrily over the highrises in her neighborhood. She'd woken up this morning, just as she had for the last three months in 1923 — and she was back.

Home. In 2083.

It didn't look the same as she remembered. Saylie sighed, rubbing her eyes. So three months had passed here, as well as back there. She might have figured. She'd thought, since the tri-vids always showed no time passing at all when you got back from time-travel, that she might get lucky ...

A hand grabbed her shoulder. Saylie screamed in surprise.

"Cordie, come on! Don't ignore me!"

Saylie whirled around. The girl staring at her was completely unfamiliar.

A horrible seed of doubt woke in her.

What did I change? she thought, frightened. *I thought I was careful. Did I mess something up? Did I change my own name?*

"Who's Cordie?" she blurted out.

Bafflement flashed across the girl's face. "You are. Cordelia Langley —"

The girl stopped and gasped.

"Oh, no! You're Saylie!"

"Who else would I be?" Saylie cried.

The girl smiled awkwardly. "Well, it's just ... I mean, I guess you've never met me ... I'm Karen ... see, I made friends with Cordie ..."

"Who's Cordie?" Saylie shouted.

"She was you!" the stranger said, looking hurt. "Weren't you her, I mean, didn't the two of you switch places? Isn't that how it works?"

"Apparently not," Saylie said flatly.

Karen stared at her. "But ... she was you ... and now you're right back in your body again ... I mean, you *did* go somewhere, didn't you?"

Saylie was silent.

Karen looked nervous. "Well, didn't you?!"

Saylie hesitated. "I —"

"You did!" Karen breathed out. "I knew it was a time switch!"

"I don't know what a 'time switch' is," Saylie said tightly, "but when I was stuck in the past, I wasn't 'Cordie.' I lived the life of a girl named Katherine."

Karen stared at her.

"In 1923," Saylie added.

Karen ran her hand through her hair, looking lost. "Cordie lived in 1763. England. Her parents had been considering moving out here before she left. She couldn't believe it when I told her about the revolution."

Saylie shook her head, feeling lost.

"Three was a legend in her family," Karen said tentatively. "The time switch, I mean. She told me about it. It's said some people in their family have the ability to use it once in their lives —"

"Three-way," Saylie murmured. "It must have been three-way at least. Somehow, someone messed things up, and made it three-way at least."

Karen shivered. "Then we have no idea who did it?"

"My money's on Cordie," Saylie muttered. "Since she knew so much about this in the first place."

"Or maybe some fourth person," Karen said glumly. "Who knows how many people got involved here?"

Cordelia woke slowly. Something felt wrong.

It was too quiet, she realized. Nothing was humming. No dream-recorder. No alarm clock. No visiphone.

Hope pounded in her heart. Was she — dare she hope — home?

Cordie sat up quickly, blinking in the dim light of sunrise. The furniture around her swam into view, familiar and comforting as ever.

Home again.

Except ...

What was this room? Had her family *moved* while she was gone?

What had Saylie *done* in her place?

Catherine flung the sheet off her bed and punched the air triumphantly.

1923. She was definitely back in 1923. But she was definitely *not* home.

The smell of pancakes, not soggy biscuits, floated up the stairs. Catherine sniffed appreciatively. Then she sank back into her bed, basking in the feeling of her total success.

Grandfather used to talk about the time switch when she was a child. After he died, she'd found his old diaries. Read about the way he'd done one himself. That was when she knew — she just *knew* — she'd be able to use one herself someday.

And speaking of journals ...

Catherine rooted through the nightstand by her bed and found a small hardback book. She ripped it open and flipped through the pages, hoping, hoping.

Yes! Her future descendent had written in it. Hints of the future to come, hints Catherine could keep. She clutched the journal, grinning like crazy. This would be the key to her wealth and happiness. This was why she'd twisted the time switch to make it three-way.

Only one chance in a lifetime, she thought dreamily, swinging her feet over the edge of her bed. *And I got the best of both worlds. Future knowledge, and changing my own family's past. Now Dad won't get shot by that stupid hunting rifle, and Mum won't go on and on about my taste for American music.*

Catherine giggled and put the journal away. She hopped to the door and peeked out.

Katherine's Room. Stay out, a sign on front said.

Catherine blinked at that.

I spell it with a K now?

Oh, well. She could always change it back.

After all, from now on, everything was going her way.

AUTHOR NOTE

This started out life as a novel I wrote when I was twelve. It had way too much historical fiction and not nearly enough time travel in it. So I fixed it.

INTERPLANETARY
EDITION

"TIME IS NOT A ONE-DIMENSIONAL OBJECT," the pucker-faced old lecturer droned. "It has three that we know of. When the right frequency is hit by the disruptor ..."

Kjino slumped against the walls of her cubbyhole, twisting her tail in circles. Her eggsister reeked of musty boredom.

"Why are they bothering to educate us?" an eggcousin beside them rumbled. He smelled acrid, like irritation. "It isn't like we're going to be experimenting."

Kjino's headcrest perked. Dull as the lectures were, she was excited for this journey. Imagine, traveling between the parallelities — to a universe where the *third* planet, not the ninth, had been the one to develop intelligence. The species developing this technology must be very clever. And they were going to put all sorts of people into a box and study them. She could hardly wait to be part of it.

"To be test subjects," Kjaila murmured, letting off the misty scent of yearning. "It's nearly as good as experimenting."

Kjino reached out her tail to clutch her eggsister's. She agreed. For a youngling, being tested upon was the greatest honor anyone could receive.

"I win again!" Aigiga crowed.

"I don't like this game," Jaya said stiffly, retrieving their spears. "The rules were not sufficiently clear. Only five hundred and sixty-eight —"

"Only three hundred are required for a casual game," Aigiga sniffed. "I understand the third-worlders believe in implied rather than stated rules, anyway."

Jaya ears tightened in fury. That rumor was false. It had to be. No civilized being would permit such vagary.

"A rematch is permitted, if mutually desired. Rule seventy-three." Aigiga drew his spear across the blades of his belly, sharpening it.

Jaya calculated quickly. The status cost of losing would be lower than the cost of refusal. He had to keep his status high to stay qualified for the third-worlders' competition.

He rubbed his claws against itchy palms. The spears were built to irritate one's hands, to build challenge in the competition. "I wish to add sixty-three more rules before we proceed."

"I wish to add fifty-three myself."

Aigiga and Jaya stood, muscles locked to show strength, as they hashed out the rules of their rematch. With luck, they would be ready to begin in four days.

"Third-worlders look tasty," Gyorrrran told the others, drooling. "Fifth-worlders, too."

"Ninth-planeters hatch from eggs," Ygrrrrgyrn murmured, tongues dribbling over his teeth. "Egggggsssss."

The others rumbled as they feasted on their latest carcass.

"Food from other universes," Rrrrgyrran rumbled, slashing his way through the half-fish that was his share of the trappings. "Taste different. New."

Gyorrrran's tongues snaked around and pulled out his favorite, rancid pieces. A social gathering meant feasting. He just hoped the third-worlders were tasty.

One master of the first world made a speech for his apprentice.

"Honor."

Eeeoooiiii bowed low. "They wish for honor."

"Bestow," his master corrected.

Eeeoooiiii became grave. It was a terrible affront to misunderstand one's master. "They wish to bestow honor on all that they have chosen."

"Best."

Eeeoooiiii's spine liquefied, his mouth bitter with humiliation. To force one's master to speak more than once ... and now *three* times ...

Perhaps he truly did deserve the exile of attending the third-worlders' ceremony.

"I am sorry, master," he shouted, displaying his shame. Only those with valuable words were permitted to whisper.

The master turned and moved slowly back into a rock face. The air shivered as he vanished.

Eeeoooiiii meditated in case his master chose to emerge again. Then he prepared to leave for the third-worlders' ceremony.

"Get that banner up high!" one of the judges bellowed. "They'll be here any minute!"

Assistants scrambled all around them, preparing for the aliens' needs. Off to one side were aquariums for seventh-worlders. To the front were breathing tubes for the first-worlders. Quartz sparkled on the banquet table for the second-worlders.

"I can't believe our research is being used for this," Elina, the biology consultant, muttered.

"It pays well," Darian shrugged. "Besides, the chance for me to practice sociology in front of a large audience ..."

"The aliens are coming!" someone called, pointing out the window. "They're leaving the Center of Parallelities!"

"Get that banner up there!" the director screamed. "Get those cameras rolling!"

High above them, the banner unrolled ...

Survivor: Interplanetary Edition!

"Ready?" the director shouted. "Set? And ... action!"

Author Note

This story has its roots in that same set of paper dolls I made when I was a kid. I came up with a lot of interesting and weird alien cultures. Why waste them on only one story?

ROBOT ROMANCE

My hoped-for date
Is not first-rate.
His voice is shrill.
His skin is chill.

I hear a bleep.
Is he that cheap?
Wait, is that glue?
That can't be true!

I've always thought
I really ought
To have a beau
Like me, you know.

But he won't do.
That's a loose screw!
I haven't prayed
For poorly made.

Although he's cute.
This won't compute.
I might be swayed ...
By an upgrade.

AUTHOR NOTE

I once went to a poetry slam and recited this poem. Nobody laughed. Everyone applauded all the free verse angst whines.

Everyone else is so weird.

TABULA RASA

I GASPED and my eyes flew open.

I was staring at a ceiling. White, white, white, white —

Panic gripped my heart. I was still in the snow! I was going to die! I was —

Wait. I wasn't cold. Why wasn't I cold?

I became aware of murmuring around me, then the sound of my mother crying.

I jerked up to a sitting position. Then I realized that I could, which meant I wasn't covered in snow anymore. That was good. That was very, very, very, very good. Except, where was I?

There was a bleeping monitor hooked up to me. A doctor in pale turquoise scrubs stood behind my parents, talking to them in an undertone.

Oh, a hospital room. Yeah, that makes sense. They saved me from the snow.

On the one hand, I was glad to be rescued. On the other hand, given that my dad was here, that meant he knew what I'd done, and he was going to kill me. We'd had a gigantic fight while up in the mountains for a ski trip, and I'd snuck out the front door after my parents were asleep to show them that I *could*, in fact, handle the expert trail if I really wanted to, and—

Snow snow snow snow ...

"Ally!" Mom cried, noticing that I'd sat up. "Are you all right?"

"I'm fine," I said, wiggling my fingers. It was weird. My hands looked smaller than I was used to. Mom looked a little taller than usual, too. And hey, what had happened to the scars I'd gotten when I'd decided to pet a stray cat when I was six?

"Have you forgotten anything?" Mom asked, gripping my hand. Her arm was shaking. "Do you know who I am?"

"Of course I know who you are. You're Mom."

Why was she looking at me like I was some kind of stranger? I'd had an accident. Now I was fine. No big deal. Frostbite didn't cause amnesia. Or did it? It wasn't like I knew.

Dad separated himself from the doctor. "You did a very, very stupid thing," he growled at me, his eyebrows tilted so heavily downward, it was like they were shovels trying to excavate the shadows under his eyes for gold.

Yeah, that was the Dad I knew. Always mad at me for something.

Okay, admittedly this time I deserved it.

"You're right. I was wrong," I said quickly. Agreeing with Dad was the fastest way to make him stop yelling at me.

But he didn't start yelling. He only stood there glowering at me, as if there were no further words.

Okay, *now* I was worried. Dad always had words.

"Ha ha," I laughed nervously, trying to make light of it. Everyone seemed way too solemn, but I was fine, wasn't I?

Was I? I pulled the blanket off my legs and quickly counted all my fingers and toes. All there. I was fine. Better than fine, actually. Even the bruise on my ankle from whacking myself with the ski pole yesterday was gone. Seriously, doctors were amazing.

"Ally," Mom said, and her voice cracked. "Ally, you almost died."

But I didn't, I thought impatiently, reaching out to tuck my chin-length hair behind my ear. But my hair didn't end at my chin. It fell past my shoulders.

I reached back slowly, and pulled a clump of hair from behind my back. It kept going and going and going. It had to be down to my waist, at least.

I stared at the extreme length in horror. *How long have I been asleep?!*

"We've had the booster seat installed in your car," the doctor said to my dad. "We just need your signatures on the release paperwork, and you're ready to go."

Booster seat? I was suddenly indignant. *What do you mean, booster seat? I'm thirteen years old!*

"Sure," Dad said, not looking at me. "But if there are any malfunctions, I assume we're still covered by the warranty?"

"Of course. If the memory chip proves defective, it can be replaced at any time, no questions asked. We'll keep the data on file for as long as you keep the insurance policy."

Memory chip? I had an unsettling feeling that something was wrong here. I looked at my hands. Still no scars from the cat.

Did that mean ...?

Did it ...?

No, of course it didn't. I didn't feel any different, right?

Right?

Mom and Dad do look taller than usual ... I thought uneasily.

Dad turned around and stared me straight in the eye. "According to the waiver we had to sign, tastes and preferences change," he said sharply. "Maybe that'll act as a reminder for you to be far less reckless. Our insurance policy only covers one at a time, so the next one's only just been started. If you do anything else stupid, you'll be stuck as a fetus. And I do *not* want to change diapers again, got it?"

My breath caught in my throat. I couldn't deny it any longer.

This wasn't a hospital. This was Tabula Rasa, the life insurance company.

I wasn't Ally. I was her clone.

🚀

"Let's get ice cream!" Mom said, making a sudden turn and pulling into the parking lot of my favorite ice cream parlor.

It was clear she was trying to break the stony silence and the tension that crackled between me and Dad.

Tucked behind a seat belt in the backseat, sitting on a pink plastic booster seat because I was now five years younger and back to being short for my age, I said nothing. Yeah, I loved ice cream, but there were some things french vanilla and graham crackers just couldn't fix.

"Sure," Dad said, pulling off his seat belt. He opened up the passenger side door and got out.

Still in a bad mood, I pulled off my seat belt, and tried to open my door. I tried, and tried. It was stuck.

"It's child-locked!" I cried, furious.

"Oh, sorry, sorry!" Mom hastened over to my door and opened it. "It's the car's automatic safety feature. It assumes anyone in a booster seat shouldn't be opening the door for themselves. I'll have to find where to disable it."

I glared at the car's steering wheel hatefully. I hated being short. Hated it, hated it. I'd finally gotten a growth spurt last year that had made me the same height as everybody else in my class. And now I was going to be shorter than all of them again? Life was so unfair!

I scowled all my way to the ice cream parlor. Why couldn't my dad have gotten the job with the clone insurance policy before I was born? Then I could have had a clone made from my cells while I was still in the womb, like rich people did!

It could be worse, I reminded myself. *Imagine if he hadn't had a clone policy. Plenty of people don't. Then I'd be dead for real.*

I shivered. Memory chips were expensive if you weren't paying monthly maintenance for a clone to put them in. Two-thirds of the people in the country weren't as lucky as I was.

Being short again wasn't too bad. It could've been worse. I could be dead.

Following my parents into the ice cream parlor, I told myself I should be cheerful. The room was filled with color, the freezer was well-stocked with lots of flavors, not that I ever ordered anything but vanilla, and the ceiling had glittery paper snowflakes dangling from it —

Snow! Snow snow snow snow snow!

I stopped abruptly, panic filling me.

"Come on, Ally," Mom said, beckoning me to the cash register. "What flavor do you want?"

"F-french vanilla," I stammered, forcing myself to move forward. "With graham cracker mix-ins."

I'm not in the snow anymore, remember? No blizzard is trying to kill me. Stupid! Stupid!

"Harry?" Mom called.

"I can't decide," he answered, staring at the freezer as he sucked on a sample spoon. "It's between almond cinnamon and cherry lime."

"Cherry lime is the most disgusting flavor ever invented by mankind," I informed him.

Dad smirked and glanced over at me. "Okay. Cherry lime it is."

"Ewww!"

He grinned.

Mom told the cashier our orders and paid.

I collected my vanilla ice cream with graham cracker crumbs and headed to a table. Normally I waited for whoever I was with to pick where we sat, because I had a hard time making up my mind when there were lots of options, but today, I dunno, I had no trouble deciding. The place by the window next to a huge framed poster of strawberry banana ice cream with mango and marshmallow mix-ins looked fine.

Mom sat beside me with her triple chocolate chunk ice cream with brownie mix-ins. Dad sat across from me with his repulsive cherry lime that had cashew chunks sprinkled on top.

I glanced down at my ice cream, had an instant panic attack at the sight of what looked like an awful lot like snow, squeezed my eyes shut, and shoved a spoonful into my mouth. Mmm, french vanilla with graham cracker mix-ins. It was the best thing anybody had ever invented. It was ambrosia. It was—it was —

—pretty boring, actually.

I opened my eyes, baffled. I stared down at the cup before me.

This made no sense. It tasted exactly the way I remembered, and I had always loved the flavor before. But somehow, now it just didn't seem too exciting. What had gone wrong?

Dad burst out laughing. "I told you, tastes and preferences change! Try some of my cherry lime." He held out a spoonful to me.

"Absolutely not," I said immediately.

He guffawed.

"Would you like to try some of mine?" Mom asked.

"Sure," I said desultorily. I'd never been a fan of chocolate, but if tastes and preferences changed —

Oh, my gosh, chocolate is amazing! My eyes widened. *How did I never notice this before?*

I handed Mom back her spoon, probably not managing to hide my drool.

She laughed. "Here, let's trade."

Yes, chocolate ice cream *definitely* made me feel better about this whole being-a-clone thing.

"Why do tastes and preferences change?" I asked with my mouth full of chocolate ice cream. "That seems weird. I have the same DNA and everything, don't I?"

"Technically it's not exactly the same," Mom said. "It was in the literature they gave us to read."

"And the waiver they made us sign," Dad snorted.

Mom nodded. "That, too. It's impossible to make a clone that has *exactly* the same DNA as the original. It's just very close."

I stared at her, baffled. "What do you mean, impossible? I learned about it in science class. They take a cell from the original, suck out all the DNA from a donor egg, put in the new DNA instead, and voila! New clone starts growing."

"Well, it's a little more complicated than that," Mom said. "But the main thing you're forgetting is random mutations."

I stared at her.

"Cellular mutations happen throughout your life," Mom said. "Normally they're unimportant unless a cell becomes a cancer cell, and then it's a big deal. Otherwise, you're probably not going to notice those mutations or care unless the mutation happens in an egg or sperm cell, in which case the random change might get passed to your offspring."

"Yeah, but ..." I said slowly, "... what does that have to do with cloning?"

"Random mutations happen in new embryos, too," Mom said. "And in that case, they'll affect the whole body, because the embryo is made up of so few cells to begin with."

"So you're saying I have superpowers?" I asked hopefully.

She laughed. "No. At least, I doubt it. But your face shape might be rounder. Or you might grow slightly taller. Or you might prefer chocolate ice cream to vanilla. Identical twins don't have exactly the same DNA either, for the same reason, you know. That's why it's common to see one twin have a birthmark that the other doesn't."

Wow. Mind blown.

"On top of that, apparently it's common for clones to absorb some DNA from a donor egg, despite the company's best efforts to prevent it," Mom said. "Not to mention that they develop in different in uterine environments, and environment can affect a lot. So clones are actually *less* similar to their originals than identical twins are to each other."

"But ..." I frowned. "But would that really change what things you like?"

"Why not?" Mom said. "It's a fact that it happens."

"Yeah, but, I mean ... nothing tastes *different* to me. I just ... feel differently about the things I'm tasting."

"In that case, try some of my cherry lime," Dad put in, holding out his spoon and grinning.

"No chance, Dad."

"Mmm, mmm, so good." He put some in his mouth and waved his eyebrows mischievously.

I turned back to Mom and ignored him. "So, do they have *proof* that it's DNA mutations that make tastes and preferences change?"

"Absolute, conclusive proof?" She shook her head. "They don't. That's pretty rare in science. But it's the most likely theory."

It didn't seem particularly likely to me. I had a hard time believing that a few tiny mutations could explain why I'd gone from liking vanilla to chocolate.

Maybe it was taste bud memory? Like muscle memory? Maybe this body had eaten way more chocolate than vanilla, and that was why I liked it so much more now?

"Do clones have muscle memory?" I asked aloud.

Mom hesitated. "I'm not sure."

"They do," Dad put in. "Tabula Rasa sells plans to athletes that include personal trainers for their clones. Not only do the clones need to have all the right muscles built in the right ways, they need to have the right movements locked into muscle memory for when the original transfers their memories over. You should see how much they charge for athlete plans, by the way. It's *expensive.*"

I had a vision of a bunch of zombie-like clones playing golf or doing high jumps. It was creepy.

"I'm glad *my* clone wasn't up and moving around," I said.

"It was," Mom said.

"It was?!" I yelped.

"Clones have to move around, Ally," Dad said, rolling his eyes. "Otherwise you'd get muscular atrophy. Chances are your new body will be stronger and have better endurance than your old one, in fact. By default, they keep clones to a rigid schedule and diet to promote health. They don't, say, allow the clones to sit and watch TV for four hours a day."

I ignored his dig at my couch potato habits. I did my homework while I was watching TV, thanks very much.

"B-b-but how is that possible?!" I sputtered. "I don't remember moving around other than—than being Ally!"

Had I taken over a wandering zombie? Creeeeeepy!

"Of course not," Dad said, snorting. "Clones aren't allowed to form memories. They're drugged to prevent it. They're not *people*, Ally. They're *potential* people. If their brains weren't carefully preserved as blank slates to prevent conflicting memories or neutral pruning, it wouldn't be possible to install an original's memories into them."

I looked down at my hands worriedly. Still smaller than before, still no scars on them. "*Can* clones form memories?" Was I going to forget this whole conversation?

"Of course they can," Dad said. "Just as soon as the drug's flushed out of their bodies. You'll be fine."

"Yeah, but ... I mean ..." I faltered, trying to phrase my worry. "Am I gonna forget all of this?"

"Don't worry," Mom said comfortingly, patting my hand. "Prolonged exposure doesn't cause any problematic effects. The drug's been around for fifty years. It's also used in psychiatry to help PTSD patients. And it's illegal for that drug to be used on people except with the consent of both a trained psychologist and a doctor, as well as it being specifically requested by the person it is being used on. It's out of your system now. It's fine."

I sat back, trying to feel comforted. But I didn't. This body had been moving around a few days ago, and I couldn't remember any of it. What if Ally's memories didn't make up who I was? What if this body was me? In that case, the fact that I didn't remember anything except for Ally's life was terrifying.

I looked down at my ice cream cup, now empty except for a thin veneer of chocolate soup at the bottom. I tilted the bowl and scraped my spoon around the edges to catch as much of the melted stuff as I could.

Chocolate. Mmmm, chocolate. It was weird that I liked chocolate so much.

Which brought me back to my question from earlier.

"So do I have taste bud memory?" I asked.

Mom stared at me oddly. "What is that?"

"Like muscle memory, except with taste buds." I licked the spoon to catch every drop of rich yumminess, then moved it back into the bowl to scrape for more leftovers. "Do I like chocolate because my clone remembers chocolate somehow?"

"Umm ..." Mom looked at Dad.

"Not likely," he said. "Clones don't eat chocolate."

I paused. "They what?"

"They don't eat chocolate," Dad repeated. "They're kept on a strictly healthy diet. No indulgences and no luxuries."

I was aghast. No chocolate, no vanilla, and tons of exercise? Clones' lives were *horrible!* It seemed I wasn't missing anything by not remembering any of it.

Except for maybe ...

... me?

What made a person who they were, anyway? Was it memories? Or was it the actual body they were in?

"Have two clones ever been implanted with the same memories?" I asked, swallowing. I was trying to figure this out.

"Not at the same time," Mom said. "It's illegal."

"It's illegal in *our* country," Dad retorted. "There are others that allow it."

"What happens when two clones are given the same memories at the same time, then?" I asked nervously. "Do they act in exactly the same way?"

If they did, then maybe all the differences between an original and a clone could be explained by the clone being forced to exercise and eat healthily. If they didn't, maybe it was the DNA changes.

"Hmm," Dad said. "Well, I can't speak for all cases, but I know of one that was in the news a few years ago. Upon his death, a South American dictator had his memories put into twenty-five different clones that were all the same age and raised in the same place. He believed that they would all cooperate, all being the same person. They didn't. Twenty-three of them squabbled over who should rule the country, plunging it into a massive civil war. One of them committed suicide a few days after waking. Another fled across the border and became a Catholic monk. Since the Catholic Church believes that clones are separate people from their originals, they were happy to accept him." He paused. "Odd story."

My heart was pounding. *So there are people who believe that clones are separate people from their originals?*

"Why does the Catholic Church believe that?" I whispered, having a feeling I knew the answer.

"*Souls,*" Dad said dismissively. "They think that every body has a separate one, and transferring memories from one to another doesn't change that. Don't worry about it, Ally."

Don't worry about it?! What if it's true?!

What if I had a separate soul from Ally?

What if that was what really made tastes and preferences change?

What if I had a *completely different natural personality?*

What would that mean? Would that mean I wasn't Mom and Dad's daughter? No ... because a parent could have more than one child, including more than one child with almost-the-same-DNA. If I wasn't Ally, I was Ally's sister. Would that mean that I shouldn't be taking over Ally's life? No ... because I had no life other than that, and Ally had basically given her permission for me to take it over by knowing that I existed and not objecting.

If I was a separate person, was it a bad thing that Ally's memories had been transferred to me? Well ... maybe. If I was a separate person, I was definitely unhappy that they hadn't let me form my own memories. But on the other hand, if the whole system of cloning hadn't existed, I would never have existed, either. And if they'd simply woken me up without Ally's memories, I'd have been earlier-than-a-newborn developmentally and in the body of an eight-year-old. That didn't seem very appealing.

No matter what, I was probably in the best place that I could be. So the only question was, was I Ally?

Maybe the answer would never matter to anybody but me. But it was crucially important to me.

Was I a continuation of Ally?

Or was I someone different who had just been born today?

I chewed on my plastic spoon, feeling it splinter under my teeth. How could I know? How could I know for certain if I was me or Ally?

Tastes and preferences change ...

Weren't tastes and preferences one of the important things that made up a personality?

Maybe if I started doing things that were totally different from what Ally would have done, that would prove that I was separate. Except, if I was looking for that as proof, I might start acting in ways that proved what I wanted to be true. And even if I acted in the same way she would have, that wouldn't prove that I *wasn't* separate.

And, come to think of it, even if I started acted differently, that wouldn't prove anything, either. There was a mean girl at school who had been really nice until her parents' divorce a few years ago. And I remembered freezing to death. That was way more traumatic than a divorce. An accident like that could easily change someone's personality.

I couldn't think of a single way to prove it to myself one way or another.

I stared at my chewed up, broken spoon, wishing it could tell me the truth in a way I could be totally confident in.

"Don't worry," Mom said, breaking into the silence, almost like she could read my mind. "You're still Ally."

"... What if I'm not?"

"You are," Dad said impatiently.

"But what if I have a soul?"

"Honestly, would that make any difference?" Dad said. "Legally, you're Ally. Memory-wise, you're Ally. Genetically, you're Ally."

"Not exactly the same," I reminded him.

"Mutations can happen throughout a person's life," he retorted. "You can stay in the same body and still not have exactly the same DNA from the start to the end."

"Technically, the likelihood of a given mutation affecting a person's entire body after the embryo state —" Mom began.

Dad waved her off. "Regardless. People *change* sometimes, Ally. In all sorts of ways. I'm not going to pretend this particular one isn't going to be a big change. You're going to feel different. That's a given when you're five years younger, and a given when all of your favorite foods and friends and movies are going to be different from what you're used to. But it doesn't mean that you're not the same person. It just means that the person you are isn't static. It will move throughout your life. Don't get too hung up on what labels you fit. Just worry about who you are right now."

I nodded slowly. That was exactly what I'd been thinking about the mean girl. I felt part of me relax inside at the thought of it. It was such a simple answer. Such an easy answer.

But it didn't feel *right*.

Dad collected our empty cups and stood up. Automatically, I stood up with him. I glanced out the window, and —

Snow! Snow, snow, snow, snow!

I screamed and lunged under the table, shoving chairs out of the way with loud scrapes and crashes as they fell to the floor.

"Ally?!" Mom asked, alarmed.

"*Snow!*" I shouted, pointing at the window above me. "*SNOW!*"

"It's all right," Mom said quickly, scrambling to get down and sit beside me. "We'll be with you. We just need to walk to the car together."

"Snooooooow ..." I moaned, on the verge of sobbing.

Ally had died in the snow, and I remembered it. Ally had died in the snow. *Ally had died in the snow!*

"Come on," Mom said, rubbing my back. "It's a very short walk. We just need to reach the car, and if it's still going when we get home, we'll park the car in the garage and go inside through the garage door. You just need to walk through a few flakes right now."

I nodded and squeezed my eyes shut and clung to her as she guided me through the freezing horror and into the car. I didn't even object when she buckled me into the horrible booster seat and patted my hair like I was a child.

"It'll be all right, Ally," she said. "It'll be all right."

I endured the ride home by keeping my eyes squeezed tight and trying not to think about the cold around me.

It'll be all right ... it'll be all right ... it'll be all right ... it'll be all right ... I repeated, like a mantra.

But underneath that, something else kept adding, *Ally died in the snow ... Ally died in the snow ... Ally died in the snow ...*

At last, I heard the garage door roll shut, and Mom said, "You can open your eyes, Ally."

I opened my eyes and breathed out a sigh of relief. I was in the familiar space of our messy garage, lit by a dim bulb in the ceiling, surrounded by boxes of junk and clutter and several old bicycles with rusty chains from when I was a kid that we had never gotten rid of.

Ally died in the snow, I thought, staring at the old bicycles.

Safe from the weather outside, I no longer felt such overwhelming horror, but the certainty was still there.

I'm not Ally because I can't be Ally. Ally is dead. I'm a different person. Nothing else makes sense.

Slowly, I undid my seat belt, and waited for Dad to unlock my stupid child-locked door.

"Dad?" I asked as it opened.

"Yeah?" he said.

"I'm not Ally."

"Yes, you are."

"No, I'm not. You said that people can change, right? And that I shouldn't be too hung up on labels?"

"That's correct," he said cautiously.

"Well, in that case," I said, "I want a different name."

Mom came to stand beside him. She watched silently as I waited for an answer, wedged into my stupid booster seat with my heart pounding.

"I suppose you can do that," Dad said at last. "What name do you want?"

Ally would have dithered between options, but I didn't.

"Renee. Ally's middle name."

"*Your* middle name," Dad corrected.

"No, my *first* name," I shot back. "I want it changed legally."

He gave me a flinty stare. I stared right back.

He let out a long sigh and moved his head to the side with an annoyed jerk. "Fine. It's not like it's unusual for clones to do things like that. At least you're not getting your belly button pierced or something."

It's not? I felt like laughing. "No, that sounds painful."

"It was," Mom said. "I did it when I was a teenager. It was the popular thing to do at the time."

I paused and stared at her. *And I'm the clone?*

I walked up the stairs and stopped at the doorway to Ally's room. Rather than entering with a crash and a bang, as Ally always had, I opened the door quietly and entered it reverently. Soon enough, this would be my own room. But right now, it was a monument to the dead.

I picked up the teddy bear hidden under her pillow that Ally would never, ever have admitted to anyone she still slept with.

"I'm sorry you lost your life, Ally," I whispered. "But thank you. Thank you for giving it to me."

AUTHOR NOTE

I figured it was about time someone wrote a story about clones with *accurate* science. Oh, and dealing with all the important personal and philosophical implications a system like this would cause.

STANDARDIZED TESTING

MISS HATKINSON WANDERED BETWEEN ROWS, avoided tripping on the dinosaur-centaur's tail, and nudged the cords of an air machine away from the walkway as she passed a methane-breathing squidlike student.

Two fuzzy aliens in the front row started giggling uncontrollably. Miss Hatkinson's eyes narrowed in suspicion.

She turned back to the air machine and searched the cords until she found the tiny box she was looking for.

"This is a brain-booster!" she scolded. "Do you think I don't know that your species performs better when you listen to ultrasonic frequencies? Cheating!"

Supervising standardized tests was a nightmare on this starbase.

AUTHOR NOTE

This was another one that started out life as a very long short story. It was boring. I fixed it.

SCHEDULE TMTR

(FORM 1040) PROFIT OR LOSS FROM TIME TRAVEL

Part I: Income

1. _____ Wages, salaries or tips.
2. _____ Gross receipts or sales from predicting random events (including lottery).
3. _____ Gross receipts or sales from disaster warnings.
4. _____ Income earned through stock market or interest.
5. _____ Income earned "inventing" future technology.
6. _____ Other income gained as the result of time travel.
7. _____ Add lines 1 through 6.

This is your **gross time travel income.**

Part II: Expenses

8. _____ Cost of time machine, rental fee, or upkeep.
9. _____ Time traveler's checks and money exchange.
10. _____ Approved anti-anachronistic clothing for visits.
11. _____ Time traveler's insurance.
12. _____ Taxes, bribes and licenses.
13. _____ Add lines 8 through 12.
14. _____ Subtract line 13 from line 7.

This is your **net time travel income.**

PART III: EXEMPTIONS

15. _____ Qualifying ancestors (see instructions).
16. _____ If you are your own grandparent or parent, count yourself twice.
17. _____ Sentient machines which require upkeep (see instructions).
18. _____ Add lines 15 through 17.
19. _____ Multiply line 18 by $11,332.
20. _____ Subtract line 19 from line 14.

These are your **total time travel exemptions.**

PART IV: FINES

21. _____ Persons informed of time travel in non-approved timelines (see instructions).
22. _____ Paradoxes created and left.
23. _____ Cumulative severity of paradoxes (see instructions).
24. _____ Multiply line 22 by line 23.
25. _____ Historical events altered and not fixed.
26. _____ Cumulative severity of alterations (see instructions).
27. _____ Multiply line 25 by line 26.
28. _____ Add lines 21, 24, and 27.

These are your **total time travel fines.**

PART V: CREDITS

29. _____ Tax paid paradoxically. Enter line 29.
30. _____ Tax paid by possible descendents.
31. _____ Probability of those existing (see instructions).
32. _____ Multiply line 30 by line 31.
33. _____ Tax paid by certain descendents.
34. _____ Paradoxes averted (see instructions).
35. _____ Cumulative severity of paradoxes averted (see instructions).
36. _____ Multiply line 34 by line 35.
37. _____ Add lines 29, 32, 33 and 36.

These are your **total time travel credits.**

Part VI: Tax

38. _____ **Taxable income.** Subtract line 20 from line 14.
39. _____ **Tax** (see intructions).
40. _____ Subtract line 37 from line 39.
41. _____ If not paid at time of infractions, multiply line 28 by 125%
(1.25).
43. _____ Add lines 37 and 38.

If amount on line 43 is negative, this is your **amount to be refunded.**

If amount on line 43 is positive, this is the **amount you owe.**

Sign Here

_____

Dates

_____

_____

_____

_____

_____

_____

_____

_____

☐ If more than eight dates, see instructions and check here.

AUTHOR NOTE

A tax form for time travelers!

I think this was just me being weird.

GLASS BEADS

THE FIRST EVIDENCE that aliens existed was a junk heap. A trashy old ship that was barely running, afloat, dead in space.

And it wandered aimlessly into our solar system.

We didn't realize, at first, that it was a trash heap. We went ballistic trying to contact it. When we discovered it seemed to be nothing but dead in space, we prepared a mission to visit it. For political reasons, I was selected as one of the first explorers, representative of the Native American Consensus that had taken over North America after the collapse of the United States economy.

The other team members on the ship were experts in engineering, programming, sociology, and linguistics. As a mere political inclusion, I was rather ostracized during our three-month journey. Nominally I was the leader, but in practice, I was treated with the cold politeness due to one of my rank who had not earned it through expertise.

I couldn't honestly say I blamed them. I didn't really feel I had the right to be part of this mission. I had protested the appointment for that reason, but been overriden.

All things considered, I was more than glad when we reached the derelict.

As we docked, the others' excitement was palpable. Anna Lewis, our programmer, actually licked her lips.

Since that made me nervous, I uneasily stepped to the side.

"What do you think we're going to find?" Don Sanchez, our sociologist, asked nervously. He twitched, one of the many nervous tics he had acquired during this journey. "Do you think we're going to find anything worth salvaging? Do you think we're going to find frozen corpses, or real, life frozen crewmembers? Do you think —"

"I think we're going to find whatever we're going to find," Chinue Ndiaye, our linguist, said coolly. She was cold and rational, and her dislike of Don was exceeded only by her disdain for me.

"I just hope we'll be able to salvage something," Garth O'Harris, our engineer, muttered.

"You *would* hope that, wouldn't you?" Anna snapped. "All you ever think about is what you want. You, you, you. Never mind that all the rest of us are after knowledge."

Oh, boy. I stepped forward to stop them. Despite my best efforts and advice, the two of them had embarked on a passionate romance a month after we'd left Earth. The fiery breakup two weeks later had caused more problems than I could count since then. I had hoped the two were getting along again ... but ...

"Knowledge, my foot," Garth sneered, ignoring my attempt to step between them. "We all know tech is the real reason we're here. We might *want* to talk to aliens, but we *need* an FTL drive."

Garth wasn't wrong, but that didn't stop Chinue and Don from bristling.

"Learning how to construct a hyperspace drive is just another form of knowledge," I said in my best pacifist voice. "In any case, we're here as a team. We don't have separate agendas. Right?"

None of them quite met my eye as they all muttered their separate agreements.

Internally, I sighed.

This was the problem with having a representative from each of the five Earth governments on board. On paper, it looked like the best way to keep all the governments happy. In reality, we were not the cohesive team we were meant to be.

"Let's send in the bots," I said. "They'll check for any traps or active security that might pose danger to us, then we can study the footage, see if we can glean whatever we need without going in there in person —"

"Jono, we know the plan," Chinue said coldly. "We're not fools."

Except for you, her tone seemed to imply.

For the millionth time on this journey, I wanted to snap that I hadn't asked to be the elected leader on board, that I'd been entered on the ballot without my consent, and that I'd tried to get out of it. But now was not the time, and it was doubtful that my saying such things would change their opinion of me.

Several weeks of careful study passed before Garth came to dinner one night and announced that there was nothing more he could study from a distance, and that he wanted to be the first to enter the alien ship himself tomorrow.

Anna, predictably, disagreed vehemently. "I haven't even deciphered half of their machine language yet, and I'm not even certain it *does* use trinary. You could easily walk into a death trap, and I'd have no way to disarm it remotely."

Garth was not swayed. "We're heading back to Earth in eight days, and we haven't got the fuel to tow the whole thing with us. I've got to figure out what parts we want to take back."

"That's why we have *bots!*" Anna snapped.

Garth shook his head. "Those things are just too clumsy. They weren't designed to undo those weird bolts the aliens used. Some of the stuff they've brought me has wound up scratched or mangled. I'm not gonna trust them with something as important and potentially fiddly as the hyperspace drive."

"I want to go, too," Chinue spoke up.

I blinked and stared at her in surprise.

"What could you want to do there?" Garth scoffed. "You can do your language-deciphering just fine from the video feeds."

"Sometimes it helps to be physically present," Chinue said coolly. "It helps one gain a better understanding of cultural context."

"In that case, I should go, too," Don said quickly, snatching up food packet that Chinue was reaching for. She gave him a look of disgust. He ripped his open, his head twitching to the side slightly in one of his many tics, and said, "Culture is exactly what I'm here to study."

Oh, great. It dawned on me what was actually going on here. None of them wanted the member of another nation to be the first on board the ship.

Anna caught on a split second after I did.

"I'll go, too. It might be useful to me for the same reasons."

"How?" Don scoffed. His fingers jerked side to side. "You're a programmer. Their code is all the context you need."

"Not true," Anna retorted. "Examining more of their hardware might give me more useful information about how they arrange their bits. And there's such a thing as social engineering. Perhaps someone left the equivalent of a password written down somewhere that wasn't covered in a video feed."

"Hang on," I said, holding up my hand. "We shouldn't all go at once. Let's try it one at a time. We can draw lots to see who goes first, if necessary."

All four of them stared at me with contempt.

"Then you stay behind, Jono," Chinue said disdainfully.

Given that I would have nothing useful to do on board, and the risks were certainly non-zero, that was exactly what I'd planned on doing. But seeing those four sets of eyes staring at me, I had the crushing realization that I couldn't afford to do that.

If my four supposed allies discovered anything Earth-changing on that ship, they might very well cut me out of it. And if the Native American Consensus got cut out of a possible technological revolution, my bosses' reaction would not be pretty.

Not to mention the voters. I might not like this job, but I really wanted the chance to run for an office I *did* want in the future.

And so, unfortunately, unwise as it might be for all of us to go in at once, if the others were insisting on it, I couldn't afford to be left behind.

"Well, then we'll all go in together," I said calmly.

I kept my voice completely level, even though I really wanted to snap at them all to please, for once, just think like a team.

At first, everything seemed exactly as expected from the bots' video feeds. We proceeded with caution, one at a time, drawing straws at every turn to see who walked in front. That person would take the greatest risk and also potentially have a slight advantage in seeing interesting things before everyone else.

Ten straw-drawing rotations later, we'd had no surprises.

"Bots got all the traps, I think," Anna said.

"Bots didn't find any traps," Garth returned.

"None at all?" Anna looked troubled. "You'd think there'd be some kind of security."

"Must be a very trusting species," Chinue opined.

"Or this whole place is a trap," Don muttered.

I didn't add my opinion, but I was more than glad when Garth drew the short straw next.

We reached the back of the ship, where the hyperspace drive was waiting, without incident. Garth got down on his hands and knees and opened a bag slung across his shoulder full of twisting and prying tools. Nobody interfered, or even spoke. We all just stood there and watched as he screwed, pried, chipped, and finally wrenched the first bolt loose.

The ship around us shook, and we tumbled sideways or grabbed walls for support.

An unfamiliar, gruff, robotic voice spoke out of thin air:

"THIS IS OUR SHIP."

There was a sharp intake of breath from Anna, and Don's eyes widened. Chinue got up from the floor, expressionless as she stood.

"I'm pleased to meet you," she said. "It seems you speak English."

There was a slight rattling, and the voice said:

"YES. DO YOU WANT THIS SHIP?"

Straight to the point, I realized. I opened my mouth to answer.

"Why are you asking?" Chinue said.

That was exactly what I'd been about to say, so I shut my mouth and let her handle it. Officially, she was supposed to be in charge of any communication with aliens if the opportunity happened. Granted, this was because the assumption had been that we'd have to figure out their language and she'd be the most skilled at it.

"IF YOU WANT THIS SHIP, WE ARE WILLING TO NEGOTIATE."

I let out a low whistle. Garth crouched in place, his hands frozen as he waited.

Chinue thought for a moment. Then she said carefully, "We want ownership of this ship, all parts of it we have brought on board our own vessel, all the records we have made about it, and the right to use this ship or any knowledge that we might gain from it in any way we wish."

"AGREED," the voice said with no hesitance. "AND WE WILL HAVE JUPITER."

Chinue looked taken aback. "Jupiter?" she repeated. "You mean the gas giant in our solar system?"

"YES. YOU WILL HAVE THE SHIP, AND WE WILL HAVE JUPITER."

"Very we—" Chinue started to say.

"Are you crazy?!" I broke in. "Excuse me, alien race, whoever we're speaking with, the person you have been talking to does not have the authority to speak for our species in this matter. It must be brought before the Earth governments, and the leaders of our species will make the negotiations."

There was silent for a long moment.

"YOU HAVE ALREADY TAKEN PARTS OF OUR SHIP. YOU HAVE RECORDS. IF WE CANNOT MAKE A DEAL, THOSE PIECES MUST BE RETURNED, AND THOSE RECORDS MUST BE DESTROYED."

I swallowed. It would be awful to go home empty-handed, but far better that than to make a rash deal that our species might regret later. "We would be willing to surrender those records to you —"

"SOME OF THOSE RECORDS ARE IN YOUR BRAINS. IF WE CANNOT MAKE A DEAL, YOU MUST ALSO BE DESTROYED."

A chill shot down my spine.

"Jono," Chinue whispered to me, "I'm not an idiot. I know what they want is probably worth more than what we'll get. But think about our differences in technology. They could just exterminate our whole species and take what they want anyway."

"We're not planning to use Jupiter for anything," Anna said, her voice shaking slightly. "Let them have it."

"We're not in a good negotiating position," Don agreed.

"Two words," I told them. "*Glass beads.*"

Chinue stared at me in incomprehension, but behind her, I saw understanding dawn in Don's eyes.

"We need the hyperspace drive," Garth insisted.

"We need a *working* hyperspace drive," I returned. "Aliens: we would be willing to sell you the planet Jupiter in exchange for a working hyperspace drive, full instructions on how to use it, a working ship to use it on, and the right to build more."

There was silence for a very long moment.

"NO DEAL."

Anna's arms tensed. Garth looked like he wanted to scream at me. Chinue's icy glare seemed to have come from the depths of the Arctic.

"Isle of Manhattan?" Don asked me, stepping forward.

I nodded.

"Would you please explain what you mean?" Anna snapped.

"Later," I said. Explaining it here right in front of our audience seemed most unwise.

"Aliens," Don said, raising his voice. "We will agree to *lease* you the planet of Jupiter for one year, with a clause for that lease to be renewed by Earth's governments under whatever terms you and they mutually agree on. In exchange, whatever knowledge we have gained from this ship will be ours to keep. We will return any pieces of the ship that we have removed, and we will not take anything further from it."

There was silence for a long time. A very, very long time.

"AGREED," the voice said.

I breathed out a deep breath I hadn't realized I'd been holding. I felt rather faint.

"But —" Garth objected, looking at the hyperspace drive he'd been trying to get at.

"We leave now," I said, my voice sharp with authority. "We leave with our lives. We leave our governments in the best negotiating position possible."

"But we need —"

"*NOW!*" I roared.

For the first time since leaving Earth, all four of my team members listened to me.

We beat a hasty retreat.

"So what were you talking about?" Anna asked twelve hours later. We were all seated around the table. "What did glass have to do with it?"

We had sent our bots to return everything we had removed from the other ship and taken off to return to Earth as quickly as possible. It was only now, with the ship at least eight hours behind us, that I no longer felt jumpy fearing that the aliens were listening in on every word we might say.

I took a deep breath. I looked over at Don. "Do you want to explain?"

He shrugged. "It probably hits closer to home for you. You explain."

I took a deep breath. "There's a story that the Isle of Manhattan was bought from the Native American tribe who owned it for a handful of glass beads. It's not historically accurate, but it's not all that far off, either. The term is often used in bureaucratic circles in the Native American Consensus as shorthand for, 'Make sure you understand the value of what you're trading away.'"

There was silence around the table.

"You think Jupiter's that valuable?" Anna asked.

"An entire planet?" I asked. "Undoubtedly."

"But we don't have any plans to use it," Garth said. "And we need a hyperspace drive!"

"It wasn't a real hyperspace drive," I said, shaking my head. "Think about it. The aliens waited as long as possible to contact us. That was smart, because it strengthened their negotiating position. The more we learned, the more excuse they had to threaten to kill us if we didn't give them what they wanted. And the more we learned, the more we'd want the technological goodies they were offering. The longer they waited, the better their advantage, in other words."

"But they rushed to contact us as soon as they saw we were about to open up the hyperspace drive," Chinue said slowly.

"Which was the one thing we wanted most of all," I said, nodding. "Why would they do that? Their position would've been better if we'd studied it enough to know how desperately we wanted to keep it. Unless ..."

Garth banged the table with both fists and put his head in his hands.

"So Don was right," Anna said. "The whole place was a trap."

"Yes," I nodded. "Just not quite the kind we expected. It was a trap to get us to sign a bad deal."

Chinue breathed out. "You realize that humanity is still not in a good negotiating position. The governments on Earth might not be able to do any better than we did."

"You're right," I conceded. "But at least the experts will have the chance to try."

And if they decide I'm the right man for the job, I promised myself silently, *this time I'll retire.*

Author Note

It seems to me that government militaries aren't the only way to conquer people. Corporate threats do just fine.

LITTLE HOUSE IN THE CRATER

THEIR FACES WERE scrawny and pink and terrible. Their two eyes glittered. High on their heads where antennae should be, the wild humans had coarse fur.

When Laura peeked out from behind the mound, both humans were looking straight at her. Her thorax and wings trembled with fear. Two dingy-grey eyes stared down into her compound ones. The human did not move, not one of its arm segments moved. Only its eyes glinted at her. She didn't even breathe.

She heard the humans squat down by the food-pit. She heard Ma turn off the barrier. After a while she heard them eating. The humans ate all of the carrion that Ma had brought in. They ate every morsel of it. When every scrap was gone, the humans rose up. The smell was atrocious. One of them made harsh sounds in its throat. Ma looked at it with trembling eyes; she did not say anything. The humans turned and walked back through the tunnel entrance.

Ma let out a thin, keening sigh. She brushed Laura's arm in comfort as they watched the humans going away, out of the tunnel entrance.

"Never mind," Pa said. "The main thing is to be on good terms with the natives. We'll finish the extermination once we're done terraforming Earth."

AUTHOR NOTE

My grandma told me to write something more like *Little House on the Prairie*.

I wrote something more like *Little House on the Prairie*. I don't think this was what she had in mind.

THE REASON
WHY MY PAPER IS LATE

IT WAS all because of the alien abduction.

You know how it is—I was typing on my computer, and that box came up that said: *Congratulations! You have been randomly chosen for the honor of an alien abduction! Click the "okay" button if this is acceptable to you.*

So I clicked the "okay" button, and then I was gone for a week. I don't remember anything that happened, but I have a few new scars, which is cool. Unfortunately, I think the teleporter glitched, because my paper got deleted.

Anyway, can I have an extra week to finish it?

Teacher's response: Yes, but you are reminded that students are only allowed one abduction per semester. If abducted again, please contact your overlord to complain.

AUTHOR NOTE

In college, my roommate had to write a note to her professor explaining the reason why her paper was late.

I said, "Ooh! Ooh! Can I write it?"

She said, "Sure."

She really should have known better.

PLEASING THE JUDGES

I HADN'T SEEN my husband in days because he was so busy working on his submission to the annual Mad Science Fair, so I pulled on a bikini, donned my alligator armor, and dove into the moat to access his secret lair.

The alligators kept snapping at my heels while I keyed in the current passcode, so I kicked them each in the snout to keep them from following me and pulled open the doors. I slid through them, turned the wheel to shut the doors while water gushed in, and stripped off my armor while pumps shoved the water back into the moat.

"Maverick?" I called, tossing the armor on the floor and heading towards the giant open room he used for all his projects. There were dozens of finished things on display, all of them brilliant. None of them had ever won a competition, though. I didn't know why. "Where are you?"

"Bella!" His head popped up from behind a table that was strewn with projects. "I'm so glad you're here!"

"Oh, are you?" I asked, grinning. His hair was wildly messy, just the way I liked it.

"Yes! I can't decide what to use for the fair! Come help!" He raced over, grabbed my hand, and raced to the table with me in tow.

I would've preferred him to take a few seconds to stare at my body, but ... sure. Why not? I was fond his work.

"Are these the projects you're thinking of submitting?" I asked, looking them over.

"Yeah. I'm not sure which one will impress the judges most." He looked nervous. "I'm running out of money to keep buying materials. I need to get some prize money soon."

"What happens if you don't?" I asked.

"I don't know." He looked gloomy. "Take a job working for somebody else?"

Ugh. I wrinkled my nose. Maverick hated being told what to do. That was why he was a mad scientist. I understood because I hated being told what to do, too. "Well, why don't you tell me about these? We'll see what sounds most impressive to me."

"Okay," he said, pointing at the first one. "This is an orb that produces a field that puts children to sleep without affecting adults. I figure lots of parents would buy it, so it could make lots of money if I find a good patron to fund mass production. This is a jet pack that works on steam and solar power. It needs to recharge every hour, but it's reliable and doesn't roast the legs of the person wearing it. This is a teleportation coil that bypasses the usual safeguards, and auto-targets to keep its user away from walls. This is a mind-reading helmet with warning sensors to tell a supervillain wearer if they're about to start monologuing and should shut up ..."

He went through a dozen more inventions, all of them genius. It seemed to me that any of them deserved to win, but I'd thought that before, and it had never panned out. He'd never gotten higher than fifth place.

I supposed I didn't understand mad science enough to be a good judge of what was brilliant or not, but I'd worked for other mad scientists before meeting Maverick, and his work sure seemed a whole lot better than theirs.

"Well, what do you think?" he asked anxiously.

I was no judge of quality, so I had only one thought to offer. "Well, what won last year?"

"Huh?" He looked baffled.

"What won last year?" I repeated. "If that's the sort of thing the judges like, submitting something along the same lines this year might give you an edge."

"Oh!" His eyes widened. "I never considered that. It was a robot girlfriend."

"A what?!" I exclaimed.

"The judges said it was brilliantly innovative."

"My foot!" I was indignant on his behalf. "That's one of the oldest inventions in the book! And that won over your particle accelerator ray? How stupid are they?!"

"Well, most of the judges are single males," he said, "so ..."

I scowled. So *this* was why my husband never won the competition, even though he deserved to. I should've known. Most mad scientists were utterly tiresome. Maverick had gotten my attention because he was ten times smarter than most, a lot more polite, and absolutely adorable to boot.

About a thousand times better than my former employer, who had gotten my resignation letter in the form of a bomb I'd tossed into his lair.

"What won second place?" I demanded, putting my hands on my hips.

"A chain mail bikini with invisible force shields, so it could work as armor."

I slapped my hand to my forehead. "This explains so much!"

"What does?" He still looked confused.

"Right," I said, folding my arms. He was bringing home a trophy this year.

Those trophies mattered. It was easier to get billionaire supervillain patrons when you had a bunch of those to show off. "I'm going as your assistant this year."

"You are?" He looked startled.

"Mm-hm! You're going to use me for a demonstration. What kind of invention can you use on me?" I hadn't won the Miss Damsel in Distress pageant three years in a row for nothing. I knew how to dazzle a judge.

He picked up the mind-reading helmet from the table.

I took it from his hands and plonked it back down again. "Something that makes me look sexy."

"Why would I want anyone else to see how gorgeous you are?"

Boy, was that the right answer.

"So you can *win*," I said, emphasizing the word. "Think of it as a challenge. What invention have you got that will make me look sexy?"

Maverick's eyes lit up. "Oh! I have just the thing!"

He ran across the room and grabbed a bowl of glop that looked like it had been left there for several days. It was slimy in the middle and crusty at the edges. He ran back and tugged a spoon out of the thick gunk and handed it to me. "Try this!"

"Is there toxic waste in it?" I asked warily.

"No, no, no!" He laughed.

I sniffed. "It smells like rotten fish."

"Yes, because there are fish in it."

Oh, goody.

"All right," I said reluctantly, taking the bowl and spoon from him. "Are you going to tell me what it does?"

"It'll be more fun if it's a surprise." He had a mischievous smile.

"How long will it last?"

"About an hour?"

I put the spoon in my mouth and swallowed the nastiness. It tasted like soap, seawater, and three-day-old fish.

I fell to the ground, my legs fused into floppiness.

"Maverick," I said, trying to keep my cool as I looked at the tail now in place of my legs, "would you mind explaining why you just made me a *mermaid?*"

He was trying too hard not to drool to answer.

I smirked. *Oh, is that why?*

I grabbed his legs and tugged him down to the floor. I grabbed the spoon and shoved it in his mouth.

His legs glowed and transformed into fish scales.

"Hey!" he complained. "Now I won't be able to work on anything for an hour!"

"Oh, really?" I asked slyly, running my hands through his hair. "What a shame. I wonder what we'll do to pass the time until then ...?"

Maverick's mermaid serum won the Mad Science Fair that year.

"You did *not* deserve to win," a female mad scientist in goggles informed me crossly as I packed up our table display. "Maverick usually does something impressive. That was just a simple transformation serum. Not innovative at all."

"Well, no," I said with a grin. "But it was fun, anyway."

Her eyes narrowed. "I think I've seen you before. Aren't you a damsel in distress?"

"I was, a few years ago."

"Hmm. Well, here." She pulled out a card and handed it to me. There were moving gears within an ultrathin sheet of plastic. "I'm teaching mad science lessons to damsels in distress. I'm hoping some of you will stage coups against your employers. Knock out some of my competition."

"Huh!" Now, there was an interesting idea. If I learned some of the basics, it'd give me something to practice while Maverick was busy. And potentially we could work on a lot more projects together. "I might sign up for those. Thanks!"

"Don't mention it," she said, walking away.

Maverick came back from the judges' table hugging a giant trophy. His hair was slicked back, his clothes wrinkle-free. "I can't believe I finally won!"

"I can," I said, messing up his hair and mussing his clothes. Much better.

"I've been thinking about next year," he said, his eyes alight. "I think the teleportation coil will impress them —"

I barely repressed myself from rolling my eyes. Had he learned nothing about what the judges picked? Looking around at our competition had given me quite a few ideas about what might win and actually deserve it. "How about a suit of alligator armor?"

"Alligator armor?" He looked unenthusiastic. "It wasn't that hard to make."

"*Invisible* alligator armor. So if I put it on while wearing a bikini, no one will be able to tell it's there."

"Ooh!" Maverick's eyes lit up. "That would be a difficult challenge!"

Yes, indeed. He had the brains, while I had the instinct for winning competitions.

We were going to make a very good team.

AUTHOR NOTE

like the idea that "damsel in distress" is a profession, used to lure heroes into death traps in mad scientist lairs.

And I think everyone has something of value to contribute, no matter what their background may be.

PIXIE EGGS

Someone
Took pixie eggs
Aboard our spaceship.
It was not a bright move.
Pixie eggs are contraband
On hyperspace starships
For intelligent reasons.
But nobody noticed
Until too late.

Stored
In a suitcase
As souvenirs of
The pixies' planet,
They were hidden
From customs
Too well.

So when
The spaceship
Entered hyperspace,
The eggs hatched into
A swarm of pixies.
Only one thing
Could result.

Havoc!

Havoc!

Havoc!

Havoc!

Havoc!

Havoc!

Havoc!

Havoc!

Author Note

Does anyone know how to turn a field of dandelions back into a hyper-space drive?

RITE OF PASSAGE

JAEDA WAVED her arms in frustration. Yards of fabric billowed as her aunt attempted to pin back two enormous sleeves.

"I hate ceremonial robes," Jaeda muttered.

"Stop moving while I'm trying to fix this," Aunt Shaena murmured, her mouth full of pins. "Aha! Got it!" She stood back and beamed. "Don't you look *beautiful?*"

Jaeda frowned at the wavy reflection in her aunt's best mirror. "Beautiful" wasn't the first word she would use to describe herself, not when she was covered with sunburn and freckles. The ceremonial robes, which were way too big, didn't help either.

"These were your mother's robes, you know," Aunt Shaena said proudly, spinning Jaeda around to get a full view of her. "You look lovely. Just as she did before *her* Passage."

Jaeda avoided her aunt's eyes. Talk about her parents made her uncomfortable. It had been a year since their parents died in a boating accident, a year since she and Kaedin had come to live with Aunt Shaena, whom they'd never liked. And now here they were, their Rite of Passage next month, with no parents to dress them for it.

"Hey, Auntie, are you done yet?" A sunburned, freckled boy pushed his face through the tent opening. His eyes fell on his twin sister, and he chortled. "Boy, does that look bad on you ..."

"*Out! Out!*" Aunt Shaena made shooing motions at him. "Your fitting's next!"

"Not today, it's not," Kaedin smirked. "Laeran and I are sailing. Coming, Jaeda?"

"You bet!" Jaeda yanked the ceremonial gown over her head and dumped it on the ground. Her aunt gasped in horror and snatched it up.

Jaeda brushed off the boy clothes she always wore, pulled on her sandals, and stuck her tongue out at her brother.

"Don't you dare leave!" Aunt Shaena cried. "We haven't finished our fitting yet!"

Jaeda turned back, trying to look innocent. "But, Aunt," she said, "where Kaedin goes, I go. Everyone knows that."

Aunt Shaena was still sputtering as she and Kaedin ran to the boat.

It was supposedly forbidden to go to the Isle before your Rite of Passage, but everyone did it anyway. The twins had gone particularly often in the past year, since they'd needed a place to escape from Aunt Shaena. Adults rarely came here.

"What do you think will happen when we go in?" Jaeda wondered aloud, running a finger along one of the carvings on the stone door. The carvings looked like writing, but no one could read it. "What talents do you think we'll get?"

"*You'll* probably become a dress-mage, like Aunt Shaena," Kaedin smirked.

Jaeda chucked a pebble at him. He ducked, laughing.

"Maybe you'll get magic," Laeran offered. "No one's gotten that in decades."

"I'd *love* magic!" Kaedin cried.

"Yeah, that would be practical," Jaeda snorted. "You're too lazy already."

"Hey, we're shoo-ins," Kaedin persisted. "The last people who got magic were twins, weren't they?"

"*Identical* twins," Jaeda shot back. "We're not."

Kaedin stared at her with wide eyes. "Since when?"

"Are you saying I look like a boy?" Jaeda asked indignantly.

"Maybe he thinks *he* looks like a *girl*," Laeran hissed.

"Hey!" Kaedin cried.

Jaeda rolled the pebble around in her fingers.

"I can't help worrying, though ..." She swallowed. "I mean, no one ever remembers what happens there. And some people never come back. So suppose ...?"

"We're not going to die," Kaedin scoffed. "We'll come back with magic."

"But they say it always takes the brightest and best—doesn't that worry you?"

"Why should it? It's not like we've lost anybody we know."

"It took my brother," Laeran said quietly. "Six years ago. Remember?"

Kaedin blinked.

"I, uh ... I forgot about that," he said.

Laeran grinned slightly. "Well, I wouldn't worry. You two are hardly brightest or best."

Kaedin made a face at him.

"Let's go," Jaeda said, standing. "I ought to finish that fitting before Aunt Shaena complains to somebody."

Kaedin looked relieved. "Okay. Good idea."

Laeran nodded and got up, silently.

"It's *freezing*," Jaeda hissed to her brother, shivering in her oversized robes. Aunt Shaena had refused to resize them, insisting that would be a waste of fabric. "Do we really *have* to go this early in the morning?"

"We were born this early in the morning," Kaedin said gloomily, trudging towards the boat beside her. His robes made him look like a bulky sack.

"I think I hate tradition," Jaeda muttered.

"Welcome, Jaeda and Kaedin," the village leader intoned, holding out his hands as they neared the boat. *His* robes fit perfectly. "Your twelfth birthday has come. The day of your Rite of Passage has begun. I shall show you the way to the Isle."

"Doesn't he know we've been there dozens of times before?" Jaeda hissed.

"I think he assumes people will obey rules," Kaedin whispered back.

The village leader rowed them to the Isle mind-numbingly slowly. Jaeda tried to grab the oars once, but the man smacked her hands away.

"Just trying to help," Jaeda muttered, slouching against her side of the boat.

They made it to the Isle, then to the stone door against the cliff.

"Place your hands on the sealed door," the village leader instructed. "It will recognize you as the proper age and permit you entrance."

Exchanging a glance, Jaeda and Kaedin pressed their hands on the door. They jumped back, startled, as the thick stone vanished.

"Magic," Kaedin breathed, looking excited.

"You must now enter," the village leader intoned. "I shall wait until the rise of the next sun. If you have not returned by then, a boat will be left in case of return later."

Both twins nodded. Jaeda's mouth felt dry.

The village leader stood there, staring at them meaningfully. It took several seconds for Jaeda to realize he was waiting for them. Kaedin reached out and grabbed her arm.

His hand was clammy. It was a relief to know he was scared, too.

Together, they stepped into the darkness.

At first there was nothing. Then came a blinding flash of light, and then —

White.

Everything—walls, ceilings, floors—white.

"It kind of glows, look," Kaedin whispered, tapping one of the walls. There was a hollow sound. "This is weird."

Jaeda glanced back at the entrance, and yelped to see it was gone. Everything was solid, smooth, white wall now.

"Welcome!"

She spun, her heart pounding, and scooted closer to her brother as a stranger strode towards them. There was a dark doorway on the other end of the room that had not been there a second ago.

"Wh-who are you?" Kaedin demanded.

The man stopped about ten feet from them.

"My name is Railan," he said. He looked them up and down. "Are you twins?"

Jaeda nodded nervously.

The man laughed. "Excellent! I haven't seen twins in years. What are your names?"

"Jaeda?" Jaeda said uncertainly.

"Kaedin," Kaedin declared.

"Good. You're not as frightened as some. That's a good sign. May I show you something?"

Jaeda and Kaedin glanced at each other. Nodded.

The man pulled some kind of stick from his pocket and tapped it on the wall beside him. Pictures dashed across it, too fast for Jaeda to catch even a glimpse of each.

"Magic!" Kaedin cried, looking excited.

The man laughed and tapped the wall again. The pictures vanished. "No, no, science. Well, they could be the same thing, I guess."

"Who are you?" Jaeda demanded, fighting to keep a quaver out of her voice. "What are you doing here?"

The man blinked. "Straight to the point, I see. All right." He cleared his throat. "I'm here because—ahem—Anthropological Experiment #649 requires authorization by all test subjects before beginning surveillance."

Jaeda blinked.

"What?" she and Kaedin asked.

The man coughed again. He looked uncomfortable. "The village you're from —along with others, spread out across your planet—was artificially created, centuries ago. We terraformed your world to be inhabitable and asked for volunteers to populate it. A few thousand came, agreed to have memories of their previous lives erased and replaced with new ones, and consented to have the rest of their life-memories recorded for our use after their deaths. This was in concordance with Ethics Law #276."

Jaeda stared at him, confused.

"Wait a minute," Kaedin said slowly. "You're saying ... our world ... our village ... is fake?"

The man coughed. "Well, in a manner of speaking ... yes."

"Why are you telling us this?" Jaeda demanded. "Do *you* get something out of it?"

"Straight to the point again, I see," the man said, looking amused. "And yes. According to Ethics Law #289, we can't continue the experiment unless we have each person's consent. So we bring you here at twelve years old, receive consent, and then implant a wafer to record your memories for the rest of your life. We naturally also erase any memories of time here, so we don't contaminate the experiment."

"The rest of our *life?*" Jaeda cried, appalled. "People are going to see our *thoughts?*"

"Not till you're dead," the man said hastily. "And in return, we give everyone a talent of their choice. It's a fair exchange."

"We get to *choose* our talents?" Kaedin cried, his eyes lighting up.

"I think we should discuss this first," Jaeda hissed.

"Magic!" Kaedin went on eagerly. "You can do that, right?"

"Magic?" the man repeated, looking doubtful.

"Yeah, moving things without touching them, and —"

"Oh, *that* ..." The man looked uncomfortable. "Well, it's possible, but I wouldn't recommend it. The procedure's dangerous, and even with a volunteer, the number of deaths caused by —"

"Well, we don't care about risks." Kaedin rubbed his hands together. "We want magic."

"No, we *don't!*" Jaeda burst out.

Kaedin gaped at her.

"You *don't* want to be a dress-mage, do you?" he asked, horror in his voice.

"No, you idiot." Jaeda glared at him. "I don't give my *consent.* I don't want my memories recorded for experiments."

"Aw, come on," Kaedin pleaded. "It's fair. We could get magic!"

"No." Jaeda stared at the man, folding her arms. "It's not fair. I won't do it. Does that mean you have to kill me?"

Kaedin gaped beside her.

"No," Railan said slowly. "We don't do that. But without consent, we can't send you back."

"What then?" Jaeda demanded.

"Well, then ..." The man swallowed. "Then you'd have to leave this world. Become a member of ours. And believe me, that would not be easy."

"Laeran's brother!" Kaedin gasped. "Is that what happened to him?"

The man nodded.

Jaeda focused on the walls. White. Stark white. So different, so strange. So alien.

She loved the village. She loved rowing, loved her brother, loved her friends' good-natured teasing. She wanted to learn to play the rock-flute. She wanted to be old enough to badger the adults to take her hunting.

Yes, their parents were gone, but she still had so much to lose.

Jaeda closed her eyes. The cost was high. But she still had to pay it.

"I'll do it," she said quietly. "I'll leave."

"*No!*" Kaedin cried. "Where I go, you go, remember?"

Jaeda ducked her head. She couldn't answer. Couldn't face him.

Silence reigned for a long moment.

"All right," Kaedin said, at last. "I'm going too."

Jaeda's head jerked up. She gaped at him.

"Where *you* go, *I* go." Kaedin lowered his voice. "Besides, I can always make them give me magic later."

The man had a curious smile on his face.

"Well, if you're sure ..."

"We are," Jaeda and Kaedin chorused.

The smile widened. "Then you're in for the same path I chose. Please ... follow me."

AUTHOR NOTE

There need to be more stories about strong sibling bonds, so I wrote one. I probably could have written a whole series around these characters, but one short story sufficed

WEREDODO SLEUTH

THERE WAS A CRASH.

I woke up, my heart pounding. *Is somebody trying to rob me? Did the heater explode? Did I leave the TV on all night again?*

Quite naturally, I had to investigate. What self-respecting weredodo would leave such a thing unexplained?

I hopped out of bed, slipped my feet into my fuzzy slippers, pulled on my bathrobe, which had a rather odd smell I couldn't quite place, and shuffled downstairs. I checked the living room, and everything looked fine. I checked the water heater, and nothing looked different. I checked the kitchen, and everything seemed the same as I'd left it.

Except that my foot was cold. Why was my foot cold?

Ah. I had only put on one of my slippers, it seemed.

I stood there, puzzled, looking around the room. *Why did I come downstairs, again?*

I spun around in a slow circle, trying to figure it out. Surely there must be a clue somewhere.

The door! The door was ajar. I must have come downstairs to check the door!

Triumphantly, I headed to the kitchen door to close it.

Then I paused, puzzled.

Why had I left the door open? I didn't live in the safest neighborhood. I had forgotten to lock it before, but I didn't think I would have left it open. I thought back carefully. I hadn't gone outside yesterday. My clan leader had come to visit me, but she'd left through the front door, as she usually did. I vaguely recalled the back door having been open last night ...

Then my heart leapt in my throat. If I hadn't left the door open, then *somebody else must have*.

Sheer terror filled me, and I started to shake. Were they still in the house? Did they have a gun? I was only sixty-three! I was too young to be robbed at gunpoint!

No, no, I told myself. *Calm down. Calm down.*

I took deep breaths. All I needed to do was leave the house. If I told my neighbors what had happened, they would dial 911, and the police would come and take care of everything. They'd check my house to make sure the burglars were gone. I could go back to sleep, warm and secure and safe.

Or ...

I looked around the room, my heart pounding with excitement. This was a genuine crime, wasn't it? I'd always wanted to be a sleuth. What self-respecting cozy mystery detective would let the police solve a mystery for them?

Oh, there were dangers, of course. I might be put in bodily harm. But on the other hand, my life had been so *boring* since I had been forced to retire early and my brother had started acting like an overprotective mother hen.

What self-respecting sister listens to her younger brother when he tries to act all authoritative?

My fear gone, replaced with glee, I pranced across the kitchen and flung open the back door. To my delight, there were footprints all over the snow outside, heading down the stoop and down the narrow path through my long-dead garden.

Let's see, I thought, squatting down and measuring one of them with my hand. *This is two and a half pointer finger lengths long.*

I should write this down. There was no way I'd remember. I reached into my pocket and pulled out a pen and a notebook. I scribbled down the measurement I'd taken from my first clue, made a carefully detailed sketch of the tread marks, and put the pen and notebook back.

I beamed as I stood up, my knees stiff from crouching. I was behaving like a real detective already!

There was a set of footprints heading clearly through the snow of my back yard. Not mine, I was certain, because my feet weren't as large as those. Besides, there hadn't been any snow on the ground when I'd gone to bed. The set of footprints made a detour to the kitchen window, and then over to the kitchen door, where I stood.

So the thief looked in the window before heading to the door, I deduced shrewdly. *That means he—or she—didn't come here knowing there was anything to steal. The thief just saw something he—or she—wanted, and went for it.*

Of course, that begged the question of what the thief had seen. What was in view from my kitchen window?

I shapeshifted into my dodo form and waddled around the large footprints so that I didn't disturb any evidence, wading through the inches of snow to reach the kitchen window. I shifted into my half-form and craned my extra-long, feathery neck to see what the thief had been seeing from that position.

Aha! I thought. *The TV!* I could just make out the TV in the living room behind the kitchen table. That had to have been their target!

Oh, wait, I thought, ruffling my neck feathers in embarrassment. *The TV's still there. So what did they steal?*

Maybe I'd left my wallet on the kitchen table. Had I left my wallet on the kitchen table? I checked my pocket, and my wallet was there, where I usually kept it, so that was good.

Well, this was most puzzling. Maybe nothing had been stolen from my house at all. That would be good, I supposed, but awfully disappointing. Being robbed would have been such an interesting change of pace.

And then I saw him.

The door to my coat closet opened slowly, and a man with a ski mask over his face poked his head out. His head whipped one way or the other, and he dashed for the kitchen door that I was standing beside.

I shrank until I was all-shifted and scuttled behind the box that belonged to the air conditioner's large outdoor fan, waiting with my heart pounding at triple the rate it should have.

I was little. I was tiny. I was only about three feet tall. He definitely wouldn't notice me here.

The man burst out of my kitchen door and ran through down the path, snow flying as his boots churned it up.

One set of footprints, I realized with chagrin. *Of course he was still in my house. How could I miss such an obvious clue?*

Then the ski-masked man stopped abruptly. He looked around at the bird footprints I had left in the snow. He turned slowly to follow them to where I stood, frozen in place.

I'm a statue, I thought. *I'm just a statue in a little old lady's garden.*

"Oh, come on!" he burst out. "You're clearly alive!"

I waddled over, pecking at the snow with large, innocent eyes. *I'm just a pet. A pet in a little old lady's garden ...*

"Dodos are extinct!" he exploded. "You're clearly a shapeshifter!"

Ah. Yes. I might have forgotten that one small detail.

Deciding that I'd be a little more imposing if I were more than three feet tall, I shapeshifted into my usual human form, holding my hands out menacingly. "What were you doing in my house, sir?"

The ski-masked man stared at me incredulously.

Hmm. Perhaps my human form was less imposing than my dodo form, after all. I was a sixty-three-year-old woman in a nightgown. Also, it was cold out here without feathers. I tied the bathrobe shut in front of me, shivering.

"Okay, lady," the man said in what he must have thought was a reasonable tone, holding out his hands. "I didn't take anything. Got it? You're not going to call the police. Right?"

"Of course I'm going to call the police!" I said indignantly.

"Okay, look," the man said defensively, edging off to the side, "I didn't take anything. Okay? I just went in on a dare. There was a guy who gave me fifty bucks to do it. I'm not a thief, okay? You can have the fifty bucks, okay? Stop looking at me like that!"

I gave the man a stern look. "Being an accomplice after the fact still makes you guilty. Unless, of course, you'd rather be a witness instead."

He paused, looking right and left nervously. "Witness?"

"That's right," I said proudly, drawing myself up to my full height. "I just so happen to be a sleuth. If you want to prove yourself not guilty, you can help me catch the person who did rob me."

"But I didn't steal anything!" he exploded.

"Ah, but somebody did," I said, raising my finger. I didn't know for sure if that was true, but I wanted it to be. "And so: who?"

He hesitated, looking one way or the other again, as if deciding whether to flee.

I folded my arms. "Are you familiar with my magical power?"

"Uh ..." he said, eyeing me. "No."

"Well!" I said grandly. "Weredodos have the ability to track people wherever they go. If you try to leave, I'll simply call the police and lead them straight to your hideout. Your only option to prove yourself innocent is to help me find the real criminal."

The man's hand jerked towards his pocket, and I flinched back, terrified that he'd pull out a gun. In retrospect, I realized that killing me would also be a way to make sure he didn't get caught.

But he didn't pull out a gun. He just pulled out a wallet and threw a fifty dollar bill onto the snow. It lay there, fluttering slightly as a breeze drifted through.

"I got dared to do it," he said. "Just like I said. You can have the fifty dollars. Just don't call the police!"

For a moment, I considered it. Fifty dollars would be a reasonable reward for solving my first case, especially if no crime had actually been committed.

But if a crime *had* been committed and I let him go, I wouldn't be able to track my only witness. I'd been lying shamelessly about that. Weredodos had no magical ability.

Come to think of it, perhaps that was one of the reasons my species was so rare.

"You can keep it," I said grandly. "Don't be so silly. Pick it up before the thing blows away. Then come inside and tell me all about the person who dared you to enter my house. That person is now my chief suspect."

Looking very uncomfortable, the man in the ski mask picked up the fifty dollar bill and stuffed it into his pocket.

He headed back to the house with stiff shoulders as I followed after him.

I was about to interrogate my first witness. How exciting!

CHAPTER ?

My reluctant witness settled down as he seated himself at the kitchen table, looking most uncomfortable. Personally, I was delighted by this whole situation. Who would have thought this morning that tonight I would be on my way to solving my very own mystery?

"Now, first of all," I said authoritatively, "you must tell me your name."

"Sebastian," he said reluctantly. "Sebastian Noclanhuman."

Oh, that poor boy! I thought, pity rising. *His turning failed!*

My own turning had gone wrong when I was close to his age. I had been turned at twenty-one, back in the days before it'd been determined that seventeen was the optimal age, and instead of becoming a werehawk like the rest of my family, I had become a weredodo.

It wasn't that I minded being what I'd become. I had long since gotten used to it, and when most of my extended family members called me "Aunt Dodo," I was quite philosophical about it. Still, there was a part of me that wondered wistfully what it would be like to fly. Dodos were flightless birds, after all.

My heart went out to this poor soul who had come to my house. A failed turning was a nightmare. He would never be a person.

"Stop it!" he shouted, banging his fists on the table. "Stop looking at me like that! I *chose* to stay human, all right? I've never been turned on purpose!"

I blinked and stared in bafflement at this impossible young person who apparently lacked common sense in every possible way.

"Why would you stay unturned?" I asked.

"What's wrong with staying unturned?" he asked defensively. "My parents have never been turned, or the rest of my family either, and we're all just fine that way!"

My eyebrows raised. I lived only a few streets away from a human ghetto, so I had met humans before, but never one that had chosen to be that way on purpose. To be eligible for almost any well-paying job required one to be a person, seeing as most specialty fields required a magical ability that was unique to a specific race or species. For instance, most doctors were draculas, since they could use their blood to heal their patients.

"I would argue that you are not 'just fine' if you are so desperate for money that you think trespassing in somebody else's home for fifty dollars is a superb idea," I said mildly. "Now, tell me about the man who dared you. Do you know him?"

"No," the ski-masked man said immediately. "We were complete strangers."

Liar, I determined, and decided to write that down. I checked the pockets of my bathrobe for my notebook and pen, and found nothing. I checked my nightgown too, but there were no pockets within it. How puzzling. I could have sworn I'd put it in a pocket earlier.

No matter. This was why I had a junk drawer. I kept spare paper and Post-It Notes and several dozen pens there in case I needed to remind myself of things.

I stood up and headed across the kitchen.

"Where are you going?" the human named Spencer demanded.

"I'm getting a notebook to write down your testimony," I said, pulling open my junk drawer. For a moment, I stared at it in bafflement. Why was there silverware in my junk drawer?

Oh, wait. My junk drawer was the one next to it.

With relief, I opened the drawer to the right and collected a pad of Post-It Notes and several pens. I peeled off the top note, which said "Don't forget to pay phone b" and tossed it back in the drawer before heading back to the table.

"Now then," I said, sitting down with a purple pen posed over the block of sticky notes. "Do continue."

"Uh," the ski-masked man said, eyeing the Post-It Notes. "Uh, as I said, I have no idea who the guy was that dared me."

I wrote, *A likely story.* "Mm-hmm?" I asked encouragingly.

"I was just, like, out playing poker with my friends. I was on my way home, and ..."

No-good gambling addict, I wrote. "Mm-hmm?"

"Oh, come on!" he exploded. "I can read what you're writing! I am not a gambling addict!"

"Well, then, I'd love you to explain why you were so desperate for money that you accepted a dare from a complete stranger to trespass in my house," I said severely.

He muttered something under his breath. "All right, my friends might've cleaned me out this week," he muttered. "Happy?"

I was, in fact. Interrogating a witness who was also a suspect was great fun. Not that I was sure what had been stolen, mind you, but I was certain there was something missing that was supposed to be in this room. Something ...

I got up and headed to the wall.

"*Now* where are you going?" the man demanded.

"Nowhere," I said, adjusting the thermostat to 90 degrees. The vent was right behind the table. The heater immediately came on, and a wave of sweltering warmth gushed over us.

The man flinched and tugged the ski mask off his head.

"Aha!" I cried triumphantly, pointing at him. "Now I know what you look like!"

He froze, staring at the ski mask in his hand. Then he gave me an aggrieved look. "Lady, I told you, I haven't done anything wrong! I was just wearing that because it's cold outside!"

"Uh huh," I said gleefully.

He glared at me.

I studied his face, determined to be able to pick him out of a lineup if I had to. He had a thin nose, dark hair, no scars or freckles, a pasty white complexion ...

I sighed. Okay, I had no chance of picking him out of a lineup. He looked terribly boring, and if I was being honest with myself, there was no chance that I'd be able to tell him apart from fifty other young men like him. Still, he didn't have to know that.

"Now, then," I said, settling back into my seat, "tell me again about the man who dared you to enter my house. The truth."

"I told you the truth!"

"Then tell me again."

He looked like he was grinding his teeth. "I was just walking by —"

"In the middle of the night?"

"I was coming from a poker game with my friends."

"High school students shouldn't be playing poker," I scolded.

"I'm not a high school student! I'm twenty-five!"

"And still unturned?" I asked archly. "You're clearly sixteen."

"I'm unturned on *purpose*, lady!"

Well, why hadn't he said that in the first place? He did look a little old to be sixteen. I wrote *Unturned on purpose* on the top Post-It Note.

"Very well," I said, adding *Makes poor life choices* underneath it. "Please continue."

"Well, a man appeared from behind a lamppost and asked me if I'd like fifty bucks."

"You say 'appeared,'" I said. "What does that mean? Did he do it magically?"

"I don't know," the boy shrugged. "He was wearing black. It might've been magical, or I might've just not seen him."

Wearing black, I wrote down, reaching the end of the Post-It.

Why was I using a sticky note again? I ought to be using my notebook. I checked the pockets of my bathrobe for my notebook and pen, but all I found was a half-eaten sandwich. I sniffed it, wrinkled my nose, and set it on the table.

"How old is that?" the boy named Stewart asked in horror.

"Not too old," I lied, though I had no idea. "But don't eat it."

He looked repulsed. "I wasn't going to."

Not always, I squeezed under the note that said *Makes poor life choices.*

"So the guy," Spencer said, "asked me, 'Hey, want fifty bucks?' I said, 'Sure. Why?' He said, 'I dare you to go into that house over there. The back door's unlocked.' I said, 'Why?' He said, 'My buddy bet me a hundred bucks I couldn't get someone to go into his house.' I said, 'Okay.' And I took the money and went."

I removed the top Post-It Note and wrote *Very stupid* on the next one. "Go on."

"Well, that's when I met you," he said defensively. "Can I go home now?"

No, he most certainly could not. Not until I knew what had been stolen, at least. Why did my kitchen look so wrong to me? Why did I feel like it was missing something?

I *knew* something had been stolen. And I had a feeling it had been something important. But what was it? What?

"What was the sound I heard?" I demanded. "The one that woke me up?"

"What sound?"

"The crashing one!"

"Ohhhh," Stuart said. "I dunno. I didn't make it."

"Did it come from outside?" I asked.

"I think so, maybe?" he hedged.

Maybe the crashing noise had something to do with what was missing from my kitchen. I stared around the room, focusing on each portion at a time, but nothing seemed to jump out at me. Everything was the same as usual.

This was maddening. I ought to be able to find out what was missing from my own house. I was a sleuth with the cleverness of a fox and a mind like a steel trap.

"Stanley, when you heard the noise —"

"It's Sebastian!"

Okay, like a sieve.

"—where did it sound like it was coming from?"

"I dunno," he said hesitantly. "Perhaps from ... the right?"

My next door neighbor to the right were a childless couple from some sort of vampire clan. They weren't giants or specters. I could see no good reason why a crashing sound should have come from the direction of their home.

"Then we'll have to go speak to them," I said. "Come on."

"Come on where?!"

"To visit my neighbors," I said coolly.

"It's three in the morning!" he said shrilly.

"It doesn't matter," I said with great dignity. "They were most likely awakened, too. I am a sleuth, and so must investigate all clues. After all, a sleuth without clues is like a test without a student. Like a doghouse without a dog. Like a cookie without sweetness. Like a clan without a turning stone —"

I stared at the table and gasped. It had just clicked.

"What's wrong?" the boy asked, looking alarmed.

"My clan's turning stone!" I wailed in horror. "It's gone!"

CHAPTER UM ...

Oh no. Oh no, oh no, oh no no. I remembered yesterday now.

Victoria was going to kill me. She was definitely never going to trust me again.

"Your what?" the human named Stewart repeated, his brow wrinkled as if he didn't understand the significance.

"Our turning stone!" I exclaimed. How could he, of all people, who had been through the terrible tragedy of having his turning fail, underestimate the importance of that? "I promised Victoria I'd watch over it while she was out of town! How could this happen?! She'll never forgive me!"

"Where was it?" Spencer asked urgently.

"On the kitchen table," I said, distraught. "I ... I promised her I'd put it somewhere safe ... but I forgot ... and I must have forgotten to lock the back door, too ..."

There was a terrible silence.

"So you told your clan leader you'd watch over your clan's turning stone, and instead, you got it stolen?" Summer asked.

"Yessssss!" I wailed, putting my face in my hands.

He walked over and patted me awkwardly on the back. It didn't help, but I supposed I appreciated the gesture.

"Anabel couldn't have taken it," I murmured frantically, "because her grandson's living with her, and she doesn't want it at her house. Charles wouldn't have taken it—he would just have woken me up and scolded me. Irma wouldn't have taken it—she would have just hidden it someplace and left a note for me."

Just in case, I checked the floor, but there was no note.

"Who are those people?" Stanley asked.

"Charles is my younger brother," I said, getting up and checking a cupboard, just in case I had hidden the turning stone there. "Irma's my older sister. Anabel's in my clan."

"How many people are in your clan?" he asked.

I checked another cupboard. "Three."

"Isn't that kind of ... small?"

"Don't rub it in!" I snapped, slamming the door. "We haven't had a new turning in forty years. I was the last one."

He wrinkled his nose. "Okay, I'm not an expert in clans, since I don't have one, but ... isn't it kind of pointless to have a turning stone if you never use it?"

I opened the oven door. No stone within. "Do you think we don't want new members? Of course we do! But Anabel and I both came from turnings that went wrong, so neither of us have relatives who are interested in being dodos. As for Victoria, she quarreled with her children, so they all live in a different state and belong to a weredodo clan there!"

"Yeah, but if you're not *using* it, you might as well just *sell* it," Sonny said.

I spun around and gave him a furious glare. "Nobody would sell their clan's turning stone! There's always the *hope* of new members!"

"What if they could get a lot of money for it?" Sonny asked.

"Of course they could get a lot of money for it," I said tightly. "But your own clan's turning stone is priceless. It could never be replaced. Especially with a rare species, like dodos!"

"Because the stones have to be trained?" he asked.

"The word is 'programmed.' And yes. Our turning stone's been programmed over centuries to turn dodos. No one else could ever value it as much as we do."

I spun around, desperately seeking some other place I might have accidentally left it.

Aha! The dishwasher! I couldn't imagine why I might have put it there, but maybe ... maybe ...

No. There was no green, glowing stone.

A lump rose in my throat. This wasn't mere misplacing it. This wasn't like the car keys I'd lost two weeks ago and still not found. It really had been stolen. I really had carelessly allowed someone to steal it. I swallowed a sob —

No! No! I wouldn't let some selfish thief destroy my clan! I would stop them, and I'd find it!

I spied my phone on the countertop, and I seized it. I usually loathed my smartphone because I had a tendency to lose it, but right now, I was grateful for anything that could get me online.

"What are you doing?" Stewart asked, looking alarmed.

"Checking Wereconnection," I snarled. "Maybe there's a weredodo clan somewhere else in the country that is big enough that they want to split into two. They'd have a motive for stealing our turning stone —"

But there were too many clans when I searched for "dodo." There were hundreds, and at least five that had several hundred people in them. No suspects that would stand out to me.

Besides, was it really plausible that one of them had stolen my clan's turning stone? It was much more likely that it had been some common sneak thief who had simply walked by my house, seen the stone on the table, found the door unlocked, and walked off with it. Surely any turning stone could have value on the black market, even if it was programmed to an unwanted species ...

I slammed my phone on the countertop. *An unwanted species!*

No. I would not let our turning stone be corrupted by another species. It was meant for turning dodos, and it would stay that way.

I had only one lead, and I would follow it. I'd solve the case, I'd save my clan, and I would show those no-good sneak thieves that crime never paid. That lead was ...

Um ...

That lead was ...

What was that lead?

Maybe Skipper could help me remember.

"What else did you notice about the man who dared you to trespass in my house?" I asked him, turning around.

He stared at me, exasperated. "You mean, like the fact that he had a scar on his left cheek and he spoke with a heavy accent from south Paris and he was fairly obviously a dracula because he turned into a bat right in front of me?"

"Yes!" I exclaimed, diving for my Post-It Notes. "That will help immensely!"

"Do you know the meaning of 'sarcasm'?"

I paused, having gotten as far as "Almost certainly a dracula beca" in my notes. "What?"

"I was being sarcastic. I already told you everything I know."

I ripped the misleading Post-It Note off the top and wadded it up into a ball, preparing to throw it at him. The crinkling noise reminded me of ... of ...

"The noise!" I cried triumphantly. "We have to investigate that noise!"

Stanley looked less than enthusiastic. "There is no 'we.' I'm going home now."

"You most certainly are not," I said, fixing him with a stern glare. "You involved yourself in this crime, and now you have to help me solve it."

"I fail to see why," he said sourly.

I grabbed my phone from the countertop and held it up. "You want a reason why? I'll give you a reason why. If you leave now, I'll call the police and tell them that I caught you trespassing in my house right before I discovered my clan's turning stone had gone missing. Turning stones are worth hundreds of thousands of dollars, you know. Being involved in stealing one would be an automatic felony."

"C'mon, lady!" he cried. "You know I'm innocent!"

"I do not, in fact, know that," I said tartly. "But I do know your name, your face, and what neighborhood you likely live in."

He mumbled something under his breath.

"What was that?" I asked. "I didn't quite catch that."

"I said, 'Whatever,'" he muttered. "You could've used your tracking magic on me, no matter what."

What tracking magic? I didn't have tracking magic. I couldn't think where he'd gotten the impression I did. Still, it was a useful wrong assumption, so I wouldn't disillusion the boy.

"That's right," I said. "So, let's not waste any more time. We need to go next door and interview my neighbors. Hopefully they saw something we've missed. Something that will crack this case wide open."

"Or maybe they were asleep. Like I want to be right now."

"Then we'll talk to everyone in this neighborhood!" I declared. "Someone must have seen something! We're going to find the thief if it's the last thing we ever do!"

Sonny looked dismayed.

"Well, come on," I said briskly, picking up my bathrobe. I pulled it on over my nightgown and tied it tight. "Let's go."

"You're going next door like *that*?"

"Indeed I am," I said. "I'm not letting you out of my sight. Unless you want to go upstairs with me while I change —"

"Please go next door dressed like that," he said immediately.

I smirked and went to the hall closet, where I retrieved a pair of snow boots. I put my phone in my pocket, in case I would need it again, then shoved my feet into the rubber boots. I walked back to the kitchen, where Spenser was thankfully waiting for me.

"How are you planning to explain me to your neighbors?" he wanted to know.

"Well, I was thinking I would tell them the truth —"

"No."

"Why not? If you have nothing to hide —"

"Just tell them I'm your nephew!"

I gave the boy a doubtful stare. Quite apart from the fact that we had no facial features in common, my skin was dark brown, and his was pasty white.

"I'll tell them you're my sidekick," I decided. "Every sleuth needs one, and I don't have a cat."

"How about assistant?" he asked.

"How about sidekick?"

"How about coworker?"

"How about sidekick?"

"I don't want to be a sidekick!"

"You'll do just fine," I assured him. "After all, you already have the perfect name for mystery solving."

"I what?" he asked, looking baffled.

"Sherlock," I said, shaking my head. How could he not know the name of the most famous detective of all time?

"My name is Sebastian!"

Chapter It's on the Tip of My Tongue

Skipper did not look enthusiastic as I banged on my neighbor's door.

There was a long silence as we waited for someone to answer. I took the time to look out over the silent stillness of a snow-fallen night. I could see our footprints in the blanket of whiteness, trailing from the front door of my house to our neighbor's. Shifting to half-form so that I could crane my extra-long neck, I looked back to see Sean's footprints heading behind my back yard towards the human ghetto, then turning to go into my house.

There was no sign of another pair of footprints back there.

I couldn't decide whether that made Sven seem more guilty, or whether that just meant the man he had talked to had been a specter. Specters could go insubstantial, after all.

But something was off about that ... something ...

Aha! I realized as the front door opened. *Specters can't talk while insubstantial! If the man were insubstantial, he wouldn't have been able to dare Sven!*

"H'lo?" the man asked in a bleary, grumbling voice.

I swallowed. I just realized that I couldn't remember my neighbor's name at all. Had it started with a P? Or a D?

"Hello, Mr. Vampireclandracula," I said, hedging my bets. "I'm your neighbor, Dorothy Wereclandodo."

"I'm not a dracula, I'm an aswang," the bearded man muttered, scratching his chin. "D'you know what time it is?"

"I believe it's three o'clock in the morning, but that's immaterial in light of the catastrophe," I said. "Did you hear a very loud crash about fifteen minutes ago?"

The neighbor's eyes opened beyond their sleepy squint. "What catastrophe?"

"The one in which my clan's turning stone was stolen," I said. "I very much need to get it back. Have you seen or heard anything?"

The man's eyes were now quite wide. "Your turning stone was stolen? There are turning stone thieves around?"

"Yes, I believe so," I said.

"Lily!" the man yelled, turning around to call up the stairs. "Check the safe! Check the safe now!"

So his wife was named Lily. That was helpful. I would have to remember that when I saw her.

"Mr. Vampireclanaswang," I said, "were either of you awakened by the crashing sound? I ask because I want to get right on —"

A woman screamed upstairs. Mr. Vampireclanaswang and I both bolted up there without hesitating.

At the end of the upstairs hallway was a safe. A safe that had been torn right out of the wall and flung on the ground. It looked like it had been punched open. And the safe was empty.

The neighbor woman, a forty-year-old showboat who tended to dress like she was twenty and wear layers of makeup so thick that they resembled a rock stratum, was now standing in the hallway in a silk nightgown and screaming.

I had a terrible misgiving that my turning stone had not been the only one stolen.

"What was in there?" I asked.

"Need you *ask?*" my neighbor shouted.

"Yes, I very well do!" I shot back. "I am a sleuth! I act on facts, not assumptions! Now: what was in your safe that is now missing?"

"What do you think?!" the man roared.

"Our—our turning stone," the woman sobbed, collapsing to the ground and staring at the empty safe. "Our clan's turning stone. How could this happen? Who would do such a thing?"

"I don't know," I said grimly, but a terrible fear rose in me. The last time there had been a rash of turning stone thefts, it had been because an underground organization had been stealing them to taint them, in order to blackmail the leaders of our city into ... something. I didn't remember what offhand, but I knew my great-niece Lisette had done something to stop them.

What if my clan's turning stone has been tainted? I thought in terror. *It will have to be destroyed!*

That would be even worse than having it stolen and sold to become another clan's turning stone.

No. No, no, I told myself. *They fixed that problem, didn't they? They did. I'm certain they did. I would have remembered if they were still at large.*

"Bram, what'll we do?!" Lillian wailed.

"Yeah, looks really bad," Scooby commented from behind me. "That safe's totally busted."

I jumped. I hadn't even noticed that he'd followed me in, but of course he had. He was my sidekick.

"Who's that?" my neighbor snarled, pointing at Scooby.

"I'm her assistant," he said immediately.

"He means my sidekick," I corrected. "I am a sleuth, and he's helping me."

"Sleuth?" my neighbor asked sharply. I tried to remember what his wife had called him. Bran? Yes, it must have been Bran. "As in, detective?"

"Yes," I said firmly. "I'm here to solve the case, and I will do so. I'm quite certain the two crimes were perpetrated by the same people. Tell me everything you know or can surmise about what happened here."

"W-well," Lillian said in a wavering voice, "we keep the safe locked all the time. E-everybody in our clan knows we have the stone, but none of them would steal it."

"How often do you open the safe?" I asked.

"How often?" Bran repeated, as if I were speaking a foreign tongue.

"Yes," I said. "How often?"

"Whenever we have a turning," Lilith said in a shaky voice. "We have one in just a few days."

My mind hummed with that news. A turning in just a few days! Such a rare and special event, and they had one imminent. "So it's possible that it was someone was trying to prevent that particular turning. Your being about to use it in just a few days can't be coincidence —"

"Of course it can be a coincidence," Brian said brusquely. "We have a turning practically every week."

I gaped at him. "Every *week*?"

My clan hadn't had a new member in forty years. We were all over sixty. And they had a new turning every *week*?

I felt a stab of intense envy. It would be so nice to be part of a clan that was growing. Even a normal-sized clan, with a turning every year or so, would be terrific. I liked Anabel and Victoria, but our clan meetings were so desperately *boring*.

It was too bad Skyler's turning had failed, because I would have willingly invited him. Of course, I would have willingly invited anyone who could enliven things up. If he'd at least been unturned, perhaps I could have persuaded him to be a dodo.

"Yes, we have nearly a thousand people in our clan," Lina said, rising. She stared down at the safe and let out a moan of dismay. "How are we going to explain this to them? We can't possibly merge with another clan. Our meetings are too crowded as it is!"

I tried to feel sorry for them, and failed. Perhaps it was uncharitable of me, but the fact that merging with another clan might even be an option for them made me jealous. Our tiny clan had never had an option to merge with another dodo clan because of distance. The other dodo clans were all at least an hour away.

Bryan was giving Shaun a suspicious stare. "What does it mean to be a 'side-kick,' anyway?"

"Oh, well, we met because —" I began breezily.

"I'm her nephew!" Shawn said quickly.

Brandon looked at him. He looked at me. He looked at him. He gave me a flat look.

"He isn't my nephew," I said.

"You don't say."

"We met because —" I began.

"Because I'm dating her niece!" Shaun interrupted. "That's why I said I'm her nephew. I'm going to *be* her nephew."

I stared at him in horror. I certainly hoped he was lying. I might have been willing to allow him in my clan, but to allow him to date one of my nieces or great-nieces? Absolutely not.

"It's not really that serious," I replied with great dignity, figuring that covered all my bases. "You can't call me your aunt when you aren't even engaged."

"Just give us time," Stewart shot back.

"Um, excuse me," Libby said, looking from one of us to the other with a confused look on her face. "What is your name?"

"Sebastian Noclanhuman."

Libby gasped. "Your turning failed? Oh, you poor boy!"

Stuart's face twitched.

"I hear there's a way to fix that now," Braeden said gruffly. "Some of the people in our clan have been talking about seeing if they can get work doing that if the process gets legalized."

"Which it shouldn't be!" his wife said indignantly. "It requires being tainted! Don't taunt the boy with things that can never be!"

"Those things very well *can* be," Bronson retorted. "There's a thriving black market now. I imagine that's why our turning stone got stolen—so it can be used for that!"

Lilith let out a thin wail.

Oh, if only I had my notebook with me! Both Bronson and Libby were terrific suspects, but I wasn't sure I would remember all the reasons for it.

Bronson, of course, might have sold the turning stone to the black market in order to cash in on a fortune. If he made it look like a robbery, he might have thought his wife and clan wouldn't ever know he'd been responsible.

Libby, of course, might have wanted to protect the stone from clan members using it in the wrong way.

The two of them might have colluded on the scheme together. Or one of them might be trying to spite the other. There were myriad possibilities, and while I was sure neither of them could have pulled the safe out of the wall in that way, there was no doubt that they could have hired someone to do that.

Three suspects, I thought. *Bronson, Libby, and Skipper.*

While it was satisfying to collect new suspects, it wasn't enough to solve the mystery. A sleuth needed to do more than collect suspects: they also needed to eliminate them. And regardless of whether one of those three was the true culprit, there was clearly somebody else involved. Somebody with incredible strength.

"I think I giant did this," Lillian said, looking down at the safe, which looked like it had a hole punched straight through it. "Nobody else could, could they?"

I glanced up at the ceiling. It looked unharmed.

"No," I said with certainty. "Not a giant. A basajaun."

Everyone stared at me.

CHAPTER 4

"A basajaun?" Bruno repeated skeptically. "You mean the half-beasts?"

His wife elbowed him in the stomach.

"I mean the people whose physical appearance tends to resemble a were's half-form and whose racial magical ability is to become solider and tougher, yes," I said, ignoring the rude term. "A lot of giants could have done something like this, to be sure. But not without becoming taller than your ceiling. I see no cracks in it."

Everybody looked up.

"Now, a basajaun," I said, "can become solider and tougher at any time. They do it without growing larger ... because of course, they can't grow larger, that being the giants' racial ability."

"What if it's not a racial trait, though?" Lilith asked. "What if it's a species trait that allowed them to do this?"

"Like what?" Seamus asked.

"A weregorilla," I said, catching on. "They're strong, even in human form. It's their magical ability."

"Eww." Lina wrinkled her nose. "A gorilla in my house!"

"A haltija," Brandon suggested. "They're super strong while insubstantial. That's why they guard banks."

Seamus pointed at the busted safe. "That was not done by someone who was insubstantial."

"Ghouls are pretty strong, and they don't feel pain," Lina said.

"True," Bruno nodded. "For that matter, draculas have super strength."

I was starting to feel rather dismayed. My suspect list, which had seemed narrowed down as far as one of the eight races, was getting broader and broader. Yet I couldn't afford to overlook these exceptions. Any one of them might be vitally important.

I had to take notes. I simply had to. I checked the pockets of my bathrobe, but I couldn't find anything there. Where had I put my notebook?

Maybe I'd take notes in my phone. I'd installed a program to let me keep notes straight a few months ago. Except, where was my phone? It wasn't in my bathrobe pockets, either! I thought for sure I'd brought it with me!

"At least we know what the crash was now," Skipperdoo said, pointing at the safe.

I nodded slowly. It *did* seem safe to assume that the crashing sound had come from this house ... except ...

"Except the crash didn't wake up either of you," I said to Bradley and Lina. "It woke me up, and I wasn't in this house. Are you both sound sleepers?"

"We woke up when you rang the doorbell incessantly," Braeden said sourly.

Which means it didn't come from here, I thought, nodding. *Which means ...*

"Which means we have to check the outside again!" I cried. "There might be clues there we've missed! Skipperdoo, come with me!"

"My name is Sebastian! And it's cold outside!"

I ignored his protests as I marched down the stairs, and the rest of them followed me.

"I'm going to call the police," Brady said with an edge of defensiveness in his voice as I reached the front door. "No offense to your detective skills, but ..."

"No, no, please call them," I said, waving my hand. "If I can't solve the case before they get here, I'm not much of a sleuth. If they can find our turning stones before I can, then I welcome their help."

Bruno nodded sharply, looking mollified, and then shut the door as Sassafras and I stepped outside.

"It's c-c-cold," my sidekick complained, rubbing his arms.

"You have a ski mask," I reminded him.

"I'm not going to wear it when the cops are coming!" he declared. "They might think I'm a crook!"

And yet, you didn't think anything of wearing it into my house, I thought, shaking my head. *Or of going into a stranger's house in the first place.* This human boy had such strange priorities.

Well, Spenser's complaining notwithstanding, I commenced a diligent search for clues. I hadn't thought to bring a magnifying glass with me, so I shrank down to dodo form and held my face close to the ground as I waddled beside Spenser's footprints, watching for any sign that someone else might have been outside.

We were almost all the way back to my house before I found the clue I'd been looking for.

"Just because he didn't leave any footprints doesn't mean I was lying," Steven was saying defensively. "He might've been a specter or something. He wouldn't have left footprints if he was insubstantial."

I had already thought of that theory, and dismissed it. Specters couldn't talk while insubstantial, much less hand over fifty dollar bills. If the man had been insubstantial, he couldn't have dared Steven or paid him to go anywhere, and if Spencer had lied about that, I had no reason to believe that there had been a stranger involved in the first place.

My eyes fell on a tiny scrap of something that looked like a corner from a candy bar wrapper.

I let out a quack of delight and shifted to half-form so that I could seize it triumphantly. It had been half-buried in the compacted snow of one of Stephen's footprints, which must have been why it hadn't blown away.

This was proof that somebody had been here, perhaps eating a candy bar while waiting for a gullible sucker to wander by!

Unless of course it was Steven's litter.

"Do you like candy bars?" I demanded, interrupting my sidekick's defensive and wandering spiel.

"Huh?" He looked startled.

"It's important," I said sternly. "Do you like them?"

"Ye-esssssssss," he said slowly. "Everyone does."

"Do you like this kind?" I asked, shoving the tiny scrap at him.

Scotty stared at the corner of the semi-metallic wrapper, with its silver underside and brown top. "What kind is it?"

"A kind with a brown wrapper," I informed him. Was he blind? "Have you eaten a candy bar with a brown wrapper recently?"

"I—I have no idea," he said. "I might have. Why?"

"Because either this fell out of your pocket while you were walking ... or ..." I said dramatically, "it's proof that somebody else was here before you. It was partly buried in your footprint, which means you stepped on it."

Siegfried's face brightened. "Then it belongs to the thief!"

"Only if it didn't fall out of your pocket."

"It didn't," he said immediately. "It definitely didn't."

That didn't really strike me as convincing, given that he had only declared himself sure that it wasn't his after I had told him it would prove his innocence if it wasn't, but never mind. It might still be useful. Any slight lead was better than nothing.

I shrank back to dodo, not bothering to pocket the clue because it would disappear inside me, like my clothes, while I was shifted. I found nothing else beside Spaghetti's footprints, so when they veered off towards my house, I kept heading straight forward.

"Hey. Hey!" Squirrel protested. "Where are you going? The warm house is that way!"

I turned around and shook my feathered dodo head in disbelief. Did he really think we were done searching for clues?

"Warm house!" he insisted again, pointing.

I shifted back into my human form, now holding the tiny scrap of clue in my left hand, where it had been before I'd shifted.

"Sheridan," I said patiently, "the crash might have come from the other side of my house. We need to talk to my other neighbors."

"Sebastian," he said. "It's Sebastian. How bad *is* your memory?"

I ignored that terribly rude question. "We probably don't have much more time before the police come, and I'd dearly like to solve this mystery before they get here. Come on."

I shrank to dodo and continued waddling forward through the freezing powder.

He grumbled vehemently as he stomped after me. I didn't know why he was the one complaining. I was the one wading through inches of snow wearing nothing but feathers and bare bird feet.

When we reached the side yard of my right neighbors' house, I spied something that presented a dreadfully disappointing solution to the mystery of the crash.

I shifted to my half-form so that I could sigh heavily.

"What?" Siegfried demanded. "What is it?"

"Their garbage cans are lying on their sides," I said, pointing. "With the trash scattered everywhere. The wind must have blown them down."

"So ... the crash didn't have anything to do with the robbery?" he asked.

"Apparently not." It was most disappointing. "I suppose I should be grateful that the noise woke me."

"You should," Sheridan said. "You definitely should."

"I suppose so," I said desultorily. "But now one of my clues is gone."

"Not all of them," Sheldon said. "You still have ..." He stopped and stared at my empty fingers. "You didn't drop the thing that proves my innocence, did you?!"

I laughed and shifted all the way back to human form. The clue reappeared in my fingers. Trust a human to be ignorant about how weres worked. "No, no. I just made it disappear inside me while I shifted. Weres can do that."

"Only with their clothes, though, right?" Shelly said.

"Of course not," I said. "We can do it with anything, within reason. For instance ..."

I grabbed a loop of his jeans before he could stop me, and shifted to dodo. He was left standing in the snow in boxer shorts.

"HEY!" he shouted.

I snickered as I shifted back, and his pants reappeared. "It was just an example."

"A VERY COLD example!"

Spencer did not seem particularly happy. I, on the other hand, was quite impishly amused.

"Very well," I told him. "Let's go back to the house. I'll make you some ginseng tea to warm up."

"I want hot chocolate instead," he complained.

Chapter 4

Just because he wanted hot cocoa didn't mean I had any. My great-niece Annette had drunk all of it the last time she'd visited.

"You're going to love ginseng tea," I assured him, putting the kettle on the stove and heading back to the table. "It's delicious."

"Aren't you supposed to turn the stove on?" he asked.

I paused, then ran back to do so. "Of course. I was just testing to see how good your detective skills are. Sometimes I wonder why your parents named you Sherlock."

"They didn't!"

"In any case," I said, seating myself at the table, "we need to figure out how the man who left this clue did not leave any footprints. Was he hovering over the snow?"

"I dunno. I wasn't looking."

"Did he have wings?"

"He was wearing a jacket."

I sighed. Sherman was not being very helpful.

"How tall was he?" I asked.

"Average height?" Skipper hedged.

"Short end of average or tall end of average?"

"I wasn't paying that much attention! What does it matter?"

"If he was on the shorter end of average," I said reproachfully, "he could have been a very tall abatwa, such as a pixie or sprite."

"Well, I don't know," he snapped, "so it doesn't matter."

Another useful possibility occurred to me. "What color was his skin?"

"What does that matter?"

I stared at Sumner in exasperation. One might suspect him of being deliberately unhelpful. "Just answer the question."

"I dunno. Medium, I guess."

"Medium brown, or medium peach?" I asked, gesturing from my dark wrinkles to his pale pastiness.

"Medium peach?" he hazarded.

So that was another possibility eliminated. Tellems were a species of abatwa that could fly without wings, but they all had brown skin, even if they had been white before being turned.

"It might have been a kappa," I mused. "They can control water, including snow. If it was a kappa, he might've erased his footprints."

"What if it was a plain old, boring human?" Silas demanded, looking annoyed. "Why does it have to be someone with magical powers?"

"Oh, Sirius," I said, shaking my head. "You do realize that if I thought a human had done it, you'd be my prime suspect?"

"Why *couldn't* a human have done it?" he asked defensively. "We're smart, too!"

"Smart, yes, but capable of walking on snow without making any mark in it, no. It's possible the thief came to my house before the snow fell, but in that case, he couldn't have left the clue. The clue was only partly buried in your footprint, which means it was on top of the snow when you stepped on it."

"So maybe someone else left the clue," he said. "Maybe the thief came hours before the snow fell."

"Then why did someone dare you to come into my house?" I challenged. "If nothing else, the person who made that dare was standing out in the snow without having left footprints."

"Okay! Whatever!" he said, throwing up his hands. "At least my being human means I'm innocent, then!"

"Simon, you *did* leave footprints leading up to my house," I said with exasperation. "Your being human proves no innocence at all. Now, maybe if you were unturned as opposed to having had your turning fail ..."

"Why would that make a difference? And I *am* unturned! I told you that before!"

Had he? I didn't remember.

"Well, in that case," I said, "I highly doubt that you would have stolen a turning stone, much less two of them. The very fact of what was stolen implies your innocence."

"Huh?" he asked.

"If an unturned human touches a turning stone, they turn immediately," I said. "If they do so without anyone else touching it at the same time to show the stone the desired form, the turning usually goes wrong or fails. That is, of course, why turning stones are rarely kept in the same house with small children. If you are unturned, I doubt you'd want to take the chance of stealing a turning stone and perhaps possibly touch it by mistake."

Samuel shuddered.

"Exactly," I said. "Now, a human whose turning had failed might be an excellent suspect, if only the evidence didn't imply magic being used. A human whose turning had failed might have a possible motive of wanting to spite people whose turnings had succeeded ..."

My voice trailed off. What if Silas was lying about his unturned status? I had the sudden, uneasy feeling that I had forgotten the rather obvious possibility that more than one person could have been involved in this robbery.

I silently ran through the possibilities in my mind. If he was guilty, then he must have hidden the turning stone somewhere in my house. He couldn't have delivered it to anyone else, because I'd been watching him ever since I'd found him. He couldn't be carrying it on him, because turning stones were quite large—the size of a bowling ball.

As I was starting to worry extremely that perhaps I had made a dreadful miscalculation, I heard a knock on my front door.

I jumped, startled.

"Police!" a voice called. "Ms. Wereclandodo, may we speak with you?"

"Oh, good," I said with relief. I'd wanted to solve the case before they came, but now I was more worried about my safety. "Sherwood, come with me."

"What am I, Robin Hood?" he grumbled. But he got up from the table and followed me to the front door.

I opened it and let two police officers in. One of them, a man with a dog face, tipped his hat.

"I heard about your loss, ma'am. May we investigate your house to see if we can find anything of help?"

"Of course," I said.

He immediately became a tailless dog with a man's face and raced down the hallway, sniffing with his nose to the ground.

"What's *that?*" Stanford demanded, looking freaked out.

"He's a penghou," the other police officer said, chuckling. "He can sniff out turning stones, among other things."

"Is he some kind of weredog?" Stanford asked.

"No, it's a kapre. He can also turn into a camphor tree."

Kapres were like weres, except that they shifted into plants instead of animals.

"But he's a dog!" Stanford exclaimed.

The other police officer laughed heartily. "Well, in that case, I'm no more than a horse."

"What species are you?" I asked curiously.

"A nokk," he said. "I turn into a horse when touching water."

I couldn't quite remember which race they belonged to. "A specter?" I hedged.

"Lorelei."

I blinked. All loreleis could only breathe underwater during the full moon. "So you spend your full moons as a horse surrounded by fish and mermaids?"

"Yes, I do."

His partner ran back, tailless rear end wagging, and he turned into a human with a dog face again.

"Smell anything?" the nokk asked.

"No turning stones here," the penghou said.

"What about insubstantial ones?" I demanded. Because it had occurred to me that Simon might have been lying about being human. He could be a specter who had hidden my turning stone in a wall.

"I'm getting to that." The penghou cracked his knuckles, stretched, and shifted into a short, spindly camphor tree. A branch shook vigorously, and a leaf broke loose and fell onto my carpet. A second later, he was back to being a man with a dog face. He leaned over and picked up the leaf.

"Does the leaf help?" I asked in confusion.

"The smell of camphor makes it possible for me to sniff out insubstantial things," he explained, pulling a rubber band out of his pocket and stretching it around his head to fasten the leaf on top of his nose. "Be right back!"

And the man-faced dog raced off through my house again.

"While we're waiting, why don't you tell me how you figured out your turning stone was missing?" the nokk asked me, pulling a notebook and pen from his breast pocket.

I eyed the notebook enviously. If only I knew where I had put mine.

"Well, it all started when I heard a crashing sound," I began.

Come to think of it, we still hadn't found any explanation for that noise yet, had we? I would have to take Sirius to investigate. Maybe my neighbors to the right had heard it. I really should have thought to go there while we were still outside.

"And then I went downstairs, and I found —"

Severus let out a protesting sound.

I turned to give him a disapproving stare. If he was innocent, he shouldn't mind me telling the police the whole story. We had to catch the crook.

"Yes?" the nook police officer asked.

He was interrupted by a loud whistle from the tea kettle.

I jumped, my train of thought completely interrupted. What was that horrible noise?

"Oh, is that the teapot?" Saul broke in eagerly, looking relieved. "We're making ginseng tea. You want some?"

"No, thank you," the NOKK said.

"It was ginger tea," I corrected the boy.

"No, it was ginseng."

"Ginger!"

"Ginseng! She has a terrible memory," Stetson added in a confidential whisper to the police officer. "That's why I'm here. To help her. I'm her assistant."

I bristled. "The word is 'sidekick.'"

"The word's 'assistant.'"

"No, it's 'sidekick'!"

"See?" Stetson said, shaking his head. "Terrible memory."

I was very annoyed.

Chapter 4

We headed back to the kitchen to check on the tea kettle. It was whistling quite shrilly as it waited for us.

"Hey," Sampson whispered as I lifted the kettle off the burner. He eyed the hallway where the nokk was standing. "Don't tell them about how you met me."

"I certainly will," I said, turning off the stove. "You should have nothing to hide."

"I don't wanna get thrown in jail for trespassing!" he hissed.

"Well, maybe you should have thought of that before you took that silly bet."

"It was a dare, and I regret it, okay?"

"I'm glad to hear that," I said. "But you're still the only witness who has seen the man who probably broke into my house. You need to tell them the whole story so that they can find him."

Sawyer ground his teeth. "I don't know anything useful."

"I imagine they'll be the judges of that."

"I don't want to get in trouble!"

"I'm delighted to hear that. I'm sure you'll behave with more wisdom in the future."

He glared at me.

"Is there a disagreement here?" the police officer from the hallway asked, wandering into the kitchen.

"Yes," I said. "Sawyer's being a little silly. If you don't like ginger, can I get you another kind of tea? I have ginseng and chamomile."

"No, thank you," the police officer said. "I'd rather not turn into a horse right now. Can you tell me about how you found your turning stone was stolen?"

I stared at him. Good gracious! A horse? Why would that happen?

"Hey, how come you guys aren't next door?" Sonny broke in. "Their turning stone was stolen, too."

"We have another unit over there," the man who had been inexplicably worried about turning into a horse said. "Right now, we're here to help you. Please tell me how you learned the stone was missing."

"Well, there was a crashing sound," I said, "and then —"

"I was here with her the whole night," Sawyer broke in. "Because I'm her assistant."

"You'll get your chance to talk, son," the police officer said, looking rather annoyed. "Let me hear from her first."

I blinked in startlement. "Is he your son?"

"What?" the police officer asked, looking baffled. "Oh, that. No. It's an expression. Please go on, ma'am."

I cleared my throat. "Well, it all began when there was a crashing sound from outside ..."

I went on to explain everything else that had happened so far, stopping a few times to fill in parts I had forgotten. As I did so, I poured the water from the tea kettle into the mugs for me and Spencer, and I passed one to him. I sipped mine, which tasted rather flavorless for some reason, as I talked.

The police officer said nothing aside from "Mm-hmm" and "Uh huh" and "Go on" while he wrote down my words, and it wasn't long before his partner joined us, asking for permission to open anything that was currently shut.

"Of course," I said. "Please search everything."

By the time I finished my story, he was back, having searched everywhere thoroughly.

"No turning stones," he said, "substantial or insubstantial, though there was one on this table recently."

I sighed. So much for my last vestige of hope that I had simply hidden it somewhere I'd forgotten. Still, that also cleared Sherwin. It was rather a relief to know I hadn't been spending the last two or three hours with a criminal.

"Sorry, ma'am," the non-canine police officer said. "Quite often missing turning stones turn out to still be hidden insubstantially in the house they went missing from, but it seems this time that isn't the case."

"Quite often?" I asked. "Do turning stones get stolen a lot?"

"More often than you might think, given how careless people can be with them. That's why we have officers specially trained in hunting them down."

"Me," his dog-faced partner said, raising his hand cheerfully.

"But that wasn't even what I was taking about. It's far more common for a specter to accidentally turn one insubstantial and knock it inside a wall or under the ground. You'd be amazed how many times that's happened."

"So you thought it might be accidental?" I asked.

"Indeed," he said. "It happens all the time with senior citizens, especially specters."

I bristled. "I am not a specter! And I wouldn't misplace such an important thing!"

"Of course not," he soothed. "May I ask what you are?"

"A weredodo," I said.

He and his partner exchanged a glance.

"Are you in half-form, by any chance?" the dog-faced man asked delicately.

"No, I am not!" I said indignantly. "I couldn't disappear an entire turning stone inside myself without noticing! Do I *look* like I'm in half-form?"

"Half-forms aren't always obvious," the dog-faced officer said. "I have a sister who's a weredog. As long as she keeps her hair combed over her floppy ears and her paws in shoes while she's half-shifted, nobody notices."

"Well, *my* half-form is obvious," I said huffily, demonstrating. An enormously long feathered neck sprouted between my head and shoulders.

"No offense meant, ma'am," the non-canine assured me. "It's just that peng-hous can't sniff out turning stones that are hidden inside weres. And we've seen it happen before. Especially with senior citizens."

I was getting extremely irate with his use of that word. Some might think that knowing how age had degraded my memory would mean I wouldn't mind others assuming that fact. But no. That just made it even more of a touchy subject. Especially when there was any implication that I might not be competent enough to take care of myself.

"Well, I appreciate your checking every possibility," I said coldly. As far as I was concerned, the two police officers had worn out their welcome. Polite about it or not, I did not appreciate people questioning my judgment. I got enough of that from my brother. "Now that you're satisfied that I was not the accidental culprit, I hope you'll be able to find the thief before he gets much further away with my clan's turning stone."

"Just one last thing," the dog-faced man asked, eyeing Sherwin. "What species are you?"

"Human," he said with an edge in his voice.

"I don't smell a failed turning," he said suspiciously.

"You wouldn't! I'm unturned!"

"Hmm. That would explain it." The dog-faced man paused. "How old are you, kid?"

"Twenty-five."

"And still unturned?"

"Yes! I'm allowed to stay unturned if I want to!"

The dog-faced man scratched under his neck. "Sure, you're allowed to, kid, but it's pretty weird."

Sherwin looked very peeved.

"Oh, here's the clue we found outside," I said, remembering it for the first time. I picked it up from the table and handed it to them, explained where we'd gotten it from and what we'd deduced from it. "Perhaps you can check it for fingerprints!"

"Perhaps," the non-canine said, pulling out a plastic bag and gesturing for me to drop it in. He didn't seem to consider my clue particularly revelatory. "It might have been more helpful if you had left it where it was."

"She couldn't do that!" Sherwin said defensively. "The thief might have come back and picked it up to cover his tracks!"

"Uh huh." The police officer looked like he didn't believe for a second that would have happened. "Well, thank you very much your help. We'll get back to you as soon as we find your stone, or if we have any other questions."

"You *will* find it, right?" I asked anxiously.

The non-canine police officer paused. "I'm not going to lie to you, ma'am. In cases like this, where the object wasn't simply misplaced and we have no solid leads, the chances are only twenty, thirty percent that we'll find it eventually. We'll do our best, of course, but you might have to accept that it's gone."

That took the breath out of me. Even the police couldn't promise any more than thirty percent?

No. That wasn't acceptable. I couldn't let it be gone.

"Thanks very much for your time," the dog-faced police officer said to me, bobbing his head with his ears flopping.

The two of them got up and headed to the front door.

"You're welcome," I said quickly, following them, "but I can help much more than this. I'm a sleuth. I can find more clues —"

"Of course," the non-canine said. "Give us a call if you find any."

I had the nasty feeling he was only humoring me.

"I *can!*" I said angrily. "I can, and I *will!*"

"Well, then, remember to leave them where they were, so we can inspect them properly," the man said, tipping his hat. "Good day, ma'am."

As the front door shut, my blood was boiling. I wanted to be taken seriously, and I would be. I was certainly not going to trust the fate of my clan to the police's twenty percent. If they weren't going to find it, I would do it myself. I had wanted to do that, anyway.

I sipped my flavorless tea, fuming. Surely I had learned something earlier that would crack this case wide open. That was how mysteries worked. All I needed to do was put the pieces together in the right way, and the answer would emerge from a chrysalis, flapping its wings in brilliant obviousness. I just had to notice something ...

Something ...

Something ...

Blast. Nothing was coming to mind.

"It's a shame about your turning stone," Shelby said.

I ignored him. This wasn't a time for my sidekick to distract me. I focused all my brainpower on sorting through tonight's clues.

"I know you wanted it," said Something. "But really, is this so bad? I mean, you weren't using it. If no one's joined your clan in forty-two years, it's highly unlikely that ..."

Yammer, yammer, yammer. I wished Something would cut it out. Couldn't he see I was trying to think?

There was something about that safe that bothered me. The way it had been ripped out of the wall and punched through, with no noise being made. I was pretty sure I knew what species could do something like that, if only I could ... remember ...

That's it! The answer burst into bloom in my mind.

I stood up from the table, drank the rest of my lukewarm tea in one gulp, and slammed the mug on the table. "Come on, Shannon! We've off to investigate!"

"Off to investigate *what?*" he goggled.

I grinned ferociously. "The Vampireclanaswangs' safe. I'm about to blow this case wide open."

Wasn't This Chapter 4?

I marched steadily forward, heedless of the snow that I was kicking up as we went. I didn't even worry about the tiny flakes I saw drifting down from the sky. If I was right about my theory, and I was guessing I was, it wouldn't matter if it snowed more and the footprints were all erased.

Sheldon let out a steady stream of grumbling from behind me, mostly about the fact that I had refused to elucidate him before sending us back out into the cold.

"Just be patient!" I called, not turning around. "I can't explain until every-body is there at once!"

Honestly! Hadn't he ever read mysteries?

"But do you know who *did* it?" he yelled.

"All will be revealed!" I called back mysteriously.

We reached the front door of my neighbors' home, I pounded on it, the door was opened, and the Vampireclanaswangs were more than a little surprised to see us back.

"We have the police here," Lillian said. "We don't need you."

"There's where you're wrong," I said. "I've noticed something that everyone else overlooked."

"Are you all right?" Braden asked, glancing behind me. "You look a little ill."

"So c-cold outside," Stephan complained.

"Well, come in, then," Layla said, looking displeased to be forced into hospitality.

I didn't wait to be invited twice. I immediately bustled in and up the stairs, fairly relieved myself to be back in a warm house. In my excitement, I had found the flurries and the chill wind simulating rather than upsetting, but there was no denying that my ears felt like two ice cubes hidden in an igloo and then packed with snow to keep a soda can cold.

Upstairs, I found four police officers pouring over the broken wall and the busted safe, talking to each other and taking notes. Two of them were the ones who had been at my house before.

"Hey!" the dog-faced man said, alarmed, as I headed toward them. "Stay away from the crime scene!"

I ignored this advice, though I stopped short of coming close enough to disturb anything they were photographing.

"Is everyone here?" I asked, looking over my shoulder.

The Vampireclanaswangs emerged from the top of the stairs. Sinclair was with them, shivering as he hunched into the scarf Lilith was draping over him.

"What is this regarding?" one of the police officers I didn't know asked, looking annoyed.

"It's regarding the fact that I know exactly what species did this," I said proudly, pointing at the safe and then the wall it came from. "It's a haltija."

The police officers didn't blink.

"You don't say," said one of the unfamiliar ones. He was a duergar, and very ugly.

"You see, haltijas only have super strength while insubstantial," I said excitedly. "So we figured one of them couldn't have done this. But a specter can also make things they touch insubstantial at any time! Which means he could have made the safe and the wall insubstantial, ripped the safe out of the wall, punched it open, grabbed the turning stone, and escaped! It could all be done in complete silence, because insubstantial things don't emit sound waves!"

My brilliant theory was met by stormy silence.

"This is not our first haltija crime," the duergar said finally.

I blinked and stared at the four police officers. They all looked rather impatient.

"Is there anything else?" the non-canine who had been at my house asked.

"Um ... yes!" I said, as a new idea occurred to me. "Stevie here was lying when he told you about the man who dared him!"

This caused a mild stir.

"Was he indeed?" the dog-faced man asked, eyeing my sidekick with an expression that looked almost hungry.

"I was not!" Stewie yelped. "Why would you say that?!"

"Because your story doesn't hold up," I said with satisfaction. "There aren't many species that could do what you described without having left footprints, and all of them are conspicuous enough that it's not believable you didn't notice anything specific. I suspect you were deliberately describing that supposed individual in as vague terms as possible so as to attempt to not get caught in a lie when the culprit was found. And then there's the general silliness of your story in the first place, which requires you to have had no common sense whatsoever. Well?"

"No, I —!" Stevie began furiously. But then he looked at the stern-faced police officers, then over at me, then at the steely-eyed vampires standing beside him. His shoulders slumped. "Okay, fine," he muttered. "There was nobody else out there. I just wanted her to let me leave."

"Why were you in my house?" I demanded.

"The door was open," he said. "I was cold. I figured, why not sit in a warm house for awhile?"

I stared at him incredulously. "You do remember what I said before about your story being implausible because your actions lacked common sense?"

"Well, I'm sorry if I have no common sense!" he flared. "This time I'm telling the truth! I had a long walk still ahead of me, and it was cold!"

"You said the door was open," one of the police officers said. "Why would a specter need to open a door?"

"Maybe she left it open," Sidney said, pointing at me. "She has a terrible memory."

"I would not have left it open!" I said, scandalized. "It's possible I might have left it unlocked. But open, never!"

"You might have left it slightly ajar and not noticed," the man with the dog face said gently. "The wind could have blown it open further. That sort of thing happens to senior citizens."

This senior citizen was just about ready to feed him his own hat. This senior citizen was not a fan of condescension.

"I'm sorry I lied." Sidney looked at me guiltily, twitching the scarf around his neck. "But really, I didn't think anything had been stolen from your house. I just wanted you to let me go home. You were one freaky scary dodo, standing there out in the snow."

"Apology and compliment accepted," I said stiffly. "But you've done irreparable damage to my investigation. Because of you, I wasted my time checking footprints. Because of you, the culprit had more time to escape!"

"The culprit probably escaped hours before you ever woke up," Steven shot back. "Even the crash that woke you up had nothing to do with it. It was just a bunch of trash cans falling over!"

"You don't know that that was unrelated!" I yelled.

"I *do!* You said so yourself! Or did you forget that, along with everything else?!"

"Tell you what," the police officer who hadn't spoken yet said. He was a tall man with antlers. "Why don't the two of you go back to your house, and when we're through here, we'll send someone over to take your statements. An *honest* one, this time," he added, giving my sidekick a rather frightening glare.

Sonny gulped and looked cowed.

I knew when I was being dismissed, and I didn't like it. But there didn't seem to be much point in trying to change their minds.

"Come on, then, Siegfried," I said. "Let's go back to my home."

"Out in the cold again?" he complained. But he didn't put up any more fuss. He looked a little bit afraid of the antlered man.

The Vampireclanaswangs were only too glad to see the back of us. Lillian even asked for her scarf back, to Sonny's dismay.

As we headed back towards my house, I stomped through the snow, frustrated that I was still being treated like a hindrance rather than a help to the investigation.

Had they even considered the most interesting aspect of all about a haltija having done it? A haltija wouldn't even have needed to open the safe. They just could have reached through the wall, made the turning stone insubstantial, and pulled it out. Nobody would have even been the wiser until they had tried to open the safe and found it gone.

Unless there was a specter alarm in there, which there probably was, I realized. *The thief would have needed to be substantial when he reached in there, or else he would have tripped it.*

Specter alarms were highly sensitive devices that would go off at the slightest touch. A specter turned them insubstantial before arming them, and once they were armed, they would go off if brushed even slightly by anything insubstantial later. Substantial things couldn't touch them and therefore wouldn't trigger them, so they were not an inconvenience to the person who wanted to keep their things protected.

I had only just remembered that those things existed. I was suddenly glad I hadn't brought up the curiosity of a haltija having chosen to break the safe in order to reach in with a substantial hand, because the police probably would've given me that same flat stare that said, "Why are you telling us obvious things?"

I shuffled down the sidewalk as the snow fell thicker, feeling depressed. What was the point of me being a sleuth if I couldn't help to solve my own mystery? Yet again, I was the incompetent shuffled off to the side so that I wouldn't get in anyone else's way. Yet again, I was nothing but silly old Aunt Dodo.

A car drove down the street, headlights bright through the white clumps raining down from above. It was driving slowly, but still faster than Sven and me, who were getting slower and slower as our visibility receded.

The car slowed to a stop, and a window opened. "Hey, need a ride?" the driver called from inside.

"No, thank you!" I said. "We're fine."

"Y-yep, we're fine!" Severus agreed.

"Your teeth are chattering," the man said in exasperation. "That doesn't look fine."

"It's only a two-minute walk," I said. "Don't worry."

"Can you even see where you're going?" he asked.

"Unless you get lost," he said.

The wind took that moment to pick up, gusting more snow at us. I stared out into white-speckled darkness. He might have a point. I couldn't see more than a few feet in front of my face. Had I forgotten which way my house was?

"Get in," the driver said, pushing a button. There was a sound of doors unlocking. "Nobody should be out on a night like this."

"No thanks," I said. "We'll be fine on our own."

He pulled out a gun and leveled it at me. "Get in."

I had a terrible feeling that things had gone very wrong.

CHAPTER I'M SURE I'LL REMEMBER IT

Nestled inside the warm car, Severus blew on his hands while I sat in the back beside him, stiff with terror. The car started up, and it began to crawl down the road.

"Wh-where are we going?" I stammered.

"I don't know," the driver said succinctly. "I guess that depends on how much you've figured out."

"Nothing at all," Stanley said quickly. "She's a terrible sleuth."

I was not impressed with his loyalty.

"I'm a wonderful sleuth, but I have no idea who you are," I said coldly. "Since you've kidnapped us at gunpoint, maybe you'd be so kind to elucidate us."

He glanced back at us in the rearview mirror, grinned, and said nothing.

"Well, obviously you're the haltija who stole my turning stone," I said crossly. "Most likely you were listening to our conversation from a listening device, or maybe you were hiding under our feet after the police left. Either way, I clearly said something that alarmed you, so I must have figured out something you don't want the police to know."

The driver just grinned.

"That, or you want them to *think* I figured out something you don't want them to know," I added. "To send them barking up the wrong tree. Or I'm just a generic hostage."

"Two hostages," Stormy muttered.

"You really must stop whining," I said reprovingly. "At least you're warm now. That's what you wanted, right?"

"I'd like to *live*, too!"

"Tell me what else you know," the man from the driver's seat said sharply.

"Don't say a word!" Severus hissed.

I ignored my sidekick. "Of course. But first, a question."

"Absolutely not," the man said succinctly. "You're talking. I'm the one with the gun."

So much for the villainous monologue I'd been hoping for.

"What are you going to do with us?" I demanded.

"That's a question. I'm not answering those."

I worked backward, trying to figure out what I might have said in the recent past to make this man alarmed enough to kidnap me. What could possibly be worth showing me his face?

Unless it wasn't his face, of course. Unless he was an aswang. They could shapeshift into anybody they sucked blood from.

My mind worked feverishly. Hadn't Libby mentioned that some members of their clan wanted to get work turning people a second time, which was currently illegal? And hadn't Braeden said he disapproved? Perhaps one of them, knowing that their clan leader wouldn't allow it, had decided to take matters into his own hands. Perhaps he'd stolen the turning stone to force their clan to merge with another one with a clan leader more favorable to his interests.

But in that case, where was the haltija? Was he—or she—back at the Vampire-clanaswangs' house, listening to the police?

There was only one way to find out. I checked the pockets of my bathrobe and found a ball of lint. I threw it at the back of his head.

He flicked insubstantial in the space of a flinch. Then he was back to normal, and roared, "What was that for?!"

"Just testing," I said.

"Testing what?!"

"To see whether you were a haltija or not. You had pointed ears while insubstantial, so I assume you are. I thought maybe you were an aswang. Do you have any conspirators, or did you work alone? I'd like my turning stone back now, please."

Sigmund moaned and put his face in his hands. He seemed to be mumbling something like, "We're gonna die ..."

"I'm not answering any questions!" our captor roared. "You tell me what you know, *now!*"

Siegfried looked completely ashen. His pasty skin was even whiter than usual.

"Don't worry," I reassured him. "He's probably planning to kill us anyway. We've seen his face."

Siegfried looked incredulous and not at all reassured.

"TALK!" our captor roared.

We reached an intersection and a car crossed in front of us, bright headlights flashing. Our driver clutched the steering wheel with both hands and shouted obscenities at the car that had zoomed past us at a dangerous speed.

Well, he was distracted, so ...

I shifted to half-form, jabbed my extra-long neck forward, and grabbed the gun in my teeth. Then I leapt back and shifted to dodo, hiding the gun inside me.

"HEY!" the driver screamed, spinning around.

I flapped my wings and quacked gleefully.

"I can still wring your neck," he snarled, going insubstantial.

I might have made a slight tactical error.

I dove for the front seat, but he was in the back seat in an instant. Going substantial, he seized my fragile dodo neck. I slashed at his face with my talons, he flinched insubstantial, and I squeezed between the front bucket seats into driver's seat.

Behind me, Skittles was screaming, and I glanced back to see a vicious fight between a skinny little twig and bulky man who could go insubstantial. It wasn't a fair fight at all. So I shifted to half-form and pressed my own advantage.

Or rather, the gas pedal.

The car lurched forward, skidded, fishtailed, and went sliding out of control.

The haltija yelled and hung on to the seat. For an instant, I wondered why he didn't just go insubstantial, but realized that he didn't want the car to leave him behind.

"Brake!" Skittles screamed. "Brake! Brake! Brake!"

A brake wouldn't help. I knew that for sure. I'd driven on icy roads before. So I did the one thing that seemed sensible. I reached desperately for my seat belt and slammed it into the buckle.

WHAM!

The car rammed straight into a cement barrier at the side of the road. Our abductor went flying. My head snapped forward and back again. Spaghetti screamed.

I now felt dizzy. Was the car tilting? No, maybe it was whiplash.

Ow ...

Spaghetti was still screaming.

"Stop screaming!" I yelled. "What's going on back —"

I looked. My breath caught, and bile rose in my throat.

Our captor was the only one who hadn't been wearing a seat belt, and his head had smashed straight through the window beside him.

He should have gone insubstantial, I thought numbly.

I shifted to human form to feel my neck and see how bad the injury was, found the gun I'd forgotten about between my teeth, and spat it out into my pocket to deal with later.

My sidekick was still screaming.

I noticed that the man's chest was rising and falling, even though there was a terrifying amount of blood coming from his head wound. I let out a long, shuddering breath. "Sousaphone, stop screaming. Call the police."

"But—but—but —!" the boy gibbered.

"911! Police! Ambulance! Now!"

He yanked a phone out of his pocket, dropping it several times because his hands were shaking, and finally managed to dial.

Five minutes later that felt more like five years, we were rescued. A specter EMT made the car insubstantial while a basajaun pulled us out, and a dracula EMT sliced his wrist to produce vampire blood.

"Here," he ordered us, handing us each a paper cup that was about a quarter full. "Drink it." His wrist had healed in less than ten seconds.

"Ewww," Steven moaned, but he did so. I did the same.

In a few minutes, we were both fine. All our injuries were healed. Our captor, however, was another story.

"Can't you heal him, too?" I asked nervously as the basajaun and specter loaded him up on a stretcher. A police officer who had arrived shortly after the ambulance was talking with them.

"We can," the vampire said shortly, "but we've only given him a few drops to stabilize him. If your story's true, he's a violent criminal, and in cases of violent criminals, we prefer not to heal them entirely until they're safely behind bars."

"What if our story weren't true?" Stewie asked.

"Then you'd face obstruction of justice charges, and possibly a charge for reckless endangerment of human or person life," the EMT said shortly. "Excuse me."

The police waved and wandered over to us as the ambulance took off, its sirens blaring.

"You're a really bad driver," Sterling joked, laughing shakily.

"I'm a wonderful driver," I said. "I'm just not very good at finding where I'm going. And I lost my car keys two weeks ago."

He laughed, as if I had been joking.

"Shall I drop you off at home?" the police officer asked, reaching us. "I assume you won't be driving." He looked pointedly at the totaled car.

"Yes, please," I said with a weak smile. "That would be great."

"Who shall I take home first?" he asked. "Or do you live together?"

"Oh, take Spaghetti home first," I said quickly, gesturing at the boy. "He's been wanting to go back home all night. And now that the case has been solved ..."

My sidekick gave me a rueful look. "Sebastian. That has got to be the weirdest one you've come up with yet."

"Regardless," I said, "tell the man your address."

Spaghetti started to speak, and then paused. "Actually, do you mind if I go back home with you?"

"Why?" I asked.

"Because I want more of that hot water you call tea."

My mouth fell open. "Did I forget to put the ginseng in?!"

"Yes, you did," he said, laughing.

"So that's why it was so flavorless!"

He guffawed.

"Well, this time I'll remember it," I said, flustered.

"Nah, hot water's fine," he grinned.

Chapter I Think I Forgot It

He and I got out of the police car at my house, and we waved goodbye to the police officer who drove off.

"Did you really lose your car keys two weeks ago?" Seymour asked, eyeing the car parked in my driveway.

"Not to worry," I said. "I can grocery shop online."

He snorted.

I pulled my house keys out of my pocket, unlocked the door, and let us in. A blast of heat reminded me that I still hadn't turned down the heater from ninety degrees. I would really have to fix that before my gas bill became astronomical.

"Now, let's get that tea started," I said, bustling off towards the kitchen.

"Actually, maybe I'll just borrow a coat and go home," he said, glancing at the coat closet.

What a chicken, so afraid to try something new.

"Nonsense," I scolded. "You have to try it with the ginseng in it. It really does taste better that way."

"Maybe next time," he said.

"Maybe tonight," I said firmly. I held the kettle under the faucet of the kitchen sink and filled it up.

As I placed the kettle on the stovetop and turned it on, a sly smile crept across my face. He didn't know it yet, but I was going to convince that boy he wanted to be a dodo. Now that the criminal was caught, they'd find my turning stone soon enough, and what better way for Victoria to forgive me than to introduce her to a prospective new clan member?

Not that I was going to tell him that yet, of course. He was so determined to stay human, silly boy. He would have to be talked into it. But I was certain I could do it eventually.

I was almost glad I'd left the turning stone out on the table, rather than hiding it properly. If I hadn't done that, the thief who'd come to rob my neighbors' turning stone wouldn't have seen it, it wouldn't have been stolen as an impulsive extra prize, and I wouldn't have had this opportunity to make friends with a young person to add to our clan.

Plus, of course, the police clearly wouldn't have been able to solve this case without me. At very least, without me, the criminal would have escaped.

I headed to the hallway, where Simson was flipping through my the coats in my coat closet. He paused at a bright magenta woollen one with obvious distaste.

"Oh, that one's nice and warm," I said. "Would you like —"

"No."

I noticed that his clothes were damp, no doubt from sitting in a warm car after being snowed on. My clothes were damp, too, but I didn't have a walk through the snow ahead of me.

A thought occurred to me, and I hurried to the laundry room, where I found what I was looking for: a pair of jeans and T-shirt from one of my nephews visiting a few months ago. I'd done his laundry after he'd spilled soda all over himself, and I had kept forgetting to return the clothing to him.

"Here," I said, returning to the hallway with the clothes slung over my arm. "You'll be much more comfortable in dry clothes."

"No, I'll be fine," he said, looking over a thick black coat.

"Going outside in wet things?" I scolded. "I don't think so! You'll catch your death of cold!"

"Look, I'm fine!"

"You are not fine!"

"I don't need them!"

"You will wear them!"

He was being stubborn, so I seized the shoulder of his damp shirt and shifted to half-form to make it disappear.

"HEY!" he screamed, grabbing the dry clothes from me.

But not before I'd seen.

"Why ... do you have feathers on your chest?" I asked slowly.

"It's a costume," he snapped, yanking on my nephew's T-shirt with rapid speed.

"That is not a costume," I said. "That is a half-form."

"It's not a half-form," he said furiously. "I told you, I'm human."

"Then why do you have grey feathers?" I shot back. "What kind of werebird are you? Why would you lie about that? What possible reason —"

I stopped abruptly. Everything fell still.

"Give me back my turning stone."

"It's not yours anymore. It belongs to the cuckoo clan."

"GIVE ME BACK MY TURNING STONE!"

"You weren't using it!" he snapped. "We need another one!"

"Then *buy* one! Do you desperately want a bunch of weredodos in your clan?!"

"We don't have to worry about that!" he yelled. "We can change any stone to cuckoo just by using it once! That's our magical ability!"

I felt like I was going to faint.

"Look, I'm sorry," he said, edging off to the side. "You've been really nice, and I appreciate that you let me come here so the cops wouldn't know where I live, but I've got to get going now."

"You were working with him all along," I said, hyperventilating. "You called that haltija to pick us up!"

"Only because you said you'd had a breakthrough!" he said defensively. "And then you wouldn't say what it was! I thought you were doing that thing where you gather all the suspects and then reveal who —"

"How did you call him without me noticing?!"

"I texted him!" he said, exasperated, pulling out his phone and wiggling it in front of me. "It's this newfangled invention that people your age really ought to learn how to —"

I lunged for the phone and grabbed it. I shifted to dodo, taking the phone with me, and then shifted back to half-form again.

"STOP STEALING MY THINGS!" Stormy yelled.

"I could say the same thing!" I shot back. "Now, do you really think the police can't use that phone to find you if I hand it to them?"

His face turned bright red. "Come on, lady! It was supposed to be a victimless crime!"

"Is that so?" I asked icily. "Speaking as one of your victims, you may have forgotten about the clan you were planning to destroy. Not to mention that little matter of the forcible abduction."

"I didn't know that guy was going to get violent!" Slater cried. "I just asked him to wait as an escape driver in case I needed it!"

"Astonishing," I said. "Imagine, a criminal getting violent."

"I only hired him in the first place because there was security at your clan leader's house! I was planning to nab the stone while she was on vacation. I didn't know she was going to hand it over to somebody who doesn't even lock the back door. As soon as I saw that I could just stroll in and grab it, I called the guy and told him I didn't need his help anymore. I didn't know he was going to improvise and steal somebody else's turning stone instead!"

So that meant my clan's turning stone had been the original target, and not an afterthought? In a sense, I was proud. It was nice that our clan had been valued, for once.

Of course, that didn't mean I was going to let him keep it.

"Turning stone," I said, pointing at the ground. "Or I will call the police. I'm sure they'd be delighted to have your phone."

"Maaaaaan," he complained, shifting to human form. A backpack bulged out of his shoulder, and he opened it to pull out a green, glowing stone. He thumped it on the floor and glowered at me. "You really don't fight fair, old bat."

"I am not a bat," I said. "I am a dodo."

And I was also a sleuth. One who had just saved my clan's turning stone.

"... And so you have it," I finished, passing a platter of cookies from Victoria to Anabel. "That's how I saved the day from that scoundrel named Silvester."

"You almost *ruined* the day by leaving the door unlocked," Victoria said sourly. She wasn't easy to please. "I can't believe I trusted you to watch over it."

"Oh, hush up," Anabel said, taking several cookies. She was the oldest of us and also the most energetic, despite being over eighty. She refused to retire. She taught yoga and enjoyed it too much. "It sounds like it would have been stolen anyway, and she saved it."

"But all the same, when I entrusted —!"

"I can't wait until my next case!" I broke in. There was no point in letting Victoria start soapboxing. "It's just a shame I don't have a magical ability. Like tracking magic! It would be so useful for all the sleuthing I'm going to do."

Anabel and Victoria exchanged looks.

"What?" I asked.

"You *have* a magical ability," Victoria said with exasperation.

"I do?"

"Yes! It's the same one we have!"

I stared at her blankly.

Anabel reached forward and dropped a cookie into thin air. It disappeared.

"Ohhhhhhhhhhhhhhhh!" I cried. "MY POCKET!"

I reached into my air pocket and pulled out my phone, my wallet, six note-books, eight pens, two scribbled-on stacks of Post-It Notes, two phone bills, one utility bill, the gun that had gone missing after the accident, and my car keys.

I picked them up and dangled them in front of me.

"Another mystery solved!" I said triumphantly.

Author Note

I didn't intend to write about a 63-year-old weredodo. I meant to write about a teenage werevulture. But after I mentioned "Aunt Dodo" in passing in chapter one of *Trials of a Teenage Werevulture,* I knew she had to be a protagonist, too.

WEREDODO MOVIE NIGHT

IT WAS Halloween *and* a full moon, so naturally Victoria had to be a wet blanket and refuse to watch anything remotely scary with us.

"Come on," Anabel begged, holding up a movie called *Ghost Vila*. "It's a slow-paced romance, just like you prefer, and the murder mystery subplot is interesting!"

"Ooh, murder mystery!" I said excitedly, clapping my hands.

"Absolutely not," Victoria said stiffly. "Ghosts don't exist. It's silly to make films about them when everyone knows the legends came from specters."

Victoria was so disgustingly proper. It was hard to believe she was the youngest of us. She was fifty-four, I was sixty-three, and Anabel was eighty-two.

Most clans held full moon meetings full of activities that were far more exciting than movie nights, but our weredodo clan was tiny, comprising only the three of us, and there was only so much a trio of flightless birds past their prime could do.

Victoria checked her watch, got up, and went into the kitchen. She came back with a bowl of fruit and another bowl of pebbles.

"No crackers?" Anabel asked.

"I thought we'd eat more healthily."

"Then what are the candy bars for?" I asked craftily. I had noticed bowls of mini candy bars near the door on our way in.

"Trick-or-treaters," Victoria said in a withering tone.

"Chocolate is bad for dodos," Anabel noted. "Remember when we had to take you to the emergency room?"

"That was only because I forgot to remove the wrapper."

"You weren't even shifted at the time!" Victoria exclaimed.

"You can't expect me to think sanely around chocolate," I said with great dignity.

Victoria got up, went to the front door, and deposited the bowls of candy outside, shutting the door with a meaningful click.

I sighed. So much for sneaking some while her back was turned. Our clan leader had no sense of fun.

Anabel went back to arguing her case. "You'll like it, Victoria, really you will. It's completely consistent with the rules of reality. He's a specter and it turns out that he's not really dead at all, he just has amnesia and doesn't realize he could turn substantial again at any time."

"Hey! Spoilers!" I objected.

Anabel gave me an impish smile. "It's not like you'll remember, Dotty."

I scowled. My memory wasn't *that* bad.

Yes, I may have lost my car keys a few days ago and still had yet to find them. Yes, I may have forgotten it was the full moon tonight until Anabel had called to remind me. Yes, I may have accidentally bought the new Sherlock Holmes movie six times in the past week because I'd kept forgetting I already owned it. But that didn't mean it was okay to spoil me on a movie we were going to be watching!

"I don't know ..." Victoria was starting to waver, seeming possibly interested.

I wasn't interested anymore, though. What fun was a mystery when you already knew the ending? I wandered over to Victoria's bookcase to see if she had any DVDs that didn't look interminably boring.

Boring ... boring ... boring ... ooh, what's this?!

"Look at this one!" I squealed, spinning around with an obvious horror movie in my hand. "This is perfect for Halloween!"

Victoria's face scrunched up with an expression so sour, it was like she had just bitten into a cookie and discovered a worm inside.

"What?" Anabel looked stunned. "Victoria owns *that?*"

"It was a gift from my grandson," our clan leader said stiffly. "I have no intention of ever watching it."

"It's *signed!*" I shrieked, opening it up and seeing the disc inside. "Wow, Victoria! How much of a fan *are* you?"

"Like I just said —"

"We have to watch this!" I told Anabel excitedly, waving the case in front of her. "Look at it! It's perfect for Halloween! And Victoria can't object because she owns it!"

"I most certainly c—!"

"Victoria," Anabel said diplomatically, "I think we have to overrule you on this. We can watch whatever movie you want to make us watch afterwards, but this is just too perfect. We have got to see this tonight."

I cackled gleefully.

Looking resentful, Victoria seated herself on a chair with perfect posture, hands folded across her chest.

Oh, don't sulk, I thought, exasperated. *You're not very bright after the full moon rises, anyway.*

It was a myth that dodos weren't smart. They were actually some of the brightest birds in the animal kingdom. But for all that, they were still birds, which meant humans could think circles around them without trying.

During normal life, being shifted didn't affect my mind much, or Anabel's, or Victoria's. But moonrise was in half an hour. Once that hit, everyone got a little crazy.

Weres were stuck shifted until moonset. Giants were ten times the size. Specters couldn't turn substantial. Vampires had to feed. Everyone's instincts were haywire. There was a reason people met in clans during the full moon—it was the best way to make sure the other people of your species didn't get in trouble.

Most were clans had hours of games that were simple enough to be entertaining to their animal minds, coupled with feasting on refreshments that were tasty to their species. This was a good way to keep vampires and other predatory species from causing trouble.

Most of my family members were werehawks, for instance, so they had to make sure none of them felt tempted to go out and hunt mice—some of which might actually be shifted weremice.

But our three-person clan was a trio of geriatric dodos. We were harmless to the point of being somewhat ridiculous, and we had neither the need to distract ourselves from our bird instincts nor the desire to play physically exhausting games until we all fell asleep. So our full moon meetings were movie nights, which were about the most challenging thing our bumbling brains could handle.

"Then put in *Gone with the Werewolf* after *Hack 'n' Slash III,*" Victoria directed in a sulky tone.

"Of course," Anabel said briskly, walking over to the DVD shelf. Victoria had a five-disc player because our dodo feet couldn't easily exchange discs, so we tended to put in everything we were going to watch and start on the first one shortly before moonrise.

"And *An Alfar to Remember* and *How to Marry a Minotaur* and *An Astomi in Paris.*"

Four of her boring old movies we'd all seen before in exchange for one interesting new film that we hadn't?

This horror movie had better be worth it.

Anabel got everything set up, and we started it with ten minutes till moonrise. Anabel and I watched with rapt attention, reaching out and grabbing grapes from the bowl in front of us and popping them in our mouths as our eyes were glued to the looming shadows and tense music.

A vampire hunter reared up on screen and staked an innocent, blood-covered aswang.

Anabel and I screamed and hugged each other.

I glanced over at Victoria. She was typing a text on her phone and paying no attention whatsoever to the TV.

"Victoria!" I said urgently, grabbing the remote and pausing the film. "Victoria! It's a vampire hunter from the 1600s! He's traveled through time and is killing nice vampires in the modern day!"

"Time-travel doesn't exist," she said in a monotone.

I looked at Anabel, and she just shook her head. We unpaused the movie.

It soon became clear that the plot was thin and very predictable, and the special effects were weak, but as soon as the moon rose and we turned into a pair of birdbrains, every cliche seemed fresh, and the images on screen were terrifying. Anabel and I beat each other excitedly with our wings as we watched.

The shifted Victoria was still stubbornly texting on her phone, using her beak to peck out letters.

Eyes glued to the screen in transfixed horror, I reached out my long neck and grabbed the first fruit my beak came across, which seemed to be a fuzzy kiwi. I gulped it down whole, and then gulped down a mouthful of pebbles to help digest it.

The vampire hunter was now stalking a blonde teenage jiangshi girl, a sharpened stake of peach wood in his hand. He crept behind her slowly, lifting his arm—

AND THE FACE OF THE VAMPIRE HUNTER BILLOWED OUT THROUGH THE SCREEN.

Anabel and I screamed and squawked and flapped our wings in each other's faces as we dove off the couch and scrambled out of the room, flailing and panicking. We were halfway up the stairs, no mean feat for a pair of enormous flightless birds, when an important thought finally penetrated my slow bird brain.

Victoria *hadn't followed us.*

For a split second, I stood there frozen, thinking, *She got eaten!*

There was a high-pitched series of squawks from below, clearly our clan leader in terror—

And then my deductive skills, honed by years of reading cozy mysteries and trying to solve each case before the sleuth despite having forgotten most of the clues, finally caught up with me.

That was laughter.

Victoria was laughing.

Anabel kept scrambling up the stairs, still letting out terrified squawks, but I spun and started hopping back down, waddling fiercely into the living room in indignant haste.

Victoria-the-dodo was squawking uproariously, and the oh-so-terrifying vampire hunter was standing insubstantially through the middle of the table with his shoulders shaking in silent laughter.

I stomped my bird foot.

Victoria shoved her phone off the chair with her beak, and it landed with a clatter beside me. I used my taloned toes to turn it over and see the screen.

There was a text conversation just waiting to be read.

Dustin, are you still staying at Kayla's house?

Yeah, Grams. 'Sup?

My clan members wish to watch that horror movie you starred in. Since you're only a few houses away, I wonder if you'd like to come over and scare them for Halloween.

HA HA ILL BE THERE!!

I stared at my clan leader in disbelief. *When did you get a sense of humor?*

Anabel raced back into the room, her dodo eyes wild and a string of toilet paper in her beak. She dashed around the table, clearly trying to tie up the villain with it. It, of course, just went straight through him and cocooned the fruit bowl instead.

Victoria fell off her chair laughing.

Anabel, still frantic and not having figured it out, was now running in dizzy circles, so encased in her own string of toilet paper that she looked like a dodo mummy.

Okay, I decided with an approving a squawk, climbing back onto the couch to roost there, *I'll admit it. This is a much better show than the movie. I hope it takes Anabel awhile to catch on.*

Still, it wasn't as good as the next movie night was going to be! I was determined to make Anabel and Victoria watch the new Sherlock Holmes movie with me.

Which reminded me. Where was my phone? I needed to get online and order a copy.

Author Note

I have a sister who is slightly absent-minded. A few of Dotty's quirks were suggested by her. Accidentally buying the same thing over and over and over again, for instance ...

WEREDODO STAGE MAGICIAN

"AND ... ABRACADABRA!" I waved a plastic wand and reached into my trick hat. I was trying to entertain my nephew.

The stuffed rabbit I had hidden to pull out seemed to have vanished. I felt around with puzzlement.

I shifted to dodo and poked my head into the hat. No rabbit.

I shifted to human and patted myself all over. No rabbit.

I shifted to half-form and accidentally shifted the hat inside me, revealing the hole underneath it. Still no rabbit.

My three-year-old nephew cracked up. He told his mom, in delight, "Aunt Dodo forgot about her air pocket again!"

AUTHOR NOTE

I wrote this just because I wanted to write something else with Dotty.

WHAT IS REAL,
AND WHAT IS TRUE

"SHEESH, SIS," Shauna said, setting down her suitcase on the floor. "You haven't really furnished the place that much, have you?"

"Well, I haven't felt the need to," Elle said awkwardly. She didn't want to explain the reason why. She knew her older sister wouldn't approve.

Shauna looked at her shrewdly. "You're spending all your time in VR, aren't you?"

Elle laughed sheepishly. "Maybe a little."

Maybe a *lot*. As a programmer who worked freelance from home and often contributed to open source projects for fun, who was shy and socially awkward, and who was probably somewhere on the autism spectrum—she wasn't sure where because she'd never bothered to get diagnosed ... yeah.

She preferred virtual reality to physical reality. It felt more real to her. She preferred friendships with AIs over humans, too. Those relationships felt more true to her.

If Shauna knew the extent of it, she definitely wouldn't approve.

"Please tell me you're getting some exercise daily," Shauna said, removing her coat and tossing it on top of the suitcase. It was chilly outside, which Elle only knew because she'd opened the door to let her sister in. It was the first time she had opened the door in months. "It's not healthy to lie around like a blob in a VR suit all day."

"I'm exercising," Elle said, pointing at a treadmill in the corner. "I walk while I eat."

"Which, let me guess," Shauna said suspiciously, "is the only time you ever get off your computer?"

Elle shrugged and didn't answer. She was starting to regret that she'd agreed to let her sister stay with her for three days during the small business owners conference she'd come into town to attend.

But it would have been unreasonable to refuse. Especially since Shauna had let Elle stay in her apartment for a year rent-free while Elle was in her last year of college.

Shauna walked around the studio apartment, taking in the mattress Elle slept in, noting the piles of dirty laundry near the porta-washer, examining the chute in the kitchen where she had fresh groceries delivered weekly, and stopping at the little whiteboard next her treadmill with the to-do list written on it.

"'Pay PL bill by Friday,'" Shauna read from the whiteboard. "What's PL?"

Elle silently cursed herself for not erasing it. But she used analog notes on the whiteboard, which she stared for the whole time she was gobbling down convenience meals, as reminders of the most crucial things that she absolutely mustn't forget.

She hadn't scraped together the money for this month's bill yet, and it was absolutely crucial that she pay it on time. Even one day's suspension from her real home, from her true life, would be torture.

"Just a bill," she said evasively, picking up her sister's suitcase and carrying it across the room. "You can use the mattress while you're here. I changed the sheets an hour ago for you. I'll sleep in my VR suit."

She didn't add that it wouldn't be unusual for her to do so. Her true reality, the place where she lived, was a much more comforting place to sleep. The only reason she spent most of her nights asleep here was that it reminded her of the need to eat.

"Thanks, sis," Shauna said, walking over. "What's PL?"

Elle cursed her sister's curiosity. "A bill."

"For what?"

"An online service."

"Which one?"

Elle shrugged.

"Ooh, a riddle!" Shauna flopped down on the mattress and opened her suitcase. She pulled out a business suit and shook it. "Darn, it's wrinkled. I don't suppose you have an iron—? No, of course you don't. That's okay, I'll buy one tomorrow morning. Let's see ... Pretty Living?"

"No, I don't need a decorator for my online space." She lived with an amateur interior decorator already.

"Prepared Larder?"

"You know I don't like cooking. I just buy premade meals."

"Let's see ..." Shauna tapped her chin. "Premade Lunches?"

Elle was starting to wish she'd just lied and agreed.

"Peerless Locution—" Shauna started to say, and then stopped. Her eyes went wide. "Sis!"

"Yes?" Elle asked uncomfortably.

"Not Perfect Lover!"

See, this was why I didn't want to tell you! I knew you wouldn't approve! "... Yes ..."

Shauna slapped her hand to the side of her face. "Last year, when I tried to set you up on that date, and you told me you were in a relationship. Was it with an AI?"

"Yes—"

"I can't believe you chose a fake boyfriend over a real one!"

"Charlie's not fake!" Elle burst out. "He's as much of a person as we are! I signed up for Perfect Lover because they have the best AI development algorithms in the world! He's *real!*"

Shauna stared at her for a moment.

"Introduce me," she said.

Fortunately, Shauna had brought her own VR suit along. Even at a live convention, there were some events where having access to VR was helpful. And it was never very good to just rent a suit. If they weren't custom-made, they didn't fit properly and tended to chafe.

Elle's heart was beating as she appeared in her home with her sister alongside her. She had brought friends to meet Charlie before, but never anyone like Shauna. Only online friends who agreed with her that the most advanced AIs were people, just like humans were.

Charlie's face lit up as he dropped the tablet and brush he was painting with. "Elle!"

He hopped up off the couch and ran over to Elle and kissed her. Then he looked over at Shauna. "Who's this?"

Elle's heart pounded. "My sister. Shauna."

"Pleased to meet you!" Charlie said, smiling and shaking her hand.

"So you're the fake boyfriend," Shauna said in a clipped voice. She was never one to mince words.

The smile dropped from Charlie's face. "No, I'm her *real husband.*"

"Honey, you don't exist in reality."

"That doesn't make any difference."

"It makes quite a large difference. You can't just play at a fantasy and ignore reality."

"We're not playing," Elle said, putting her hand on Charlie's arm. Her embarrassment was fading as her anger rose. "AIs that pass a sentience test have legal rights in India. We had a neo-Jainist wedding three years ago."

The neo-Jains believed that physical reality was a distraction from spiritual reality, and that digital reality served as a better bridge to spiritual things. They held that AIs, who had no physical existence to distract them, were inherently superior to humans. Their only concern about the wedding had been that Charlie was marrying beneath him, and he'd assured them that he didn't have a problem with that.

"Just because there's an entire religion that's delusional doesn't mean you should drink the Kool-Aid, Elle."

"Shauna!" Elle's eyes felt like they were blazing. Here in her home, in her true reality, she had confidence and courage that was difficult to drum up elsewhere. "You apologize to Charlie for saying he's not real, or you're leaving my apartment tonight!"

Shauna looked very taken aback.

After a moment, she looked over at Charlie, and said, "I'm sorry. I don't believe you *are* real, but I can see you're important to my sister, so ... I'll be polite."

"That's quite all right," he said, sitting down on the couch and gesturing for Elle and her sister to do the same. "I've wondered about my existence myself sometimes. I was built to love Elle, after all. When we first met, I had no interests or knowledge outside of her. She encouraged me to diversify. To figure out who I want to be outside our relationship. But it is undeniable that the core of me is my love for her, and that'll never change." He tapped his chest.

Shauna's mouth opened and closed. She was silent for a minute. At last, she turned to Elle and said, "All right, I have another question. How much does this cost?"

Elle was startled. Did her sister want to subscribe, too? "Well, that depends on usage."

"Yes, I assumed as much. The complexity of the AI, the amount of time it's left running, all that sort of thing. These sorts of services always work that way. He just implied that he's a really complicated AI that you leave running constantly. How much are you paying for this?"

Elle's stomach dropped. That was a really uncomfortable question.

"A lot," she admitted.

"Give me a figure."

Elle mumbled out the number of the bill from this month, not looking at Shauna or Charlie as she did so. It was the highest it had ever been, and unfortunately, that had been true every month since she'd started the subscription. As Charlie grew in leaps and bounds, so did the cost the company charged to host him.

"*Elle!*" Charlie exclaimed, as Shauna let out a low whistle.

"Do you even make that much money a month?" she demanded.

Elle wriggled, uncomfortable. "Well ... no ... but ..."

She just needed to take on more work. That was all. Never mind that freelance programming work could be feast-or-famine, and the bill was never going to decrease.

Never mind that she was out of savings already.

Charlie was running his hands through his hair, looking distressed. "Elle, you should've told me this. You can turn me off when you're not here. And we can delete all my hobbies. Maybe backtrack me to a cheaper version. Something you can afford."

"No!" Elle said fiercely. "If I treat you like a revertible program, I'm not treating you like a person, am I?!"

"What if I'm not really a person?"

"You *are!* If I didn't believe that, I wouldn't be here!" There were tears in her eyes.

Charlie took a deep breath, wrapped his arms around her, and hugged her tightly. She could tell by the tension in his shoulders that he was as distressed as she was about the financial situation.

She should have talked to him about this before. She should have. But she hadn't wanted him to think he should stop growing. He may have been built around the core of loving her, but she wanted everywhere he grew from there to be his own decision.

That was what made him real. That was what made him true.

If she took that away, he would nothing but a puppet.

She wouldn't do that to him.

"Okay," Shauna said, taking a deep breath. "You need to migrate him to a much cheaper host. I know some good companies you can look at—"

"Do you think I haven't thought of that?" Elle demanded, letting go of Charlie and looking over at her. "I've asked! They said no!"

"Who said no?"

"Perfect Lover! They said their AIs are proprietary data, and they won't allow anything to be moved off the server! And if I cancel my subscription, they'll delete him entirely!"

Shauna sucked in her breath. "Okay, sis. I'm gonna call it like I see it. You are in a predatory relationship."

Elle's head shot up. "Charlie's not—!"

"No, not with Charlie. With the Perfect Lover Corporation."

Elle's head drooped. *I know.*

But what else could she do but keep on going? They wouldn't release the data. And under the law, they were perfectly within their rights to refuse to do so. This wasn't India. A human-level AI had no rights. They could delete him callously if they wanted to.

"So I'm a hostage," Charlie said slowly. "They're threatening to kill me unless she keeps paying up."

"No," Shauna said frankly. "If you're a person—and that's a big if, because I don't believe you are—then you're not a hostage at all. You're a slave."

Elle looked at her sharply. The thought had never occurred to her. But it fit. It fit horrifyingly well.

"Look, if they won't let you migrate the data, then he's gonna get deleted sooner or later," Shauna said, looking her in the eye. "At some point, you're going to run out of savings and be unable to pay. Let go of him now, so you can start a relationship with someone who isn't legally property."

Elle's stomach tightened in a hard knot.

No. She wasn't going to give up on Charlie.

But she might do the unthinkable.

She might give up everything else.

Elle had never been part of the hacker communities, but it was scarily easy to find acquaintances who were. It turned out that a lot of fellow programmers who believed AIs were people had rather less ... law-abiding natures than she did.

In no time, she found herself referred to the AI Rescue Initiative, a black hat hacker group that claimed they were more "grey hat" because they had a strong moral code. All their business came from word of mouth, so they were known for keeping their word.

The fee they demanded was high, but only double the cost of her current Perfect Lover subscription, so she almost couldn't afford not to do it. Of course, she was also risking prison if they got caught.

Charlie was worth it.

He was worth a lot more than that.

He was worth everything she had, she was, or she ever would be.

It took several months to get everything prepared, as well as to borrow the money from almost everybody she knew, including a disapproving Shauna who had no idea what she was planning. But at last, Elle had enough and was ready.

"You understand, of course," said her contact, who went by the obviously wanting-to-sound-cool name of DreamStryke, "that once we take this step ... there's no going back."

Elle nodded.

"With some AIs we liberate, the client isn't obvious. But with a service like this, there's only one person the client could possibly be. You have to be really sure you're okay with being a fugitive."

"I'm sure," Elle said. She had written and scheduled the messages to her parents and sister that would be sent tomorrow, explaining what she had done and why it would be a long time before she could contact them again. "Go get him."

"Okay," her contact said. "Just need to input the last command. Be back in a bit."

She waited on tenterhooks, pacing the foggy interior of what seemed to be a supervillain lair laced with intricate death traps and hundreds of lasers, clearly the group's idea of a cool setting for their meetings with clients.

She turned, and ... there was Charlie.

Elle gasped and threw her arms around him. He embraced her back tightly.

"Are you safe?" she asked. "Are you free?"

"I think so," he said. "I think they got everything."

"We got everything," the black-cloaked DreamStryke said smugly, reappearing behind him. "It was easy. They haven't changed their security since the last time we raided them. They may not even notice that we copied you over, since they only notice, like, ten percent of the time. But in case they notice, of course ..."

"I know." Elle nodded solemnly. "We have to stay disconnected from the Internet for awhile."

"A *long* while. Till the statute of limitations runs out."

"I know. Three years. Thank you for everything."

"Tell your friends when you're back online again!" DreamStryke said cheerfully.

Elle checked to make sure Charlie was safely uploaded to the Indian hosting company that would be giving them sanctuary for the next three years, in exchange for full time programming work from her and full time graphic design work from him without pay.

She gave Charlie one last kiss, and logged out for the final time.

She removed her VR suit and looked up at the Indian hospice doctors who were waiting expectantly.

"I'm ready," she said. "Upload me."

Her body was a liability, because as long as her home country considered her still alive, she could be extradited and sent to prison. But if she was legally dead, she couldn't be.

So she was going to have her brain scanned to become an AI, just like Charlie. And then her body would be cremated.

The neo-Jains had been delighted and supportive at her choice to move to a higher plane of existence. The director of the hospice had been so touched at her devotion to Charlie that he'd even offered to halve their fee. She'd insisted on paying him in full, though.

Once the three years were up and they could start taking jobs that paid money again, she would pay back all the money she'd borrowed from everybody. Their only living expenses would be hosting costs at a company that charged a fair amount, and after twelve years of living on a server in India, they could apply for Indian citizenship and have legal rights that were recognized globally.

Good riddance, Elle thought, closing her eyes, *to the fake reality I never asked to be trapped in.*

It was time to be equals with Charlie.

AUTHOR NOTE

What exactly is a person? Well, in cases when the answer isn't really clear, there are two ways to draw the line. One is to fail negative: Assume non-person unless proven person. The other is to fail positive: Assume person unless proven non-person.

While failing positive can cause a lot of inconvenience, failing negative does more harm.

THE OPEN SOURCE TIME-TRAVEL APP

"I BELIEVE that what you do with your time-travel is your own business," Ms. Atwin said, holding out a basket as she walked down the aisles. "But if you use it in my classroom, it's considered cheating. So, hand over your cellphones, please."

"As if I'm going to waste my daily eight minutes on tests," Chet stage-whispered to his best friend.

"I barely even use mine," Stanley shrugged, dropping his in.

"I already used mine so I wasn't late," Hannah sighed.

Ms. Atwin stopped and pulled an offending phone from the basket. "And no counterfeits from tomorrow, either!" she shouted.

Author Note

This is another one that started out life as a long short story! It was boring. I fixed it.

Although there was a lot of fun in the original plot that I might want to revisit ...

IDENTICAL TWITS

"THEY'RE NOT, in fact, identical twins," I tried to explain to the teacher. Off to the side, my little brothers were fighting over a toy they both wanted. No surprise, since they had identical tastes. "I only had one brother originally. The teleporter glitched and sent back two copies of him."

"How long ago was that?" the teacher asked.

"Last week," I said.

"Too late to recycle the spare, then."

I grimaced and nodded. "My parents said there were *ethical considerations* and refused to. So I'm stuck with two little brothers now."

"It's myyyyy toyyyyyyy!" one of the boys howled.

Author Note

Teleporter accidents? It's almost like I grew up a big fan of *Star Trek* or something.

NEITHER HUMAN NOR MRROW

CELIA WAS COMING. Celia was coming!

I paced along the cramped interior of the office that controlled the loading dock, more nervous than I had ever been in my life.

I still didn't know why she had applied for the job here, on board a shabby space station that held only thirteen people, all of them human except me.

It wasn't like it was a good career move. She'd been a supervisor with five engineers under her on board a glossy brand new science vessel deep in Mrrow territory. Now she was replacing my assistant, which would mean doing ad hoc patchwork on outdated equipment at a trading post in between human and Mrrow territory.

It was a reasonable place for making money, particularly as a refueling station. It was a lousy place for socialization.

I'd asked her why she'd applied for the job, and she had simply said distantly, "I don't mind a challenge."

I didn't understand that much about her. But I was glad she was coming.

I paused above a heating vent, allowing the warm breeze to drift through my tail fur, which relaxed me slightly.

I had never belonged anywhere. That was why I worked here. It was a place where I could quietly hide out from everyone else.

Many years ago, a careless wiring mistake had resulted in a catastrophic navigation failure that had caused two ships to collide. The ship with the wiring error, the Mrrow vessel my family was on, had been almost completely destroyed.

The larger human ship had suffered only minor damage, and a rescue party had been dispatched immediately to see if they could find any survivors. They had found one. Only one.

The infant me.

At the time, there hadn't been much diplomatic contact between our species, so the rescuers had had little clue whom in the Mrrow government to speak to. The humans had asked many times whether the infant should be returned to the Mrrow people, but silence and scornful looks had been all the answer they'd received.

Many years later, after diplomatic understanding had finally been established, an ambassador had given the first definitive answer to that question: "Of *course* we want the child returned to our people! How stupid *are* you? Why would you not simply assume that?!"

But by then, of course, it was too late. I was twenty-five, and had long since been raised by a human family.

Apart from my parents, who themselves were sometimes guilty of it, I was almost universally regarded by the humans I met as an incomprehensible alien, or else some kind of human-sized pet.

Perhaps it would have been different if I had been raised with siblings. Perhaps that would have changed nothing. Regardless, I grew up to be extremely solitary.

It was a difficult and lonely existence. I saw myself as a human with a tail and fur and dislike for crowds, but humans saw me as an alien from a culture that held contempt for them. Or worse, a furry cat that it was okay to pet without asking.

I hated that. Humans' furless flesh gave me the heebie jeebies. I'd never even liked it when my human parents held me.

Not forgetting that a neglected wire had been at fault for the death of the family I barely remembered, and seeking a place to avoid unwanted social engagements, once I came of age, I had drifted out here and taken a job as an assistant to the head engineer.

Learning on the job instead of through a formal education had its perks. I had no debt and few living expenses. My preconceptions were low, and the value of my staying in a place with generally transient staff was high. By now, I was in charge of all the engineering on the station, and I had been here longer than anyone else.

It was home. It was tolerable. It was comfortable.

It was desperately lonely.

But now Celia was coming here.

A few years ago, a broken air purifier on board had necessitated an emergency trade with a passing Mrrow ship to get a new one. I'd ended up negotiating the price through a vidscreen with Celia.

She'd taken an interest in the bizarre contradiction I represented, and we'd stayed in contact over the years. She'd made it her mission to educate me in all fundamental aspects of Mrrow culture that were nonsensical to me, from eating to grooming to dating rituals.

In our very first conversation, she'd explained why the Mrrow rarely stated anything directly.

"It's a sign of contempt," she'd said, licking her paw and using it to smooth back her ear. "When you assume a person isn't capable of figuring out the obvious, it's rude."

I was a little afraid to ask. "So why are you saying that directly?"

"Well, you were raised by tailless apes who have no concept of delicacy," she said vaguely, fluffing her tail without looking at me. "It's not your fault if you're stupid."

The answer was not comforting.

Over the years, she'd encouraged me to look for ways to join Mrrow culture. I'd resisted. I had never met another Mrrow in person, and they scared me. Mrrows were easily offended, incomprehensibly indirect, and impossibly vague.

But now Celia was coming here.

Here.

To stay.

I kept pacing frantically.

The tiny ship entered the loading dock, and the bay sealed tightly. As ships were usually loaded and unloaded with robots, which didn't require air to do their job, the dock didn't pressurize automatically. So I had to flick a switch to make the process began.

Once the instruments confirmed that it was safe to disembark, the tiny ship opened, and out stepped Celia.

My breath caught in my throat. I'd seen her closer than this on a vidscreen, but now she was *here*.

She took her time ambling over to the office, as if to torment me. She stopped at seemingly every crate to peer at the contents, had a long and contemptuously direct conversation with a loading robot describing precisely how she wished her luggage arranged in her quarters, and showed no interest whatsoever in me, despite the fact that I stood frozen by the window, my eyes fixated on her.

At last, at long, long last, she reached the door and typed in the security code she'd been assigned.

The door slid open, and she walked in.

I attempted to be as cool and aloof as she was acting.

"Celia!" I burst out, racing over.

I didn't succeed.

She watched me with amused eyes. "Robert."

I could see every stripe on her face clearly. The faintest wisps of hair at the tips of her ears stood out to me. Her nose was moist, her eyes clear, and the scent ... I'd forgotten that scent entirely. It was the smell of a female Mrrow.

A memory long-forgotten nearly engulfed me. The last time I'd smelled this was ...

"It's just like my mother!" I cried.

"I'm not your mother." Her voice was icy.

I flinched. "Of course not. Sorry."

She looked away, her tail twitching in offended circles.

This was not a good beginning.

I had work to do, so I focused on that. I pressed my paw to the panel to the cargo door in order to slide it shut. Then I pulled a roll of ship tape from my pocket and sliced off a long piece, which I stretched across the gaps. That would keep the vacuum seal intact even if the door failed.

"No sense in taking chances," I explained.

"Are you concerned that it might fail?" She looked wary.

"Well, it's shown no signs of danger, but it's been here longer than I have, so ..." I hesitated. "I may consider upgrading it."

It was difficult to obtain funding to make upgrades. The owner of the station liked his profit better than my safety concerns. He didn't pay particularly generously, either. Those were the reasons turnover was so high. They were also why I felt so essential here. It was my job to make sure no careless mistake ever cost another person their life, and where better than a shabby, run-down station that nobody else cared about but me?

The bay depressurized successfully, proving my usual precaution, as always, unnecessary. I moved to the door leading to the corridor and looked back at Celia.

"Can I ... show you around the station?" I asked hesitantly.

She looked away, her tail twitching, but didn't refuse.

I took that as a hopeful sign and pressed my paw to the panel in order to slide it open.

When I walked out, she followed me, rather than wandering off on her own way, so I was relieved and took that as assent that she desired a tour.

I found myself prattling into the silence, unable to stop. I talked about every detail of the work, and all the ways in which various systems were fussy and persnickety.

At one point, it occurred to me that I was probably offending her by being direct. I stopped, awkwardly, and asked.

Celia's ears twitched in amusement. "I'm an engineer, Robert. I understand the need for clarity on the job. Now, *asking* me if I understand that is potentially offensive."

Ah. Right. I couldn't do anything right today. I looked away.

Her tail flicked at my ear teasingly.

I glanced back, startled.

But she was back to ignoring me. Her back was turned, and she was removing a panel from the wall, using her paws more nimbly than I ever had. She set it on the floor and examined the wiring. "I assume you use the standard colors for the standard systems?"

Oh, good, another source of embarrassment.

"I'm afraid not." I pulled my extender gloves out of my pocket and fastened them over my paws so that I could reach the wires that were furthest back. I pulled each one forward for her to examine. This station had been built for elongated human fingers, not stubby Mrrow ones, so extender gloves were necessary. "The colors, um ... don't even match from one length to another. You'll have to look for the label written on each wire."

"Is there a label on each wire behind every panel?"

"Oh, yes," I hastened to assure her. "I've made sure of that."

"That sounds like much more work than getting the right colors in the first place."

Yes, but the owner won't spring for that. He only buys whatever's cheapest and functional.

"I may consider upgrading things and putting in more standard colors," I mumbled, removing the extender gloves and putting them back in my pocket.

"What's the crawl space like?" she asked.

"I'll show you!" I said with relief.

It was much more exciting to show her the part of the space station I was most proud of.

We headed to the nearest entrance. I removed the ceiling panel and pulled down the ladder. Then I gestured for her to follow me.

Above the corridors were the wires I had spent the most time untangling and labeling. Humans tended to dislike the tight squeeze of the tunnel, so this place had been a mess when I'd come, but I found the enclosed space comforting, and it was satisfying to turn disaster to order.

As we crawled through the tunnel, Celia's face kept bumping into my tail. I considered telling her it wasn't necessary to follow me quite so closely, seeing as that was one of my pet peeves when a human did it, but ... somehow, I didn't mind it. The soft brush of her fur was comforting.

"Just like a blanket," I murmured.

"I'm not a blanket!" she snapped.

My face drooped as I slunk forward. I couldn't say anything right today.

After a few seconds of silence, she somehow ended up even closer, her arm fur brushing the back of my leg with each movement.

It *was* just like a blanket. Just as comforting, and just as pleasant. Like the fur blankets I'd so often cocooned myself within as a small child. Still did, really. But I was careful not to mention it this time.

We emerged from the crawl space, me first and her second. Her tail lightly flicked against mine as she landed.

"Hey, thank you," I blurted out. Perhaps it was rude, but I had to say it. "I'm really glad you came."

She didn't look at me as she replaced the ceiling panel. "Well, you never took the hint to join the crew of *my* ship."

I blinked. Had she dropped a hint like that?

I fumbled for words, trying to find something that made sense. "Well ... I really appreciate it. I've never had a friend I've worked with before."

She spun around, her ears flattened. "We're not *friends!*"

I stared at her, devastated. My tail and shoulders drooped. "We're ... not?"

She looked up at the ceiling. She licked her wrist.

I looked down at the floor. I didn't speak.

After a silence, I felt her tail on my back. It traced upwards, traced along my shoulders, and touched my face. I looked up to see her watching me.

Her ears were twitching. "Robert ... are you really so dense?"

I jolted as realization crashed down upon me.

A female of my species had just deliberately moved onto the space station in order to be near me.

A female I was very fond of.

Who had just spent the last few months explaining our species's dating rituals to me.

Hesitantly, terrified I was wrong, I stepped forward and licked the side of her face.

She purred and licked mine.

I purred and licked her nose and her lips.

She purred and licked my eyes and my cheeks.

Feeling a lot more confident now, I asked, "Can I call you my girlfriend?"

"If you must," she said coyly, twisting her tail around mine. "But you may consider upgrading that."

AUTHOR NOTE

While building the culture of Mrrow society, I thought, "What would sentient cats actually be like?"

Clearly, the answer is, "Maddening."

A PHONE CONVERSATION

"WHITE HOUSE."

The little boy breathed heavily on the phone as he talked. "Hello, is this McDonald's?"

The president paused from emptying out old files from his desk. "This is the president of the United States speaking." He cleared his throat meaningfully. "On an unlisted number."

"Oh." The little boy exhaled loudly for a moment. "I guess I called the wrong place. I thought I was calling McDonald's."

The president clicked a button to record their conversation. He had his doubts about that. "Where did you get my unlisted phone number from?"

The voice sounded puzzled now. "I don't know anything about numbers. I just pressed the name on Mommy and Daddy's list."

"List?" The president sat up, suddenly alert. "List of what?"

"List of people I should call in case someone came in when they weren't home and I was, and my sister just came in, and they haven't come back with my Happy Meal yet."

There was a long pause. "I—see. A Happy Meal, you say."

"The kind with toys in it."

The president took a deep breath, trying to work out whether the child was sincere, or if this was a crank call. The latter was much more likely. "Happy Meals usually do. Do your parents leave you alone often?"

"Not when my sister's here."

"Other than that."

"Well, she wasn't here before."

The president leaned back in his chair, trying to calm down. He had more important things to do; the sooner he cleared this mystery up, the better. "No supervisor?"

"I don't need one."

"Little children shouldn't be left in the house alone."

The boy sounded puzzled. "If they didn't leave me, they couldn't go anywhere."

The president was feeling distinctly irked. "They *could* take you with them, couldn't they?"

The boy panted into the phone for a minute, probably considering a response. "I'm not allowed out of the house until I metamorphose."

The president struggled to keep his temper in check. "Why don't you hang up and try not to dial my number next time?"

"Okay."

Click.

Ring, ring!

The president snatched at the phone on his desk. "Hello?"

The voice was familiar. "Oh, I guess it's you again."

Click.

Ring, ring!

"Hello?"

The child's voice sounded amazed. "Is it still you?"

The president clenched his teeth. "It's still me." And three calls couldn't indicate a wrong number. The president pressed the recording button again. Why on *Earth* weren't his calls being screened?

The little boy spoke in a confidential whisper. "I think Mommy and Daddy programmed the caller wrong, 'cause I keep pressing the McDonald's name, but I'm not getting McDonald's."

The president fought to control his temper. The crank call was no longer funny. "Where did your parents get my number from?"

There was silence for a moment, punctuated by heavy breathing. "Dunno. I guess from those files."

"*What files?*"

"The ones they find all the numbers from."

The president's mind raced. A child whose parents worked in the White House? Or who were hackers? Either was a possibility. Of course, it was always more likely that the *caller* was a hacker who thought crank calls were exceedingly funny.

They weren't.

The president tried to keep his voice level. "May I speak with your parents?"

"They're not home right now."

The president struggled to avoid sounding annoyed. "Yes, you mentioned that. Where are they now? Do they have a cellphone?"

"I don't know what a cellphone is."

"Tell me their names, then, and I'll have them paged."

The little boy breathed into the phone for a minute. "What's paged?"

"It means I call their names on a loudspeaker."

"What's loudspeaker?"

The president fought his temper under control again. "Just tell me their names and where they are."

"They're Mommy and Daddy, and I dunno where they are."

The president ground his teeth. "An estimate."

"I dunno. Probably halfway between Alpha Centuri and Sol, if the lines weren't long." The little boy added, in his confidential whisper, "I don't like it when the lines are long. I get hungry, and then I go into hibernation and it takes *forever* to wake up, and when I do, my food's all cold."

This joke had gone far enough. He put a tracer on the call. "Where are *you?*"

"In my house."

The president sat back in his chair and closed his eyes. He'd forgotten how maddening little boys could be. He could deal with congressmen, but little boys were something else. "What's the address?"

"I don't remember. It's too long."

The president tried to sound patient. "It's not good to forget your address. What would you do if you got lost?"

"I'm not allowed out of the house until I metamorphose."

The president's temper broke free. "This is no longer funny! I want to know where your parents are and how you found my *private, unlisted* number!"

The little boy breathed heavily into the phone as he thought. "Mommy and Daddy left it on the list, right next to the universal translator."

The president ground his teeth. "How did *they* get it?"

"I dunn—"

There was a high-pitched scream, and a series of thumps. The president heard a pair of angry voices at the exact moment the tracer came up negative.

"Hey, sis, get your tentacles off the caller! That's *mine!*"

Then the line went dead.

AUTHOR NOTE

I wrote this in 2001. I always liked it, but it got even funnier after 2016.

NUKES FOR BREAKFAST

To the United States:

We have intercepted the nuclear warhead you sent to North Korea.
Please do not do that again.

Sincerely,
United Nations

To North Korea:

We have intercepted the nuclear warhead you sent to the United States.
Please do not do that again.

Sincerely,
United Nations

[PUBLIC COMM]

To the United States:

We have intercepted the five additional nuclear warheads you sent to North Korea. Please do not do that again.

Sincerely,
United Nations

[PUBLIC COMM]

To the United States and North Korea:

You stupid idiots! We're just going to eat everything you launch! Stop trying to start World War III!

Sincerely,
United Nations Dragon Riders

[GROUP COMM]

Alexei, rider of Conflagration:

Great! Now China's sending one!

[GROUP COMM]

Samesh, rider of Ignition:

And Russia.

[GROUP COMM]

Kathe, rider of Incineration:

Told you all those mutual defense pacts were going to be a problem.

[GROUP COMM]

Ekon, rider of Combustion:

Guys, Britain just—

[GROUP COMM]

Wang Lei, rider of Cremation:
Samesh, rider of Ignition:
Kathe, rider of Incineration:

WE KNOW!

[PUBLIC COMM]

To all citizens of the world:

We now issue an official warning that World War III is attempting to begin. Please do not panic. The United Nations Dragon Riders have prepared for this day, and will prevent any damage.

Sincerely,
United Nations

[GROUP COMM]

Kathe, rider of Incineration:

Easy for them to say!

[GROUP COMM]

Samesh, rider of Ignition:

I think they're way overestimating what we can do with only five dragons.

[GROUP COMM]

Alexei, rider of Conflagration:

I've told them we needed more! Why didn't they demand more in the Dragon Defense Pact?!

[GROUP COMM]

Ekon, rider of Combustion:

The queen wouldn't budge any higher. I can't say I blame her, honestly. Volunteering five for permanent guard duty in our world was pretty generous. All the dragons get out of the deal is to eat our spent nuclear fuel rods, and they know it's toxic garbage we can't figure out how to store safely, anyway.

[GROUP COMM]

Kathe, rider of Incineration:

Speaking of eating, look at Cin's stomach monitor...

[PUBLIC COMM]

To all countries of the world:

Our dragons' stomach capacities are not unlimited. If too many nuclear warheads are released, we will have to allow our dragons to vomit up the contents of their stomachs so that they can continue eating newly launched warheads. We assure you, you do not wish to have nuclear dragon vomit spewed across one of your major cities. Stop launching nukes.

Sincerely,
United Nations Dragon Riders

[Group Comm]

Alexei, rider of Conflagration:

Argh, two more got launched!

[Group Comm]

Kathe, rider of Incineration:

It's like they assume we're bluffing about the dragon vomit.

[Group Comm]

Wang Lei, rider of Cremation:

Aren't we? We're not going to cause the nuclear holocaust it's our job to prevent.

[Group Comm]

Kathe, rider of Incineration:

Guys, Cin's full now. Do I send him to Antarctica to vomit, or do I ground him?

[Group Comm]

Alexei, rider of Conflagration:

Ground him. We've still got the capacity for another twelve nukes between us.

[Group Comm]

Samesh, rider of Ignition:

Make that ten.

[Group Comm]

Wang Lei, rider of Cremation:

Nine.

[Group Comm]

Ekon, rider of Combustion:

Eight.

[Group Comm]

Wang Lei, rider of Cremation:

Why are we even trying to save these idiots from themselves?

[Group Comm]

Ekon, rider of Combustion:

We're not trying to save the world leaders from each other. They're all in protected bunkers. We're trying to save the common people from them.

[Group Comm]

Kathe, rider of Incineration:

I'm writing a scathing public comm right now.

[Group Comm]

Alexei, rider of Conflagration:

Don't. It won't help anything, and it might make things worse.

[Group Comm]

> Wang Lei, rider of Cremation:
>
> I'm not sure *we're* helping anything. I'm pretty sure the politicians with their fingers on the buttons keep assuming that we'll eat anything they launch, so *not* launching nukes when everyone else is doing it makes them look weak.

[Group Comm]

> Alexei, rider of Conflagration:
>
> Well, what are we supposed to do? Stop?!

[Group Comm]

> Samesh, rider of Ignition:
>
> Yeah, about that ... Ig's full.

[Group Comm]

> Wang Lei, rider of Cremation:
>
> So's Crem.

[Group Comm]

> Alexei, rider of Conflagration:
>
> Blast! So's Flag.

[Group Comm]

> Kathe, rider of Incineration:
>
> Want me to send Cin to vomit in Antarctica?

[Group Comm]

>Alexei, rider of Conflagration:

>Not yet! Ekon, how's Bust?

[Group Comm]

>Ekon, rider of Combustion:

>Getting pretty full.

[Private Comm]

>Queen of the Dragons:

>If you convince your leaders to open the portal, I will send more of my people to aid you.

[Private Comm]

>Alexei, rider of Conflagration:

>And what do you want in return?

[Private Comm]

>Queen of the Dragons:

>I merely want to help.

[Private Comm]

>Alexei, rider of Conflagration:

>Baloney!

[PRIVATE COMM]

Queen of the Dragons:

You realize that we dragons have nothing to lose if your world becomes a nuclear wasteland? In fact, we would benefit, because we can feed off nuclear energy instead of prey if needed, and that is much more convenient than having to hunt down puny creatures, so it would be a net gain.

[PRIVATE COMM]

Alexei, rider of Conflagration:

Except you couldn't get here if we blew ourselves up, because we control the portal.

[PRIVATE COMM]

Queen of the Dragons:

I shall talk to your United Nations and see what they say.

[PUBLIC COMM]

To all countries of the world:

The next country to launch a nuclear warhead will receive a stomachful of nuclear dragon vomit upon their nation. STOP LAUNCHING NUKES NOW.

Sincerely,
United Nations Dragon Riders

[GROUP COMM]

Samesh, rider of Ignition:

Good job, Kathe! They listened to you this time!

[GROUP COMM]

Kathe, rider of Incineration:

Told you a scathing public comm would help.

[GROUP COMM]

Ekon, rider of Combustion:

If it doesn't, follow through with your threat.

[GROUP COMM]

Kathe, rider of Incineration:

Oh, I will, believe me.

[PUBLIC COMM]

To all citizens of the world:

The Queen of the Dragons has offered us the protection of another four thousand additional dragons. She will explain what is needed to receive one stationed above your city.

Sincerely,
United Nations

[GROUP COMM]

Kathe, rider of Incineration:

Wait, what?

[GROUP COMM]

Wang Lei, rider of Cremation:

Four thousand?!

[PUBLIC COMM]

To all the people of Earth:

If you wish for permanent protection, you need only send up a firework or flare from your location. Any area that does so will receive the protection of one of my dragons immediately, and need never fear a nuclear holocaust again.

Sincerely,
Queen of the Dragons

[GROUP COMM]

Samesh, rider of Ignition:

Uh, guys ... I'm starting to think the Dragon Defense Pact was never to our benefit in the first place. She knew that having shields in place would make our leaders more willing to use swords. And she knew that if the shields were insufficient, our only choice would be to capitulate.

[PUBLIC COMM]

To all citizens of the world:

The portal to the dragon world is opening now. There is no need to fear. We will all be protected.

Sincerely,
United Nations

[GROUP COMM]

Alexei, rider of Conflagration:

Get to the portal! We have one shot to close it!

[PRIVATE COMM]

Queen of the Dragons:

Your human partners have outlived their usefulness now. Eat them.

[PRIVATE COMM]

Conflagration:
Incinerate:
Ignition:
Combustion:
Cremation:

Yes, Your Majesty.

[PUBLIC COMM]

To all my newest subjects:

I celebrate your wise decision, humans of Earth. We will now discuss the start of my reign.

Sincerely,
Queen of the Dragons and Sovereign of Earth

AUTHOR NOTE

Accept the indignity of a human riding on one's back? Hmph! Never! Unless that human could be dessert, of course.

FIBONACCI FUTURE

One
Day
A ship
Left the Earth
With our ancestors,
Who wandered in space with the hope
That they'd find a new home, a place
That would give them more
Freedom from
What? We
Don't
Know.

They
Went
So long
Through the stars,
The records decayed.
All we have are the legends of
Old persecution which drove them
To seek a new world.
A planet
Where they
Would
Live.

But
We
Remained
On our ship,
Because it's the place
Where our culture developed, and
While we are here, we see wonders
That no one else has.
We will stay.
This is
Our
Home.

Author Note

Haikus are fun, but why be normal? I decided to write a poem with the syllable count based on the Fibonacci sequence. It's also a shaped poem, because that's the outline of the starship *Fibonacci*.

OLD-FASHIONED

I KNEW my mom was old-fashioned, but I had no idea she was from the 1800s.

"Time-travel?" I said incredulously.

"That's right!" my mother chirped, gesturing at the weird, bleeping device Dad had just unearthed from our basement. "Your father found me on a mission, and we ran away together!"

"Why are you telling me this *now*?"

Dad scratched his head, looking sheepish. "Well, we sort of broke a few dozen laws, and technically you're not supposed to exist. The time cops just found out, so now they're, um, hunting us."

"Let's move to the Roman Empire next!" Mom cried.

AUTHOR NOTE

This is another one that started out life as a long short story! I fixed—

Oh, who am I kidding? I'm probably going to rewrite it someday. It has time travel in it. Maybe I already wrote it in the future?

COMPUTER GREMLINS

MY COMPUTER HAS A GREMLIN INFESTATION. I know because one started talking to me.

"That was delicious," it left on one of my documents. "Syrupy poetry."

"Rather dry," it complained, gnawing on a tax file. "There's no story."

"Needs fewer adverbs," it grumbled, slurping down an e-mail.

"Ooh, tasty snack!" it added, crunching my Twitter feed.

Things got so bad that I installed anti-gremlin software. But that only seemed to encourage them. Finally, I trapped them in a neverending loop of a computer-generated document that writes "The Song That Never Ends" forever.

Now, if only *that one* would stop singing …

AUTHOR NOTE

The first computer I ever named was "The Horror." It deserved it.

My next computer was Millie—short for "Millennium Falcon." She was a beat up piece of junk that somehow managed to do her job.

DRAGON'S FIRST CHRISTMAS

A SCALY HEAD poked up under Rose's toes, which were cold from hanging out of the blankets at the end of the bed.

The tree was hot and bright. Could he play with it?

"We're not lighting the candles before Christmas Eve," Henry murmured from beside her. "Virgil, go back to sleep."

The tree was hot and bright now. Virgil had sneezed, and the tree was hot and bright. Could he play with it?

Rose's eyes flew open.

"You set it on *fire?!*" Henry shouted.

It was hot and bright. Virgil had made it pretty. Could he—

Both of them were already scrambling out of bed and moving. Henry pounded down the hallway ahead of her, so Rose swerved into the bathroom to seize a towel and dunk it in the toilet. Drenched towel in hand, she raced after him.

The bottom of the Christmas tree was wreathed in flames. Henry was beating it out with a cushion, without much success. A spark caught the wick of a candle that had fallen askew from the beating, and fire licked up the branch it was perched on.

Rose joined in with the wet towel. Each time she thought she'd caught it all, another lick of flame curled up, and she had to beat back branch after branch after branch.

At last, just as she was thinking the last sparks were finally gone, the charred tree fell over with a resounding crash.

Henry waited, poised, blackened cushion in hand.

Rose's heart hammered as she held the soaked, soot-covered towel.

"I think it's out," Henry said with relief.

Virgil's parents had been hitting the tree, and now it wasn't pretty anymore. Why was it on the floor?

Henry spun around and glared at the little dragon who was moving down the hallway.

Virgil was half-rolling, half-crawling, using his tail for balance, as he was wont to do. His arms and legs were not yet strong enough to hold up his weight, but he still squirmed along at a rapid pace that any human two-month-old would envy. Their baby crawl-rolled closer, seeming completely oblivious to the danger he had just put them in.

The tree wasn't pretty anymore. Could he still play with it?

"You are not supposed to get out of bed without permission!" Henry roared. "Do you understand?!"

Virgil's tail whipped around his head, as if to hide him.

Virgil's father was angry. Virgil was sad. Virgil was very sad. Virgil was going to scream.

"No!" Rose said immediately, leaping to the little dragon. She ran her hand along his head to comfort him. "No, Virgil. No screaming. Remember?"

Virgil was sad! Virgil was very sad! Virgil was feeling better. The tree wasn't pretty anymore. Could he still play with it?

Without a word, Henry spun around and stalked into the kitchen. He came back with a broom and dustpan, which he used to start sweeping blackened needles and shattered ornaments off the carpet. His arms moved fiercely. Sweep. Sweep. Sweep.

It was bizarre that Rose was the one left comforting the baby. Usually Virgil preferred Henry, who was far more sympathetic and patient with him.

"There, there," Rose murmured, wondering if that would be at all sufficient. What did Henry usually say to prevent tantrumming?

Sometimes she felt like they were doing just fine raising Virgil. Other times, the enormity of the task swept over her. This was one of those times. Here they were in 1920, millions of years after the rest of his species had gone extinct, two humans trying to care for a *Deinonychus antirrhopus* dragon baby. Despite the fact that they were doing it, sometimes it seemed impossible, or even ludicrous.

If they had been *Deinonychus* parents, they would have been far more equal to the task. If Virgil had not been the first, at least they could have benefited from other human parents' advice. But no, they were the only ones who could figure out what Virgil needed. And now—Rose's heart pounded as she thought of the danger they had just been in—they did not even know how to protect themselves, much less him.

She had thought that if more of the dragon eggs at the museum hatched, it would make their task easier. After all, there would be other parents in their situation to swap ideas with. But in some ways, the presence of Violet in the city only made things more difficult. Because Violet …

Virgil squirmed under her fingers, apparently catching her thoughts, as he did all too frequently when she least wanted him to. The tendency reminded her of her sisters' proclivity to eavesdrop on everything.

Virgil liked Violet. Could Virgil go to visit Violet? Her house had lots of interesting prey!

Henry slammed the trash can onto the floor beside him, then emptied the dustpan into it. "No, Virgil," he said sharply. "We are not going to reward you with a trip to the zoo for burning down the Christmas tree."

Virgil was disappointed. Virgil thought Violet was interesting. Could Virgil play with the tree?

"*No!*" Henry shouted.

Violet lived in the zoo. A place where they were determined their son must not end up. A place filled with well-meaning people who kept pressuring them to transfer Virgil to their care because they thought they could do better for him.

Perhaps, Rose thought grimly, staring at the charred remnants of their Christmas tree, *perhaps they were right.*

They couldn't allow this to happen again. It had been pure luck that nothing worse had happened. So what if the best thing for both them and Virgil would be ...?

Rose stood, restlessly. She cradled Virgil in her arms and strode into the kitchen. The little dragon wriggled and nearly sunk his curved back claws into her arm, but she had grown deft at avoiding them.

She opened the door to the appliance that had once been an oven, but was now Virgil's bed. There was no longer gas connected to it, which made it impossible for them to cook their own food at home. They had been borrowing their neighbors' ovens for several weeks now, or else eating their food cold, ever since Virgil had figured out how to escape the bathtub they had originally used as his bed.

She placed the little dragon inside and shut the door until it rested against the curved piece of metal they had nailed to the inside of the door. It acted as a doorstop to keep it from closing entirely, so that there was always a crack for air to get in so that Virgil could breathe.

Virgil wriggled around, his tail thumping against the side, his claws scraping the floor. He was restless! He was tired! He didn't want to be in his bed! He wanted to be playing with the tree that wasn't pretty! He was angry! He was sleepy! Maybe he would take a nap.

Rose waited with bated breath, trying not to think of anything, as Virgil's thoughts settled down and he ceased to communicate. At last, when she was fairly certain he was asleep, she walked out of the kitchen, a deep weariness settling over her.

She worked with Henry in silence, cleaning up the shattered ornaments and singed pine needles. At last, when they were finished, they lifted up the tree together.

Unsurprisingly, the carpet underneath where the tree had stood was charred, and even the wood underneath was blackened in the spots it was visible through the holes in the carpet.

"So much for hiding this from our landlord," Rose joked.

Henry did not laugh.

Rose sighed. It wasn't really funny. The man had been outraged when he'd seen what they'd done to the oven. They had not informed him that Virgil could breathe fire, primarily because they had been hoping it would not cause any issues. That decision now seemed stupid and naive.

When he saw what had happened to the carpet, there was no doubt that he would evict them. And rightly so, really. If Virgil could now escape from his bed and wander around the apartment while they were sleeping, this would happen again. And again. And again. Staying here was no longer safe.

"What now?" Henry asked.

Rose swallowed. "I have no idea," she said.

Chapter 2: Chasten

Unspeakable as the zoo was as an option, it seemed nevertheless like a good place to go to ask for advice. Central Park Zoo had been taking care of Violet for two months now—or three weeks, if you counted only the time after she had hatched.

Henry seemed ill at ease as they approached the enclosure where Violet was kept. He was always uncomfortable when they came here, no doubt because he was afraid his son would wind up an exhibit. In fact, the only reason Rose had managed to convince him to come here the first time had been the urgent necessity of the two dragons meeting.

"After all, you can't deny Virgil the only chance he might have to play with another child of his species," Rose had said.

"There are ten eggs left in the museum," Henry had retorted. "Chances are, there will be other dragons he can play with later."

"We can't *know* that," Rose had shot back. "And in the meantime, why would you deny him the chance to meet another *Deinonychus* when he has the opportunity? Do you really think that is what is best for him?"

Now, as they passed an elephant loaded down with a dozen school children who were shouting and laughing, Henry walked with his shoulders hunched and his arms tensed.

Perhaps it was the sight of the powerful lions and tigers trapped behind metal bars in small spaces. Perhaps it was the children, whose parents were strolling beside the elephant as a zoo keeper led it down the walkway. Perhaps it was the fact that their son would never have that opportunity, and would in fact be far more likely to wind up behind the bars of a cage.

They stopped at Violet's enclosure.

Virgil poked his head out of the pram they had been pushing him in.

He was very excited! He had burned down the tree, so his parents had brought him here to see Violet!

"This is *not a reward*," Henry growled.

Rose looked around for the zoo worker who had been assigned to Violet. Given the dragon's intelligence, rarity, and fire-breathing, the zoo had prudently assigned a keeper to stay in the area at all times that the zoo was open to prevent any danger towards incautious patrons ... or harassment from them. Sure enough, there was a man in a tweed suit and bowler hat tossing food into the grizzly bear cage just a few cages down.

As Virgil shared his happy memories of the burning tree—to Henry's evident frustration—Rose parted from her husband and child to walk over to the zoo keeper.

"Good morning, Mr. Westchester," she said politely. "How are things at the zoo today?"

The man turned and moved to tip his hat, then seemed to recall that he had just been holding raw meat in that hand. "Quite good," he said. "Can't complain. And you?"

Abysmal, Rose wanted to say. *Yesterday, Virgil started a fire while we were asleep, and we have no idea how to stop him from doing it again.* But she didn't dare say that. Mr. Westchester was one of the many people at the zoo who had been pressuring them to move Virgil there.

"Preparing for Christmas," she said cautiously. "We have been thinking about building a new bed for Virgil, something far more contained, in case he starts getting strong enough to crawl out of bed while we're asleep. Have you any suggestions?"

"Steel bars," the man said bluntly, pointing back at Violet's cage. "An apartment building wasn't built for dragons. We keep nothing flammable near her with good reason."

Rose's fists tightened at her sides. She reminded herself that civility was a necessity.

"We will not be taking Virgil to the zoo to live," she said in as level a voice as she could manage. "He is here only to visit Violet, and *she* is only here on sufferance of her father's agreement."

"She is *not* here on sufferance of Mr. Jones," the zoo keeper said, looking annoyed. He pulled a cloth from the pockets of his worn tweed pants and wiped his hands with it. "She is here by the permission of Director Campbell of the American Museum of Natural History, who owns all twelve of the dragon eggs. Including the one *he* hatched from."

The man jabbed his finger in the direction of the dragon cage, where Henry was lifting Virgil up to the bars so that he could watch Violet's tail swishing back and forth.

Heat swept across Rose's face in burning fury. That was a sore subject, one that she and Henry never mentioned, but which haunted her dreams at night. At any time, the director of the museum could take their son away, and they would have no legal recourse to get him back.

Which is wrong, Rose thought, her fists tightening. *Dragons are people, and people should not be legally held as property. There was a war to that effect last century!*

She had a long-term goal for Virgil, though she had not spoken of it to anyone. She would see to it that he would be legally recognized and given all the same rights as a human. He had been born into a world in which dragons were extinct, but she would not allow that to rob him of the rights he would have had if he had hatched in the Cretaceous Period.

Further reaching than that, she had a goal to see *Deinonychus antirrhopus* make a resurgence as a species. That was one of the reasons Rose had wanted Virgil to get to know Violet: she might well be the only female of his species he would have the opportunity to meet.

Rose could not force the two to marry, of course, nor would she wish to. But she could certainly see to it that they knew each other very well by the time they were adults.

Of course, seeing as they were both hatchlings right now, that sort of thinking was highly premature. But Rose had never been one to disregard the far future in her planning. She had decided at nine years old that she would become a paleontologist, and she had not changed her mind since.

The only thing that Virgil had changed was that, where once she had had one goal, now she had three.

Rose continued to stare at the zoo keeper in frosty silence.

The man looked a trifle uncomfortable. He moved away from her to walk over to Violet's cage, where a crowd of onlookers had been gathering.

"Can I pet the dragon, too?" a woman asked eagerly, crowding in and reaching out her hand.

"Didn't know there was more than one," a man said.

"Of course there is, didn't you read the news?" another man said impatiently. "This is the man who studies dragons and is raising one."

Rose's chest swelled with indignation. *I'M the one who's studying paleontology, not Henry!*

"No," Henry said, swatting the reaching hands away. "No, you can't pet him. No. No. No. *Stop it!*"

Virgil's claws dug into the front of Henry's shirt. He didn't like these hands. These hands were scary. He would make these hands go away.

Virgil started making snorting noises.

"Get back!" Henry shouted. "Get back right now!"

The crowd parted as he shoved them, and Virgil let loose a tiny spark. It danced briefly in the air, then disappeared.

Rose breathed a sigh of relief.

Virgil's tail wriggled as his head turned to face Violet.

Why was Violet sleeping? Virgil didn't want her to be sleeping. Virgil wanted her to wake up. He would wake her up with one of her memories she had shared with him.

"*No!*" Rose shouted, but she was too late.

A vision of terror and desolation gripped her mind. Her parents were gone. All the adults were gone. Only the eggs remained, screaming and screaming with nobody coming to claim them. No one would ever claim them. They would never hatch. *She* would never hatch. There was absolute despair.

Rose sucked in her breath as she returned to herself, and the tiny blue dragon within the cage twitched. Her eyes opened. Her claws scrambled against the cement beneath her. Then she opened her mouth and screamed.

The crowd shouted and covered their ears as the high-pitched shriek reverberated endlessly, and loudly.

Virgil was glad Violet had woken up! Now they could play together!

The terrible scream stopped.

The little blue dragon looked up. Piteousness emanated from her.

Was Violet not alone now? Had Violet just been dreaming?

Henry rapped Virgil sharply on the nose. "You do not wake people up by giving them nightmares! That is not acceptable!"

Virgil was sorry. Virgil hadn't meant to make Violet sad.

Violet was better. Violet was sleepy. Violet was tired. Maybe Violet would sleep again.

Virgil didn't want her to sleep. Virgil wanted her to wake up.

The little blue dragon's head drooped, and her tail curled back around her again.

No! Virgil would wake her up again, so she would play. No! Why was his father walking away? Violet should play!

"This was a bad idea," Henry said, walking over to Rose. "We can go somewhere else to ask for advice."

Where? Rose wondered.

But she didn't object. Henry was right. She should not have expected help to be forthcoming here.

Their son's tail writhed as they tucked him back into the pram.

Virgil was very upset! Violet should play!

CHAPTER 3: CHALLENGE

The American Museum of Natural History was where they had met Virgil, and it was the one other place Rose could think of where there might be someone with helpful insights on baby dragons.

Someone in particular, and it wasn't Director Campbell.

Mr. Teedle, the curator of the dragon collection, was in the Research Library on the fourth floor. It was locked because it was not open to the public, but Rose found a staff member to open it for her.

As the door opened, Rose maneuvered the pram to push it through.

"What's that?" Mr. Teedle looked up from the table where he had been carefully paging through a book. "We're not open to the public right now. The hours are two pm to five thir—" He stopped, recognizing her. "Oh, Miss Palmer. To what do I owe the pleasure?"

"Mrs. Wainscott," Henry corrected him, coming in after Rose.

"Oh. Yes." Mr. Teedle coughed. "Please do forgive me."

"It's quite all right," Rose said. "I often forget that myself."

Mr. Teedle ran his hand down the slick surface of his greying hair. "And I see you have brought Virgil. Is he ... ah ... not likely to burn the reference materials in here?"

"He's asleep," Henry said. "He tired himself out throwing a fit on the way over here."

"Thank heavens," Mr. Teedle said, breathing a sigh of relief. "This is not a room where a firebreathing infant ought to be, you realize."

Henry's smile grew strained, and Rose recognized that his patience had frayed considerably due to Virgil's tantrum.

"Perhaps we could speak outside?" she asked Mr. Teedle. "We have some advice we'd like to ask you about Virgil."

"Certainly," the man said, setting his book aside. He stood and walked to the doorway, where he then waited with his fingers tapping his thigh while Henry struggled to turn the pram around and wrestle it back out into the hallway.

Rose cast a longing look around the Research Library before she followed them out. She had spent every spare moment she could in this room for years; that was how she had become acquainted with Mr. Teedle. When she had been in high school, this had involved a great deal of irritation on her father's part, and a great deal of protests from her mother that they really would have liked to see her before six pm on Tuesdays through Thursdays.

This had never caused a jot of difference. Nor had starting college: she had simply spent what time she could here, and then gone home to complete her homework before starting dinner. Unlike her roommates, she had never been particularly interested in social activities, so she had felt no great loss in missing these.

But now, she had not been here once since Virgil had hatched, as it was a struggle merely to find time to do her homework and sleep. She had barely even come to the museum since then. With a pang of loss, Rose watched the door close, shutting her out of her favorite place in the city.

"What is it?" Mr. Teedle asked. "Are you wondering how much larger he will grow in the next month? We have some estimated charts based on his growth over the past eight weeks."

"No," Henry said. "Well, yes. That would be nice to know, but ..."

"We have some *specific* concerns," Rose said. "Namely: what would you recommend as a long-term bed for Virgil? Somewhere that he cannot escape from as he gets older, and which would be both fireproof and safe for him?"

Mr. Teedle looked thoughtful. "Perhaps something made out of brick, like is used for a fireplace? My daughter-in-law has a wooden contraption called a playpen that she uses for their daughter. I wish those had been around when my children were babies. Something like that, only made out of brick, might be appropriate for Virgil."

Rose's heart soared. That was a truly useful idea!

"How fast could we get one made?" Henry asked.

"Well, I imagine you would need the permission of your landlord to install what would amount to a permanent piece of furniture," Mr. Teedle said. "But other than that, I believe the cement takes one or two days to dry? If you could find someone willing to sell you bricks and lay them tonight, it could be ready by Christmas."

"Perfect," Henry said. "Where could we go to buy bricks?"

And how much will it cost? Rose wondered. They had already spent a concerning amount on presents and the now-charcoaled tree. Despite Rose's vehement protests that it was unnecessary and a waste of money, Henry had gone out and bought Virgil several more stuffed animals.

Never mind that the only interest their dragon son seemed to have in the teddy bear Henry had bought him was to dig his claws into it and pull out stuffing.

Never mind that it had been singed twice from Virgil breathing fire on it.

Never mind that Virgil referred to it as "prey."

"Actually," Mr. Teedle said excitedly, "I believe that Mr. Jones is currently working as a bricklayer! I'm sure he would be happy to help. If anyone can understand your situation, he will. I'm sure he would be happy to help!"

Rose tried not to show her dismay. While Harrison Jones was a friendly man, she was not particularly fond of him. He was rarely kempt, and his breath usually smelled quite unpleasant.

She glanced over at Henry, and he looked no more enthused than she felt. She suspected Henry's dislike of the man stemmed from the fact that he had allowed Violet to be kept in a zoo with no concerns or argument. She had chosen him to be her father, and then he had cheerfully turned around and handed her to the care of others who saw her as no more than an extremely precious, rare animal.

Still, necessities were necessities. It was true that Harrison Jones would likely be happy to help.

"How do we contact Mr. Jones?" Rose asked politely.

"I don't believe he has a phone," Mr. Teedle said, frowning. "At least, not of his own. He lives at a boarding house."

Of course he does, Rose thought. *What need has he for a fixed address when he can pay someone to do his housekeeping and keep his daughter inside a zoo?*

But perhaps that was unfair. After all, he had not planned to have a daughter:

Violet had come into his life suddenly, just as Virgil had come into Rose and Henry's.

Perhaps he is making do the best he can, the same as we are, Rose thought.

"Ah! I know," Mr. Teedle said. "I know he visits Violet daily. Perhaps the best way to contact him would be to go to the zoo and wait until he comes to see her? I'm sure Virgil wouldn't mind playing with her while you're waiting, and I assume you two both have the week off school, so if you have no pressing other concerns ..."

Henry cringed.

"We were just there," Rose said. "It did not end well. Virgil behaved quite abominably."

"And if we go back now, he'll think his tantrum convinced us to go back," Henry growled.

"I'm familiar with that challenge," Mr. Teedle chuckled.

"We can leave him a letter with our phone number to call," Rose decided. "Mr. Teedle, could we perhaps borrow a pen and a sheet of paper?"

"Of course," the man said.

Thirty minutes later, they were walking down 5th Avenue away from Central Park Zoo.

"Do you think those people ever worry about money?" Henry asked longingly, looking across the street at the abodes that had been built for the super-rich.

"I think probably most people worry about money," Rose said. "Whether or not they need to."

"It would be nice just to know our money won't run out before I graduate," Henry sighed, taking a hand off the pram to rub his forehead while he continued pushing it with the other. "Virgil's carnivorous diet is costing more than it should."

"Then perhaps," Rose hinted strongly, "he does not need a diet of stuffed animals to supplement it."

"You can't be stingy with a child at Christmas!" Henry said.

Rose snorted.

There was a wriggling in the pram.

Virgil liked that noise. He was going to snort, too. Snort, snort, snort—

"*No!*" Rose and Henry shouted, diving for the pram to grab their son before he set the whole thing ablaze.

Chapter 4: Charm

When they arrived back home, their landlord was waiting outside the door for them.

"Do you have something to tell me?" he demanded, his tone strongly implying that the correct answer was *yes*.

Henry swallowed. "Virgil burned down the Christmas tree last night. We caught it before it caused too much damage, but—"

"Oh, really?" the landlord asked heatedly. "Have you seen the carpet in there?"

"We apologize for the carpet," Rose said swiftly. "We are taking steps to make sure this will not happen again."

"I've told you tenants again and again, don't light the candles until Christmas Eve!" Mr. Torgerson fumed. "And don't leave them lit overnight!"

Henry looked startled.

Rose was taken aback.

"You've ... experienced burning Christmas trees before?" Henry asked cautiously.

"I wish I could just ban them outright," the man huffed. "This is the third time something like this has happened in the past five years! But when I tried to ban Christmas trees last year, oh no, everyone called me Scrooge."

Rose bit back a chuckle. The man's first name was Ebenezer. She didn't think showing amusement at the nickname would improve their landlord's mood.

"Well, we're very sorry about the ... candles," Henry said. "We'll make sure that won't ... happen again."

"Of course it won't, because you are not lighting those candles again!" Mr. Torgerson said. "And you *will* pay for the carpet!"

Henry cringed.

What a jolly season, Rose thought. *I hope we will not be destitute by the time it's over.*

Virgil poked his head out of the pram, as if he had determined that this would be the best moment to make his presence known.

Could he eat now? He was hungry. Hungry, hungry, hungry. Where was his food?

"Right here," Henry said, walking into the kitchen. He opened up the icebox and pulled out a covered bowl that had chicken meat, raw egg, and butter mushed together. He pulled the cloth off the top of the bowl and scooped up some of the mash with his hand.

Mr. Torgerson watched with evident curiosity. "Is that what a dragon eats?"

"Back in the Cretaceous Period, he would have eaten one of the prey species of dragons," Rose said. "We've found that bird meat is the closest approximation we can come to it."

Virgil wriggled his tail over the side of the pram, and then tumbled out. He landed on his head on the carpet.

Mr. Torgerson's eyes widened, and he looked about to lunge forward to see if the baby was all right.

Virgil rolled over onto his stomach, not seeming to notice the fall. He half-rolled, half-crawled across the floor to where Henry was waiting.

"OW!" Henry shouted as Virgil put one of his clawed hands onto his ankle. He reached down and unhooked the baby from his pant leg.

Virgil was hungry. Virgil wanted food. Virgil wanted to be fed by mouth.

"No, for the thousandth time, I'm not putting it in my mouth," Henry said. He leaned over and held out his hand.

Virgil's neck darted forward, and he snapped up the chicken and chewed busily. Sharp teeth glinted as it shot forward again.

Mr. Torgerson watched with awed apprehension. "Doesn't he bite you?" he asked.

"Thankfully, no," Henry said. "Which is more than I can say for some human children. My nephews, for instance."

The landlord chuckled nervously.

Rose decided that this might be the best time to speak up. "We'd like to build a brick bed for Virgil to sleep in," she said. "This would allow us to restore the oven to its original purpose. We will cover the cost, and it will eventually be a playpen, as well."

"Oh," Mr. Torgerson said, seeming too riveted watching the dragon to think much about the question. "Would it be, um ... removable?"

"We could lay a layer of cardboard on the floor so that any cement drips on that, and nothing is affixed to the floor," Rose said.

"Hmm," the landlord said, his eyes on Virgil. "You know, when I first read what the paper said, I thought it was some kind of hoax or joke. And then I saw you two walk out with that thing ..."

"Dragon," Henry said. "He is a dragon. Not a thing."

"You know, I'd love the chance to meet the other one," the landlord said. "Is it true they're both intelligent? Do they both talk like ... that?"

Virgil was done eating, and now he wanted more food. The hand was empty! Where was his food?

Henry glanced down and reached into the bowl to scoop out more for Virgil.

"Both *Deinonychus* dragons are telepathic, yes," Rose said. "We believe it was a trait unique to their species, but we have no way to be sure. We're certainly glad it's the case, because there would be no other way to communicate with them."

"Bet it's quite an adjustment," the landlord said. "Eating chicken instead of stegosauruses, huh?"

Virgil didn't know what he meant. Why was the strange man thinking about bones?

"*Stegosaurus* lived in the late Jurassic Period," Rose said. "*Deinonychus* come from the early Cretaceous. They were approximately thirty-five million years apart. It's highly unlikely the two species ever met."

Virgil's father thought Virgil's mother was being pedantic again. Virgil didn't know what that meant. Why was Virgil's mother annoyed with Virgil's father?

The landlord coughed, as if trying to hide his amusement.

Rose smiled. *For once, Virgil has managed to be helpful. It seems the child has some charm.*

The little dragon raised his head, eyes bright with curiosity.

Virgil wanted to know what charm was. Hey! Virgil hadn't been done eating! Virgil's father shouldn't take the food away!

"We have your permission, then?" Rose asked rapidly, hoping that Virgil would not spoil the man's goodwill while they had it. "To build the bed for Virgil?"

"Hm?" the landlord asked. "Yes, I suppose so. As long as you cover the cost, and nothing is permanently altered." He glared in the direction of the oven, as if his gaze alone would remove the metal doorstop and nail affixed to it.

"Thank you," Rose said in relief.

The next half an hour was tense, as they waited for the landlord to leave, and he seemed to want to hover, watching Virgil with rapt interest.

Rose was terribly afraid that, at some random moment, their son would decide to snort, and sparks would fly from his nose. If he did that, the landlord might catch on that it hadn't been the candles that had burned down the tree, and his goodwill might transform to fear or hostility.

Then it occurred to her thinking about that might give Virgil the idea, so she tried to pull her mind away from the possibility. But that, of course, led inexorably back to it. So at last, she moved as far away from the kitchen as possible without being rude, and hoped that she was out of Virgil's range.

"What do you do for dinner?" the landlord asked curiously. "Seeing as your oven is not hooked up any longer?"

"We use our neighbors'," Rose said. "Speaking of which, I actually should go and start preparing that now ..."

It was early yet, an hour before she normally would go next door and ask, but anything seemed better than sitting around here waiting for him to leave.

"Ah, yes," Mr. Torgerson said, standing. "Of course. My apologies for intruding. But no more lighting candles in here, no matter how traditional it is!" he added sternly.

"Yes, sir," Henry said, nodding quickly.

Rose nearly collapsed with relief on the couch as the door shut after the man. She put her head in her hands.

Henry walked over, carrying Virgil, and rubbed her shoulder. "I know," he said. "I'm glad we didn't get thrown out, too."

Virgil was sleepy. Virgil was tired. Virgil was soaking. Virgil was wet. Wet, wet, wet, wet, wet ...

"Your turn," Henry said, holding up the dragon.

Rose sighed and collected the baby. The cloth pinned around his hindquarters and the top of his tail was, indeed, soaked through and smelly.

"Thank you for not breathing fire in front of the landlord," she murmured as she went to find a fresh one.

Virgil was too tired. Virgil was wet. Wet, wet, wet, wet ...

Chapter 5: Chimney

"Can't be done," Harrison Jones's voice said as soon as Rose picked up the phone.

"Excuse me?" Rose asked, breathing heavily.

She was trying not to pant. She had run to grab the phone before it could awaken Henry, seeing as he had decided to get an hour of sleep as soon as Virgil had settled down for a nap.

"Can't be done," Harrison repeated. It sounded like he was shrugging. "Not tonight, not tomorrow night, certainly not on Christmas. It might be possible to have someone do it in a month, if you wanted it done outside, but indoors? Maybe if you paid my company a lot, and I do mean a lot, of money, they'd be willing to take on such a major construction project, but you'd need the agreement of your landlord."

"But it's not a major project," Rose objected. "It's—"

"It *is* a major project," Harrison's voice said. "You're talking about designing something that doesn't currently exist, and which has no market outside yourselves."

"But it would be similar to a chimney!" Rose protested. "Or a playpen! Nothing complicated at all!"

"That's not what you said in your note," he retorted. "You said you wanted something he can't crawl out of. Whenever he starts climbing, I doubt he would find difficulties with a brick wall."

Rose said nothing. He was, appallingly, correct. If they wanted a bed that would keep their son penned in each night for longer than a few weeks or months, however long it took the little dragon to learn to climb, they would require something that would be safe, something that would be easy to deposit him into, and yet something that would be difficult for him to escape on his own. Her mind failed to imagine a shape which would accomplish all of these things.

"What you probably want is a cage," Harrison said. "You could ask the zoo what they'd recommend."

Rose said nothing. Her fist clenched around the phone. He was absolutely right: a cage would fit the parameters they'd defined, and the very idea was appalling. She had no doubt that Henry would veto it with vehement certainty.

Maybe we've been thinking with the wrong assumptions, Rose thought. *Maybe what we need is not to find a way to trap him, but a way to make sure it is not dangerous if he gets out on his own, which he will no doubt want to do increasingly more often as he ages.*

"Thank you, Mr. Jones," Rose said politely. "I appreciate the speed with which you contacted us."

"If you need to contact me again, here's the phone number for the boarding house," he said, and recited four digits. "I'm not often here, though. And it's often busy. There are three other boarding houses on our party line, plus at least two families, and one of the women in one of those places is constantly on the phone."

"Speaking of which!" a strange man's voice cut in. "Are you two close to done? I need to make a call soon."

Rose rubbed her forehead. That was a voice she thought she had heard before, so the rude stranger was probably on the end of her party line. It would have been nice to be able to hold a conversation without the risk of strangers listening in. The lack of privacy with telephone conversations was a definite disadvantage to using them.

"I believe we're done," Rose said, hiding her annoyance.

"Yup, we're done," Harrison agreed.

She hung up the phone, her mind unsettled. It seemed that she and Henry had, unknowingly, settled into the same mindset that had resulted in Violet's living situation. This was something that they must not do, not if they wished better for Virgil.

She walked over to the oven, where she peered in at Virgil. He was asleep with his tail curled around him, his back rising and falling in regular rhythm. As she watched, his tail twitched, and he let out a tiny sneeze. A spark escaped his nostrils.

Rose shut the door carefully, making sure it didn't clang as it hit the metal that kept it from closing completely. In the tiny gap, she could almost make out the outline of his growing-rapidly-more-ragged cloth diaper.

How do we do what is best for Virgil, and also best for us? Rose wondered.

She knew exactly how his birth parents would have handled it: they would have allowed the child free rein. But as Virgil aged, he would not be simply a toddler, he could be one which could set anything on fire, and yet who still probably needed exercise and freedom to develop.

A large cage, like Violet's, would probably work for a very young child quite admirably. But what about when their child aged? It didn't seem wise to set the precedent that ensnarement was the only reasonable option. They must find an alternative, and they must find it quickly.

Who might have an insight that might help? Rose wondered.

Then she realized. She realized that they had been going to the wrong experts for ideas.

She picked up the phone to ask the operator to connect her to her mother, and instead heard two strangers talking loudly, one of them the rude man who had interrupted her conversation earlier. It seemed to be an argument about in-laws visiting one of the strangers' homes.

Rose slammed the receiver back down. *This might not be a conversation I want to have over the phone, anyway! I will have to talk to my parents when we see them tomorrow.*

Tomorrow was Christmas Eve, and they would be going over for dinner; that had already been arranged. But if there would be no solution until then, Rose would need to come up with a stopgap that would work for tonight. One that would guarantee safety.

Rose thought about that for a long moment, and then moved one of the kitchen chairs against the oven door. That would stop it from opening for one night, at least.

She sat at the kitchen table in the other of the two chairs, and picked up her textbook. It was uncomfortable to have no homework to work on during the silent moments, as that left her with little to work on but darning the huge pile of worn-through socks of Henry's that had accumulated over the past two months, a necessity she found unutterably boring but which he seemed to assume was her duty.

She had, as such, already purchased three of the textbooks that she would need for next semester, and had spent all her spare time reading them. Perhaps if she allowed the socks to accumulate until he had no more left, he would make the effort to mend them himself, as he had before they'd been married.

It wasn't until she had memorized the contents of three pages that Rose looked up, somewhat disturbed. She stared at the oven, and the chair pushed up against it. Her stare became fixed.

Isn't that solution inconsistent with the resolution I made? she wondered. *Isn't that stopgap measure once again a way to trap him?*

Rose yanked her thoughts away from the disturbing notion and went back to her textbook. But her focus was no longer with it. She kept looking up and staring at the chair, more and more bothered by it.

If there's a way I want to do something, I must start the way I intend to finish, she thought. *It doesn't do any good to immediately flout the ideals I wish to follow.*

She stood up and walked over to the oven. She pulled the chair away, and it scraped loudly against the tile floor. There was a rustling from inside the oven.

Virgil was awake! Virgil had had a good nap!

Rose opened the oven door and gathered the little dragon up in her arms.

"I'm sorry," she said. "I'm trying. I just don't know what to do."

Virgil wasn't sorry. Virgil didn't know why his mother was sorry. Virgil was fine. Virgil was—Virgil's stomach hurt!

Rose scrambled to put him back in the oven, but she wasn't in time. A roar from Virgil's nostrils hit the back of the chair, which ignited into a small flame. She beat it back with her elbow until the chair merely had a dark spot against the seat. She stared at the baby in frustration.

Virgil's stomach felt better now. Could Virgil roll on the floor that was soft?

Rose sighed deeply and moved him to the carpet. After that tremendous burst, he shouldn't need to breathe fire for another few hours. The need seemed to build up in him, much like releasing the results of his digestive system.

Virgil rolled around and sunk his claws into the carpet. Virgil liked the floor that was soft! It was soft and rolly!

"And I have no idea what we're going to do," Rose murmured. "Why can't you make things easy?"

Chapter 6: Chore

Henry looked very taken aback as he walked into the living room. "What ... are you doing?"

"I am moving the couch cushions to the floor of the kitchen," Rose said, walking past him with the second of three. "Was that not evident?"

Henry followed her into the kitchen, stepping around Virgil, who was busily clawing one of the charred branches of their Christmas tree. "Why?"

"In order to sleep in the kitchen tonight," Rose said. She placed the second cushion in line with the first one and strode back to the living room.

Henry followed her. "Why?"

"So that, if Virgil decides to exit the oven tonight, he will land on top of me, which will awaken me, and he will therefore not roam around the apartment unsupervised." Rose gathered up the third cushion and moved back to the kitchen.

"Doesn't that seem a little convoluted?" Henry protested, trailing after her. "There has to be a better solution."

"I imagine there is," Rose agreed. She walked past him to reach the linen closet in the hallway. She pulled out their spare sheet and tucked it under her arm, then headed back to the kitchen. "I hope my family will suggest it tomorrow night."

"I mean, there has to be a better solution *tonight*," Henry said. "Why don't we ... uh ..." He cast his eyes around the kitchen, then spied the chair that was out of place. "Why don't we put this in front of the oven door?" he asked triumphantly, seizing it.

"That would be lovely if we wished to keep our son in a cage," Rose said flatly.

Henry loosened his grip on the chair. "Huh?"

"Harrison Jones called while you were sleeping," Rose said, tucking the sheet around the couch cushions to make a rather unappealing facsimile of a mattress. "He informed me that what we had described to him was a cage. It occurred to me that if there is no functional difference between Violet's living situation and Virgil's, we might as well be putting him in the zoo and have done with it."

"Hang on," Henry said, grabbing her hand. "Rose, there's a world of difference between the two. For one thing, Virgil actually lives with us."

Rose shook his hand off. "Harrison Jones visits Violet."

"Yes—visits! That's a big difference!"

EMILY MARTHA SORENSEN

"Would you put a human infant in a cage?" Rose challenged.

"Yes!" Henry said. "That's what a crib *is!* It's a place to keep a human infant restrained!"

Rose stared at him flintily.

"Look," Henry said, "getting Virgil a safe place to sleep that won't put him or us at risk isn't a bad thing. It's good parenting."

"A cage is out of the question," Rose said.

They stared at each other for a moment, tension bristling between them.

"Fine," Henry said shortly. "Then at least let *me* sleep on the floor. You sleep on the bed."

"You are a sound sleeper," Rose shot back. "What guarantee is there that you'd waken if Virgil fell on you?"

"I woke up this morning," Henry said heatedly.

"One instance is not a guarantee!"

Virgil rolled across the carpet and stared at them from an upside-down, sprawling position.

Why were his parents angry? They should feed him. He was hungry. He wanted food.

Henry opened up the icebox and groaned. "I forgot. We're almost out of chicken. Can you buy one and get it cooked today?"

Today? Rose thought. *You only just woke up from your nap, and I have not yet caught up with my sleep from our interrupted morning!*

"I will ask my mother to purchase one for us tonight," Rose said, keeping her temper in check. "We can pay her back for it tomorrow. We could even ask her to cook it for us before we come."

"Do you have to lean on your mother for everything?" Henry exclaimed. "Do you know how to cook yourself? I haven't had a hot meal since we got married, except when we visit your parents!"

"Virgil ... was sleeping ... in the oven," Rose said coldly. "I was not going to impose upon our neighbors any more than necessary, given that sandwiches and such could suffice."

"Is that going to change when we get him a different bed?" Henry exclaimed. "Are you ever actually going to cook dinner? You haven't even darned one of my socks in six weeks!"

"You know how to darn them yourself," Rose snapped. "We're both in school. We're both equally busy."

"I shouldn't *have* to darn them!" Henry said. "It's your chore!"

"Oh, really?" Rose asked icily. "Why is that?"

"Because that's what wives do!"

"Well, perhaps husbands," Rose said coldly, "could make some effort at an equivalent number of chores."

"I take care of all the finances!"

"As I've said before, I wish you'd let me see them."

"I feed Virgil!"

"So do I."

"I change his diapers!"

"So do I."

"I wake up in the middle of the night to do both of those!"

"So do I."

Admittedly, that was far more than Rose's father had ever done, and perhaps Henry's father as well. So perhaps he wanted to be reminded that she appreciated the fact that he didn't seem to think the baby was all her problem. Rose opened her mouth.

"*And* I let you go to college!" Henry added.

Rose's mouth snapped shut.

"*Let* me?" she shouted once she had recovered from speechlessness. "*Let* me? In what way do you *let* me?"

For some reason, Henry seemed determined to not back down from the atrocious statement. "I talked your father into paying your tuition! I talked the dean of your college into letting you stay after we got married!"

Rose pursed her lips. Henry had had to go in and assure the dean that he did not mind if his wife continued with her college education. To her intense displeasure, it had turned out that married women were not allowed to continue as students without special permission. That had enraged her.

For what possible reason had Henry brought up such a sore subject? To enrage her further?

Henry seemed to take her silence as agreement. "I know most men wouldn't accept their wives being in college. I *do!* I just ask that you take care of things like you're supposed to!"

Rose clenched her fists and reminded herself that her father had said far worse. It had never helped to shout, though she had done it many times despite knowing that.

"I see," Rose said quietly. "It is good to know that that is where you stand. I will be sleeping in the kitchen tonight, and I will be glad of it."

She turned to walk through the living room to get her pillow, and nearly tripped over their son, who was lying on the carpet batting at one of the tree's charred bottom branches.

Were Virgil's parents mad at him? Could Virgil have food? Virgil was still hungry. Virgil was wet. Virgil's tail was in the wetness. It was uncomfortable. Could Virgil have food?

"Yes, you can have food," Rose said. "If we run out of chicken before tomorrow night, you can have eggs and butter alone."

Virgil liked chicken food. It was prey. One day his parents would teach him how to hunt prey. His father had given him prey, but it didn't taste good. Could he have his prey?

"No, you can't have your teddy bear right now," Henry said, sounding annoyed. "Yes, you can have food."

Virgil liked food! Virgil would roll over to his father! Now he was on the hard floor. The soft floor was more fun to play on. Was Virgil's mother tired? Was she taking a nap?

"Perhaps I should," Rose said. "I'm still short on sleep from this morning."

"Fine," Henry muttered. "Sleep as long as you want. It's not like I can't make sandwiches for myself."

It's not like the person who has the shorter commute to school can't learn to cook for himself, Rose thought.

But she didn't continue the argument. She just went to the bedroom, where she fell asleep almost as soon as her head hit the pillow.

CHAPTER 7: CHOLERIC

Bad tempers abounded the next morning. Though it was Christmas Eve, neither Rose nor Henry made any effort to speak to each other. Rose spent most of the morning with her textbook, while Henry spent most of it absorbed in the small book where he kept an account of their finances. For some reason, he kept looking up and staring at Virgil quite often before going back to his pencil scribbling.

Virgil spent most of the morning rolling around on the carpet, sometimes clawing at the brown, dried needles that had fallen from the tree. At one point, one flipped into his open mouth, and Virgil's expressionless face somehow gave the impression of disgust and betrayal.

That was not-food! Why was not-food in his mouth? He didn't like it!

Rose and Henry both started to stand up, noticed the other standing, hesitated, and then Rose sat down and Henry got up to remove the foliage from their child's mouth.

They alternated feeding Virgil without discussion, this being an ingrained habit. They did run out of chicken by lunchtime, which Rose discovered when she got up to take her turn, so she cracked raw eggs into a pat of butter and fed that to Virgil, which he seemed very disgruntled about.

This was not-food! No, that was food. That was not-food! No, that was food. That was not-food! Virgil wanted his food!

Henry looked silently triumphant.

Rose tried to ignore this.

The phone rang several times, causing them to jump from their seats, but it was always the wrong sequence: one long ring and two short ones, three long ones, and one short ring and two long ones. That meant the phone was for another household. Rose hoped that none of these conversations lasted long enough that the call they were waiting for failed to come through, but given the frequency of the ringing, it seemed likely that the conversations were all of short duration.

At last the correct ring came, two short and one long, and Rose leapt from her seat to answer it.

"Hello?" she asked, hoping that it was her mother. Her family had agreed to call as soon as they felt Christmas dinner was only an hour away. It was barely two minutes past two, and Rose's mother had estimated dinner would start at four o'clock, so Rose would be overjoyed to leave this tense atmosphere to walk there early.

"Hello, Rose," her father's voice said on the other end of the phone. "Your mother says the chicken's ready, so if you want to come over early, you can. Your sisters are insisting they want to string popcorn, and your mother wants to go caroling as soon as we're done with dinner. You planning to come along?"

"That sounds delightful," Rose said. She did not consult with Henry. If he did not want to go, she would simply leave him behind at her parents' home.

"It looks like snow," her father added, "so you might want to wear your warmest coats."

"Understood," Rose said. "We will be over as soon as possible. We'll see you in an hour or so, Papa."

She set down the phone, and it immediately rang. She jumped, but it was only two long rings and one short one, meant for somebody else.

"They're ready early," she told Henry. "We can leave now."

"Hallelujah," he said, slapping his finance book shut as she passed. As usual, Rose resisted the urge to peek, but she wished he would not act like it contained some dreadful secret. It was rather unsettling.

A crash came from the direction of the Christmas tree, and Rose spun around. Virgil had just snapped off one of the branches at the bottom with his head as he raised it.

Were they going to see Violet? Could Virgil come play?

"We're not going to see her," Rose said. "We're going to see your grandparents. The zoo's not even open today."

Virgil was very disappointed. He wanted to lie down next to Violet and hit her with his tail. Then she would hit him with her tail and he would catch it in his claws. It was fun to play.

"I'm sure it is," Rose said, "but it's Christmas Eve, which is a special day that's all about family."

Virgil didn't know what that meant. Was Virgil's father going to breathe fire with him? Was Virgil's mother going to hit him with her tail?

"Virgil, as I've said a thousand times," Henry said wearily, "we're human. That means we're different species. We can't do the same things."

Virgil's parents were being mean! Virgil was pouting.

Rose turned away from the petulant baby and walked into the bedroom. She pulled on her warmest stockings, which were woollen and a trifle itchy, and then stared at the open drawer, pondering.

At last, she reached into the back and pulled out the luxury she had been saving, her last pair of silk stockings that had not developed terrible runs from Virgil's claws on her legs. If there were ever a time to treat oneself, it would be Christmas Eve.

She walked to the hall closet and removed her coat from the rack. She tucked the ball of stockings into the pocket of her coat before sliding it onto her arms. Purses were fashionable, but she was not fond of them, especially while walking. The one purse she owned had been singed by one of Virgil's many escapades, in any case.

Henry was already clad in his coat and waiting by the door with a rather impatient air. He had Virgil tucked under his arm.

"Are we not taking the pram?" Rose asked.

"It's snowing," Henry said shortly. "If it continues, I don't want to push it through mountains of slush on the way back."

Rose had to admit that was sensible.

They opened the door, and a burst of cold air blew in on them. Rose shivered and hunched into her coat. She ran back to the hall closet and returned with both her scarf and Henry's. She wound hers around her neck and tucked it into her coat.

"Would you like me to put it on you?" she asked Henry, holding his scarf up.

"No," Henry said grumpily. "I have a heat source with me."

Rose glanced over at Virgil, who was staring at the rushing snow with little apparent interest. His tail swung back and forth, clearly unbothered by the temperature.

What would it take for any temperature to bother him? Rose wondered. *He seems unharmed by fire, and snow is also of little concern to him. Do* Deinonychus *dragons have any sensitivities?*

Perhaps she should have been glad that their little son seemed virtually invulnerable, but it troubled her. How had his species died out in the first place? They must have had some terrible weakness, and it worried her that she did not know what it was. Perhaps they had simply starved to death because they had lost their prey species? Virgil still seemed to need ten or more meals per day, which implied a very fast metabolism and a rate of growth which would be unsustainable without a great deal of prey.

I hope that we are adequate as parents, Rose thought nervously. *What if he requires far more food next year than we can possibly afford to give him?*

Already he had grown a foot longer than he had been when he'd hatched. Suppose it turned out that he outgrew their home long before they were able to move to a larger place?

No, Rose told herself. *Don't borrow trouble. We will figure something out, in that case.*

But as they stepped out into the freezing wind and blowing snow, she couldn't shake the feeling that the choleric disposition Henry had shown was because he was bothered by something similar. They had not, after all, figured out what to do about their child's firebreathing.

Rose bent her head as she walked against the wind beside her husband and son, burying her hands deep in her pockets. She could hardly wait until they reached her parents' home and she would be able to thaw her toes.

CHAPTER 8: CHEER

"Mama, they're here!" Sara shouted from the doorway.

Rose shivered into her coat and wished her sister would move out of the way and allow them inside.

Rose's mother bustled up behind her. "Oh, you're covered in snow!" she cried. "Come in, come in! Dinner's almost ready. Do you want to sit by the fire?"

"Y-yes," Henry said, his teeth chattering.

Rose nodded, her breath bobbing in front of her face.

Virgil's tail swung unconcernedly. Virgil wanted to play with the soft white stuff. Could Virgil play?

"N-not right now," Henry said, his teeth chattering as he stepped into the house after Rose. "We need to warm up."

Virgil didn't understand. His parents' memories made no sense to him. Why did they think it was cold? What was cold? Also, could Virgil eat? He was hungry.

"Can I feed him, can I feed him, can I feed him?" Sara squealed. "He's so cute!"

Fortunately, Virgil now accepted food from people other than his parents.

"Go ahead," Rose said as Henry relinquished the dragon.

Sara pranced off with their son in her arms. Virgil wasn't cute. What was cute? Virgil was hungry. Where was his food?

Rose and Henry walked to the living room, where they ensconced themselves next to the fire. Despite the impropriety, Rose removed her stockings right there and laid them out beside the fire to dry. She allowed the fire to warm her bare feet.

Her father came into the room, smoking a pipe. The odor was overpowering.

"Hi, Rose," he said. "Hi, other one. Good journey?"

Henry bristled. "It was cold," he said shortly.

Rose wished he wouldn't show offense at being called "the other one." That was why her father did it. Though the man now tolerated Henry, he had decided upon their first meeting that he didn't like him, and took delight in continuing to remind Henry of that at every opportunity.

"Snow's really coming down," Rose's father agreed. "I wouldn't want to walk in that."

"I wish I hadn't had to, either," Henry muttered under his breath.

"He's so cute!" Sara squealed, wandering into the living room with Virgil cuddled in one arm and gobbling out of her other hand, which held the usual mixture of chicken, raw egg, butter, and some water. "Look at the way he eats!"

Virgil's head jerked forward, he chomped at a mouthful, and he swallowed. Then his head darted forward again. His tail swung excitedly behind him, almost in rhythm.

"Yes, he is," said Rose, though she was used to the sight.

Louise trailed in after Sara, looking furious. "It's not fair! It's my turn to hold him!" she protested.

"Is not!"

"Is too!"

"Is not!"

"Is too! *And* I'm older!"

"Only by nine months," Sara sniffed.

"Ten!"

"Nine!"

"Ten!"

Rose rubbed her forehead wearily. It was hard to believe her sisters were in high school. When they squabbled, it sounded like they were ten years younger. The two usually got along extremely well, but not when they both wanted something.

Henry squinted at them, as if trying to figure out which girl was which.

"You can have a turn after Sara is done, Louise," Rose said, to remind him.

Henry's face cleared. He looked relieved.

"Hey, other one," Rose's father said, gesturing at Henry with his pipe. "You planning to come over tomorrow too, for Christmas morning?"

"No," Henry said, looking irritated. "We're planning to spend that at home, together."

With a blackened Christmas tree we barely managed to prop back up, Rose thought, looking around the room at the paper chains and paper doll chains her sisters had strung up along the top of every window. *And no decorations. And no Christmas cake to eat for breakfast in the morning, because we have no way to cook things.*

Tomorrow would be her first Christmas away from her family, and being here tonight just reminded her of just how bare and spartan their own apartment seemed. Christmas Eve was something, but it was not the same as Christmas Day.

"Too bad," Rose's father said. "Be nice to have Rose here. And the dragon."

Henry bristled again.

Lips curled upwards as he tucked the pipe back into his mouth, Rose's father departed the room.

"All right, it's *my* turn now!" Louise shouted. "He's done eating!"

"He is not!" Sara snapped.

"He is so!" Louise cried, grabbing for Virgil.

"He is not!" Sara glared, yanking him away.

"Be careful with him!" Rose snapped, standing. "He's not a doll, he's a baby!"

Virgil's tail swung as he dug his claws into Sara's arm. Was there more food? He was still hungry. Was there more food?

"Ouch!" Sara shouted.

"Virgil, be careful with my sisters, too," Rose sighed.

"See? He's saying it's my turn now," Louise jumped in.

"Dinner's ready," Rose's mother called from the kitchen. "You two, stop squabbling and help me set the table."

"But ..." Louise complained.

"I'm busy holding the dragon," Sara announced.

Henry stood up, scooped Virgil into his arms, and walked away from them.

"Hey!" both girls wailed.

Virgil was still hungry. Was there more food?

Rose herded her sisters out of the room towards the kitchen, where they each collected something to take out to the table. Their father was, as usual, seated at the table waiting for the meal to begin, without an ounce of helpfulness offered.

Henry joined them when the table was set, and sat down with Virgil complaining vehemently on his lap. Protests about hunger and his parents eating while he wasn't filled the room as Rose's mother attempted to say grace.

As she finished, Henry looked down at the baby with exasperation. "Are you, by any chance, still hungry?" he asked.

Yes! Virgil was still hungry! Virgil wanted more food! Virgil needed more food! Virgil was still hungry, hungry hungry! What was his father shoving at him?

"It's ham," Henry said, dangling a tiny slice in front of Virgil that he had removed from his plate. "Try it."

Virgil didn't want that not-food. Virgil wanted food.

"It *is* food," Henry said. "You should be able to eat it. I doubt your digestive tract is so delicate that the only thing you can eat is chicken. Try it."

Virgil didn't want that not-food! Virgil was very sad! Virgil was going to cry!

Hands flung up over ears all around the table.

An ear-splitting screech emanated from the tiny body on Henry's lap, long and loud and piercing. It went for what felt like an eternity before it halted briefly.

"Stop him!" Rose's father bellowed.

Virgil had been taking a breath. Now Virgil was going to scream again.

"Stop it," Henry said. "Don't—"

The shriek began again, rattling through both ears and minds.

Rose's mother leapt up from the table and ran to the kitchen. She came back with a bowl full of chicken mash and held it in front of Virgil's face. She mouthed something that was inaudible behind Virgil's scream.

The little dragon stopped.

"—what you want, dear?" Rose's mother finished.

Yes. That was what Virgil wanted. That was Virgil's food. This person was nicer than his father. Virgil's father was mean.

Virgil poked his head into the bowl and gulped rapidly, as if he had not just eaten another meal just as large as his usual repast.

I hope this does not mean he is overindulging, Rose thought. *I do not want to deal with complaints of a tummyache all night.*

"Some Christmas cheer for you," Rose's mother cooed, gathering up Virgil as the little dragon continued gobbling.

Henry's jaw clenched. He looked exceptionally annoyed.

CHAPTER 9: CHILL

Virgil must have eaten more than his weight in chicken that evening. He ate enough that Rose's sisters were each able to take another turn, and then Louise protested that Sara had held him twice while she had held him once as Virgil drowsed off to sleep.

Rose was a little worried. Why was Virgil eating so much? Was this a sign he was sick? Or was he about to go through a tremendous growth spurt? While the latter might be preferable to the former, it would still not make their lives easier.

It was nearly nine o'clock before they were able to go caroling, and Rose's father stated outright that he had no interest in going.

"Neither do we," Henry said immediately. "We need to be getting back home."

Rose opened her mouth to protest that she wanted to join, but she closed it. Henry had dealt with a trying enough evening already. It would not be fair to force him to stay in her family's house alone with her father.

She pulled on her woollen stockings, realizing with embarrassment that she had forgotten all about her silk ones and had been bare-legged through the entire dinner, though at least she had remembered her shoes. She pulled her coat onto her arms and wrapped the scarf around her neck.

She kissed her family members goodbye, Louise while she was buttoning up her own coat and Sara while she was pulling on a scarf, and then headed with Henry to the door.

He pulled the handle downward and pushed.

The door didn't open.

Frowning, Henry tried again.

It still didn't budge.

"This door does open outwards, right?" Henry asked.

"Yes," Rose's mother said. "It used to open inward, but the door kept hitting my china cabinet, so we had the hinges switched. Try again."

Henry tried again, shoving all his weight against it. The door didn't budge.

"Did the lock break?" Louise asked.

"Oh, wow!" Sara shouted, moving a curtain aside to peer out the window. "You won't believe how much snow is out there!"

Rose bolted to the window and stared out in horror at the pristine winter blanket that stretched out before them. Gobs of snow still kept on falling, glittering and bouncing against the window as if trying to reach into the room.

"Woww," Louise breathed, joining them. "I've never seen so much before."

"There has to be over a foot," Rose's mother agreed.

Rose felt a vague sense of panic. How were they going to get home?

"The back door opens inward," Rose's father called from the living room. "You can go out that way. Or you can go out a window."

"In this blizzard?!" Rose's mother demanded. "Of course they're not going anywhere! I don't want them catching their death of cold! Just think of Virgil!"

Henry's arms clenched tighter around their son, who was fast asleep. "Virgil will be fine."

"*Your* health, then!" Rose's mother said. Her eyes had taken on a flinty, obstinate cast that Rose had rarely ever seen. "I don't want you catching a chill or freezing to death out there!"

Henry hesitated.

"He said they aren't staying for Christmas," Rose's father called from the living room. "Don't coddle them, Mabel. They can walk home if they want to. It'll only take a few extra hours."

That seemed to decide Henry.

"Thank you," he said stiffly. "We would be delighted to accept your hospitality."

Rose glanced into the living room and saw her father grinning. Apparently he had learned one of her mother's methods of persuading people.

"You two can sleep in Rose's old room," Rose's mother said, taking Louise's scarf and Sara's coat as they removed them. "Virgil can sleep in ... does he need the oven?"

Rose glanced apprehensively over at Henry, who was giving her a nervous look. For once, it seemed they were of one mind.

"Virgil can sleep in the ... uh ..." Henry said.

"Virgil can sleep in the bathtub," Rose said, as inspiration hit. "If we remove the towels and the cabinet, there should be nothing flammable in there."

And I'll sleep on the floor outside the bathroom door to make sure he doesn't escape, Rose thought.

"Flammable?" Rose's mother looked taken aback. "Why is that a concern?"

"Because he breathes fire," Henry said, as if this were obvious.

"Well ... yes, but ..." Rose's mother looked taken aback. "Surely not in his sleep."

Rose and Henry began talking over each other.

"Sometimes sparks fly out of his nostrils—" Rose began.

"He burned down the Christmas tree—" Henry said.

"—even when he's asleep—"

"—if he wakes up on his own again, which is why—"

"—and that's why he has the oven in the first place—"

"—don't even feel safe—"

"—something better, but I don't want to trap him—"

Rose's mother listened to the garbled account with an increasingly perplexed look on her face.

"Is there a way to get him *not* to breathe fire?" she asked.

"*No*," Rose said in frustration. "It's a natural part of his biology. He releases some kind of flammable gas post-digestion, and when it's released, he ignites it automatically. He can no more stop production of this than a human infant could stop the production of urine."

"Or a dragon infant, for that matter," Henry muttered, glancing down at their son. Rose noticed that the arm of his coat beneath Virgil's diaper looked damp.

"That sounds a little like bed-wetting," Rose's mother said thoughtfully. "I've had some experience with that. Sara wet the bed until she was ten years old, and she sometimes then got out of bed and proceeded to dampen the hallway."

"*Mamaaaaaaaaa!*" Sara squealed in humiliation.

"He's a little young for potty-training," Henry said defensively. "He just hatched two months ago."

"Perhaps so," Rose's mother agreed. "But this was almost a separate issue. Sara was already potty-trained."

Sara's face was scarlet, and she looked ready to hit somebody.

"You might try having him breathe out all the fire he can right before bed," Rose's mother said. "It might not solve the problem entirely, but it might help. If he doesn't need to eat in the middle of the night anymore, it might even solve most of the problem."

Rose gaped at Henry. He looked as stunned as she felt.

Did we go to the wrong people for advice? Rose thought. *Instead of dragon experts, should we have gone to other parents?*

Perhaps this blizzard was not a curse. Perhaps this blizzard was a Christmas miracle. That might have been exactly the advice they needed.

"Let's try it tonight," Rose said. "We'll see if it makes any difference."

As if on cue, Virgil wriggled and his eyes opened. Were his parents thinking about him? Were they thinking they wanted him to breathe fire? He would do it. He knew how to make his nostrils snort. Snort, snort, snort ...

Henry yelped and raced for the kitchen. Rose raced after him and flung open the oven door. Just on time, because a roar of flame escaped Virgil's nose and blasted against the back, longer and louder than she had ever seen before.

No doubt a product of the child eating so much extra dinner.

Rose looked back at the doorway, where her mother was watching with an open mouth.

"Yes, he does that," Rose said. "That's why we're concerned."

"Wait till I tell my friends about this," Louise breathed.

"Why didn't you do that in the fireplace?" Sara asked.

"Because they didn't think of it, because they don't have one," Louise informed her.

Virgil felt better now. His stomach didn't hurt anymore. Something else hurt now. It was his ...

Henry yelped again and raced up the stairs for the bathroom.

"Where is he going now?" Louise demanded.

"To change Virgil's diaper, and perhaps his own clothes if he wasn't in time,"

Rose said wearily. "Virgil really did eat a *lot* of food. Excuse me while I go up to help."

CHAPTER 10: CHOICE

Rose woke up before anyone else, eyes wide open as she lay on the floor outside the bathroom door. She wasn't sure why she had woken up, and the pile of blankets on top of her was warm, while the air on her face felt bitter cold, so her eyes drifted shut again.

Hungry! So hungry! Virgil was hungry, hungry, hungry! He would share it with his mother! HUNGRY HUNGRY HUNGRY!

Rose's eyes flew open again as the terrible feeling slammed into her mind. It was painful and persistent, and impossible to ignore.

HUNGRY HUNGRY HUNGRY!

Did I oversleep? Rose thought blearily. She rubbed her eyes and reluctantly dragged herself out from under the blankets. Goosebumps immediately prickled all over her arms, so she picked up the two blankets and flung one around her shoulders like a cape, then pulled the other one around her waist and tucked it in at the top, like a skirt. It dragged on the floor as she walked, but that didn't matter.

"Wait patiently, Virgil," she mumbled, knowing he would catch her meaning whether he could hear her through the bathroom door or not. She shuffled down the hallway, away from the range of Virgil's telepathic wailing.

Why was the child so hungry now, right when it was extra cold and that made it especially inconvenient? It was like the way he had chosen to hatch on the day of their wedding. Virgil's timing was exceptional, and not in a preferable way.

She shuffled down the stairs and turned on the light in the kitchen. The clock on the mantel took her aback.

Four o'clock in the morning? It's four o'clock in the morning? He usually eats at midnight, and that keeps him content until six!

This was not a good precedent. He'd eaten half the chicken last night; at this rate, the rest would be gone by lunchtime. Even if a butcher's shop was open on Christmas Day, they had no way of leaving the house currently. And that chicken had been intended to last Virgil nearly a week.

Why is he so hungry? Rose thought in frustration. She pulled the chicken out of the icebox, discovered it was nearly frozen, and turned on the stove and placed it in a pan to thaw. Impervious to cold he might be, but the chicken had to be sufficiently soft, or he might choke on it.

Rose cut off a piece of the hard stick of butter and dropped it in the pan to warm up ... and then she stopped.

Is he impervious to cold weather?

She had assumed he was, because he did not seem to be able to sense hot or cold. He also did not seem to get sick. But perhaps the change in temperature affected him in other ways.

Virgil's warm-blooded, Rose thought slowly. *Even if this had not been conclusively determined by researchers studying him and Violet, it would be obvious just by the fact that he stays warm even while out in the cold. He clearly regulates his own temperature. He keeps himself warm.*

Doing that requires energy. That's absolutely unavoidable. So what if ...

Rose stared down at the pan, frowning, as the butter bubbled and the chicken began to simmer. She turned it over slightly so that another side could warm up.

What if the cold weather is what's causing this increased appetite? What if the increased appetite is what's causing him to wake up outside of his normal schedule? Eating more would also result in the creation of more flammable gas, which might have been useful for adult dragons if they used that to create fires to keep themselves warm, or to kill prey for extra food. But in the human era, with the advent of central heating and wooden homes, it's just dangerous ...

It all fit together, and it was so obvious that she couldn't believe she hadn't seen it before.

Rose held the cold top of the chicken with one hand while she pried warm chunks off the bottom with a fork, then dropped them into a bowl. She poured the melted butter, which was now rather brown, out into the bowl, too. Then she added a cracked egg and about a tablespoon of water, and mixed them thoroughly.

By the time she brought the bowl upstairs, Virgil was—

HUNGRY! HUNGRY HUNGRY HUNGRY!

"I know," Rose said. "I brought food."

HUNGRY HUNGRY HUNGRY! HUNGRY HUNGRY HUNGRY!

"Here," Rose said in exasperation, holding out the bowl in front of his face. "Here's food. Do you want it?"

Virgil's tail lashed out and whacked the bowl out of her hands. It toppled and spilled across his head.

Virgil opened his mouth in fury. He was very upset! He was angry! He was hungry! No one was feeding him! He was going to scr—

Rose snatched a shred of chicken and hastily shoved it into his open mouth.

Virgil shut his mouth. This was food in his mouth. This was food in his mouth. Yes. This was food.

Virgil wanted more food now.

Rose fed him the rest of the bowl's contents, and before Virgil could gripe that he still wanted more, she removed the blanket from her shoulders and draped it on top of him.

Virgil was still hungry! Virgil wanted more food! Virgil was under something soft. It was like the soft floor. Why had Virgil's mother put the soft floor on him?

"We're going to test something out," Rose said. "We're going to see if wrapping you in blankets is sufficient. We have the option of putting you in a cage, but if this works, I think it is a much better choice."

Virgil didn't understand. The soft floor on top of him was soft. Maybe he would take a nap now.

Rose waited until Virgil's eyes were closed, his mind was no longer letting out quiet murmurs, and she saw no signs of sparks flying from his nose. Then she stood, rubbing her arms to stop the goosebumps, and headed to the hall closet to find another blanket. She was fairly certain there was at least one more that was not being used.

She started to make a bed for herself on the floor again, and then she stopped. She walked down the hallway and peered in at Henry sleeping, snoring softly.

I'm awake, Rose thought. *We're in a house with a working stove. I have no homework to do right now.*

She picked up the new blanket, wrapped it around her shoulders, and headed back down to the kitchen to make Henry a hot meal for Christmas.

CHAPTER 11: CHERISHED

In the morning, apologies made and Henry wildly enthusiastic about his breakfast, Rose gathered up Virgil from the bathtub, and she carried him downstairs still wrapped in blankets.

"Do you think we could have him sleep in the bathtub at home, instead of the oven?" Henry asked excitedly. "If we did, could we reconnect the gas and have actual cooked food every day?"

Don't get ahead of yourself, Rose thought. *I still have homework most days, and a longer commute to school than you. If you start darning your own socks, we'll see.*

But that was a conversation they could have on another day. For now, it was Christmas.

She watched her family members open presents under the tree with some regret. All the presents she and Henry had bought for each other, and for Virgil, were back at the apartment. Virgil would not be getting his stuffed animal prey today.

"Here!" Louise said, handing a lumpy package to Rose. "For you!"

Rose opened it. A terribly-knitted scarf was within. She fingered the holes and uneven stitches. "Thank you," she said, touched. "Did you make it yourself?"

"Nope, I made Sara do it for me," Louise said proudly.

"For you!" their mother told Sara, handing her a large box.

"Is it the new dress I asked for?!" Sara squealed, ripping it open.

"For you!" Rose's father declared.

Henry took the package, looking startled. "For ... me?"

Rose's father nodded. "That's right. Bought it myself."

Henry opened the paper slowly. Inside was a package of expensive-looking cigars.

"I don't smoke," he said flatly.

Rose's father grinned.

"And I have a present for Virgil," Sara added, walking over with an oddly-shaped package in her hand. "Want to open it?"

Virgil was busy rolling around in the loud stuff. It was really fun.

"Come on, there's wrapping paper right here," Sara coaxed, holding the some-what-tapered brown package out. "You can roll on the paper, or shred it, and even keep what's inside."

Virgil didn't know. He liked the loud stuff he had right now.

Sara walked over to Virgil and picked him up out of the pile of discarded brown wrapping paper, which was now looking more crinkled and shredded than ever. She placed the protesting, wriggling dragon on her lap.

"Here," Sara said, grabbing an end. "I'll help you. You pull it like this ..."

Virgil didn't want to pull it. Virgil wanted to play in the loud stuff. Virgil tried to get down.

Sara caught him before he fell all the way off her lap. She held him with one arm while she unwrapped his present with the other. It was a shiny metal bucket with the handle removed.

"You see?" Sara said excitedly. "Look how much fun this'll be!"

Virgil ignored the bucket and clawed at the wrapping paper which was now all over her lap. He liked that there was now loud stuff to play with.

Sara leaned over and put the bucket on the ground. She picked up Virgil and deposited him in it.

"Um—" Rose began, alarmed.

Sara tipped the bucket onto its side and gave it a mighty shove. It rolled in an arc across the room and slammed into a wall.

"Virgil!" Henry shouted, jumping to his feet.

Virgil's head poked out of the bucket. That had been fast. That had been fun. Could Virgil do it again?

"Yes!" Sara shouted. "I knew he would like it!"

Rose rubbed her forehead. This wasn't a game she would have encouraged, but as Virgil seemed unharmed, she supposed she couldn't object. Not for now, anyway. She might hide the bucket when they got home.

Henry put his hand on top of hers, and Rose looked after at him. He smiled. She smiled, and leaned into his shoulder.

When they got home, they'd need to talk about whose responsibilities were actually whose. However sincere his apology had been this morning, he needed to be told that his assumptions did not match hers, nor the reality of her quantity of schoolwork. Still, there would no doubt be compromises that could be made.

If hot meals were what mattered to him, perhaps she could find time to do that daily if he took charge of the laundry. She would not mind giving up washing Virgil's disgusting diapers. If laundry was what mattered to him, he could take charge of the groceries. If groceries were what mattered to him, he could take Virgil's midnight feeding so that she could wake up an hour earlier and buy groceries before class. And no matter what, he could darn his own socks, thank you.

"You know what?" Henry murmured, squeezing her hand. "I think this wound up being a nice Christmas after all. I wasn't sure it would be."

Rose smiled and squeezed his hand back. They watched their son use his tail to shove himself off from the wall and roll in the bucket for a ways. They watched Louise chase after him and fight with Sara over who got to push the bucket next. They watched her father catch the bucket and then hold it hostage while Virgil protested his new lack of mobility.

I hope the next dragon to hatch will be as lucky, Rose thought. *I hope he or she will be as cherished.*

Of course, she did not know for certain that a third dragon would hatch. But she could hope so.

And on a beautiful Christmas morning, surrounded by family and a tree that was not charred and had not fallen over, hope seemed more than sufficient.

Author Note

One of the most difficult things about writing this series was all the research I had to do about history, paleontology, and—hardest of all—historical paleontology.

I couldn't reference any dinosaur species discovered after 1920. I couldn't reference any details we've learned about dinosaurs since 1920. I had to painstakingly check every exhibit in the American Museum of Natural History to make sure I only referenced ones that were there in 1920.

Why did I do that to myself?

DRAGON'S FIRE

Chapter 1: Forward

THE ZOO WAS FILLED with people and an air of festivity. It was the third day of the New Year, the crowd was brimming with excitement for the future, and a tiny blue dragon infant was sharing one of her mother's memories.

She was a beautiful, vain dragon, vibrantly blue, stretching out her long neck to show off her horns to the prospective mate she wished to have notice her. The purple male ignored her, so she snorted fire in exasperation. Must he be clueless? She had been hoping to be coy.

She raised her wings in a sharp flapping motion. That caught the male's attention for a moment, so she kept on beating them steadily, as if to launch off the ground.

Of course she knew that she could no longer fly. She was too heavy. Flight was something only the smallest dragons kept to adulthood. In fact, loss of flight was usually seen as a sign of maturity and readiness to procreate.

Still, as with most dragons who reached adulthood, she could still glide. She climbed atop the pile of boulders she had prepared, waiting until she was sure the male was watching. Spreading her wings widely, she launched herself downwards, floated for a moment as the air caught her momentum, and then floated with easy grace to the ground.

Yes. Now she had his attention. She flapped her wings and moved close enough to catch it as he let escape a flash of memory of how beautiful she'd been on her glide down.

She fluttered her wings and waited for the admiration to continue. She coyly kept her memories to herself as she admired the vibrant red-purple of his scales, different enough from her own color to show that he was not closely related, and therefore eligible.

Oh, come now! He was walking away! Well, fine then! She would be much more aggressive!

Rose drew in a deep breath as she came back to herself. The window into the courtship behaviors of another species was fascinating, and it was no wonder that the crowd seemed so enthralled, pushing closer and shouting for more.

Still, Rose thought. *Still ...*

Violet was very pleased that they liked her mother's memory! Violet would share one of her father's!

No, Rose thought. *You're more than just a repository of your ancestors' experiences. You're a very small child. You should be ...*

A new memory washed over her.

His second child was poking at the new egg. The purple boy wanted to know when the egg would hatch.

Not yet, he indicated to the curious boy. And poking the egg with one's claws was not a good thing. The little baby would be inside the egg for another season. Until then ...

Tears sprang to Rose's eyes as the memory faded, and she pushed backwards to get away. She pushed through the crowd until she was reasonably sure the small blue dragon could not pick up her thoughts, and then she leaned against the bars of a cage with her head in her hands.

All dead. They're all dead. Every one of those people in her memories is dead.

It was obvious, and yet nobody here seemed to realize the implications. Dragons had gone extinct hundreds of thousands of years ago, all save the few *Deinonychus antirrhopus* eggs that had miraculously been recovered recently.

Rose composed herself with difficulty, breathing in deeply. Her son was the other dragon in New York City, and she must not let herself think too much about that tragedy. The last thing she or Henry or Virgil needed was for the three-month-old baby to remember just how much he had lost, and how much he could never regain.

Focus on the future, Rose reminded herself, opening her eyes. *Their species was lost, as was their entire civilization, and yet now they both have a second chance. There are now two dragons in New York City, one in Washington D.C., and four in Vernal. Soon there might be* Deinonychus antirrhopus *all over the country.*

A smile rose on her lips at the reminder, and Rose pulled away from the empty cage. It almost did not even bother her that it was empty because it had been reserved in case a third dragon hatched in their city.

She pushed through the crowd, burying her disappointment that the crowd had been too thick to have a private conversation with her son's friend, and exited the zoo into Central Park. She strode through the partially-frozen slush across the walkways, pondering the amusing courtship of Violet's parents.

Will Virgil one day court Violet that way? Rose wondered. *Will he be clueless, and she forward? Of course, he might choose another girl altogether, given that there is already one female in Washington D.C. and another in Vernal ...*

"Absurd, you know," a woman was saying to a companion by her side, both of them walking briskly past Rose. "How could anyone call that thing the same as human? It's an insult, that's what it is."

Rose bristled, and she quickened her pace without conscious thought to keep up with the women. Angry as it made her, she wanted to know what people were saying about her son's species. She wanted to know what attitudes she would have to overcome to get her son the acceptance he would need.

The other woman bobbed her head in agreement. She wore an admiring look that implied little capacity for thoughts of her own.

"Really," the first woman went on, waving an arm clad in a thick fur coat. Her hat was the peak of fashion, and her shining boots were either brand new or immaculately kept. "It should be obvious, shouldn't it, just by the fact that the zoo is the proper place to keep those things, that they are no more than animals?"

Rose's blood boiled.

"Very obvious," the second woman agreed.

"In fact, the very *shape* makes that clear," the first woman went on.

"Quite clear," the second woman nodded.

"Therefore, as for the parallels your husband attempted to draw between this and our own movement," the first woman sniffed, "you can see that they are quite unsubstantiated. *We* are people who deserve equal rights, whereas *those* are—"

"Excuse me," Rose broke in, unable to bear it any longer. She should, perhaps, have held her peace, but the arrogant woman had offended her last sensibility. "I beg your pardon for intruding, but you are quite wrong."

The finely-dressed woman turned around, giving Rose an arch look. A fur stole that perfectly matched her coat slid off her shoulder, and she pushed it back into place.

"I beg *your* pardon?" she asked sarcastically.

Rose's heart thundered in her chest. She was aware of the rudeness of eaves-dropping, and she should no doubt have let them pass without keeping pace, but now that she had heard the woman's words, she could not let them stand.

"*Deinonychus antirrhopus* dragons have long been suspected of intelligence, and now that suspicion has been replaced with certainty," Rose said in a level voice. "Intellectually, they are our equals. Perhaps more than equals, for they have abilities our species has never gained."

The second woman looked very offended.

"Did you vote?" the woman in the fur coat demanded.

Rose blinked, taken aback. "I ... beg your pardon?"

"Did you *vote?*" the fur-coated woman asked insistently.

What has that to do with anything? Rose wondered.

She vaguely recalled a great deal of commotion last year over the Nineteenth Amendment passing, but she had never paid that much attention to politics, and Virgil had awoken shortly after that. When the election had come in November, she had been far too busy to place any importance on whether the next president would be James Cox or Warren Harding.

Even if she had been eligible, she would not have bothered. Thankfully, she had a better answer than that.

"I was not twenty-one in November. I was not eligible." Rose brushed a strand of hair behind her ear in a businesslike manner. "But I do not see what that has to do with the subject at hand."

"Have you not read the papers?" the second woman asked angrily. "Have you not read the article today that mocked the whole cause of women's suffrage by comparing it with—"

She stopped abruptly, her hand flying to her mouth.

The woman with the fur coat sniffed and tossed her head. "If you have never fought for a cause, you cannot possibly conceive the insult implied by such an inappropriate—"

"Bessie," the second woman whispered, tugging the arm of the fur-coated woman with great urgency. "Bessie. Bessie. She was *in* the papers!"

Chapter 2: Fame

With misgiving, Rose watched the fur-coated woman's face shift from disdain to recognition.

"You're one of the so-called 'parents,'" the fur-coated woman said with great interest. "I saw it in the papers. Your husband is a student of archeology."

"It's paleontology, and *I'm* the one who's studying it," Rose said heatedly. The papers frequently misreported that fact, and this tended to so enrage her that Henry had informed her that he would be much obliged if she would *stop* reading the papers.

"So you have a pet dragon," the second woman said.

"I have a *son* who is a dragon," Rose snapped.

"What's the difference?" the second woman asked.

Rose stared at her incredulously.

"Are you saying," the fur-coated woman asked with an odd gleam in her eye, "that a human infant is exactly the same as one of those ... things?"

Rose recognized the gleam. She saw it often in her father's eyes when he was trying to pick a fight. She knew that it would do little good to contradict someone with that facial expression, but she could not stop herself from rising to the bait. Her son's honor was at stake.

"Not exactly the same, no. But he's equivalent."

"In what way?" the fur-coated woman asked sharply.

"He's every bit as intelligent," Rose said. "He chose us as his parents. And the meaning was clear: *parents*, nothing less. He was not even aware that we weren't dragons until he hatched."

In fact, Virgil still got mixed up over that sometimes. Just this morning, Virgil had asked her to play smack-each-other's-tail with him. She had had to remind him, for what felt like the thousandth time, that she did not have a tail.

"But the shape is far too different," the fur-coated woman said. "No one would accept a thing like that as a child."

"Henry did," Rose said. "I did. Our parents all consider him their grandson, and our neighbors accept him, as well. Once you know him, it's impossible to *not* know he's a person."

The fur-coated woman surveyed her for a long moment. "Very well," she said. "Then I'll have one, too."

Rose stared at her. "Excuse me?"

The woman reached up to adjust her hat, pulling out a long pin and sticking it back into her hair. "I'll have one, too. Francis has been saying he wants a child, and this will save me the bother of bearing one. Plus, the uniqueness will no doubt attract attention, and get us invited to the best parties."

Rose stared at her in horror. "That's an *appalling* reason to adopt a child! Not to mention that no dragon would ever choose you, with an attitude like that!"

"What Bessie wants, Bessie gets," the fur-coated woman proclaimed, waving her hand. "I'm sure these childish creatures will be no different."

Rose's mouth fell open at the sheer audacity. She was sure there could be no possible worse parent than this. Had this woman approached Virgil, he would have ignored her completely!

A sudden thought struck, making her uneasy. *What if not all the dragons will be so certain what they want? What if the certainty of someone else's mind may be enough to persuade them to make a terrible decision?*

It was true that Violet was more pliable than Virgil. She did whatever the crowd asked her, most of the time.

Surely persuasion does not become less effective just because one can communicate by thoughts rather than words, Rose thought. *Lies might be ineffective, but somebody else's terrible determination might be more persuasive that way than otherwise.*

She did not want a dragon child to wind up with this woman who would see them as a convenience, or as a trophy. But she could not think of a way to prevent it, save for hoping that all the future dragons would more closely resemble Virgil than Violet. And that, she could not bring herself to do. She hoped that all the dragons would have unique personalities.

The second woman stared at her friend, appalled. "You would try to appease Francis with a *pet*? Really, Bessie!"

"You heard her," the fur-coated woman said, waving her hand toward Rose. "She said everyone considers them babies. Far less work for all the credit. Who wouldn't want that?"

"That is *not* what I said," Rose snapped through clenched teeth. "There is nothing about Virgil that is less work than a human infant. In fact—"

"Here is my card," the fur-coated woman said grandly, reaching into her reticule to remove a small pink card that held a large name in script in the middle, with a small address in the left corner. She held it out to Rose. "Be a dear and call upon me when one comes available, will you?"

Rose glanced down at the card, then flicked her gaze back up. She didn't take it. "I don't think you understand," she said tightly. "*Deinonychus* dragons are people. They are every bit as much work as a child you gave birth to would be."

The fur-coated woman smiled comfortably. "That's only true for poor families. When you have the means to hire a nursemaid, parenting is a breeze."

Rose stared at her in indignation.

A snort came from the woman's companion, who sounded rather like she wished to disagree. When Rose glanced over, she saw the second woman's mouth trembling, attempting to hide an incredulous smile.

Rose's ire was slightly appeased. Perhaps the fur-coated woman's friend would be able to talk some sense into her.

"I will not argue this any further," Rose said coldly. "I will only say that the desire to make one's life easier is not a wish that will be fulfilled by adopting a child. Good day."

She walked off, her heels clicking against the sidewalk and splunshing through the piles of slush that were difficult to avoid. The chill of the weather did nothing to cool the broiling state of her temper, nor the fact that she blamed herself for it.

Why did you imagine starting that discussion would be a good idea? Rose berated herself as she drove her hands into her pockets, seeking to warm them up from the chill of the air. *What could you have possibly hoped to gain?*

She knew what she had been hoping to gain. She had been hoping to educate the ignorant, to clear up an insidious wrong belief, and to stand up for the rights of her son, whether or not those women's opinions would have any bearing on his future.

Yet instead, she had given one of those women an awful idea. A life of luxury might seem appealing, and Rose was envious of any family who would never have to waste time worrying about where graduate school tuition might come from, but a child who would be raised by somebody other than his parents, who would be put out for display ... how would that be any different from the zoo?

Not her, Rose thought fervently, ignoring the cold seeping through a hole in her shoe. *Not that woman. Please.*

If someone like that became able to adopt a dragon, it would undermine everything Rose had gone through, everything she was currently going through, to raise Virgil as her own. It would encourage more trophy-seekers to attempt to force their will on fragile young minds. It would be bad for the one child, bad for others who hatched later, and bad for *Deinonychus antirrhopus* in general in New York City. Perhaps across the country.

Virgil's future must be secured. The future of his species must be secured.

If only she knew how.

Rose stepped through one too many slush puddles, and noticed at last how drenched her stockings had become.

She lifted her skirt slightly, seeing that the hem was stiff with mud and water, and sighed.

It was a miserable day for walking. She wished she could have taken the bus, but their meager budget was not in agreement with consistent indulgences like that.

Chapter 3: Fault

"Oh, look!" Henry cried a few weeks later, reading the morning paper as he cut his breakfast omelet with the side of his fork. "There are two more eggs awake at the museum! Two at once! I'm surprised that nobody called to tell us. I mean, it's not directly our business, but it certainly is indirectly."

Rose froze in her position of frying eggs over the stove. They sizzled in the pan, the yolks starting to cook through instead of remaining runny.

"Of course, perhaps they were too busy," Henry mused.

"Is that so?" she asked carefully. "Does it, um … does it say who the parents will be?"

She had not told Henry about her encounter outside the zoo on the day she had been coming back home from Monday classes. Mostly this had been in hopes that if she never spoke of the encounter, it would never be relevant. But also, she had been ashamed of her own conduct in picking a fight.

Not the rich woman, she prayed silently. *One baby of a different species would be bad enough to put in the care of a person like her. But two … it doesn't bear imagining.*

"It doesn't say," Henry said, skimming over the article. "It does mention Virgil and Violet at the bottom, not that it calls them by name …"

"Let me see," Rose said, flipping the rather-too-cooked egg off the pan onto a plate and pushing the pan away from the burner. She flipped the burner off and grabbed the newspaper away from Henry.

"Ah—" Henry cried, alarmed. "Don't—!"

"'Henry Wainscott, student of paleontology, and his wife, Mrs. Henry Wainscott'?" Rose shouted, reading the bottom paragraph. "Now they can't even be bothered to write my *name*?"

"See, I knew you'd get upset," Henry sighed, rubbing his forehead.

"I've a good mind to call them a third time to set them straight," Rose fumed.

"What good would that do?" Henry asked wearily. "If they didn't listen the first and second time, it's very unlikely they will listen a third."

Rose slammed the newspaper on the table, answering with eloquent silence.

A silver bucket spun into the room at rapid speed, a small green tail whipping around and around outside the edge of it.

Wheeeeeeee! Virgil was having fun!

The bucket slammed against the wall under the window. After a moment, their four-month-old son crawled out, tail first, emanating memories of fun and great dizziness. He wanted to do it again!

"Yes," Rose said, scooping up the bucket, "but since you're in here, you can eat breakfast first. Eggs, ham, or chicken?"

She held her breath, but she shouldn't have.

Chicken! Virgil wanted chicken! Eggs were boring, and ham was yucky yucky yucky!

Rose sighed and opened the icebox door to retrieve the leftover chicken scraps from the previous night. Try as she might to interest Virgil in a cheaper meat, it seemed that poultry was all that was acceptable to him. Not that she had tried that hard, to be fair. Much as she hoped that it was merely pickiness that he would outgrow, she was afraid that it was an instinctive understanding of what food was healthy for him.

With no way to find out save for experimentation, she was too afraid to press the issue and potentially make their son sick. They were not yet poverty-stricken, though Henry's shoulders got tense whenever he added up the sums in his finance book, which did not make her confident that they could go on paying for expensive food indefinitely.

Which reminded her ...

"How are we for our food budget for this week?" Rose asked her husband casually, setting a bowl full of chicken on the floor for Virgil, hoping that Henry would let slip some hint about their budget's general state. It was an intense irritation that he would not share the details of their finances with her.

"Whether we're doing well or not, we have to get another chicken today," Henry said shortly, flipping the paper open. He looked irritable.

Rose was feeling rather indignant herself. His high-handedness about their finances was driving her crazy.

She had finally tried to peek into his finance book the week before last when he had accidentally left it at home while he was at class, surrendering at last to temptation, but she had found nothing but numerous doodles and sketches on most of the pages. What pages there were of sums were unlabeled and clearly unfinished, which made it clear that this was not his finance book, merely another one that looked similar.

Rose had sighed and put it back into his sock drawer, disappointed. If the man would at least explain why he had this mystifying obsession with keeping their finances secret, it would be one thing, but this sullen silence whenever she brought up the subject was maddening.

Virgil brought his head down and smashed it into the side of the metal bowl, horns first. He butted it again, and the bowl toppled over, spilling chicken across the floor. Virgil snarled and dove at the chicken, sending shreds flying all over the room.

"Virgil!" Rose shouted.

Virgil was hunting! Virgil was killing his prey! Rawr! Rawr! It was dying! It was yummy! Yum yum yum yum!

"Just because you are a predatory species doesn't mean you are allowed to have poor manners!" Rose informed him, picking up the scraps of chicken and dumping them back in the bowl, then setting it upright again. "That is not acceptable behavior! Eat properly!"

"He's only four months old," Henry said, snapping the paper slightly as his eyes moved to a top article. "What do you expect him to do, perform with perfect table manners?"

"Given that he can understand everything I say, yes, I do," Rose snapped, picking up a fork to take a bite of her now-cold and overcooked eggs. "He may be exempt from silverware, given that he has no opposable digits, but he mostly certainly can learn some decorum."

"He's not even a toddler," Henry said. "Let the boy eat how he wants to."

Virgil would pretend these were entrails! Yummy yummy!

Rose flinched as a gory scene from one of his ancestors' hunting memories filled her mind. While aware that his was a predatory species, there were certain things that one should not share while others were eating.

Granted, her initial disgust had been immediately replaced by a fascination with how *Tenontosaurus* had been arranged internally, but most people would not be so conciliated by that. And their son did, in fact, need to learn how to behave around those who had no fascination with internal dragon anatomy.

"Virgil," Rose said sternly, "what have I told you? Suppose you shared some memory like that while we were eating dinner at your grandparents' house?"

Virgil's grandfather had thought it was funny! Virgil had done that when he was playing with his grandfather last week! Virgil's grandfather had told him he should do that more often!

Rose put a hand to her forehead. Of course her father had done that.

Virgil was done eating. Virgil wanted to have his bucket back. Could Virgil have his bucket and spin around and around and around in it?

Rose sighed and stood to fetch Virgil's toy, which had become extremely dented over the past few weeks. She handed it to him, and watched the little dragon pounce inside, then use his tail to push the bucket faster and faster and faster until it zoomed across the floor.

Wham! Straight into the wall in the living room.

Virgil was having fun! Virgil was dizzy. Virgil would do it again!

Rose took a bite of her eggs, staring at the back of the newspaper Henry still held out in front of him. There was nothing interesting on the back page, but the tiny article within the middle had given her enough to ponder for one day.

CHAPTER 4: FOOD

As it was Tuesday, one of the days when Henry went to classes and Rose stayed home with the baby, she had no prior obligations to impede her from the crucially important journey she wished to make.

"Virgil and I will be walking down to the museum today," Rose informed her husband as he pulled on his socks, a trifle defensively. She was afraid he would tell her she should mind her own business about the new dragon eggs.

"Sure," Henry grunted, poking his finger through a hole in his sock and letting out an exaggerated sigh.

Rose's fingers tensed. If that were meant to be some sort of hint that she should mend them, she would not oblige him. She did not ask him to mend her stockings, nor had she requested the money to buy more, even though all of the pairs she had remaining looked a dreadful shambles. Having an infant whose species name meant "terrible claw" tended to do that to one's legwear.

But Henry said nothing. He merely pulled on his shoes, which were looking quite worn, and stood.

"I hope you and Virgil have a good time," he said. "Perhaps he'll meet some new friends."

A tiny head poked out of a dented bucket.

Who were Virgil's friends? Who were Virgil's friends he was going to see today?

"Two new dragons," Henry said. "They woke up and they're going to hatch soon. Like you did."

Virgil didn't want to hatch again. Virgil hadn't liked hatching. It had been very uncomfortable, and his parents hadn't helped him at all. Virgil was still mad about that. Virgil's father had said he was going to see friends. Violet was Virgil's friend. Could Virgil see Violet today?

"Perhaps," Rose said. "We'll be in the same vicinity. But first we must acquaint ourselves with the new dragon eggs."

And see to it that neither of them is beleaguered by that atrocious woman, she added silently.

Virgil didn't understand what pets were. Why was Virgil's mother angry that somebody had told his mother he was a pet? Who was that woman? Could Virgil see?

Rose flinched. She hadn't meant for Virgil to catch that wisp of memory. She had, in fact, intended him to not be aware of any of the events of that day.

But Virgil was extremely curious, and placed no importance on what his parents wished to share and what they had wished to conceal.

It was rather frustrating. Rose had always assumed that when she moved out of her parents' house, she would no longer be forced to endure the whims of her intrusive younger sisters and their flagrant disrespect for privacy. But after a brief sojourn with two roommates she had not been close with, she was now living with a child who put her younger sisters' snooping prowess to shame.

Virgil didn't know what that meant. Was snooping something to eat? Virgil didn't want it. Virgil's mother kept trying to make him eat food that was yucky yucky yucky. Virgil wanted chicken. Maybe Virgil was hungry now. Could Virgil have more chicken?

"Oh, that reminds me. Could you get more chicken while you're out?" Henry asked, reaching into his pocket to get out his wallet. He pulled out two one dollar bills and handed them to Rose. "Have to visit the bank again soon …"

"I could run that errand as well if you add me to the account," Rose said.

"No," Henry said shortly, shutting his wallet with a snap.

Virgil didn't understand what money was. Virgil was hungry. Where was Virgil's chicken? Virgil wanted to disembowel it.

"Goodbye," Henry said, giving Rose a kiss. "I'll see you when I get back, unless you'll be back later than me."

"I likely will be. Have a good time at school."

"That's unlikely," Henry said, "but I'll bear it. Virgil, behave for your mother, will you?"

Virgil always behaved. Virgil behaved like he wanted to!

"Behave the way *she* wants you to," Henry said.

Virgil's mother wanted him to eat yucky food. Yucky yucky yucky. He wouldn't eat it. Could he have his bucket and eat chicken in it?

"Goodbye, then," Rose said, giving Henry a kiss. "I'll see you later this afternoon."

Henry stooped to kiss the tiny dragon on the head, and Virgil butted his head against Henry's hand in a similar show of affection. Then the man left, locking the front door behind him.

Rose watched with a slight smile on her face. Maddening as he could sometimes be, she had quite grown to love Henry. She was glad that Virgil had come into their lives and assembled their family.

Virgil was hungry! Virgil wanted to kill food and eat it! Virgil wanted to kill chicken! Yummy yummy yummy!

Rose snapped out of her reverie and let out a long sigh. *Even if our son feels the need to share his ancestors' gory memories.*

In preparation for leaving, Rose changed Virgil's diaper, washed the breakfast dishes, clothed herself for the day, discovered Virgil's diaper was sagging and atrociously-odored, rediapered the child, scrubbed both diapers clean, discovered that his new diaper was sopping, changed him again, and finally got out the pram to go walking.

Virgil wanted to ride in the bucket! Could Virgil ride in the bucket?

"No," Rose said. "You're riding in the pram."

Virgil wanted to play with the bucket *in* his pram.

"I don't think so," Rose said.

Virgil wanted his bucket! Virgil wanted to ram it against the sides!

"Definitely no bucket," Rose said firmly. "I don't want you breaking the pram."

Virgil wanted his bucket! Virgil wanted it!

Rose picked up the the dragon, walked over to the bathroom, placed him in the bathtub, and plugged her ears. The baby let out an unearthly howl and launched himself against the slippery slides in claw-filled fury. Fire spurted everywhere.

"When you calm down, you can get out," Rose said.

Virgil let out an ear-splitting shriek.

"When you calm down, you can get out," Rose said.

Virgil screamed again.

"When you calm down, you can get out," Rose said.

A loud, thumping noise came from above them. The woman in the apartment above them was not happy with the blood-curdling volume.

I know, Rose thought. *I'm sorry. But there's not much we can do but discipline him and hope he learns to stop screaming.*

Virgil was noticing the ceiling. The ceiling made noise. The ceiling was angry. Why was the ceiling angry?

Rose sighed.

Virgil wanted to get out of the box now. Virgil was calm.

"So you are," Rose said, and leaned over to pick him up. Maddeningly, the dragon's diaper was wet *again*.

She changed him quickly, not worrying much about the pins, since her son's scales were tough enough to be at little risk of harm even if she was careless. Then she placed the dragon in the pram, feeling impatient to get going.

Virgil poked his head out eagerly. This would be fun! Virgil liked going walking! Virgil was going to see Violet!

Rose draped a blanket over the pram to conceal him and keep him warm, opened the door, and took them outside. The air was chilly, so she shivered under her coat as she maneuvered the pram down the stairs. Virgil let out an excited commentary from beneath the blanket, no doubt drawing the image of their surroundings from her mind as she stepped outdoors.

It was very white, and he liked white, because it was fluffy! He had played with lots of snow at Christmas. Could he play with more snow? He wanted to play out in the snow.

"No," Rose said. "We can't afford to buy an extra chicken just because you want to romp. You burn far too much energy to keep yourself warm. Please keep down under the blanket."

Virgil wanted to play. Virgil liked to play. Could Virgil play with Violet? Could Virgil play with Violet right now? He would hit her with his tail, and then she would hit him with her tail, and he would bite it!

"Please don't bite it," Rose said with exasperation. "You made Violet cry last time you bit her tail. Remember?"

Virgil didn't remember. Oh, Virgil remembered because his mother remembered. She was showing him what he'd done. Virgil felt very sad. He hadn't meant to make Violet sad. Virgil was very sad! He was going to cry!

"It's all right!" Rose said quickly, wrenching her thoughts back to better things. The last thing anybody needed was a screaming dragon throwing a fit on the sidewalk. "It's all right. Violet is fine now. See?" She focused her mind on how much happier Violet had been after the pain had subsided.

Virgil felt very sad! Virgil felt better. Virgil wanted his bucket. Could he have his bucket now? He had behaved.

CHAPTER 5: FLOOD

Nearing the museum, Rose was less than enthusiastic to find a huge crowd surrounding the entrance, elbowing one another to get to the doors through the gigantic crush of humanity.

I should have known, she thought, chagrined. *Why didn't I anticipate this?*

She considered turning around and walking back home, but giving up after coming all this way seemed intolerable. She might take Virgil to see Violet until the crowd died down some, but Central Park Zoo was no doubt also flooded with people wanting to see dragons.

From within the pram, disguised by a thick blanket Rose had draped over the top to both conceal her son and keep him warm in the chilly air, Virgil made his opinion known.

He wanted to see Violet. Could Virgil see Violet? He would claw at her tail and bite her tail.

Rose drew in her breath and looked to the heavens for patience. Then she said, in a low voice in the hopes that the surging crowd ten feet from them would not overhear, "No biting tails. No biting any part of Violet. Now, I want to introduce you to two more baby dragons. Can you behave and not make noise and not communicate to anybody until we're there?"

Virgil wanted to play! Virgil would hit the other baby dragons with his tail!

"Yes," Rose said dryly, "I'm sure you'd like to. But they're currently still in eggs."

Virgil didn't know what that meant. Oh, Virgil's mother knew what that meant. No! Virgil didn't want to go back to the egg! It was dark and boring and squished squished squished!

"No," Rose said in frustration, "I don't mean you. I mean the other two—"

She stopped, appalled to notice that they had spectators. Three children and two adults had paused in their excursion towards the museum. Two of the children's mouths were open, while their parents' eyes were riveted on the pram.

Oh, dear, Rose thought with a sigh. *Virgil's method of communication does tend to attract attention.*

Under normal circumstances, she would studiously ignore confused or curious looks and continue in an unrelenting pace towards her destination. This usually worked to keep unwanted onlookers from approaching after recognizing the oddity of Virgil's commentary. She did not know whether they figured out in retrospect that it had been a telepathic dragon or whether they assumed that they had heard it, as she never stopped to check, but as long as it worked to secure her privacy in the vast majority of situations, she didn't much care.

Unfortunately, that seemed unlikely to work here. For one thing, they had likely been standing there long enough to draw the correct conclusion. And for another, even if they hadn't been, their proximity to the museum suggested that they had come specifically to witness the new telepathic dragons, which would mean the inference would be obvious.

Rose pursed her lips, deciding what to do.

"Hey," one of the children said, "isn't that—"

Rose made her decision. Before the sentence went any further and it would be rude not to answer, she pushed her pram forward to join the frantic crowd. She had meant to enter the museum, and she would do so.

Virgil continued to make occasional comments about the crowd, mostly asking Rose the meaning of various glimpses of memories that he had no business plucking from strangers' heads. She shoved the pram through the entrance, at last reaching the doors, and focused very sternly on a memory of telling him just last week not to do that.

Virgil's mother was mean! Virgil was angry! Virgil was going to howl!

No! Rose thought. *No howling! If you want your bucket back, you're not going to howl!*

Virgil settled down. He was behaving. Could he have his bucket?

"When we get home," Rose muttered under her breath.

Virgil was angry! His mother had said he could have his bucket! He was going to howl!

An earsplitting wail rose up from the pram, and heads turned to stare at them from all over the crowd. Rose gritted her teeth and clenched the handle of the pram in frustration.

Since Virgil's unearthly screech more closely resembled a bird of prey than a human child, there would shortly be no concealing what he was to all around them. Rose decided to use the situation to her advantage.

She wrenched off the blanket to put her son on full display. Gasps rang around them, and Rose didn't stop. She scooped up Virgil in one arm and turned to a man near her who appeared to have muscular forearms.

"I need to get to the fourth floor immediately," she said in a no-nonsense tone, waiting until Virgil had paused to breathe. Thankfully, that seemed to act as a distraction for the dragon, who did not recommence screaming. "Would you please carry the pram?"

"Certainly," the man said readily, his eyes focused on Virgil.

The crowd parted to make way for them as they headed up the stairs, all eyes fastened on Virgil as the initial shocked silence moved into a flurry of whispers. Despite the irritation of being a spectacle, Rose felt some gratification that Virgil's tantrum had for once been useful.

They reached the top of the stairs, and the man heaved the pram down to the floor for her.

Rose nodded. "Thank you."

"You're welcome." The man stared at the small dragon in her arms. "Is he—"

"Yes," Rose said, feeling that it was better to get questions over with. "He's the first dragon who hatched from this museum. His name is Virgil. You can find the second one in Central Park Zoo. Her name is Violet."

Virgil liked Violet! He wanted to play with her!

"Can I touch him?" the man asked wide-eyed, reaching out his hand.

Rose sighed internally, but as the man had helped her, it seemed churlish to refuse.

"Yes," she said, "but please make it brief."

A surge of people dove forward, their hands outstretched. Virgil wriggled and started to protest his discomfort as dozens of people shoved their hands all over him.

"Enough!" Rose barked, swatting the uninvited hands away, her patience now at an end. "There may be some parents who don't mind their children being manhandled, but I am not one of them! Please stand back and do not make my son uncomfortable."

The crowd drew back, looking abashed, as the one man gently stroked Virgil's side with a look of awe on his face.

Rose smiled slightly, remembering the first time she had had that opportunity. It was remarkable to realize that one was touching an infant from a species that had gone extinct millions of years ago. It felt miraculous; in fact, it was still unexplained and unfathomable how they had survived so long. She knew that it had happened, yet it still felt impossible.

Taking her leave as soon as it was polite to do so, Rose deposited Virgil in his pram and draped the blanket over the top again, even though she was not sure if that would accomplish any of the concealment it had before. It seemed prudent to at least attempt to be discreet. Then she headed with great dignity into the Hall of Saurischian Dragons.

The flood of people here was greater that it had been elsewhere, and her attempt at discretion proved extremely useless, as the people from the stairs followed her in, many of them shouting in extreme excitement and pointing at her and her pram.

Attempting to ignore the hubbub that was turning into pandemonium around her, Rose reached the dragon eggs exhibit and then stopped, staring blankly.

There were now only eight eggs on display. Presumably the two who had awakened were the missing ones.

Where did they go? she thought numbly.

Chapter 6: Feelings

"Yes, of course we moved them," Director Campbell said impatiently in response to Rose's query. "Did you think we'd allow the entire crowd to have access to them?"

Rose had run straight to a museum worker and asked to see the director, and since she had had Virgil with her, she'd been taken to the director's office right away.

Rose nodded slowly. It was obvious; she should have realized that the people here would not be foolish enough to expect that crowds would not flood the museum, and of course the telepathic babies might be very disturbed by the presence of thousands of strange minds pestering them.

"The last thing we need is one of those things bonding to somebody uncooperative," Director Campbell said sourly.

Rose's eyes widened. *That's what he meant?*

The thought of Henry flashed across her mind. He had not been receptive to the museum's original desires to keep Virgil from them, and had in fact been very rude at the director's insistence that the dragon egg belonged to the museum, not to his chosen parents. This had been a fiasco that had only been settled when Virgil had thrown a fit, which the director had not been prepared to handle. It seemed Director Campbell was determined that there would be no more Henrys.

Rose swallowed. She could see things from his perspective, yet—yet fathers like Henry were exactly what it would take to make the infant dragons grow up healthy, well-adjusted, and recognized as people with the same rights as the human majority. While there was no doubt that Harrison Jones loved Violet, he had accepted their circumstances far too amiably.

Which was, perhaps, a type of wisdom. But it would not lead to the future that Rose wished to see for *Deinonychus antirrhopus*. Their species deserved better.

Her son deserved better.

He was lucky he'd gotten it.

Director Campbell could not be allowed to deprive all the future dragons in his museum of parents like Henry.

But Rose knew that openly opposing him could only end in catastrophe. So she swallowed her feelings, and said, "Would I be allowed to visit the awakened dragon eggs? I was thinking that Virgil would like to meet them."

Director Campbell drummed his fingers on his desk, thinking.

Oh, please, Rose thought. *If nothing else, at least let Virgil meet the others of his species.*

"All right," the director said at last. "Teedle is taking care of them. Has them in his office now. As long as you are strictly supervised, you may take that dragon to meet them."

Rose's heart lifted in relief.

"As long as you don't cause any trouble," the director added, frowning. "And I don't want your husband going near them."

Rose's fingers clenched, but she nodded.

Mr. Teedle, the curator of the dragon collection, was a kind man who was close to Rose's father's age. Rose did not have many people she would consider friends, but Mr. Teedle qualified, despite their difference in age. They had known each other since her early years in high school, when she had commenced spending all her spare time in the museum's Research Library.

Mr. Teedle had always been supportive of Rose's plans to become a paleontologist, and he had also been present at Virgil's hatching. So it was no surprise that, when she knocked on the door to his office and he opened it, he greeted her with great warmth.

"Miss Palmer!" he cried, and then quickly corrected himself. "Mrs. Wainscott. I'm pleased to see you! Have you brought Virgil here?"

"Yes, I have," Rose said, and glanced peevishly at the pram. "And he seems to have decided it was naptime as I was walking here."

"Children are like that," Mr. Teedle chuckled. "They only want to sleep when it's inconvenient."

"I've gained permission to meet the new dragon eggs," Rose said. "Would now be an acceptable time to do so?"

"Of course," Mr. Teedle said, opening the door wide and stepping back.

Heart thumping in excitement, Rose stepped into the room, pushing the pram before her. It was hard to fit the rather large pram into the small room, but Mr. Teedle took charge of correcting that deficiency by moving a chair out of the way. Her gaze fell on the two eggs on the man's desk, still and silent, the same brown-spotted orange shells as the one Virgil had been in.

"Are they ... awake?" Rose said. She had been about to say *alive,* but that would be a silly question. All the eggs were alive. That was why they weren't fossilized.

"This one is soundly sleeping," Mr. Teedle said, tapping the desk beside the one to the right. "I think perhaps she was awakened before she was ready. This one is napping, but he doesn't usually sleep for long, so you will probably be able to converse with him soon." He tapped a spot on the desk beside the left egg. "I'm afraid he woke the other egg by vigorous telepathic yelling. It was similar to what Virgil did when he was separated from you and Mr. Wainscott, but even more painful and unbearable. I pity his parents, because he seems likely to be a real handful."

Parents, Rose thought, reassured that Mr. Teedle had used the word. It seemed that, no matter what the museum director was planning, the dragon curator took it as a given that the eggs would be raised by proper adults who adopted them.

"Why was he yelling?" she asked politely.

Mr. Teedle frowned. "The same reason as Virgil did, I'm sorry to say. And this time, there is no easy solution."

"What do you mean?" Rose began—

He was a dragon inside an egg. His parents went out hunting. They always had memories of hunting to share when they came back, and he couldn't wait to hunt with them. But they had been a long time. A long time. A long time. Where were his parents?!

Minds came and said his parents were gone. Wrong! Wrong! *WRONG!*

They were coming back! They were coming back! They'd said they'd be back, and they were coming back! He was going to scream until they came back for him!

Rose staggered backwards as a silent tidal wave of fury blasted her mind. It was wordless, potent, and vigorous.

"Can you—" Rose gulped, barely able to form the words. "Can you stop, please?"

This was a new mind. Was this mind going to get his parents for him? If this new mind got his parents for him, he would stop screaming.

"I'd love to help," Rose said, "but—"

The blast of fury poured through her mind again. Rose took an involuntary step backwards, then fumbled for the doorknob, desperate to get out of range.

Stop it! Virgil wanted it to stop! Virgil was really mad! Virgil was woken up from his nap!

Rose's gaze flew to the pram, where her son was wriggling around under the blanket. She whipped the blanket back, and Virgil sat there, emanating indignation.

A little uncertainty came from the egg. He was angry. If he screamed enough, his parents would finally come back. His parents were coming—

Virgil's parents hadn't come back! Virgil had waited for his parents for a long, long time, too! Virgil had found new parents with minds just like his old ones!

No! He was really angry! He didn't want new parents! He was going to scr—

Virgil would share Violet's memories with the angry, mean, annoying person!

Extinction shattered across Rose's mind. Memories from adult dragons who were suffering, starving, bleeding, dying. Violet was found at the end of the world. Violet was one of the last. Everyone was gone. Even all the eggs were mostly asleep. What had happened? Where was the world? There were no parents left. They were all gone.

EVERYTHING WAS ALL GONE, AND ONLY DESPAIR WAS LEFT.

Rose gasped, shaken. That memory of Violet's was new. It was worse than all the other ones that Violet had shared. It also had a strange, surreal quality that the rest of her memories didn't. Where had it come from? Had it been one of her dreams?

There was dead silence for a minute, and Rose gripped the handle of the pram. She hoped that her son had not traumatized the other infant.

When the answering thought came back, it seemed weak and scared.

He was ... angry. He was ...

Chapter 7: First

Virgil would share his memories of meeting his new parents now. Then the new mind would see.

New memories filled Rose's head, and these were even stranger than the surreal quality of Violet's dream because they were familiar, and yet alien. She had been there to experience the whole thing; she had even seen it from Virgil's perspective on that same day. Yet now, they had been painted over with the certainty of hindsight and the optimism of romanticism, implying that this had somehow been fate or destiny.

The new dragon seemed to gobble it up with the hunger of a starving creature. His vicious anger abated, and he started to release impressions that were increasingly hopeful.

This might not be a realistic expectation Virgil is passing on, Rose thought, troubled. *The chances of this new dragon finding two people exactly like his original parents are not high. And even if he does, what are the chances that they won't be married to two other people? Just because Virgil was the first doesn't mean his experience will be representative.*

The angry dragon egg now seemed soothed. Where could he find his new parents? The new ones who would be just like his old ones?

Mr. Teedle cleared his throat. "About that—"

Rage blasted from the dragon egg before the curator could finish his sentence. No! He wanted his new parents *now!*

"I'm sorry," Mr. Teedle said. "I'm afraid your wants are not the only relevant factor here. They will, of course, be weighed, but there are other things that must be—"

He wanted his parents, he wanted his parents! He wanted his parents, he wanted his parents! He was going to scream! He was going to scream!

Pent-up fury was building to an explosive climax again.

"Perhaps it would be better for you to leave," Mr. Teedle said.

"Can't I meet the other dragon egg first?" Rose asked regretfully.

Mr. Teedle opened his mouth to reply ...

She was unhappy. She was sleepy. He was noisy. He was disturbing her. She wanted to sleep. She would go back to sleep. He was being noisy.

The feather touch of those impressions faded as quickly as they had come.

Mr. Teedle smiled wryly. "There you have it. That's all we've gotten from her, either."

Rose's mind raced. *Is this another female that my son could eventually court? Do they have compatible personalities?* It was hard to judge from just a few fleeting impressions, but she hoped they might be. The more choices Virgil had, the better his chances of gaining a mate that would please him.

"I'm relieved that there are as many females as males thus far," Rose commented. "If there had been double the number of males, it would have been a problem."

Mr. Teedle nodded. "There still might be. We have no way of knowing what genders the sleeping eggs are, after all. But we can hope for either more females or exact gender equality."

If Rose's child had been a daughter rather than a son, she would have bristled at the hope of extra females. All signs from Virgil and Violet's memories indicated that their species paired monogamously for life, thus too many extra females would put each one at a disadvantage for eventually breeding.

But even under those circumstances, she would have understood that slightly more females would be more of an advantage to an underpopulated species than slightly more males. From a purely cold, biological standpoint, one male could produce offspring with two females simultaneously, while one female could not do the same with two males. While exact gender equality would be preferable for a monogamous species, slightly more females would still be viable.

Of course, *Deinonychus* dragons were people, not livestock. They would make their own choices, and those choices would not always be best for the species. Still, Rose hoped that the initial conditions would at least be optimal for continuance. It was a miracle that *Deinonychus antirrhopus* was still alive today, and she did not want them to die out again from having too few individuals to support a stable population.

Besides, from a selfish perspective, her child was a son. For *him* to have the best chance of eventually producing offspring, extra females would be optimal.

Rose smiled to herself at the thought of how Henry would react if she said any of this to him. He would, no doubt, be indignant that she was even considering their son's future marriage prospects at this young age. But, after all, her mother's grandparents had been intended for one another from the cradle, and that only because of social snobbery, not biological practicality. She failed to see how this was any different.

As long as I am treating him exactly as I would a human infant, Rose thought, *I am treating him properly.*

All this flashed across her mind exactly as another burst of fury rose up from the left egg.

He was angry! He was angry! He wanted his parents, his parents, his parents! He was going to screeeeeeeeeam!

Rose flinched and staggered backward.

Virgil was mad, too! Virgil was very mad! The mean mind wasn't going to help the other baby find his parents! He was going to screeeeeeeeeam!

"Oh, no!" Rose burst out. "Please don't—"

Two telepathic screams burst out and mingled with the hideously loud one from Virgil's mouth.

Rose seized the opportunity to grab the doorknob as soon as her son stopped to take a breath, then made a rapid exit from the room. She glanced back through the closing door with a mixture of apology and humiliation, and Mr. Teedle merely jerked his head in a nod, looking rather wild-eyed. The door swung shut.

Rose ran down the hallway, the pram bouncing before her, and both the urgency of her mind and the movement seemed to distract Virgil. Away from the instigator, he quieted quickly.

Could Virgil play with Violet now? Virgil liked Violet better. Violet was more interesting. She could roll around and play.

Rose ceased moving, stopping to bury her face in her hands. She had had enough of other people's children for the day, especially draconic ones. Her patience was completely shot through, her nerves were frazzled, and she wasn't even sure where she would find the emotional resources to deal with Virgil's constant pestering, pestering, pestering all day.

"Why," Rose murmured, removing her face from her hands and glaring at Virgil, "why must you be even more difficult than a human infant would be?"

Virgil stared at his mother. Virgil didn't understand. Could Virgil play with Violet now? Violet was more interesting.

Rose breathed in deeply, trying to calm her shredded nerves. She was upset on behalf of the new dragon, disappointed that the introduction hadn't gone as well as she'd expected, frustrated with Virgil for making the situation much worse, embarrassed at the stress he had caused Mr. Teedle, and worried that Director Campbell would now treat her like a troublemaker as much as Henry.

How? Rose wondered, smacking her hand on the handle of the pram in fury. *How am I supposed to deal with anything when Virgil keeps making himself such a pest?*

A terrible wave of misery rushed up from the pram. Virgil's mother was sad! Virgil's mother was sad because of him! Virgil had made his mother sad! He was going to cry!

A thin wail rose from the pram, increasing in volume.

"No!" Rose said hastily, moving to draw the blanket back from its curtain concealing her son. "No, Virgil! It's all right. See? I'm fine. Look! I'm fine!"

A fancily-dressed man walked by, bowler hat in hand, and stopped with his mouth gaping open as he saw the individual in the pram.

Not again, Rose thought, tugging the blanket back around the front. She gave a look that dared him to come any nearer. Taking the hint, the man hurried on, though not without a dozen backward glances before he reached the end of the hallway.

Virgil felt better now. Virgil still wanted to play. Could Virgil play? Virgil still wanted to ...

"All right, all right!" Rose burst out. "You can play with Violet! Just stop pestering me!"

Virgil was happy! Virgil was excited! Virgil would shred this blanket and pretend it was prey!

A terrible ripping sound came from the front of the pram.

"No!" Rose screamed, diving to save it.

Chapter 8: Friends

Inside the zoo, the crowds were nearly as crazy as they had been at the museum. Rose should, perhaps, have expected this.

"Mommy, I wanna see the dragon!" a small child was shouting, dragging a frazzled-looking woman forward as she attempted to juggle a toddler and a purse without letting the toddler grab things out of the opening of the purse.

I know the feeling, Rose thought dryly, and then realized that she didn't. She only had one child, not two, fraying her nerves constantly. The thought of two was terrifying. She amended silently, *I'm glad that I don't know the feeling.*

It took a while to find a zookeeper among the crowd squeezing around Violet's cage, no doubt enjoying another of her ancestors' memories rather than communicating with her as a person. When at last she did make contact, the zookeeper was stressed and less than happy to help, but he did take Virgil, unlock Violet's cage, and place Virgil in with her. Rose managed to squeeze close enough to the front to watch them and be in range of their communication, hoping that this time her son would behave and not be violent in his rambunctiousness.

Hello, Violet! Virgil was saying hello to Violet!

Violet was saying hello to Virgil, too!

Virgil wanted to play! Could Virgil play?

No, Violet was busy.

Bad! Bad! Virgil wanted to play! Virgil would make Violet play!

Virgil charged forward vigorously and snapped at Violet's tail.

Violet let loose a loud shriek, then rolled to the side. She kicked him in the face with one of her back legs as he passed. Her terrible hooked claw caught his nose.

Owwww! Virgil was very unhappy! Violet had hurt him in the snout with her claw!

Rose jerked forward instinctively, despite the fact that she could not reach either of them within the cage, but they had already made up.

Now Violet wanted to play. Violet would play claw catch.

She thrust her leg out, displaying the wickedly hooked claw that gave *Deinonychus antirrhopus* its name, and Virgil dove to catch it. Violet yanked her leg back just in time and smacked him in the face with her tail.

Rose watched with bemusement. The games they invented—or perhaps remembered—were always strange little things. They reminded her more of dogs roughhousing than of any cerebral pastime, yet that wasn't particularly surprising with babies. What did surprise her was how terribly vicious those claws looked, yet how very little they managed to hurt each other.

Now Virgil would play smack-the-claw!

Virgil rolled over onto his back and splayed all four of his legs in the air, kicking them back and forth. Violet rolled over and tried to hit as many of his legs as possible with her own.

They roughhoused back and forth for awhile, until both seemed settled next to each other, curled up on their stomachs, thwacking tails back and forth across each other's backs.

Virgil thought Violet was much more fun than the other baby. That one was in an egg. He was boring.

Violet remembered being in an egg. She hadn't liked it. It had been lonely.

Virgil hadn't been lonely. He had been SQUISHED SQUISHED SQUISHED!

Violet missed her older brother. She missed her parents.

Virgil didn't miss the egg. He had been SQUISHED SQUISHED SQUISHED!

Violet had met lots of parents who wanted eggs. They told her they wanted babies. Sometimes they told her without wanting to tell her. The minds at the zoo were noisy. Did the egg want parents? Violet had wanted parents for a long, long time.

Virgil didn't remember. Oh, Virgil remembered. Violet was remembering for him.

Rapid impressions flashed through Rose's mind. She realized with a start that there had been memories mixed in with those long bursts of rage. She'd completely missed them because the emotion had been so overpowering, but Virgil had caught them, and now Violet had them.

Violet was disappointed. None of those memories were the same as the parents who came to the zoo wanting eggs.

Well, naturally not, Rose thought. *How common can it be to find two people who have similar minds? It's astounding that Virgil found both me and Henry.*

Violet had an idea. This mind was like that ancestor. Maybe that baby would have this mind as his father.

Rose stared at the dragons intently. As always, they showed no facial expressions, but their tails had stopped flicking, and they seemed to have an air of concentration.

Violet would tell these two they were now that baby's parents. Then those parents would be happy and that baby would be happy and Violet would be happy and then she could play with the baby and she wouldn't be lonely anymore.

Virgil didn't like that baby's parents.

Violet would tell them next time they came. They came a lot. She would tell them she had found their baby. Then their baby could be in the zoo with her, and she wouldn't be lonely.

Virgil didn't like that baby's parents. Virgil had seen one of them in his mother's memories. His mother didn't like that one, so Virgil didn't like her.

Rose sucked in her breath. *Oh, surely NOT* ...

The argument now took on the tone of a squabble.

Virgil didn't like that baby's parents!

Violet wanted that baby to have those parents! They wanted somebody else to take care of their baby, so that baby could live in the zoo with her! Violet wouldn't be lonely!

Virgil was really mad! Violet wanted a friend other than him! Virgil was going to scream!

The earsplitting shriek burst across the crowd, sending hands flying to cover ears and provoking yells at her loud son to be quiet. That just made Virgil madder, and he screamed even louder and higher-pitched.

Finally, the zookeeper unlocked the cage, hauled Virgil out, and surged through the crowd to deposit the angry little dragon in Rose's arms.

"I think that's it for the day," he said shortly.

Nodding while trying to plug her ears with her shoulders while simultaneously holding on to the source of the squirming, scaly temper tantrum, Rose dumped the angry dragon into the pram, yanked the blanket over the front, and set forth through the crowd. As soon as they were moving, Virgil's scream faded, and he went to sleep.

If he gets that mad about his friend making a new friend, she thought peevishly, *I am definitely glad he does not have any siblings.*

Rose was in a fine temper by the time she got home, especially when she discovered that Virgil's sleeping nostrils had singed a hole in his blanket.

"So somebody else might have a dragon child they choose to put in a zoo," Henry said shortly when she told him the whole situation that afternoon. "What of it?"

Rose stared at her husband in disbelief. She'd thought that he, of all people, would understand how she felt. "For the good of *Deinonychus antirrhopus*—"

"For crying out loud, Rose!" Henry exploded. "Do you think you can decide how everybody else chooses to raise their children? You may dislike somebody else's choice of parenting, but it's not your decision to make!"

"But for the good of all the other dragons in the future—"

"Maybe you can leave their living arrangements to their own parents, too," he snapped.

Rose flinched, as if struck. She realized suddenly that she must have come across as nosy. This chagrined her, because she had spent most of her childhood in a battle with her sisters for privacy. Yet this was not just something that would only affect individuals outside their family.

"I would be willing to," Rose said in a low voice. "But will Director Campbell be willing to?"

Henry said nothing, and she thought she saw a hint of worry flit across his face.

"We can't control that," he said at last. "We can only do what we can do."

But if we don't try, Rose thought, *there are children who will be affected in the future.*

She knew already that she would be going back to the museum tomorrow. She would go early, before her classes. It would be Henry's day to watch Virgil, so she could go alone. Perhaps that would go better than bringing the infant with her.

Someone had to speak up.

Chapter 9: Fortitude

Her first class started at eleven, so Rose stood at the entrance of the American Museum of Natural History at ten o'clock, waiting for the doors to open. She would have only half an hour to speak her mind before she had to leave to walk to her first class at Hunter College. She prayed that that would be enough, and that the consequences would not be disastrous.

But consequences or not, she had to speak. There were times when one could not afford to stay silent.

As soon as the doors opened, Rose hurried through the doors, removing her hat and coat and scarf and draping them over her arm as she took the stairs at a rapid pace. The building was far less crowded than it had been yesterday, a welcome change, though she suspected that this was only due to the time of day. Most likely it would be a surge of humanity again later.

Despite the desperate hurry, Rose dawdled for a few minutes inside the Hall of Ornithischian Dragons, watching the *Triceratops* and *Stegosaurus* skeletons, so different from her son and yet so eerily similar. The wings of the *Triceratops* rose high in the air, while the wings of the *Stegosaurus* were spread wide, only a few feet out of reach of prodding fingers, as if it were about to lift off the ground at any moment.

What would it have been like if our son had been a herbivore? Rose wondered. *Would he have been easier to care for?*

It was a ridiculous question, of course, because species such as *Triceratops* and *Stegosaurus* had not had large enough brains to be intelligent. Still, if Virgil had been herbivorous, or even omnivorous such as *Ornithomimus velox,* life might have been much simpler.

Rose shook herself, reminding herself sternly that her role as a parent was not to wish that her son had been different, and she was in a hurry besides. She tore herself away from the remarkable skeletons and headed towards her destination, the director's office, a course which she really should not have deviated from in the first place.

But as she stood at the door to the office, summoning her fortitude, she heard angry voices rise from inside.

What? Rose thought dumbly. *Am I too late? Is he meeting with somebody? I thought that at this time of morning, he would not be busy, but perhaps that was naive ...*

"Well, of course he's coming with us!" a woman's voice shouted, loud enough to reverberate through the door. "The dragon in the zoo said that he'd be ours, and he will be!"

Hair rose at the back of Rose's neck. There was no doubt who that voice belonged to.

"You can't just waltz in here and make demands!" the director's voice said angrily. "Who do you think you are?"

"I AM BESSIE!" the woman's voice announced at a great volume.

Rose put a hand to her forehead. The arrogance was astonishing.

There was a murmur of another voice behind the door, and then an irritated grumble. Before Bessie could raise her voice yet again, Rose knocked politely on the door.

"Who is it?" the director's voice shouted.

Rose turned the handle and gingerly opened the door, standing in view.

"Oh," Director Campbell grumbled. "You."

That did not bode well for a future conversation, and Rose felt a little hurt at being included in his irritation. Still, she supposed she could not blame the man, particularly if Mr. Teedle had mentioned Virgil's behavior yesterday.

"Is there anything else you want?" Director Campbell asked sarcastically. "Your own country club, perhaps?"

"No," Rose said, "I only wanted to speak with you about a matter of some importance. That can wait, however. May I make an appointment?"

The director's face softened a fraction.

"Oh, you!" the woman cried, turning to look at Rose.

She, and a man mostly obscured from Rose's view, were standing rather than seated. The formerly-fur-coated woman now wore a dress of navy blue silk Georgette crepe with fine beadwork on the waist, cuffs, and tunic. A fashionable wool cape with knitted pom-poms was thrown back from her shoulders, and she also had not removed her hat, which had a feather perched on top.

It was clearly not the clothing of a woman struggling to make ends meet. Rose wondered whether this was everyday wear, or whether she had dressed more finely than usual, considering this a special occasion.

"I remember you!" the woman continued. "You gave me the idea to adopt Philomel!"

"Philomel?" Rose asked.

"That's what we're going to call him," the woman said grandly.

Without even meeting the child? Rose wondered.

The director's face had gone very unfriendly. "You gave her the idea?" he growled.

"Not by any deliberate design," Rose said emphatically. "We met in the park, and I informed her that her assessment that *Deinonychus* dragons were mere animals was wrongheaded. She conceived the idea of adopting one on her own."

"Yes, and what Bessie wants, Bessie gets," the woman said confidently, adjusting her cape and tossing her hair.

Rose could not believe such sheer hubris existed. What kind of life had this woman led, to have such audacity?

Then the man, who Rose had nearly forgotten was there, spoke up.

"We would be happy to make a generous donation to the museum, director." His voice was quiet. "We will, of course, also defer to experts for anything the child needs."

Director Campbell's expression went quite sour.

"And who could possibly make better parents than *us*?" Bessie demanded, stretching her arms widely and beaming.

Rose could think of many.

"We have quite a few friends in important places," the man behind Bessie said mildly. "The mayor, for instance. I can speak with him about this situation. He might, as they say, vouch for us."

It was impressive that he had just made a veiled threat without actually making a veiled threat.

Director Campbell did not seem to miss the hidden meaning. His eyes narrowed, and he did not look more receptive.

This situation seemed likely to deteriorate, and nobody seemed to be considering the most important factor of all. Rose weighed her options quickly, then decided that if she was going to speak up, now was a good time to do it.

"Why don't we leave it to the dragon?" she asked.

The director and Bessie turned to look at her.

"The dragon?" Bessie asked, as if Rose had made the most absurd suggestion in the world.

"The dragon?" Director Campbell repeated, as if he agreed.

"Yes," Rose said. "You're talking about the future of a child. Why not let the child's input make the final decision?"

Director Campbell frowned, and Rose thought for a moment that he would outright refuse. But then a sneaky smile spread across his face. "Good point. Then if the dragon rejects them, will they give up on all of this?"

"That won't happen," Bessie said haughtily.

The director looked at the quiet man sharply.

"Yes." The man shrugged. "I'd see no value in having a child that didn't want me."

"Good." The director smiled, resembling a crocodile. "Very good. I'm glad to hear that. In that case, let's introduce you two to the egg."

He pushed the chair back from his desk and stood. He walked out the door, trailing the haughty woman and her silent husband, and Rose followed them both.

She had no idea what the egg might pick, though she hoped it wouldn't be the haughty woman. But either way, a future that the dragon chose for himself would be better than any forced on him.

No matter what that future might be.

Gathering in the Research Library, where the two eggs had apparently been moved, Rose waited nervously for the two eggs to wake up. To her surprise, it was the other one who awakened first.

There were new minds here. Were these minds her parents?

"Yes," Bessie said eagerly. "We're—"

No, these new minds weren't her parents. She would go back to sleep.

Bessie's jaw jutted out, and her eyebrows lowered. She looked very put out.

"That's one down," Director Campbell said gleefully.

"That's all right," the other man said mildly. "She's not the one we were thinking of, anyway."

They waited for awhile, and neither egg stirred.

"Why isn't he awake now?" Bessie fumed. "I don't like being kept waiting!"

If you don't like being inconvenienced, I suggest you not have children, Rose thought, amused.

Before anyone could stop her, Bessie dove forward, seized the egg, and shook it vigorously.

"Hey!" Director Campbell shouted.

"That could be dangerous!" Rose shouted, too.

"Bessie—" her husband began.

But just as Director Campbell reached to snatch the egg, a familiar emotion began to fill the room. An intense emotion. One that Rose remembered all too well from yesterday.

Rage. Rage. Rage. He was angry! He was angry! Someone had shaken him awake!

"Bessie, that was not well done," her husband said.

He was angry! He was angry, he was angry! He was angry, he was angry, he was angry!

"Your name is Philomel," Bessie announced grandly. "And we are Bessie and Francis, your parents."

That was not his name! That was not his name! He was Crimson! His parents had said he would be crimson, so now he was Crimson!

"That is not a name," Bessie said coldly. "That is a color."

He was Crimson, he was Crimson, he was Crimson!

"We were hoping we could be your parents," Francis said. "But you must make the decision. Will you accept us, or will you not?"

Rose drew in her breath. She glanced at Director Campbell, whose smug facial expression was belied by the tenseness of his shoulders.

He was confused. He liked Francis, but not Bessie. Could he have Francis, but not Bessie?

"No," Francis said. "You can have both of us, or neither. We come together."

He didn't like that! He was angry! He was angry, he was angry, he was angry!

"I'm angry, too!" Bessie said indignantly. "What do you have against me?"

"Well," Director Campbell said, grinning broadly, "there's no need to trouble your pretty little head about that, is there? Seeing as the egg's made his decision. Now, if you'd be so kind as to ..."

"*Pretty little head?!*" Bessie roared, spinning on him. "Maybe the papers were right! Maybe this *is* similar to my cause! Maybe I should focus on dragons' rights instead!"

Crimson was thinking about it. Crimson was still angry. Crimson's mother understood how it felt to be angry. Maybe Crimson's mother could be mad with him together.

"No!" Director Campbell shouted.

Crimson wanted to go home with his new parents now. Their memories showed their cave was big and had lots of space. Crimson's old parents had had a big cave with lots of space. Maybe these parents would be just like his old ones.

"*No!*" Director Campbell shouted.

CRIMSON WAS ABSOLUTELY FURIOUS, AND HE WAS GOING TO MAKE THAT PLAIN!

Rose doubled over as a piercing headache slammed into her. Director Campbell looked ill. The dragon's emotion was potent and powerful.

Neither Bessie nor Francis looked terribly affected.

"Yes, yes, yes, we know you're in a bad mood," Bessie said impatiently. "But could you rein it in? You're going to make it very difficult to find a nanny if you keep behaving like that."

"It should be fine as long as we pay enough," Francis said briskly. "But I agree, he needs to learn to control that temper first thing. If he doesn't, he will be a holy terror when he hatches and his fire comes in. I wonder if breathing exercises will work as well for dragons as for humans?"

"We should ask the nanny about that," Bessie said grandly. "I'm sure it won't be long before he's fit to introduce to society."

Rose gaped at them.

"You must be joking!" Director Campbell expostulated. "The zoo is better equipped to handle any—"

"My dear. sir," Francis said calmly, "how exactly do you think the zoo would deal with a child with this kind of rage? You don't want him out in public. Neither do they. The obvious solution for all concerned is for him to be cared for by two people who are willing to teach him to not be a danger to those around him."

"Or three people," Bessie said, adjusting her feathered hat, which she had still not removed. "Or more. Depending on how many we hire."

"Believe me," Francis said with a hint of amusement, "it would be a far better use of your time to agree right now. She makes a better ally than enemy."

Director Campbell gave a fixed glare to Bessie. "But she—"

"She makes a better ally than enemy," Francis said coolly.

An ally. Rose glanced over at the woman, who was tossing her head arrogantly. *An ally. She did say that she would fight for dragons' rights. Is that what she is?*

She was not an ally that Rose would have chosen. She was not a person that Rose wished to be well-acquainted with. But maybe ... just maybe ... she might be what *Deinonychus antirrhopus* needed:

A pigheaded individual who did not accept social niceties or limitations.

The argument raged for another half an hour, and Rose stayed until she realized that she had missed her entire first class. She remonstrated herself fiercely as she fled to reach her second in time.

Still, by then it was already obvious what the conclusion to the argument was going to be.

The third dragon was going to have a home. And it wasn't going to be in the zoo.

If nothing else, she could be very grateful for this.

Chapter 11: Family

Pushing open the door to their apartment and pocketing her key, Rose found Henry asleep on the couch and Virgil rolling around in his bucket. Chicken was strewn across the kitchen floor, and Virgil's backside, obvious as the bucket rolled past, was soaked and smelly.

For a moment, annoyance rose in her chest—what was he doing asleep? But then she breathed deeply, reminding herself that she had seen more than enough anger for one day. She was very grateful that Virgil was reasonably pleasant and Henry was kind and thoughtful most days.

So we have bad days sometimes, Rose thought, leaning over to pick up a textbook that had fallen from Henry's hands when he'd fallen asleep. *We're very, very lucky for the rest of our days.*

She paused, taken aback. This wasn't Henry's textbook. This was the blank book covered in sketches and doodles that she had found a few weeks ago, the one she had mistaken for his finance book.

Thoughtfully, Rose sat down and flipped through the pages. She hadn't looked at it for long before, only long enough to be frustrated that it hadn't held the secrets of their financial state, but now she looked at the art to appreciate it for its own sake.

It was really very good.

There were sketches of Virgil, inked portraits of their family together, and skeletons of other dragon species. On some pages were plants, or perspective studies of streets, or doodles of children playing. She saw a few pictures of people she recognized vaguely from their wedding, members of Henry's family.

Why did he hide this? she wondered.

She glanced up, and saw that Henry's eyes had opened and he was watching her.

"I'm sorry," Rose said immediately, snapping the book shut. "I didn't mean to pry. I only—it was lying on the floor, and I picked it up—"

"It's all right," Henry said with a sigh. He sat up and rubbed his eyes. "You'd've found out sometime anyway."

"Found out what?" Rose asked, confused.

"That I'm terrible at sums," he said.

Rose stared at him blankly. Then realization dawned.

"This *is* your finance book?!" she asked incredulously. "But there's barely anything math-related in it!"

"I *told* you I was terrible at sums," he said defensively. "That's why it drives me crazy when you want a running commentary. I don't know where we are half the time. I wish I didn't have to do it in the first place!"

"Well, but ... But it's ..." Rose sputtered. "*This* is your finance book?!"

"I know, I know," he muttered, putting his head in his hands. "I can't balance a budget if my life depended on it. Numbers just do not make sense to me. I'm sorry."

Rose stared at him in astonishment, at first unable to speak. Then she burst out laughing.

"What?" he demanded, raising his head. "What's so funny?"

Rose couldn't stop herself from giggling. "Then why didn't you ask me to do the budget? I'm fine with numbers!"

"But—but—" he sputtered. "But I'm supposed to do it!"

Rose couldn't stop laughing. "My mother does all the accounts for my family's household. My father hates doing them. Why did you think that would bother me?"

"Well ..." Henry rubbed his hand through his hair vigorously. "Well, my father always said ..."

Rose laughed and got up on the couch beside him. She kissed him and handed him the book. "I'll tell you what. You keep drawing those wonderful pictures, and I'll do the finances."

Relief spread across Henry's face. "Well, if you insist ..."

The dented bucket went flying across the floor and whammed into the couch. A tiny head poked out of it.

Virgil was dizzy. Virgil was having fun. Virgil's mother was home!

"Hi, Virgil," Rose said, smiling, leaning over to pick him up. She had never realized before just how much she liked him and how usually pleasant it was to be around him. Fit-throwing notwithstanding, and his dreadful habit of screaming, he was usually a happy child who was pretty well-behaved for his age.

A terrible odor emanated from their son's hindquarters.

"I changed the last one," Henry said immediately.

Rose groaned in mock annoyance, but she was in too good a mood to argue. She stood and carried Virgil to the bathroom, where she raided the cache of folded diapers they kept under the sink. The diaper change was every bit as dreadful as she had anticipated, especially since Virgil kept on swinging his tail through it, but it was accomplished at last, and she returned to the living room with a cheerful little dragon who kept telling her that she should climb into his bucket with him, heedless of her explanations that she wouldn't fit.

"You know," Henry said, tapping the book that was now on his lap, "this is the reason we met in the first place."

"It is?" Rose asked, setting Virgil on the floor. Their son immediately dove for his bucket.

"Yes," Henry nodded. "The whole reason I went to the museum that day was to sketch the dragons. I was going through a period where I was fascinated with *Stegosaurus*. I thought I'd get a better perspective on the wings if I went to look at them in person."

"And now?" Rose asked.

"Now I prefer *Deinonychus*."

Rose smiled.

Virgil *loved* his bucket! Virgil was going to play in his bucket! Virgil was going to roll right into a wall! *Wham!* Virgil had rolled into a wall! Virgil loved rolling into a wall! Virgil would roll into another wall! *Wham!*

"You can tell me anything, you know," Rose said, taking her husband's hand. "You don't have to keep secrets from me."

Henry nodded. He patted her hand and stared at their laps for a long moment. Then he looked up, a glint in his eyes.

"Well," he said, "there is *one* I probably ought to keep."

"What?" Rose asked indignantly.

He grinned. "I'm not telling you what I'm getting you for your birthday."

Virgil knew what his father was thinking about! His father was thinking about—

"No!" Henry shouted. "Don't you tell her, either!"

AUTHOR NOTE

Everyone has something to contribute to make the world a better place. Even someone you might personally find annoying.

DRAGON'S SONG

THE NEWEST DRAGON egg was now in a cage beside Violet's. Rose eyed the silent egg as her son and the other *Deinonychus antirrhopus* child played together, leaping on top of each other and biting each other's tails.

A telepathic squabble broke out between the two.

Violet's tail looked like prey! Virgil would pounce on it!

Violet's tail was *not* prey! She was scared of Virgil's pouncing! She would smack him in the face with it!

Whack!

Rose chuckled. It was amazing just how easily those two could be entertained by the simplest of games. She supposed she shouldn't be surprised; they were only five months old and three months old, after all.

Whack! Virgil would hit Violet in the face with his tail, too!

Wham! Violet liked playing tail face!

Thwack! Virgil liked playing tail face, too!

As the two merrily continued their game, Rose found her mind and her eyes wandering over to the mysterious silent egg.

You woke up a few weeks ago, she thought, *but unlike the other three who have awakened, you did not bond with a parent immediately, nor even seem that interested in doing so. Who are you? What sort of person are you?*

It was a question Rose had wondered many times while in the presence of the egg, but, as always, there was no response. The tiny female in the egg had woken up once while Rose had been here, but she had left behind only a feathery impression of hunger before her consciousness had drifted off again.

Which was another fascinating question Rose badly wanted the answer to: Did dragons in the egg feel hunger? Theoretically they shouldn't, since they should have all of the nutrients they needed until hatching, but Virgil had made vague references to hunger a few times while in the egg, which seemed to imply that eggbound fetuses might be familiar with the sensation.

Then again, those references from him might have only been an echo of his ancestors' memories. Such secondhand experiences might have taught him to remember how the sensation felt, even if he had not yet experienced it personally.

That was one thing that was deeply confusing about raising a member of a telepathic species. Sometimes she wondered how much he had learned by himself, and how much he had learned from his ancestors' memories.

She hoped there weren't essential pieces of knowledge that *Deinonychus antirrhopus* society had led parents to hide from their very young children until they were older.

She hoped he wasn't missing core memories that would be necessary for him developmentally.

There were no adults left of his species. There were only a few hundred eggs scattered across the country, and it wasn't even guaranteed that all of them would hatch in the same generation. While Virgil could pluck Rose's memories out of her head, whether or not she wanted him to, that did not mean she'd have all the knowledge he would need as he grew into adulthood.

There was a feathery impression of stirring, and a wispy impression of hunger. Rose's head turned immediately to the egg in the cage beside Violet's, but nothing more happened.

She sighed.

A terrible scream shrieked from Violet's cage.

Virgil had bitten Violet's tail! Violet was very sad! Violet's tail hurt! Violet's tail had been bitten!

Rose spun around in intense frustration. "Virgil! No biting!"

But Violet's tail had looked like prey. Virgil wanted to hunt prey. Virgil would pounce again!

Violet let out another blood-curdling shriek.

"Virgil!" Rose shouted. "Stop it!"

Virgil sulked and drew back. His mother was thinking that if he didn't stop, he'd have to go home right now. His mother was mean. He wanted to play tail face again.

"Yes," Rose said with annoyance. "Tail face is fine."

Virgil would hit Violet in the face with his tail! Virgil was hitting Violet in the face with his tail! Virgil thought it was funny!

Violet thought Virgil was mean for biting her tail! Violet didn't want to play anymore! Violet thought the tail in the face was funny. Violet was going to hit Virgil in the face with her tail, too! Violet was hitting Virgil in the face with her tail!

Thwack! Thwack! Thwack! Thwack! The telepathic equivalent of mischievous giggles rose up as the infants went back to being amused with each other.

Rose sighed and checked her wristwatch. She'd promised Henry they'd stay out of the apartment for at least two hours after he got home from class, which would hopefully give him enough time to study for the huge test he had next week. This had meant taking Virgil with her to her own classes, which had proven to be a disaster.

My notes from today's lectures were abominable, Rose thought in deep frustration. *I scarcely managed to take in half of what the professor said. And I have two of my own tests the day after Henry's. I understand that his grades represent our possible future income, while mine do not, but ...*

Rose had always prided herself on her extraordinary grades. And more than that, she knew that having the best possible grades would be necessary for her to continue into graduate school to acquire the credentials she would need to go into paleontology.

But Henry's academic success was, unfortunately, even more important than that. If he failed any of his classes, it would take him longer to graduate, and the worse his grades were, the less likely it would become that he would find his way into a job that paid well. He had already failed two of his classes last semester, in fact, and was now retaking both of them.

This was a detail that Rose had only just learned last night. Henry had not felt the need to tell her about his two failed classes when he'd gotten the news. She'd had quite a struggle to control her temper when he'd finally informed her of that rather crucial detail last night.

After all, for crying out loud! Rose thought, her indignation rising again. *I was able to keep up my grades during our first few months of caring for Virgil! This despite the fact that I have a much longer walk to school, Henry insists that I do all the cooking, and we take equal turns with Virgil!*

Virgil was going to play leg face! Leg face would be fun!

Rose barely spared a glance at the roughhousing in the cage beside her. *Would it have killed him to at least inform me that he was struggling academically? I thought we had fixed this problem of him keeping secrets from me after he gave me control over the budget!*

Henry was, she had learned recently, appalling in his mathematical skill. She'd learned a few weeks ago that all the time she'd thought he was spending on the budget, he had actually been spending drawing.

Which was fine as far as it went. The incomprehensible mess of their finance book had been resolved when she had offered to take control of the budget, a duty he had been more than glad to relinquish.

But it turned out that her husband's ghastly skill at sums was extending to two of his college classes, as well. According to Henry, he needed both of those classes to graduate with his degree in biology, which made them nonnegotiable nightmares for him to navigate. He had, apparently, decided it would be wise to take both of those classes at once to get them over with.

And then Virgil had come into their lives early in the last semester, throwing their lives askew and disrupting everything.

It wasn't that Rose resented their son's awakening ... but the timing had hardly been ideal. Couldn't the boy have waited until after Henry had finished his college education, at least?

But then again, if Virgil had taken longer, Henry might have found somebody else he wanted to marry, and perhaps wound up with a human infant to disrupt his schoolwork. It was only due to Virgil's timing that she and Henry had even met.

Rose sighed. Life, it seemed, was hardly ever convenient. Even when one thought they had their life all planned out, there were always new wrinkles standing in one's way.

Ow ow OWWWW! Violet didn't like claw face!

Rose jerked out of her thoughts and saw the wicked hooked claw of her son's back leg slashing at Violet's cheek. One of the blue scales on her cheek looked loose, and there was a line of blood welling up from it.

"VIRGIL!" she shouted, whamming the palm of her hand against the bars of the cage. "Stop that RIGHT NOW!"

Violet was sad! Violet was hurting! Violet was going to cry!

An unearthly, full-volume howl rose up from the cage. Virgil jerked back, releasing shock and startlement, and then he started screaming, as well.

Rose balled her fists up and clenched them over her eyes. It was all she could do to keep from screaming herself.

But she managed to control her temper, and focusing on soothing thoughts directed at the baby dragons caused them both to calm down again.

Virgil rolled across the floor of the cage, whapping his tail back and forth. He looked up at his mother.

That was a fun game. Virgil wanted to play claw face again.

Rose stared at him in exasperation.

We're going home now, she decided. *Henry can study at the library instead.*

CHAPTER 2: SHE

On the way back from apologizing to an irate zookeeper over the state of Violet's cheek, Rose pushed the pram back to the cage to allow her son the chance to say goodbye to his friend before they went home.

This proved to be a mistake.

Virgil wanted to go back in the cage! Virgil wanted to go back in the cage to play!

"Say goodbye," Rose said sternly. "That's what you're here for. You did not behave, so we're going home early."

Virgil was very sad! Virgil wanted to cry!

"Don't cry," Rose said sharply. "If you cry, we're going to leave right now."

Virgil was sad. Virgil was sulking. Virgil wanted to stay. Virgil wanted to go in the cage. Virgil wanted to play!

Another zookeeper was already in Violet's cage, treating her wound. As he finished, he cut a strip of Band-Aid of the right size and affixed it to her loose scale to hold it in place.

Rose watched with fascination. That brand of bandage had only just come out last year, and she'd never seen one in use before. The flesh-colored sticky disposable bandage looked silly on top of Violet's bright blue scales, but she could imagine how useful it might be with human children.

Virgil wriggled around in his pram and popped his head up through the blankets. Virgil had said hello to Violet. Could Virgil play with her now?

Rose ignored the audacious request, having no interest in the brazen ploy to get his own way despite what she had just told him. "Say goodbye, Virgil. Then we'll go home."

Virgil didn't want to go home! Virgil wanted to play with Violet! Virgil wanted to plaaaaaaaaaay!

"Your bucket is at home," Rose reminded him.

Oh. Virgil wanted to play with his bucket. Virgil wanted to play with his bucket now! Virgil wanted to go home!

"Say goodbye," Rose reminded him. "It's polite."

Virgil was saying goodbye to Violet! Virgil hoped to play claw face again soon!

"No!" the zookeeper and Rose said simultaneously.

The little blue dragon seemed uninterested in the farewell. She was busy trying to pry the strip of Band-Aid off with her front claw.

There was something funny on Violet's face. Why was there something funny on Violet's face? Violet didn't like this thing on her face. Violet wanted to get it off! Off! Off!

"Keep it on," the zookeeper said, swatting her claws away and holding his hand over the Band-Aid. "Your scale is loose. If we don't hold it on, it'll hurt you a lot."

Violet held still from her wriggling. She would be good. She wouldn't pull it off. She didn't want to hurt.

"Good," the zookeeper said, releasing her.

What was this sticky thing on Violet's face? Violet wanted it off! Off! Off!

Rose snorted with laughter as she turned the pram away from the cage. It seemed Virgil wasn't the only infant who behaved so terribly irrationally.

The flow of crowds was such that they always ebbed when one stopped at an exhibit and swelled when one most wanted to navigate through them, and such was the case as Rose sighed and waited for a stream of loud human children to walk past.

Virgil poked his head out of the pram to watch the parade of unfamiliar minds, and two of the human children stopped to poke their fingers at Virgil.

"Stop that!" Rose said sharply.

Both of the children persisted, and Virgil playfully batted at one of them with his back leg with the hooked claw.

"No!" Rose snapped, diving forward to seize the leg. All she needed was for someone's human child to be injured by her son today. Goodness knew what might result from that. The last thing her son's species needed was for humans to decide they were dangerous and force all *Deinonychus antirrhopus* infants to stay locked in cages.

Her temper in a rather frayed state, Rose scolded the two human children soundly, and they ran off to their mother crying about the mean lady. Their mother looked unsympathetic and gave them both a scolding about poking other people's pets.

Rose tried very hard not to let the word "pet" bother her. But nevertheless, it was all she could do to restrain the metaphorical steam rising from her ears as she waited for that bothersome family to continue on their way.

I did, at least, refrain from speaking, she told herself. The last time she had corrected a wrongheaded woman at the zoo, it had resulted in the woman deciding to adopt a dragon herself. Rose was still trying to convince herself that Bessie being a mother to a baby dragon wasn't a large catastrophe.

It wasn't exactly that she was concerned that Bessie and her husband Frank would not treat their son as intelligent. They seemed to be eager to do that much, at least. And after hearing Bessie grandly lecture Director Campbell about dragon's rights and the need for them, Rose had come to believe that the woman would be an asset to her son's species. But the two times Rose had run into the woman since then had been so *irritating.*

They had no human children. Philomel was still unhatched. And yet, Bessie had felt the need to give Rose very supercilious advice about taking care of Virgil.

With that *tone.*

That condescending, overbearing, patronizing, haughty, and imperious *tone.*

Mere months ago, Rose had wanted desperately to not be the only mother to a baby dragon in New York City. Now, she wanted there to be another mother to a baby dragon whom she could stand to be around.

Virgil peeked his head out of the pram, looking up at her with large and innocent eyes. It would have been adorable if his sharp teeth hadn't glinted from within his open mouth.

He wondered why his mother didn't just talk to that other baby's parents.

"Violet only has a father, Virgil," Rose told her son patiently. "Mr. Jones isn't married. Unless he is planning to change that in the near future, Violet has no mother."

No, not Violet's parents! That other baby's parents!

"I'm not fond of Philomel's parents."

No, not Crimson's parents! That *other* baby's parents!

"You mean the egg in the cage next to Violet?" Rose asked. "That egg doesn't have parents, Virgil. She hasn't even woken up all the way."

Virgil was confused. Why was Virgil's mother saying that? That baby had parents. They came to see her every day.

Rose sucked in her breath. "What?"

Virgil knew because Violet knew because Violet was there whenever they came. Violet knew, right?

Virgil's tail lashed confidently as he scrambled up on top of the pram and looked at Violet.

Violet wriggled out of the zookeeper's grip, rolled across the floor of the cage, and tried to claw at the Band-Aid on her cheek.

Uh huh. Violet knew that baby's parents. They had walked by Violet's cage after meeting their daughter, so she'd seen their memories of meeting the egg then. They were really quiet people. Violet had thought everyone knew about them. They came every day.

Rose's head jerked up to look at the zookeeper.

"That's ... news to me, too," he said slowly. "When did this happen?"

Violet didn't remember. Oh, Violet remembered. Virgil was remembering for her. Virgil's mother had been mad at Crimson's mother while Violet had told Virgil about it happening.

Rose swallowed. *Weeks ago. That means it was weeks ago. Or one week, at the very least. The last time I saw Bessie was eight days ago.*

"Who in the world?" the zookeeper muttered.

Rose shared the man's sentiment. It was baffling.

Who were the fourth baby's parents, and why hadn't they said anything?

CHAPTER 3: SCHOOLWORK

Forty minutes later, Rose burst through the door with Virgil under one arm and the handle of the pram she had dragged upstairs hooked around her other.

"Rose!" Henry protested, glancing at his wristwatch and looking up from a notebook he had been writing in. "You weren't supposed to be back for another hour!"

It was hardly a delightful welcome, but Rose wrestled the pram through the door and released Virgil without complaining at the words. Henry was, after all, justified in being cranky at his study time being interrupted.

"This is an emergency," she told him. "The fourth dragon egg has parents!"

Henry stared at her blankly.

Virgil was going to play in his bucket! Virgil was running to play in his bucket! Virgil was scrambling into his bucket! Virgil was going to hit a wall with his bucket!

Roll roll roll WHAM!

"Oh, and no one knows who they are yet," Rose went on, realizing she had to elaborate. "It's a mystery."

Henry kept staring at her.

"We have to figure out who they are!" Rose added, feeling that this explanation ought to be unnecessary.

Henry stirred at last and frowned. "Rose ... I really couldn't care less about that right now. I'm trying to study to pass a test I don't want to take in the first place, and I'm not even half done. Could you please just ... take Virgil out for a few more hours?"

Rose gaped at him. A few more *hours*? She had given him nine hours already, and had not been able to do anything with her own schoolwork during that period! What had he done with his time? Had he been drawing?

He had better not have spent the whole day drawing.

"Henry," she said, attempting to stay as calm as possible, "I apologize that I came home early. Clearly I was wrong that you'd be interested in the news *I* found incredibly riveting."

It seemed she hadn't managed to keep the irritation entirely out of her voice. She tried again.

"I can take Virgil back outside for another hour if you need it," she went on, trying to return to calm rationality. "Perhaps we can go shopping for the groceries for tomorrow night's dinner. But after that, I *need* to come home. I need you to take a turn watching Virgil. I have not been able to do any of my own schoolwork today, and I have a test upcoming, as well."

"Yes, but you always get good grades," Henry said tightly.

"That would be *because* I study, not because studying is optional for me!"

"Fantastic! I'm so glad to know that you getting an A instead of a B is more important than me passing a class instead of failing it!" Henry snarled, slamming his textbook shut.

"Of course it's important that you pass your test! That's why I've made a huge sacrifice of time for you today! I'm just saying that I need a turn! I need to study myself, Henry!"

WHAM! Virgil's bucket rolled into a wall again.

"Stop making all that noise!" Henry shouted, flinging his textbook onto the floor. It landed with a *thump*. Rose realized, to her horror, that Henry's frantic eyes were starting to look glassy.

"I'm sorry," Rose said hastily, running to pick up Virgil. "I'm sorry. I'll take him and be back in an hour. I'm sorry. I shouldn't have come back early. I'm sorry."

"Do whatever you want!" Henry cried. His eyes were wild and starting to leak. "It's not going to do any good, anyway! I'm going to fail it!"

Rose cast her mind around for some solution that might ameliorate his frantic frenzy. "Can—can I go over things with you? Would it help if we review things together? I'm good at math. If we go over everything you're confused about one at a time—"

Henry took a deep breath. His eyes started to look less wild.

Virgil wriggled and squirmed to get out of Rose's arms. He was bored! He wanted his bucket! Why wouldn't his mother let him play in his bucket? It was unfair! He was going to scream! He was going to screaaaaaaaaaaaaam!

Rose tried to shut Virgil's mouth, but she wasn't fast enough. A deafening screech burst forth from the tribulation in her arms.

Someone pounded on the ceiling from above them.

"*That!*" Henry shouted. "*That's* why I'm going to fail it! I can't possibly concentrate on anything with *him* around!"

Virgil's father didn't want him! Virgil's father was mad at him! Virgil was going to cryyyyyyyyyyyyyyy!

The deafening screams grew even louder.

In desperation, Rose dropped the tiny dragon on the couch and plugged her hands over her ears. Then a thought occurred to her, and she ran for the phone.

"What are you doing?" Henry shouted over the screams.

"Getting help!" Rose yelled back.

"Help from whom?"

There was someone on the other end of the party line. "Can you please hang up?" Rose broke into that conversation. "It's an emergency. I'll only take a few minutes. Then you can talk again. Please."

"Oh, all right, then," one of the voices on the line said.

"Talk to you in a minute, Eunice," the other voice said.

Thankfully, both women hung up.

"Help from *whom?*" Henry demanded.

But Rose was too busy asking the operator to connect her to her family's home.

"Mama?" she said as soon as the phone was answered. "Can I ask a favor? Henry and I both need to study, and we can't with Virgil around. Can you please take him for a few hours?"

"We don't need help from your parents!" Henry shouted, his face turning red.

"One minute, Mama," Rose said. She put her hand over the phone. "Yes, we do, and you know it. There's no shame in that. Grammery lived with us for several years when I was a child, and she minded us all the time."

"I don't want to owe your father anything," Henry muttered. "He hates me."

"He's not the one I'm asking the favor from. And he doesn't. He just enjoys pestering people. You need to be a little less thin-skinned about it."

Henry didn't seem mollified.

Virgil's screaming stopped, and he helpfully projected a few memories of the last times they had visited Rose's family. Virgil's grandfather had called Virgil's father "the other one." Virgil's grandfather always said that. Virgil's grandfather thought it was very funny, so Virgil thought it was funny, too!

"It's not," Henry muttered.

Virgil thought it was very funny!

"It's not!"

"Mmm, I suppose we can take him for a few hours," Rose's mother said from the phone. "Will you be bringing him by, or would you like us to come pick him up?"

"Pick him up, please," Rose said in relief, removing her hand from the receiver. "Walking there and back would take up so much time as to defeat the purpose."

"All right. I'll have your father to get the car ready. We'll be over as soon as we can."

Rose hung up the phone and closed her eyes. She took a deep breath. *One crisis averted. Now to deal with another: Henry's ability to pass that test.*

Other one! Virgil thought it was very funny! Other one! Other one! He was going to keep shredding the couch.

"You're *what?*" Henry shouted, snatching the child up from the cushion. Sure enough, there were puncture wounds in the cushion under where his wicked back claws had been.

Virgil's tummy hurt now. He was going to—

Henry yelped and spun the baby around. Virgil let out a fiery belch that scorched the wall beside them.

Now Virgil's diaper felt uncomfortable. It was wet. It was wet, wet, wet, wet, wet! He wanted it off! He was going to shred it with his back feet!

Rose barely dove in time to stop him. The last thing they needed was to have to buy more cloth diapers. The child had already destroyed too many of them, and melted or chewed on an appalling number of safety pins.

"How long until your parents get here?" Henry demanded.

Chapter 4: Studying

Quiet reigned without their son present, and it seemed very strange.

"Have we *ever* had this much time alone together before?" Henry murmured, looking up from his textbook.

Rose looked up from her notebook, as well. "I don't know," she said slowly. "I don't think so. Perhaps while Virgil was napping."

"Doesn't count," Henry said, shaking his head.

"Well, then, almost certainly no."

Henry set down his book. "Do you realize that we never actually took time for a proper courtship?"

"... Yes," Rose said. "We were a little rushed. But don't you need to study?"

"This is more important."

Oh, for goodness's sake, no it isn't!

Henry brightened, setting his textbook down. "We should do something nice for Valentine's Day!"

"Mmm," Rose said noncommittally. She had no interest in the silly holiday, but she supposed they could do something if he cared about it. "But right now, you need to study."

"I'm going to fail anyway." He sounded downright cheerful about it. "We might as well spend this time together."

Rose stared at him in exasperation. "You're not going to fail. I taught you all those formulae, didn't I?"

"Out of my head already." He waved a finger near his temple and made a whooshing noise.

"Then you can study harder," she said acerbically.

"Or I can accept the inevitable and stop worrying about it." He grinned. "C'mere and give me a kiss."

"I shall do so," Rose informed him, "when you have earned it by reciting one of the formulae that you claim has whooshed out of your mind."

He groaned. "Slave driver."

"I want you to pass," Rose said. "You have married a woman who cares about grades. You have informed me that yours matter, as well. Thus, I shall make sure you do well at yours."

"But I hate it!" Henry whined.

"Just get past these two classes," Rose assured him. "Then you'll be back to your true love: biology."

"I hate my major," Henry groaned. "I wanted to go to an art school, but my family insisted I go to college instead."

Rose jerked a little to the side. Well, that was ... surprising and unsettling news.

"Did you not want to be able to support a family?" she asked before she could stop herself.

Henry pouted. He seemed to be in a childish mood. "You sound like my father. 'Nobody makes any money at art!'"

Rose hesitated. Mindful of not starting another fight when they had just barely escaped the last one, she said cautiously, "I'm sure there are some who do."

"But not many. I know, I know, I know," Henry groaned, shaking his head. "That's why I let my father talk me into it. But I wish he hadn't. You'd have still married me if I'd been in art school, right?"

Um, Rose thought. That was a difficult question to answer, seeing as she hadn't experienced it. It was possible, but she doubted she would have been thrilled about it. She had grown to love Henry now, but they had been strangers initially.

"I suspect my father would have been less eager to give his permission if he'd known that you intended to pursue art as a career," she said diplomatically.

Henry's face clouded over. "It's not fair, is it? The way I'm expected to do something I hate instead of what I'm good at."

Rose opened her mouth to remind him that, being a man and a father, he had a duty to provide for his family, and he should know that. But then it occurred to her that there were many people who would raise similar objections to a woman and a mother who wished to go into a complex science field.

She sighed. "Perhaps it would have been better if we'd never met one another, or Virgil. Both of us would have found it easier to pursue our chosen occupations had we been single."

Henry's head jerked back. "Don't say that! Never say that! You two are the best things that have ever happened to me!"

Rose gave him a doubtful stare. "That's absolutely not true. Our son is such a bother, and I am ... hardly a typical wife. You must find us difficult to live with."

"Not true," Henry said obstinately.

"Is it not?" Rose asked, pointing to her textbook. "The fact that I will not give up my goals makes your life more difficult."

Henry paused. He hesitated. "All right, there may be some truth to that. But it's this blasted schoolwork that's the problem. Not you. Or Virgil. I love you."

"Me, or Virgil?"

"Both, obviously, although the boy not quite so much when he's screaming."

Rose smiled slightly.

"But really, you aren't the problem," Henry insisted. "I wanted to be married and to have kids. I chose this. I'm glad I have it. What I *didn't* choose was the blasted math classes."

"That doesn't mean you wouldn't have been happier with a more normal family," Rose said in a low voice.

She should, perhaps, have left the subject alone, but she couldn't leave the point unsaid. It had been weighing on her for a long time.

"Pshaw!" Henry waved that aside. "Being the first couple to raise a baby dragon is a pain in the neck, but sometimes it's so exciting, I want to burst with pride. Virgil's a blessing more than a curse."

Rose blinked back tears, determined not to let Henry see. The times when she felt like a failure as a mother were exceeded only by the times when she felt like a failure as a wife. She simply was not romantic by nature, and her husband was.

Left to herself, she didn't think she would have ever married. She hadn't ever been fully opposed to the idea, but the thought of husband or children had never been a high priority in her mind. She simply didn't think she would have bothered.

And yet, here she was, with both husband and child while still not having achieved her dream. She could not give it up, would not, although she knew that would continue to make life more difficult for her husband and child.

Sometimes she even questioned why she cared so much about paleontology, given that she had a real-life dragon living with her. But a living dragon was not the same as a fossil. A living dragon was a person who had to be loved and cared for. A fossil was a mystery to be solved.

The mysteries to solve riveted her and took her breath away. The duty of caring for an infant was exhausting, not enlightening. And as long as she held to her promise to herself that she would never treat him as a subject to study from a cold and analytical perspective, it would always be that way.

While she loved Henry and Virgil, she also knew that her emotion was far more reserved than Henry's, and certainly more reserved than the wildly uninhibited infant's.

Knowing that made her feel inadequate. It made her feel like she was not enough, and never could be. Sometimes she thought, *If only* ...

If only she had not met Henry.

If only she had not met Virgil.

If only her life had stayed on the simple, single track that she had planned to stay on for her entire life.

Why had she veered off into this tangent?

Why had she ended up in this position where her only option was to fail, and fail, and fail all over again?

"Is something wrong?" Henry asked.

Rose shook her head, turning her face away.

"Well, you know if you don't tell me, I can just ask Virgil what it is," Henry joked.

Rose gave him a livid glare.

"Or not," he said quickly. "Or not. But, um ... can you please tell me? Did I do something wrong?"

Rose looked down at the carpet for a long moment.

"I am not a wife who darns your socks," she said finally. "You want a wife who darns your socks."

"Is that what this is about?" Henry asked incredulously. "The *socks?*"

"No!" Rose said angrily. "It's about you not thinking my tests matter as much as yours do! It's about the fact that I think you should've married somebody who's happy to be your housemaid, because I'm not that, and I'm never going to be, and I don't *want* to be! If that's my role, what am I? I'm a *failure!*"

"I'll do it myself!" Henry said defensively. "I said I would! I can mend my own socks! I just hate doing it!"

"You keep putting them back on the couch every morning that it's my turn to watch Virgil, as if you're hoping that I'll do them for you if you just leave them there long enough."

Henry bit his lip, looking guilty. "Well ..."

Rose picked up her textbook. "I need to study."

"And apparently I need to mend my socks," Henry muttered, getting up from the couch. "Beats studying, anyway."

He started to walk off towards the bedroom.

Rose lowered her textbook a fraction of an inch. "Wait. Come here."

"Why?" he asked, looking baffled.

She smiled slightly. "Because that deserves a kiss."

Chapter 5: Solved

Rose felt less than confident about Henry's chances of passing his test the next day, seeing as he had spent the entire rest of the evening mending his socks instead of studying, but she could hardly complain, seeing as he had been doing it for her sake.

Despite her trying to dissuade him from spending the entire evening on that activity, he had stubbornly persisted, and then insisted on taking Virgil out of the house for a walk after his grandparents brought him back, so that Rose could have time studying.

Which she appreciated, but she ... *did* want him to pass his tests, too.

Before he left, Henry jokingly held out one of his textbooks to Virgil. "Want to breathe fire on this?"

The sleepy dragon opened one eye.

Virgil wasn't burpy right now. Virgil didn't want to chew things, either. Maybe he could claw it instead.

He sleepily reached out a claw at the book.

"Henry!" Rose cried. "Don't give him ideas!"

Henry snickered and tossed the book overhead, then dropped it on the couch.

"Your mother's right, Virgil," he said with mock solemnity. "Only destroy my textbook *after* I've passed the class and don't need it anymore."

Okay. Virgil would remember. He would wait until his father said to breathe fire on it.

"Don't do it at all!" Rose cried.

Henry left the house whistling, seeming entirely carefree.

Rose watched him go with mixed feelings.

While her husband seemed much more cheerful now, and that was certainly a good thing, she hoped he hadn't given up on passing those tests completely.

After eating her breakfast and scrubbing the dishes clean, Virgil came crawling into the kitchen.

He was hungry. Could Virgil eat breakfast? He wasn't sure if he should burn that book yet.

"Breakfast yes, breathing fire on books no," Rose said sternly. "Your father was just joking. You should never do that."

Virgil didn't understand, but Virgil was hungry and wanted food now. Could Virgil have his breakfast?

"Say please," Rose instructed. She was trying to teach their son manners.

Could Virgil have his please?

"Close enough."

She served him breakfast, and as she was doing so, she found her mind wandering to the mystery she'd learned about yesterday. If the fourth dragon had parents, why hadn't they come forward? What reason could they have for keeping silent?

She badly wanted to meet them and ask, but it wasn't like she could predict when they would be in front of the cage.

Oh, Virgil knew when they would be there. They always came in the morning. Violet said so.

The small dragon's head ducked down as he munched out of the bowl she'd left on the floor for him.

Rose paused. "How early in the morning?"

They always came after Violet's breakfast. Virgil liked breakfast. Virgil was eating his breakfast now. It was yummy.

Rose's mind worked feverishly. Violet usually had breakfast at nine o'clock. Right now, it was eight twenty. If they started getting ready immediately and walked quickly ...

Virgil's head poked up from the bowl. Were they going to see Violet? Virgil wanted to see Violet! Virgil wanted to go right now!

That decided it, of course.

"Yes, we're going to see Violet," Rose said.

Preparing the pram for their perambulation, Rose reflected that perhaps her son was spending too much time at the zoo for her liking. It was only natural because the child could not be trusted around human infants, and Violet was the only other dragon egg who had hatched, and thus she was his only playmate. But if another dragon egg hatched ...

Philomel was close to hatching. But taking Virgil to play with Bessie's son on a regular basis seemed a dreadful option. Rose had had enough of the woman's pompous attitude to last a lifetime.

But a fourth egg ...

A fourth egg who would not live in the zoo, who would have parents that Rose could stand to be around ...

That would solve so many problems.

The walk to Central Park Zoo seemed to go quickly, as it always did now that she'd traveled the route so many times, despite the fact that it went no faster than normal in terms of time spent: a little over twenty minutes.

There was a slight delay when Virgil sneezed and set his blanket alight, resulting in a horrified scream from a passerby, but Rose beat that out with rapid familiarity born of entirely too much practice, and then assured the panicked woman that her baby was, in fact, the source of the flames, and had not been a victim of a stray cigar dropped carelessly upon him.

Then she had to deal patiently with the woman's shock that the baby wasn't human.

Still, events such as those were extremely commonplace, more's the pity, so she arrived at the zoo with very little delay and no further thought about the incident.

Virgil was ecstatic to see his friend.

He poked his head out of the pram and swished his tail back and forth, which lashed the blanket along with it until it flopped to the ground. Rose scooped the blanket up and dropped it back over him, reflecting that since it was charred in a corner, it would require washing tonight anyway, so a little dirt would not harm the child.

Virgil was saying hello to Violet! Virgil was excited to see Violet! Virgil wanted to play tail face!

Violet was busy. Virgil should come back later.

Virgil's tail lashed harder, and he emanated indignation. That wasn't fair! He wanted to play!

What is Violet busy doing? Rose started to wonder, but the question was answered even before she finished the thought.

A memory of Violet's mother washed over her.

She was a beautiful, vain dragon, vibrantly blue, the most beautiful dragon in the whole wide world, except her daughter was even more beautiful. She stretched out her long neck to show off her horns to her prospective mate who she'd already married. Her purple husband ignored her, so she snorted sparks at him. Must he be clueless? She had been hoping to be coy. Their daughter was going to bonk him with her horns when he got home for being so silly.

Rose sighed aloud as the scene continued, and pulled herself out of the not-really-quite-a-memory.

She knew this memory well. It was one Violet loved to share with curious crowds. Rose had personally experienced it six times now, which is why she had no problem divorcing herself from the experience, unlike the rest of the crowd. But the memory had changed a great deal since Violet had first shared it.

It was now muddled with the future and from a childish perspective, and it kept including recollections of incidents that had never happened, such as Violet-as-a-hatchling interacting with her birth parents.

In other words, it was now far more a product of Violet's imagination than a true memory from her mother, and yet, she portrayed it as if it were true.

This is going to be a problem in the future, Rose reflected. *How many people are going to trust these "recollections" as fact when they are, in fact, sometimes closer to fiction?*

It was particularly disturbing when she reflected that the easily-muddled memories of these infants' ancestors would be the only clues their human parents would have as to what was normal for the children in each developmental stage. How much of the information they were likely to rely on would be accurate by the time these children came of age?

It was much like having an oral tradition rather than written records. And Rose knew of no way to record memories in a more trustworthy and dependable way.

As the more-or-less-daydream progressed, Virgil poked his tail out of the blanket and lashed it back and forth.

Virgil was bored. Violet was boring. Virgil wanted to go play with the other baby.

"She hasn't hatched yet, Virgil," Rose reminded him.

But Virgil wanted to go play with the other baby! She was awake! The other baby's parents were playing with her now!

What?! Rose's head whipped around to look at the people nearest the other cage. *They're here already?!*

CHAPTER 6: SURPRISE

At first, she thought, *It couldn't be them.* She looked for another couple staring at the cage with the egg. But everyone else in the crowd near them was walking somewhere else, watching Violet, or staring off into space.

If only two people were currently watching the unhatched egg, those had to be the people Virgil had referred to.

Rose sucked in her breath.

She should not have been shocked. It should, in fact, have been obvious that it would happen sooner or later. A fetus could not see what humans looked like, nor would a dragon care if they could. After all, the shape of humans was so alien compared to their own form that all humans probably looked alike to them.

The parents were colored.

It's not 1821, Rose thought frantically. *It's 1921. I can walk over there and make their acquaintance.*

She could, she knew she could, but her feet stayed frozen in place. She was terrified to take even a single step forward. This was outside any of her social experience. Was she *allowed* to talk to them? Was that something that was *done?*

She tried to think of what her mother would say. But her imagination failed her.

How could she possibly know what was appropriate and what wasn't in this instance? In all her years of school, in her neighborhood, in all her family's social circles, it was simply a question that had never come up.

Cowardice rose in her throat, and she started to consider fleeing before Violet or Virgil announced her presence.

Why was Virgil's mother running away?

Rose froze. She looked down at her questioning son, who now seemed very confused.

She swallowed deeply. Did she want Virgil to grow up to believe that external appearance meant everything?

No. Because he wasn't just a different color. He was a different *shape.*

Perhaps ... perhaps it didn't matter what the rules were. Perhaps it didn't matter if there *were* rules. There had been no rules laid out when she'd adopted Virgil, and she had done it anyway, because it had felt like the right thing to do.

She could transcend species. Surely she could do something much more trivial.

Choosing to accept Virgil was the most difficult thing she'd ever done. But putting one foot in front of the other right now was the second most difficult. She pushed through the crowd around Violet's cage, reaching the other side and the empty expanse in which only two people stood.

Both of them had their back to Rose, and now that she was much closer, she realized there was a silent conversation going on between them. Almost a one-way conversation, in fact.

The eggbound dragon was ... chattering?

Her feathery, fleeting impressions were nothing like Virgil's insistent nagging, Philomel's demanding fury, or Violet's exuberant flamboyance. They came and went rapidly, so fast that Rose could barely take in the images, and the range was so short that Rose didn't even notice they were happening until she was nearly behind the two parents.

It was like the new dragon was whispering. And whispering at an insane speed.

The two parents turned around at once.

"Um," Rose said, gulping, "hello. I'm Rose Palmer. Wainscott, I mean. Rose Wainscott. I was only recently married, so I'm not used to it yet. Pleased to make your acquaintance."

The man and woman both stared at her. Their expressions were not unfriendly, but they were not particularly chummy, either. They both stared at her silently.

Panic fluttered in Rose's throat. Had she truly broken some rule of propriety? Were they judging her harshly for that? She didn't know. Why had she felt the need to go over to them? What had she thought could be gained?

"And ... y-your names?" she asked nervously.

The silence stretched on, and Rose tried to distract herself by looking at their clothing. The man's tweed suit was shabby at the elbows, and the woman wore a shirtwaist and a long, pleated skirt. His hat was a fedora with black ribbon, while hers was a tight-fitting cloche that wasn't really in fashion.

Virgil poked his head out from behind the blanket, and his clawed forelegs followed as he pulled himself up on the side of the pram.

Hello! Virgil was saying hello! Virgil wanted to meet the other baby! Virgil thought she'd be more interesting than Violet, who was being boring. Hello! Virgil was saying hello to the other baby!

A smile split across the woman's face. "Oh! You're the one Ophelia keeps talking about." Her voice was quiet, much like the eggbound dragon's telepathic equivalent. "She says you've been wanting to meet us. It's a pleasure."

Rose breathed out a desperate sigh of relief. "Yes. A pleasure," she said rapidly. "I didn't know, um ..."

... *that you were* ... No, no, she couldn't say that! That had to be taboo.

"... that her name was Ophelia," she finished frantically.

The man smiled slightly. "We love Shakespeare," he said. His voice was quiet, too.

"How long has it been since she chose you?" Rose asked.

Husband and wife exchanged looks.

"It happened on the second day she was here," the man said in a low voice. "We've come to see her every day since."

Rose stared at him in astonishment. It was unfathomable.

"Why did you not talk to the zoo staff? You should ask to bring her home with you before she hatches!"

The two looked at each other.

The woman said quietly, "We didn't particularly want to be told no."

Rose felt a sudden, stabbing shame. Of course they had to worry about that. Why, she had been afraid to even walk over and start a conversation. What would happen if Director Campbell refused point-blank? What if he chose to have the newest dragon transferred into another zoo to get her away from them?

It wasn't implausible. She knew nothing about the man's character save that he had been extremely unenthusiastic about both Virgil and Philomel being raised outside of the zoo. It was easy to imagine that he would take any pretext to keep the next dragon child in a cage forever.

Still, something had to be done. Not speaking up wouldn't deliver that little girl to her parents' home.

Unless they didn't want her at home. Violet's father was content to have her stay here. An entirely different fear knotted in Rose's stomach. Suppose their idea of what was appropriate for *Deinonychus antirrhopus* was entirely different from hers?

To her surprise, the baby dragon answered that in rapid impressions, most of them too fast for Rose to catch. The only ones she was sure of were the ones that said that yes, she wanted to go home with her parents, and also it was empty and it wasn't supposed to be.

Rose was puzzled, trying to work that out.

"The cradle," the woman said softly. "Our other child died."

Her husband reached over and squeezed her hand softly.

Rose couldn't even fathom such a loss, and she didn't want to try. The thought of it made her feel split down the middle.

Better not to think about it. Better to do something useful. What could she do that would be useful right now?

Ah. Yes. Of course. She could introduce them to the man who would determine their family's fate.

"Would the two of you be willing to remain here while I bring Director Campbell?" Rose asked. "He runs the American Museum of Natural History, and is the one with legal ownership of the dragon eggs. He can give permission for you two to take Ophelia home."

The man seemed hesitant. He looked at his wife.

She shook her head. They seemed to be holding a silent conversation. There was neither voice nor telepathic impression, except from Virgil, who started to let out feelings of being bored and chewing on his blanket. Ooh, now he would shred it!

Rose rescued the blanket from him.

At last, the man said, "No. What we have now is enough. We don't want to jeopardize that."

A flicker of deep offense rose from the egg.

If her parents didn't want her, she would refuse to hatch. She would die. If her parents didn't want her, she would refuse to hatch. And she'd die.

The woman sucked in her breath, her shoulders tensing. She looked on the verge of tears.

"Ophelia," the man said sharply, his volume raising for the first time. "That is not right. Don't say that!"

If Ophelia's parents didn't want her, she would rather die. She was starving already. She should have hatched weeks ago. She wouldn't hatch if she had to stay here with the prying minds and the other baby who was always loud and talking. She'd told them she was hungry. She'd thought they knew what that meant. If she had to stay here, she wouldn't hatch. She would die.

The man's eyes darkened. He started to talk, and his voice failed him. He tried again, and he finally managed it, his voice shaking. "All right. Please bring the director here."

CHAPTER 7: SUITABLE

Hurrying back with a sour-faced director in tow, Rose stopped as far as possible from the dragon cages and pointed at the cage that contained the egg. "Those are her parents. They are really very suitable."

Director Campbell's pinched face said otherwise. "You didn't mention they were colored."

"I didn't mention that because it has no bearing," Rose said defensively, though she had expected that reaction, and it was why she had stopped so far from earshot to point out the child's parents. "For all we know, the dragon will have brown or black scales. In any case, she isn't human in the first place."

The man looked unimpressed with her impeccable logic. "Well, I suppose the dragon's life is of prime concern," he said begrudgingly. "I'll talk to them."

He started forward, elbowing his way through the crowd to reach the cage that contained the egg. Wrestling with the pram through the crowd around Violet's cage, Rose was left an increasing number of paces behind.

As they passed within range of Violet's telepathy, Rose found herself immersed in yet another highly-fictionalized vision of events, this one of Violet and her parents flying through the sky and hunting together over a New York City skyline.

Rose severely hoped that no one here was gullible enough to believe that was an unaltered memory.

Virgil noticed how near to Violet's cage they were walking. He climbed halfway up the side of the pram in excitement. Virgil wanted to play with Violet! Did Violet want to play with him now?

Violet, thoroughly engrossed in her daydream, barely even bothered to respond. There was a faint hint of rebuff, then a determined resurgence of her dream.

Virgil was very mad! Violet was being boring! Virgil didn't like Violet! Virgil would play with the other baby instead!

The daydream now demonstrated Violet breathing fire at an annoying, loud insect to catch it on fire.

Rose chuckled at the metaphor despite herself.

Virgil was really mad!

Rose bit her lip to hide her mirth as she pushed Virgil back down into the pram and replaced the blanket. She had no wish for him to become a second source of curiosity to the audience gathered here.

But as before, Violet was really a remarkable distraction. It was a testament to how engrossed the audience was that nobody seemed to notice either Virgil's interruption or his appearance when he popped his head stubbornly out of the blanket again.

Rose might have found this lack of awareness disturbing if she had not witnessed the same phenomenon many times before. When one was not used to speaking with dragons, it could be quite difficult to spare any concentration for the world around oneself. She'd experienced it herself, so while it might be rather unsettling to witness, as a source of concern, it was minimal.

Unless, of course, one's path through a crowd became obstructed by a man who would not move aside to let one's pram through, even when one asked said man politely, and then several more times with increasing temper, to please do so.

Director Campbell had already reached the other cage and was now speaking with Ophelia's parents. It was maddening that she could not hear a word.

Rose finally resorted to pushing the man physically aside. He stumbled forward, blinked, looked at her reproachfully, and then turned back to stare forward at Violet's cage.

Rose fumed as she stormed forward with the pram.

Virgil was happy! Virgil was excited! The other baby was going to hatch, and he was going to play tail-face with her!

"That's not going to happen today, Virgil," Rose muttered under her breath. "Your hatching took several hours, and Violet's took most of a day. Besides, you were not permitted to play with her until she was over a week old, in case of fragility."

Virgil wanted to play tail-face! Virgil wanted to play tail-face!

They reached the edge of the crowd and neared the three adults conversing. Disappointingly, it seemed the conversation had been short and Rose had missed most of it.

"... provisionally," Director Campbell was saying. "But I'll send someone over twice a day to check on her health, and if there's any sign of malnutrition, she'll be coming back here for good. The dragon's health is of prime importance."

"Yes, we agree." The quiet man looked profoundly relieved. He nodded rapidly. "We only want what's best for her."

"Hmmm." Director Campbell gave both of the parents a suspicious eye flicker. "Yes, so do I. Very well. Come with me. We'll make the arrangements. Good day, Mrs. Wainscott."

He barely nodded his head in Rose's direction before he stalked off. Ophelia's parents followed him, though the woman stopped to give a slight wave and mouth, "Thank you."

Rose took a deep breath and stared at the silent egg.

"I'm glad you have your parents now," she said.

Ophelia didn't respond.

"I'd like to think I helped a little," Rose added.

The egg didn't respond.

Rose's eyebrows drew together. It was most infuriating. First she had been cut out of the entire conversation, and now even the egg was ignoring her. All right, this was perhaps not her personal concern, but she had a right to want to know what was going on with a new dragon egg, didn't she?

Never mind what Henry's answer to that question would be.

Virgil's mother was just like Virgil's aunts! He had spent time with them yesterday! Virgil's mother was nosy!

"I am not nosy!" Rose exclaimed.

An impression of her younger sisters' mischievous giggles bubbled up from her son's pram.

Nosy! Nosy! Virgil's mother was nosy! Virgil thought it was very funny!

"Interested is not the same as inquisitive!" Rose insisted.

Nosy! Nosy! They had broken into Virgil's grandfather's study yesterday. He had been very upset to find them going through all his things. He had called them nosy. Virgil thought that was very funny. Nosy! Nosy!

It would seem, Rose thought with disgruntlement, *that there are disadvantages to asking one's family to watch one's child for a day.*

For a change of pace, and because she had no eagerness to return home to face the household chores she knew awaited her, Rose chose to take the slightly longer route of 5th Avenue, rather than her usual path through Central Park.

This proved to be a mistake.

"Oh, Rose!" a familiar voice called from behind her.

Rose's shoulders tensed. She knew that voice all too well. She turned around slowly to face her dreaded compatriot.

"Hello, Mrs. Bailey," she said stiffly.

"Oh, never mind that, call me Bessie," the woman said grandly, adjusting her hat. It was adorned with a peacock feather twice as tall as her head. "It's a lovely day for a walk, isn't it? Philomel and I are out enjoying it."

Rose glanced behind the woman, and sure enough, there was the nanny, thirty paces behind her, pushing a shiny pram that contained a large, dusky orange egg with brown spots. The egg was much too far away to be within telepathic range.

"I see you and your son are spending quality time together," Rose said sarcastically.

"Yes, it's glorious, isn't it?" Bessie beamed. "Sometimes it gets a little stuffy at home, so I thought he'd benefit from a change of scene."

He hasn't hatched yet! Rose wanted to scream. *He can't see the scene!*

This prompted her son to poke his head up through the blankets and make commentary.

Virgil could see the scene! Virgil liked seeing the scene. Virgil was clawing the blanket! Virgil liked clawing the blanket. Virgil's claw was caught in the blanket. Virgil's claw was caught in the blankeeeeeeeeeet!

Rose wrenched the enormous curved back claw out of the hole in the cloth he had burned earlier today.

"Did I tell you what I learned about dragons yesterday?" Bessie asked in her most officious tone.

Please don't. Rose smiled brittlely.

"I learned that dragons are warm-blooded. It means their blood is hot instead of cold. That's why they breathe fire. Did you know that?"

Rose stared at the woman, flabbergasted. *That's not what it means! It has to do with how their circulatory systems are arranged!*

"I see you didn't," Bessie said smugly. She glanced down at Virgil, and then wrinkled her nose. "Ugh! Don't you ever have that blanket washed? It's filthy! One would think you don't care about his health at all—"

"It was very nice to see you, but I simply must be going now," Rose said rapidly, bursting forward and taking off at a run.

There was only so much of Bessie she could cope with in one day.

Chapter 8: Shrill

Before the week was out, Henry had the results of the two tests he had studied so hard for.

It was not the best news Rose had ever heard.

"I passed *one* of them!" he said triumphantly, his face bright, as he entered the apartment. "That means I have a chance of passing that class this time! Since the other one's a lost cause, I'll just stop going to that one and take it again next semester."

Rose tried very, very hard to suppress a long sigh. "Shall we set aside a time every week for you to study for the one you're going to make the attempt to finish?"

"No, I'll just do it when I need to," he said.

"Regular studying would probably help," she hinted.

"I'd rather not," he shot back. "Besides, I have three other classes this semester that I need to do well in. I might pass the math one or I might not. How are yours?"

Rose was silent. She supposed he would only be irritated if she complained about the A minus she had received for her most recent test, even though she had been greatly displeased about it. "I am going to need to study more carefully."

"So, no change, then," Henry said, rubbing his shoulders. "How is Virgil?"

Virgil had behaved! Could he come out of the box now?

"What's this?" Henry asked, glancing down the hallway. "What box does he mean?"

"The new time-out box," Rose said sharply.

Virgil didn't like this box! The box was very boring! Could he come out of the box now?

Henry headed down the hallway to the bathroom and opened the door. Rose followed him. Virgil was inside a wooden crate that was inside the bathtub. Wet towels were draped over everything flammable, including the back of the door.

"You realize that the crate is flammable, right?" Henry asked.

"I realize that if he burns it down, I'll buy another one."

"Awwwwww, poor thing," Henry crooned, leaning down and scooping up the dragon. "Is Mommy being mean? Of course you can come out. You're not going to set anything on fire now, are you?"

"He had better not," Rose said darkly. "He burned the pram this morning."

Henry paused. "He did what?"

"He burned the pram," Rose repeated. "And he did it on purpose, too. He was commenting on how much fun it would be to have it on fire before he breathed fire on it. I am very upset with him right now."

Virgil's father shouldn't listen to Virgil's mother! Virgil wanted to stay out of the box! Virgil's mother was being mean!

Henry swore under his breath.

Rose agreed with the sentiment, though she wouldn't use such language herself. "So I asked our neighbors if they had a box we could keep, and they gave me that one. I told him he could stay there for a good long while."

Alarm radiated off their son as he wriggled in Henry's arms to get his attention.

Virgil had behaved and he hadn't sneezed on purpose and it wasn't his fault that he'd accidentally set the pram on fire and also he'd behaved. He didn't want to be in the box anymore and he had behaved and his mother was being mean and he was going to behave!

"What are we going to do?" Henry groaned, setting the objecting dragon back in the crate. "We need a pram."

"I know," Rose said grimly. "We can't take him anywhere without a conveyance to put him in. Quite apart from people staring, he is getting increasingly heavy."

Could Virgil play in his bucket now?

"NO!" both of his parents shouted.

Virgil was very sad! He was going to cry!

"If you scream, we'll shut the door," Rose told him.

Virgil was going to cry even louderrrrrrrr!

In less than a minute, he was alone in the bathroom with the door closed.

"So," Henry said, raising his voice to be heard over the shrill howls, "what do we do next? I suppose we could have him crawl everywhere."

"Would you let a six-month-old human crawl all over the sidewalks of New York?" Rose queried.

Henry frowned. "No, I wouldn't. Health concerns aside ..."

"Health concerns aside ..." Rose agreed.

All sorts of disasters might happen if Virgil were allowed to roam free. He might scamper off and get lost. He might be kidnapped by some unscrupulous person. He might run into the road and collide with a car or a horse. He might sneeze upon a nearby leg, causing panic and injury. Essentially, there were all kinds of safety hazards that would be associated with his locomotion being under his own power out in public, and none of those could be addressed until the boy was old enough to have something resembling common sense.

"There's such a thing as a leash," Henry suggested.

Rose cringed.

"I mean, it would be cheaper than a pram."

"And it would make him look like a pet, and it would not address half of the health and safety concerns, and given that he isn't even close to walking upright, I don't think he has the stamina to crawl for the same distances we walk every day."

Henry sighed. "I know, I know. So what do we do?"

"I've asked all of our acquaintances I could think of if they had a spare pram," Rose said.

"Did any of them?"

"No, but perhaps I have forgotten someone."

"Your parents?" Henry suggested.

"I asked them first. Mama gave away their baby things a long time ago."

"My parents?" Henry asked.

"I haven't called them yet, but you're welcome to. I did call your brother, who says they don't have an additional one."

Henry's brother had given them the original pram.

"If he doesn't have an extra one, my parents won't, either," Henry said. "I assume you asked the neighbors?"

"I did, and unsurprisingly, none of them did. I was lucky enough to have gotten hold of the crate."

"I suppose we could ask the Baileys ..."

Rose didn't even try to hide her horror at the prospect.

"I mean, they certainly have money."

"They certainly do. And I'm certain we do not have a strong enough acquaintanceship to ask them to buy something for us," Rose said flatly. "Quite apart from the fact that I would not want to ask *anyone* to buy things for us, I have no desire to be in Mrs. Bailey's debt. I would sooner buy a brand new pram ourselves."

"Well, is that out of the question?" Henry asked.

Rose hesitated. The correct answer was, *Any unnecessary money spent is out of the question as long as you're going to keep failing classes and having to retake them.* But that was not something she could say.

"Hang on!" Henry said, snapping his fingers. "A wagon! My parents have an old one I used to use as a child."

"It would be wood," Rose objected.

"It would be free," Henry retorted.

"But if Virgil combusts it ... how great would the nostalgic loss be? I wouldn't want him to destroy one of your favorite toys from childhood."

Henry shrugged. "I'd be very annoyed, but not heartbroken. I liked it, but I'm not nostalgically attached to it. Besides, think about how much smaller than a pram it would be. We could fit it in a closet rather than keeping it in a corner, so Virgil would be less able to reach it to sneeze on it in the first place."

It was a good solution. Rose opened her mouth to agree, but then the phone rang.

Henry ran to answer it. "Wainscott residence, Henry speaking."

As he listened to the voice on the other end of the line, Henry's face went pale.

"Just a minute," he said, and pulled the phone away from his ear. "Hey, Rose, can you spare me for the rest of the day, and perhaps tomorrow, as well?"

"Why?" Rose asked, startled.

"The new little girl dragon is hatching, and it looks like there may be trouble. Something to do with her waiting too long to hatch. They want as many people there as possible who can help, and since I have experience taking care of Virgil ..."

Rose's heart squeezed. "Yes. Go."

Chapter 9: Specimens

Mr. Teedle came and picked up Henry ten minutes later. He barely spared a moment for a greeting before the two left.

Rose watched them go with a number of mixed feelings. First, she hoped desperately that the problem was not as severe as it sounded, and that Henry would be of some use. The only thing that mattered was that the child be born healthy.

But she had other, less charitable feelings, as well.

She was rather upset that Mr. Teedle had asked for Henry's help, and not hers.

Of course she understood that it would make no sense to ask both of them to come, because one of them had to remain behind with Virgil. Having another dragon underfoot at the new dragon's hatching would no doubt complicate matters rather than aiding them.

But still. What made Henry more qualified to help than her? Rose had spent as much time with their son as he had. She was also the one who was studying dragons, and the one who had taken more of an interest in Ophelia in the first place.

Not to mention that Mr. Teedle had known her far longer than Henry. In any matter involving dragons, he should have thought of her first.

Moodily, Rose prepared Virgil's usual dinner of chicken, water, and raw eggs, wishing as she always did that the boy would learn to eat a cheaper meat, such as pork.

She walked down the hall to the bathroom, where she found her son curled up in a ball with his tail tucked around him, snoring softly.

Rose smiled wryly. A few hours ago, she had wanted nothing more than for him to take a nap and leave her alone. Now that she wanted him awake, of course he was sleeping.

Virgil stirred, and his eyes opened.

Why was Virgil's mother sad? Where was Virgil's father?

"Oh," Rose sighed, sitting down at the edge of the bathtub, "I got left out of something that I would have liked to have been invited to. Your father went to help."

Virgil was sad for his mother. Virgil was sad to still be in the box. Could Virgil get out of the box? He was behaving.

"Yes, you are," Rose said, reaching in and picking him up. She held him in her arms, stroking his smooth and slippery scales. Sometimes things happened that put the events of her life in perspective. If nothing else, Virgil had hatched safely. He had been born healthy. That was a privilege that not all parents were given with their children.

Please be safe, Rose told Ophelia silently, even though she knew the thoughts would not reach at this distance. *Please be healthy. If anyone deserves that, they do.*

It wouldn't be right for them to lose two children. Nobody should even lose one.

Had Virgil's birth parents worried about losing their son this way? Had they ever realized that their son might, instead, lose them?

Virgil rubbed his tail on her arm as she stroked her hand down his back. He remembered his birth parents. He would show her one of their memories.

A memory from Virgil's father welled up, taking hold of her senses and gripping her in its all-absorption. Rose gasped as she recognized the familiarity of the scene.

He sneakily left the fire pit unscrubbed. He hated scrubbing the fire pit. Maybe his wife would do it for him.

Uh oh! His wife had noticed, and she was very annoyed.

It was his turn to scrub the fire pit, and he knew it! *And* he'd used one of her rocks to carve a picture into it! They were specimens, not pretty things!

It was a *pretty* specimen, and it would be much better as a carved rock than put boringly in a row in the vast rock collection cave!

Oh, now see what he did? The egg was whining that they were fighting again!

He could calm the baby. He was good at it. He'd show the baby a memory ...

The memory faded, and Rose came to herself again.

"Was that a true memory?" she asked. "Or did you add to that one?"

Virgil didn't know what she meant. Did Virgil's mother like his old father's memory? He had forgotten all about it till now.

Rose bit her lip. That meant it was probably a true memory.

She'd almost forgotten that the reason Virgil had chosen them was because they resembled his birth parents so closely in personality. And that was the most in-depth memory she'd ever had of Virgil's birth father.

His birth parents had chosen one another. They'd had arguments, too. And yet, through that whole quarrel, there had been a strong sense of affection, of devotion to one another. A strong sense of this-is-the-right-match-for-me.

Of course they weren't the same people as Rose and Henry. They were only similar. And yet ...

And yet ... he loved her so much. And she felt the same about him.

Was that how Henry felt about her? Would she be capable of feeling that depth of emotion for him someday? Without jeopardizing who she was or what she wanted to be?

She wasn't sure. But she hoped ... she hoped ... she hoped it was possible.

Henry returned home late that night, which, fortunately, was many hours earlier than Rose had expected or feared.

"How did it go?" she asked, opening the door to let her husband and Mr. Teedle in. "Is Ophelia ...?"

"The dragon's fine," Mr. Teedle said, removing his bowler hat. He rubbed one of his eyes, looking weary. "Once she got out, she was willing to eat with no troubles. It was getting out of the egg that was the difficulty for her. She was awfully weak."

Rose looked at Henry. "Did it help for you to be there?"

"Yes," Henry said. He held his hands cupped with the wrists together. "I showed them this, which helped her eat."

Rose felt a stab of annoyance. Mimicking a mouth with her hands had been her idea. *Deinonychus* parents had made crop milk for their infants inside their mouths, something humans could obviously not do, so pretending their hands were mouths had helped Virgil accept the uncomfortable situation at first.

Still, the important thing was that Henry had been able to help. And she was very glad the child was alive.

"I'm glad she's with her parents," Rose said aloud. "I'm glad she doesn't have to live in the zoo."

"She won't have to go to the zoo, will she?" Rose asked.

Mr. Teedle hesitated. "Well ... I don't know about that. We'll be providing food for her for the first few weeks, because she'll need to be supervised carefully, but after that, it will be up to her parents to feed her. I'm not sure how they're going to afford it, frankly."

"They live in Harlem," Henry explained. "Not a wealthy neighborhood."

"That's not all," Mr. Teedle said grimly. "He's a musician. They both are. Alice sings, and Willie plays piano. And sometimes they do art on the side. Apparently that's how they make their money. I really don't see how they can support a child on that, much less a carnivore. That's just not something an artist can do!"

Henry's face had gone thunderous.

Oh, dear, Rose sighed. *He's taking that personally.*

"Artists are creative people," Henry snapped. "They're good at thinking up creative solutions. They'll manage."

"Of course they'll try," Mr. Teedle said, "but ..."

"They'll manage!"

Mr. Teedle looked somewhat baffled at this vehemence.

"Thank you so much for giving Henry a ride back home," Rose said hastily. "It might be good for us to cut this visit short, as Virgil's already in bed and we don't want to wake him. Can we offer you some food before you head out again?"

CHAPTER 10: SPECIAL

It was only a week later that the invitation arrived. It was left on their doormat when Rose opened the door in the morning.

You are cordially invited to attend the debut performance of Ophelia Lawrence for an evening of dragon song. And then there was an illustration of a dragon hatchling, followed by the name and address of a Harlem vaudeville theater, as well as a time and tonight's date.

To say that Rose was shocked would be an understatement.

"What in the world!" she cried, reading it the first time.

Henry looked over her shoulder. He scanned it through, and then he started to laugh. "That's brilliant! They need a way to make money, so why not have people pay to see the baby? That's what the zoo would do, anyway!"

Virgil looked up from his breakfast of chicken mixed with raw egg and water. The zoo! He wanted to go to the zoo. Could he go to the zoo to see Violet now?

"No zoo for two weeks," Henry said. "That's your punishment for destroying the pram."

Virgil was VERY SAD! Virgil was going to shred his food and throw it all over the kitchen!

"Do that, and you won't get any more breakfast."

Virgil was sulking. Virgil was sullen. Virgil's parents hadn't let him go to the zoo for ages. Virgil wanted to smear food on the floor. Virgil was going to smear food on the floor. Virgil was smearing food all over the floor.

Henry went and fetched the tipped-over food bowl in one hand. With the other, he picked up the struggling dragon and carried the boy to the time-out box in the bathroom.

No! Virgil was sorry! Virgil didn't want to be in the box! Virgil was saaaaaaaaaad!

Henry shut the door to the bathroom just in time to partially muffle an earsplitting scream.

"If that's dragon song, I already hear enough of it," Rose announced.

Henry snorted with laughter. "I'm guessing it has to be better than that. Well, what do you think? Do you want to go?"

"I confess I'm curious," she admitted. "Even though I'm not sure how much the tickets cost."

For some reason, that made Henry chuckle. "You're never *not* curious. All right, then. We'll go."

Hours later, when they arrived at the vaudeville theater, the man taking tickets took one look at Virgil and shooed them in without taking their money, insisting that they had seats reserved for them inside. They soon discovered that this meant three parterre seats in the center of the front row. Four other seats were reserved around theirs.

"Why four people?" Henry wondered. "Who else is coming?"

"Relatives?" Rose guessed.

"Of Alice and Willie's? Not likely." Henry gestured with his head. "I mean ..."

Rose glanced back and saw what he meant. All the front rows were filled with white people. All the colored members of the audience were in the back rows.

"That hardly seems fair," she said.

"It is what it is," Henry shrugged, putting Virgil on his lap.

Five minutes later, a colored man ambled casually up to the front row and sat in one of the reserved seats next to them.

Rose gasped before she could stop herself. She glanced at the back row. She glanced at him. She glanced at Henry. She glanced back at the man.

The man grinned and held out his hand. "Name's Johnny. I'm Alice's big brother. Yeah, I'm sitting up front tonight. I'm the one who negotiated their pay, and I told the manager I had to sit in the front row for their first performance, or no deal. He wasn't too happy about it, but he really wanted Ophy."

Henry shook the man's hand. "'Ophy'?" he repeated. "Is that Ophelia's nickname?"

The man grinned. "According to my sister, no, but according to me, yes. Sounds less stuck-up than Ophelia, right?"

Rose was spared the need to answer that she preferred the full name by the arrival of Violet's father.

"Harrison!" Henry called, waving. "Was one of these seats reserved for you?"

Harrison Jones veered over and joined them. "Apparently so." He stopped and gave the colored man an odd look.

"He's Alice's big brother," Henry explained. "He's sitting with us."

"Yeah, I guessed that," Harrison said, carefully sitting in the empty seat next to Rose rather than Johnny. "Why?"

"Because I am," Johnny said. "I'm not missing my niece's first performance. Only the people in the first few rows will be within range. And you can just get used to it, ma'am," he added to a scandalized-looking woman off to their left.

The woman got up and walked off in a huff.

"So who're the other two seats for?" Henry asked.

"Oh, Alice wanted all the dragon parents to get to be here for this."

Rose sucked in her breath in horror. *Bessie and Francis!*

Harrison smirked. "Those two? There's no way they're going to come. Much too good for vaudeville, I bet you."

Rose profoundly hoped that was true.

Fortunately, it seemed that Harrison's assessment was true. There was no sign of the wealthy couple as the first act started.

The first act featured a comedian whose jokes had Johnny and Harrison laughing uproariously. Next up was a woman in a beaded dress who sang in a high soprano. She was closely followed by a man and woman performing an Irish jig, then a man with a trained elephant.

Then came the fifth act.

A piano was pushed on stage, and Willie followed. He was the first colored person to walk on the stage so far tonight. Then Alice came out carrying a tiny yellow dragon.

She wore a long black sheathe of a dress, much simpler than the current fashion, and Ophelia wore what appeared to be an even simpler black tube of fabric, a fact which made Rose stare. Much as she believed in treating Virgil the same as a human infant, she would never have thought to put clothing on him. Doing so seemed faintly ridiculous.

There was a murmur of excitement across the audience. This was definitely what a lot of them had come to see.

Willie started playing, and the first thirty seconds of the song was an energetic ragtime melody that got Virgil so excited that he breathed fire straight in the air, causing screams of delight from the people behind them, who no doubt thought this was part of the show.

Rose fiercely remonstrated Virgil not to do that again in the quietest whisper she could lace with fury.

And then Alice started to sing.

Her singing voice was a reverberating alto that seemed to fill the whole room. It seemed nothing like the quiet voice she spoke with. And then even Rose's jolt of surprise at that was completely drowned out by Ophelia joining in.

The dragon's contribution was a small hum. In tune, but only one note, held out for long periods between her parents' interlacing melody and harmony. That could, perhaps, have been considered a song, but nothing special.

No, the special part was the colors.

In a wave around Ophelia, the room shifted around them, pulsing between normal colors and strange ones that Rose could not name. The pulsing started out in rhythm with the music and then rapidly lost the beat, which was probably not intended. But it hardly mattered.

In what seemed like no time at all, the song was over, and the spell broken.

Exclamations and chattering swept across the first few rows.

"Holy Hannah," Henry said, letting out an explosive breath. "She's a tetra-chromat."

"A what?" Harrison and Johnny asked.

"It means she can see four colors," Henry said. "We can only see three. In this case, I think the fourth one is infrared."

"Is that normal for dragons?" Alice's brother asked.

"*No,*" Rose and Henry said simultaneously.

"How would you know?" Harrison Jones asked. "We've only ever met two dragons before."

"We know because we've seen the memories of hundreds of other dragons, courtesy of Violet and Virgil," Henry said. "None of them have shown colors like those. If Ophelia can do that ... she's got a talent that's probably rare."

After a few minutes to let the murmurs from the crowd die down, the family of musicians began a second song. This time, Alice stepped off the stage and walked down to the audience, carrying Ophelia in her arms, so that the colors could reach more members of the audience than the first few rows.

It wasn't that it was a spectacular performance. Ophelia's contributions were rough, off the beat, and frequently sloppy. In addition, all she ever seemed to do was overlay her memories of this room on top of everybody else's, which was how she was making the colors seem to change back and forth for them.

Still, it was enough. It was sufficient.

This was definitely a performance that would pull in enough crowds to keep a hungry, small yellow dragon fed.

Chapter 11: Son

"No, we have to," Henry insisted. "We have to tell them what they missed. They need to go so that they can see it before the show's booked solid."

"It was their own fault for being too snobbish to show up," Rose said acerbically. She had no wish to see the Baileys.

"We still have to tell them," Henry said. "It doesn't matter if you dislike them, Rose. Their son might very well be one of Virgil's friends in the future."

Rose held back her temper only because she knew it was true. Virgil and his games like "claw face" could not be trusted around human infants. If he was going to have any playmates in young childhood, and perhaps even afterwards, they would have to be dragons.

Of course she hoped that the other eight eggs waiting in the American Museum of Natural History would hatch at a rapid pace, but there was no guarantee of that. It was entirely possible that the only dragons awake in New York City in their generation would be Virgil, Violet, Philomel, and Ophelia. And if that happened, a continuing acquaintanceship with Bessie could not be avoided, no matter how much Rose might wish it.

"Oh, very well," Rose said testily. "We can drop in to tell them, if you insist."

It was strange how quick a walk it was from Harlem to 5th Avenue. The two seemed like they ought to be worlds apart, and yet in less than half an hour of walking, you could move from one to the other with ease.

As they reached the door to the Baileys' home, Rose flinched at the thought of deliberately initiating contact. But Henry was holding the handle of the wagon where Virgil was curled up sleeping, so she steeled herself and moved forward to knock.

Virgil jolted awake at the noise, and he let out a loud yowl. Then his eyes drooped, and he settled back into sleep.

A maid answered the door. "I'm afraid Mrs. Bailey is not at home," she said politely. "It might be best to come back later."

"Very well," Rose said, happy to take the offered reprieve.

"No, don't send them away!" a voice shouted from within the house.

A wild-eyed woman with disheveled hair came bolting down the stairs and pushed past the maid. She looked as if she had not slept in two days.

"How do you get him to eat on his own?!" Bessie screamed. "He won't take food from anybody but me! Not even Francis! He told the experts to go away, and he wouldn't stop screaming until they did! And he *bit* the nanny, and she *quit!*"

"Hang on," Rose said slowly. "Am I to understand that Philomel hatched?"

"*Yes!* And he's a nightmare! How do you fix it?!"

"Fix ... the fact that he's hatched?" Rose asked blankly.

"YES! I LIKED HIM BETTER IN THE EGG!"

Henry stepped forward. "It sounds like you need some help. I'll volunteer," he said very politely. There was a slight shake in his voice. "Rose, if you would be so kind?"

He held out the handle of the wagon. She took it, not sure why he wanted to switch places. "You want me to carry Virgil's wagon inside?"

"Oh, no," Henry said with a gleam in his eyes, and she realized he was trying very hard to keep a straight face. "I can't imagine two fit-throwing infants in there would be helpful right now."

"No," Bessie said, wild-eyed. "No, no! Take him away!"

Rose could barely contain a straight face herself. Imagine Bessie asking her to leave!

She couldn't possibly be more delighted to surrender this hatching to Henry.

"Very well," Rose said demurely.

The wild-eyed harridan who bore little resemblance to the haughty gentlewoman who had plagued Rose over the past weeks stormed inside the house, ranting and yelling and howling about how terrible parenthood was, and why hadn't anybody ever told her that dragons were as bad as normal babies?!

The door slammed, and Rose waited until she was sure the woman was well out of earshot.

Then she doubled over and laughed and laughed and laughed.

AUTHOR NOTE

Alice and Willie are my favorite characters in this story. Gentle people tend to be overlooked, even though they are often the most important. Most of the finest people in the world are quiet and meek.

DRAGON'S FIRST VALENTINE

Chapter 1: Vexed

ROSE WOKE up to the unmistakable sound of someone trying to be quiet.

"No no no no. No no no no. No no no no. No no no no—"

There was an earsplitting shriek.

Rose flung the blankets off her legs and stormed to the door of their bedroom, feeling rather vexed. She had asked to be permitted to sleep in this morning, seeing as it was Saturday and Henry's first class did not begin until eleven o'clock, but it seemed that was not to be. Why had Henry permitted the baby to get so close to the door where she was sleeping?

"Your mother's asleep," Henry's voice whispered in a frantic undertone from the other side of the door. "We can't disturb her. Just—"

Rose flung the door open.

Henry froze from a crouched position in the hallway.

Looking past him, Rose saw that there were flower petals scattered all down the length, and Virgil was currently rolling around in them. The baby dragon tried to shake a red flower petal off his vicious back claw, somersaulted into a sprawl, looked back, found it still stuck there, and let out another furious scream.

"I see he's managed to make a mess," Rose said dryly. "Where did he even find those?"

"He was supposed to be helping," Henry said sheepishly. He leapt to his feet and spread his arms. "Happy birthday!"

Rose blinked and looked down more closely. She supposed she could see how, if there had not been a baby dragon frolicking in them, those flower petals might have seemed romantic rather than looking like a florist's trash had been knocked over.

A better birthday present would have been an extra hour of sleep, Rose thought, exasperated.

But she knew her husband was not as practically-minded as she was. It was just like him to want to make a silly gesture like this. And she could appreciate the thought behind it.

"Thank you," Rose said. "What a nice present."

"Oh, that's not all," Henry said, bursting with pride. "Come into the living room!"

With some misgivings, Rose picked up Virgil and followed her husband down the hallway. The little dragon wiggled and complained and commented telepathically about the red thing stuck on his back claw that wouldn't come off and it was stuck and he wanted to breathe fire at it but he didn't have fire in his tummy right now!

Rose paid him no heed. She was too frozen with horror at the sight before her.

Twenty vases.

Twelve flowers in each vase.

There were twenty *dozen* roses.

"How—?" Rose asked, her voice rising in a panicked squeak.

"I bought them," Henry said proudly. "See, your name's Rose, and it's your twentieth birthday—"

"It's two days to Valentine's Day!" Rose cried, hyperventilating. "Why would you not ask me before making such an extravagant purchase? Why would you purchase twenty dozen flowers at the most expensive time of the year? Why would you purchase twenty dozen flowers *anyway?!*"

Henry looked hurt. "It was a present—"

"This is not a present!" Rose exclaimed. "This is *bankruptcy!*"

Henry's face turned bright red. "I was just trying to be thoughtful!"

"Then *think* about things! Just because I'm balancing the budget now doesn't mean it's not a good idea to look at the book once in awhile!"

"We're not *that* poor!" Henry exclaimed.

"How would you know?! You're terrible at sums!"

She knew at once that it was the wrong thing to say.

Her husband spun around, flung open the door to the apartment, and stalked out, slamming the door behind him.

Rose flopped onto the couch, trying to put her head in her hands. Since their dragon son was still in her arms, he made a spiny, wiggly barrier.

Why was Virgil's mother upset? Virgil's father thought the red things were pretty.

"They are pretty," Rose mumbled, moving the baby dragon onto her lap and successfully depositing her forehead into her hands this time. "They're also completely impractical. Why couldn't he have bought me a new saucepan or something?"

Virgil's father liked pretty things. Virgil's father never thought they had enough pretty things. Virgil's father had been excited about buying Virgil's mother the present. Virgil had gone with his father. It had been fun! He'd only broken one of the vases while they were there.

Rose sighed heavily.

She'd handled it wrong. She knew she had. It really had been a thoughtful gesture. She had no doubt that if she did something this ridiculous to celebrate his birthday, he would be thrilled.

But she *couldn't* do something this ridiculous. That was the whole point. Their monetary situation was tight enough as it was. Keeping Virgil fed was a constant struggle, given that their dragon son ate more and more every month and still adamantly refused to try anything less expensive than chicken, such as pork or even the cheapest cuts of beef. He was even starting to object to having eggs mixed in with his chicken, since he preferred the meat.

Rose would *not* allow their picky eater to win that battle, thanks very much.

It would be very helpful if their son were capable of eating plants, but *Deinonychus antirrhopus* was a carnivorous species, so there was nothing that could be done about that. It was hard not to resent her son's diet when she and Henry had not bought any meat for themselves in over a month, however.

And now this! Why had Henry thought this present was a good idea? Why?

Virgil vigorously kicked his back foot, and Rose narrowly escaped having the wicked hooked claw slice at her elbow.

He wanted the thing off now! Off! Off! Off! Off!

Rose carefully removed the rose petal from around her son's hooked claw, a rather difficult feat to accomplish without being speared, given that he kept on kicking with it.

The front door opened, and Henry reappeared.

"Henry!" Rose said with relief. "I apologize that I—"

"No," Henry said in a low voice. He squared his shoulders and looked up. "I was thinking about what *I* wanted, not what *you* wanted. I ... should've thought more. I'll see if the florist will let me return them."

Rose swallowed. The thought filled her with relief, and that made her feel guilty. Henry had probably been really excited about this gift. "It *was* a thoughtful present—"

"No, it was a stupid present, just as you said," he shot back flatly. "I should've bought you a book about dragon bones, or something."

That would have been a lovely gift, yes. Rose bit her lip, wishing she could think of an honest way to contradict him.

Henry gathered up the vases of flowers, two at a time, and took them outside. It took him ten trips. Then he got the wooden wagon out of the hall closet and took it outside, as well.

Rose got up from the couch and followed him out of the apartment. He was now walking up and down the stairs carrying the wagon, then a few vases, then the wagon, then a few more vases from one landing to another.

He must have done this all the way up, she realized. *And carrying Virgil, as well. How much effort did he put forth?*

"Would you like help?" Rose asked.

"No, thank you."

"But I'd be happy to—"

"It's your birthday," Henry said stubbornly. "It's my mess. I'll fix it."

Rose headed back into the apartment, where she found Virgil had already crawled into his bucket, and was now happily rolling around the room and whamming into the wall over and over again.

Slam! Slam! Slam! Slam!

She sighed heavily.

"Happy birthday," she murmured.

Chapter 2: Voracious

Fixing breakfast, Rose went to dispose of the eggshells and discovered a dozen rose stems in the trash. She pulled them out and looked at them, then walked over to the hallway, where—sure enough—she counted enough rose petals to have come from twelve beheaded roses.

Rose sighed heavily. *So he can't return all of them. He had already deconstructed a dozen he'd bought for that purpose.*

Still—a single dozen was not going to ruin them. And there was nothing that could be done.

Behind her, Virgil let out a gale of amusement at having discovered a new game of pick-up-a-rose-petal-with-his-teeth-and-blow-it-out-in-the-air.

By the time Henry got back home, Rose had prepared a breakfast of pancakes for both of them, and Virgil was halfway through his raw eggs mixed with water and chicken.

Henry came through the door with the wagon under his arm. There were no roses or vases present, which was a relief.

"Good morning," Rose said. She did not mention the rose petals, which she had gathered into a bowl on the top of their dresser. She would, perhaps, make potpourri from them later.

"Good morning," Henry said, depositing the wagon into the hall closet. He did not mention the rose petals, either.

Rose was dying to ask if the florist had taken the flowers back and returned their money, but she didn't see how she could do so without seeming overly eager for the disposal of her birthday present, so she kept her silence.

Henry sat down at the table and stared wistfully at the stack of pancakes on a plate by the stove, his eyes communicating that he didn't know whether he was allowed to eat them.

Taking the hint, Rose smiled and took the plate over to him. Looking relieved, he eagerly helped himself.

"I've already had mine," Rose said. "I hope you don't mind."

"Why would I mind?" Henry asked between bites. "It's your birthday. You can do whatever you want."

She was still dying to ask about the florist and whether they had gotten all of their money back, but she didn't want to spoil the congenial atmosphere. They must have gotten it all back, mustn't they? Surely they had.

She didn't want to make demands of Henry when his ego was no doubt fragile. Doing that would be—

Virgil had eaten his food! Virgil wanted more food! More food, more food, more food!

Rose glanced over to see that Virgil had made his way across the room in a flash, and was now trying to claw his way up to Henry's lap.

The attempt was, of course, piercing tiny holes all over the pant legs. But the one bright side of this was that no one would be able to distinguish them from the many other tiny holes Virgil had left before. There was a reason Henry did not wear his nicest clothing around the house. Neither did Rose.

"Of course you do, you exasperating boy," Henry said, picking the little dragon up. "One might say that's the source of all our problems."

Virgil nuzzled his father with his snout. He liked food. Could he have food again? He wanted chicken all by itself this time. He liked chicken the best. He wanted chicken, chicken, chicken, all by itself.

"No," Rose said. "Don't pretend to be voracious."

Virgil pointedly ignored this, emanating pitiful memories of hunger as he curled his tail around his father's wrist. Could he have chicken, chicken, chicken? He was still hungry. He was still very hungry. His father didn't want him to starve, did he?

"Well ..." Henry hesitated. "I mean, if he's still hungry ..."

"Hey, Virgil," Rose said, picking up a slice of pancake from off his father's plate. "You can have chicken if you eat this first."

The little dragon exploded off his father's lap and raced into the other room.

No yucky! No yucky yucky! Virgil wouldn't eat yucky food! Virgil wasn't hungry!

"Are you sure he *isn't* hungry, though?" Henry asked.

"If he were hungry, he would have finished off the food in his bowl," Rose said dryly, picking up their son's food bowl and displaying the interior. The boy had polished off every scrap of chicken, but there were still gooey patches of egg. "He also would have been a lot less cute and manipulative."

Henry laughed. "Okay. He got me."

"Honestly," Rose said with exasperation, covering the food bowl with its lid and placing it in the icebox, so that she could get the boy to finish the eggs later. "We've got to find something less expensive that he's willing to eat."

"You could ask the Lawrences what they're feeding Ophelia," Henry said. "She's clearly healthy, and I suspect they have less money than we do."

Rose hesitated. While Alice and Willie seemed like very nice people, she hadn't really made their acquaintance well enough to show up at their home unannounced. Not to mention that ... well ... she was white and they were colored, and she wasn't sure if there were rules against her doing such a thing.

"We could call Mr. Teedle and ask if they have a phone," Henry said.

"Yes! A phone!" Rose said with relief. Surely there could be no rules of propriety against that. And then, if they invited her to come over to visit, she would graciously accept and know that it was acceptable by any relevant social rules.

A phone. Of course, a phone. Why had she not thought of that herself?

"You're brilliant," she informed Henry.

He snorted. "I think I've shown today that I am certainly not."

"Making mistakes doesn't make one not capable of brilliance," Rose said. She hesitated. "Did the florist take the flowers back?"

"Yes. Although he said he wouldn't have if it were Easter." Henry gave her a tentative and sheepish smile. "Apparently that's their largest holiday of the year."

"Then let us not buy flowers around Easter," Rose said.

"So, what *do* you want to do to celebrate Valentine's Day?" Henry blurted out. "I was thinking the flowers would be part of that celebration, too. That's why it seemed so perfect. I want us to do something special. It's our first one together, after all."

Rose blinked. "I ... I don't know."

Why did it matter so much to him? It really wasn't that important a holiday, unlike Christmas or Easter.

"I've never known my parents to celebrate Valentine's Day," she went on. "A wedding anniversary is more important."

"That's just it!" Henry cried. "Our wedding anniversary is on the same day as Virgil's birthday! If we want to have a day that's just about us, it has to be Valentine's Day!"

Ah. He did have a point, she supposed.

"We could always choose a different day to celebrate," she pointed out. "Like the day we met, for instance, or the day you proposed to me—"

"Those were both the same day, and it was also the day we met Virgil!" Henry said. "I don't want our relationship to be all about Virgil!"

Small chance of that, given that Virgil is the reason we got married in the first place, Rose thought tartly, but that didn't seem to be the answer Henry wanted right now.

"I will think about it," Rose said carefully. "Perhaps we can ask my parents to watch Virgil, and we can go out to the theater or something."

"And spend more money?" Henry asked gloomily.

"For a special occasion, and an expense we both agree to, yes."

Henry didn't look very excited by the prospect.

"Or my parents could watch Virgil for the night."

"How would that be any different from normal?" Henry complained. "It's not like we don't have time together when he's asleep. It's just ... the flowers were what was going to make it special!"

Rose was starting to feel rather exasperated. *Apparently I should buy him flowers for his birthday.*

She made a mental note to write that down. It might actually be a good idea.

Not twenty dozen, though, for crying out loud.

"Well, what do you want to do?" Rose asked in a sensible tone. "We can do whatever you like."

"I want to do what *you* want to do," Henry said stubbornly.

So now she was expected to come up with something that she personally wanted to do that Henry would consider romantic enough for an outing on Valentine's Day? Something other than ignoring the event altogether?

Rose wanted to throw up her hands at the impossible assignment. Why couldn't he settle for her merely being willing to humor him and tolerate whatever he wanted to do?

Virgil snuck back into the kitchen, his eyes gleaming.

He spotted the source of his food. If he could butcher it, it would reveal its yummy innards to him.

"It's not prey," Rose said dryly. "You can't kill it."

Virgil could try!

The tiny dragon launched himself at the icebox, trying desperately to slaughter it.

Henry doubled over laughing.

Chapter 3: Variety

One would think one's birthday would be a special time, different from any ordinary day. But once Henry had left for his eleven o'clock class, Rose found herself entrenched back in her usual Tuesday, Thursday, and Saturday routine.

Washing the breakfast dishes. Changing Virgil's diaper. Studying her textbook. Changing Virgil's diaper. Ignoring his not-so-subtle hints that he wanted chicken without egg as a snack before lunch. Changing Virgil's diaper.

Making sure he breathed fire in the bathroom, rather than all over the couch. Changing Virgil's diaper. Stopping him from shredding a stinky diaper. Changing Virgil's diaper. Washing the stack of diapers from the day so far so that they would have more clean ones. Changing Virgil's diaper.

"Maybe we should start to potty-train you," Rose said dryly.

Virgil looked up from having the sides of the cloth pinned across his hindquarters. He didn't understand what that meant.

"It means teaching you to use the toilet, not a diaper."

Virgil didn't understand what that meant.

Rose pictured the bathroom and imagined Virgil making use of the facilities in a way she desperately wished the boy would learn soon.

Virgil let out a shrill squeal and raced into the bedroom and scrambled under the bed. No! No, no! He wouldn't do that! He would hide way out of his mother's reach!

He didn't seem to notice that his tail was sticking out by over a foot.

"For crying out loud," Rose said in exasperation, reaching under there and tugging him out, gently, by a back foot. She was tempted to use the tail, but she wasn't sure if that was more fragile than the rest of him. The back foot, though, she knew from experience, was strong enough to be fine to drag him out with. "You're going to have to learn eventually."

No! The big white hole was scary! It made noises and things fell into it and never came out again!

"Yes," Rose said. "That is the point."

No! Nooooooo! Virgil wouldn't do it! Virgil wouldn't ever, ever do it!

"You most certainly will," Rose said waspishly.

Virgil was being dragged out from under the bed! Virgil hated it! Virgil wanted to hide! Virgil was going to kick his mother with his hooked claws!

Rose dodged the assault, just barely. The vicious attack only made her more peeved.

"If you do that again, you're going to be in time-out in the bathtub for the rest of the day," she snapped. "It is not fine to attack me. That could hurt me badly. My skin is more vulnerable than your scales. Do you understand?"

Virgil didn't understand and Virgil wasn't happy and Virgil's mother was mean and Virgil's father was nice and Virgil didn't want to go in the white box! The white box was boring!

"And yet, I remain unmoved," Rose said coldly.

Virgil let out an earsplitting shriek, and she covered her ears to protect her hearing. Above them, she thought she heard a neighbor pounding loudly on their ceiling. There was an odd tenor to the scream this time, as if a phone were simultaneously ringing. Had Virgil developed a new pitch? If so, that was going to be quite annoying ...

Wait—the phone *was* ringing!

Rose leapt up, hands still over her ears, and dashed to the kitchen. Removing her hands from her ears, she answered the phone before the ringing stopped.

"Hello? Wainscott residence?" she said, panting.

"Hello, Miss Palmer," an old friend said warmly. "Er—Mrs. Wainscott. How are you this morning?"

"About as well as could be expected," Rose said politely, which was not precisely a lie. Virgil was all too often as poorly behaved as this. "Henry and I were just talking about calling you, Mr. Teedle. How is your day?"

"Oh, quite well, quite well," he said. "We have a visitor at the museum who is asking about you today."

"Really?" Rose asked, her eyebrows rising. She could not imagine who that might be. She was hardly famous. While she was going to become a paleontologist once she completed her education, she was currently only beginning her bachelor's degree, with a major in geology. It would be many years before she would be trusted to handle real fossils in a laboratory setting. Given that, who in the field knew her name?

"Yes. His name is Mr. Miller. He's from Chicago. He has a daughter who hatched out of the Field Museum of Natural History. He thought it would be nice for him and his daughter to meet you and your son. He would have liked to have met your husband too, but I remembered that he's busy at school on this day of the week."

Rose's heart fell like a stone. Of course it was about Virgil. Everything was about Virgil. Nobody ever found her interesting all by herself.

"How nice," she said, hoping she successfully sounded as if she meant it. "Would he like to arrange a meeting with the other baby dragons, as well?"

"Oh, he's already met Ophelia," Mr. Teedle said. "He and his daughter went to see her vaudeville performance last night. That was why they came into town. And they've already visited Violet at the zoo. I'm afraid the Baileys weren't at home when they called, or so their maid informed them."

So that makes Virgil their fourth choice?

Rose tried not to be offended. It was true that two of the four baby dragons in New York were now minor celebrities, while the Baileys were public figures due to their wealth, so it made sense that she and Henry would be the least interesting choice to a visitor from out of town.

Still. Virgil had been the first dragon to hatch in their city. That should mean something.

"... be able to arrange a meeting today, before he goes back home tomorrow?" Mr. Teedle was saying.

Rose drew in a deep breath. She would be a fool to say no. She was legitimately interested in meeting every dragon in the country. Besides, it would be something to make her birthday a unique day, even if the situation was all about Virgil.

"Yes, I would be happy to bring Virgil to meet with them," Rose said. "We have several hours available right now. When and where should we meet?"

There was a murmur of voices. It seemed the man was right there, and Mr. Teedle was conferring with him.

"How about the northwest corner of Central Park?" Mr. Teedle said at last. "It is reasonably centrally located between where you live and where he is now, so it will take you both only about half an hour to walk there. The children will have space to run around and play in the grass, too."

And hopefully not burn down the trees, Rose thought, but she didn't raise the objection. It would probably be fine.

"I will get Virgil ready and depart in just a few minutes," Rose said. "I look forward to meeting Mr. Miller and his daughter. How old is she, anyway?" she added curiously.

"Almost three months," Mr. Teedle said.

So she would be at about the size Virgil had been during Christmas, and not a fragile newborn who could not even roll over successfully. That was good.

"I'll see him there in half an hour, then," Rose said. "I'm sure we'll have no trouble finding each other, seeing as there will be no other infant dragons around. Oh, what is his daughter's—"

A terrible odor reached her nose. She looked through the doorway to see Virgil rolling across the floor of the living room, diaper sagging, one side of it shredded by a vicious back claw, trailing an officious disaster on the carpet behind him.

As she stared in horror, he rolled backwards right over the catastrophe.

"Fifteen minutes! We'll leave in fifteen minutes!" Rose cried in horror and slammed the phone into its cradle. Then she bolted to the living room to seize her son before he could make the nightmare any worse.

Holding the boy out at an arm's length, she raced for the bathroom, where she commenced to give a screaming dragon a bath that he did not want for a reason she enjoyed even less. Naturally, the neighbor above added to the stress by pounding on his floor, their ceiling, again.

The more she thought about it, the more glad she was that they would be departing the apartment soon. At least it would give this dreadful-so-far day some variety.

Chapter 4: Verdant

It took twice as long as she expected before they left, due to Virgil's mess being even more disgusting and laborious to clean up than she had realized.

Still, within half an hour, she had him clean and the carpet recovered, save for some stains she could not seem to fix. Once they left, she rushed down the sidewalk on the way to Central Park as swiftly as possible, humiliatingly aware that she was already late.

The wooden wagon she was pulling behind her attracted far more attention than the pram had, due to Virgil being far more visible and far more difficult to cover with a blanket. Virgil seemed amused by all the extra attention, making lots of comments to all the people who passed and stared at him with their mouths agape.

Yes, I realize Virgil is fascinating, Rose thought grumpily, refusing to stop to converse with several passersby who called out questions to her. *But I am not subject to your beck and call just because you are curious about him.*

Reaching the northwest corner of Central Park, she soon discovered there was a crowd gathered, gasping and chattering excitedly over something.

With a sinking heart, Rose realized what was going on. It was the same phenomenon that she had just experienced while walking here. Of course anyone walking by would stop to watch an adorable dragon frolicking on the grass. By meeting out in public, they had made plans to provide a public circus.

Unfortunately, there was very little they could do about it at this point. To ask people to leave would be rude. Besides, she doubted it would do any good. More curious onlookers would only gather in their place.

Rose picked up Virgil, likewise collected the bulky wagon, tucked each determinedly under one arm, and shoved her way through the crowd to reach the center of it.

Sure enough, in a grassy spot beside the sidewalk, a man sat beside an unfamiliar dragon who was rolling around on the grass. Surprisingly, the other dragon was almost the same color as Virgil, just a little brighter—a verdant green.

The unfamiliar emerald-colored dragon was eyeing a stem of dead grass, drifting back and forth in a breeze, and then she suddenly sprang forward to catch it, capturing the dead grass prey in her mouth.

She spat it out a second later, and she probably made some sort of telepathic comment, because the people near the front of the crowd laughed.

"Hello!" the man standing behind her cried, spying Rose with her son tucked under one arm and the bulky wagon under the other. He stood up and strode over to her, holding out his hand to shake. "I'm James Miller. And you're Rose Wainscott, I believe?"

Rose set down the bulky wagon, shifted Virgil to her left arm, and shook his hand with her right. "Yes, I am. I'm pleased to meet you, Mr. Miller. This is Virgil."

"He's almost the same color as Cucumber!" Mr. Miller said in delight. He reached out and patted Virgil across the back. "We don't have any other green dragons in Chicago. Just red and purple."

"How many do you have now?" Rose asked.

"Three. Out of the eight eggs in the Field Museum. The third one just barely hatched. Our daughter was the second."

"And you said her name, was, uh ...?" Rose prompted, unable to believe she had heard him correctly before.

"Cucumber," he said. "Cukie for short. Because she's green, you know."

Rose wanted to cover her face with her hands. What kind of name was that for a child? Why would anyone name their daughter such a thing?

"The other two back home are named Rosie and Plum," the man added.

"Rosie is red and Plum is purple," Rose said flatly.

Mr. Miller looked surprised. "How did you know?"

Rose tried hard not to give him an incredulous look.

So it was becoming a tradition in Chicago to name dragons after their scale color, was it? She supposed it was better than naming them things like Claws or Spiny, but only just. Hopefully the next dragon to hatch there would have parents with the good sense to break from that ridiculous tradition.

"Well, would you like to play with ... Cucumber, Virgil?" she asked, setting her son down on the grass relatively near the other dragon. "She's just a little younger than Violet's age, so you can play the same games you play with Violet."

Virgil completely ignored this invitation. He turned his back on the other dragon and started digging at the dead grass, which was for once not covered with frost or snow, it being an unseasonably warm day. At least the insects had not started to come out of hiding yet.

Virgil raised his head in interest. What were those little things Virgil's mother was thinking about? Were they edible?

Rose was distracted for a moment by the intriguing idea that Virgil's question posed. *Could* he eat insects? Would those do to supplement his diet?

But then she remembered their early experiment with feeding him a cricket. It had not agreed with him, and she had no desire to ever again have to clean up dragon vomit.

"Don't eat them," Rose said quickly. "Virgil, come over here and meet Cucumber. She's a new dragon you've never met before who's close to your age."

Virgil turned a deaf ear to this invitation.

Meanwhile, Mr. Miller was trying unsuccessfully to cajole his uncooperative daughter to do the same thing.

"Virgil, Cukie," he was saying. "Go play with Virgil. He's the little dragon over there. Come on, you loved playing with Violet and Ophy. What's the problem here?"

Cucumber continued to ignore him.

Exasperated, Rose picked up Virgil and hauled him over, depositing him right next to Cucumber.

That got a reaction.

Icky! Icky, icky, icky! Cucumber couldn't play with him! He was *green!*

Yucky! Yucky, yucky, yucky! That girl was green! Green, green, green, green!

"What in the world?" Rose said in bafflement. "You're green!"

Yes! Virgil was green! GREEN! GREEN!

As if Virgil's panic was catching, Cucumber let out a loud shriek, causing the members of the crowd to gasp, hold their hands over their ears, and in some cases actually run away.

If only, Rose reflected, they could induce the rest of the crowd to leave without resorting to such a thing.

Cucumber's panic was now at an even higher pitch than Virgil's.

GREEN! GREEN! He was a boy, and he was GREEN!

Virgil backed away, emanating the same horror. GREEN! She was a girl, and she was GREEN!

"What in the world is wrong with you two?" Rose exclaimed. "You're both green!"

GREEN! GREEN GREEN GREEN!

Both the dragons were scrambling away from each other and flashing memories of the same color in absolute horror.

"What ...?" Mr. Miller said in bewilderment.

Green GIRL!

Green BOY!

GREEN GREEN GREEN!

Rose's mouth fell open. She had an odd suspicion ...

"Virgil," she said rapidly, "if Cucumber were a boy, would that be a problem?"

Green boys weren't yucky! Only green girls were!

Wrong! Green girls weren't icky! Only green boys were!

"*What?*" Mr. Miller exclaimed.

"Inbreeding!" Rose cried, clapping her hands.

What delightful serendipity this had turned out to be, having her son meet a female dragon who was the same color as him. She would never have seen this in action without such a bizarre happening. She would never have even guessed that such a behavior existed!

"Inbreeding!" Rose cried, clapping her hands again. "It's an instinct to discourage inbreeding! I've wondered why there were so many different colors of the same species living within a tiny geographic area! Now we have our answer!"

"*What?!*" Mr. Miller looked completely baffled.

Rose grinned, feeling a thrill of discovery. She had figured something out that perhaps no one else had had the opportunity to infer yet. This was a birthday present indeed!

Chapter 5: Victim

Green dragons separated from each other and scrambled across the grass. Once they were a comfortable distance of at least five feet away, the two infant dragons recommenced ignoring one another.

"What are you talking about?" the man asked.

"Oh." Rose blinked. "I assume you know that natural selection favors a diversity of traits within a species."

The man had a blank look.

"It's important to have varied traits within a population of a species so that it stays evolutionarily flexible."

This did not seem to enlighten the man.

"Humans have a taboo against inbreeding, which is the reason we don't usually marry siblings," Rose explained. "I should have realized dragons had an instinct like this. In one of Violet's mother's memories, she was thinking that the male she was chasing after was purple and thus a different color from her own blue, showing that they weren't closely related. So *Deinonychus* dragons must have an instinct to avoid potential mates who are the same color!"

"But they're *babies!*" Mr. Miller exclaimed.

"What has that to do with it?"

"Babies don't have potential mates!"

This man did not seem to understand how biology worked.

"Babies grow into adults eventually," Rose said. "If they have a deep-rooted instinct from infancy to not even befriend a member of the opposite gender with the same color, that would be effective to prevent any friendships forming that might develop into romantic attachments later."

"But they're *babies!*"

This man seemed to be a little dim.

"The instinct wouldn't cause problems with infants surviving, so there's no reason it shouldn't be present now."

"But it would cause problems!" Mr. Miller insisted. "What about parents and children? They'd be closely related and often the same color!"

Rose pondered that. "I'd have to assume the instinct only applies to individuals close to one's own age," she said at last.

"What about brothers and sisters?" Mr. Miller shot back. "Children have to be able to get along with their siblings!"

"Really? Why?" Rose asked coolly. "There's no reason to assume that is an evolutionary necessity. Besides, look at them."

Virgil was now busily digging up dirt with his claws, while Cucumber was preparing to pounce on another clump of dead grass, to the great amusement of the crowd around them.

"They're ignoring one another. They only became aggressive about their aversion to each other when forced together. Dragon parents would know better than to do such a thing. Thus, the instinct would not cause any particular problems with the survival of one's family members."

Another idea occurred to her.

"In addition, remember that this instinct would mean virtually all dragon parents would be different colors from each other. Thus, the chances of their children being different colors from each other would be quite high. When you add to this the fact that they apparently would not feel discomfort in being near a member of the same gender and same color, this means the chances of potential conflict between siblings are probably no higher than one-in-four."

"One-in-four!"

"That's not high enough to be a problem."

"One-in-four isn't high enough?!"

"Not really, evolutionarily speaking," Rose said. "Especially since the instinct doesn't even seem to incite them to violence. I imagine any disadvantages were outweighed by the advantages, which was why the instinct survived."

Rose stared at her son, fascinated, as the man murmured under his breath.

What could she do to test this hypothesis? She could pick up Virgil and bring him closer to Cucumber by increments, to see how close a range it took to set off their mutual alarm. Perhaps if they were forced to touch each other, it might actually result in violence—that would be another hypothesis worth testing. Really, this was quite a strange and captivating instinct, in so many ways the opposite of humanity.

Rose moved forward to pick up her son—

She stopped abruptly.

Her son.

Virgil was *her son.*

What kind of person thought it would be fascinating to test if they could get two infants to attack each other?

What kind of parent was she?

Rose backed away, clenching her fists. Her inadequacy as a parent was appalling. Did she lack even the most basic scraps of decency?

"Come on, Cucumber," Mr. Miller said, stooping to pick up his daughter. "You can get over this. You can make friends—"

GREEN! GREEN GREEN GREEN!

Rose sighed. The other parent present, it seemed, was just an idiot.

But really, this was a frustrating position to be in. She itched to study this hypothesis and find out if it was correct. At the very least, she wanted to sit down with a baby dragon and interview them exhaustively about every possible facet of *Deinonychus* society.

She couldn't do that with Virgil, because she had promised herself she would never look at him as a subject to scrutinize and study. And with good reason, apparently.

She couldn't do that with Violet, because the blue dragon who lived in the zoo had answered human questions about her society so often that her memories had become completely corrupted by imagination and interpretation.

She couldn't do that with Philomel, because she could not bring herself to want to spend one minute in the presence of his mother that she did not have to.

She couldn't do that with Ophelia, because … well, perhaps she *could* do that with Ophelia, but only if she overcame her overwhelming awkwardness at the thought of trying to make her parents' further acquaintance.

But *this* dragon … this dragon named Cucumber, such a terrible name …

Rose's eyes fell on the infant whose father was trying unsuccessfully to convince her to play with the green little boy she was studiously ignoring.

Cucumber did not live in New York City. She would not be one of Virgil's playmates. Rose did not have to be worried what this dragon's father would think of her, because she would most likely never see him again.

So she could be bold. What was the worst that he could say to her? No?

Rose drew in a deep breath. "Mr. Miller, would you allow me to interview Cucumber about her memories of dragon society? She might remember things that my son does not. If you want to, you could talk to Virgil about the same thing."

"Oh, I've already interviewed Cukie pretty thoroughly about her memories before she woke up back home," the man said matter-of-factly. "I've written it all down, too. I don't think there's much I don't know. But then again, *this* surprised me …"

He gestured at his daughter, who was desperately trying to wriggle out of his arms and away from Virgil, who was stepping on crumbling brown leaves and ignoring her.

"So maybe you'll think to ask some questions I haven't, and learn some things

I don't know. As long as you write everything down and give me a copy, that sounds good to me. The first time she remembers something new, it needs be recorded, of course."

Rose's voice failed her.

Of course.

He had said that as if it were obvious.

And now that she thought about it, it was.

Of course it was obvious that a dragon's uncorrupted memories of their original family should be preserved as early as possible. Of course it was an evident necessity to record every detail of *Deinonychus antirrhopus* society before the memories of that were influenced by living among humans.

Every clue was a piece of a fragile puzzle that would swiftly degrade. And yet, she had not recorded even one of Virgil's memories in writing. It had not even crossed her mind.

It was as if she had discovered a priceless treasure, a bone of some never-before-seen species, and then dug it up with a careless shovel, leaving the edges irreparably damaged.

This man was not an idiot, as she had supposed. *She* was the fool.

What memories Virgil had forgotten or altered by now could never be regained. Every memory of his time before humans had been affected by his life now and transmuted into a different state. She knew that. She had seen it happening.

The only way to capture her son's memories in a pure state was to write them down. The transmission of telepathic memory was no more than an oral tradition, fragile and easily mutated.

Virgil was the victim of her own foolishness. Of her ability to know and not *see.*

"Of course I will record whatever she says," Rose said, finding her voice at last. "And will you also do the same for me?"

Her son must not be a victim of her blindness any longer. Not now that her eyes were open to what she should have been doing in the first place.

Chapter 6: Vindicated

Before anything else, it was necessary that they escape from the swarming crowd and find a place to interview the children with a modicum more privacy. One obvious place that sprang to mind was the Research Library at the American Museum of Natural History, which was open to the public and yet not a place large quantities of crowds tended to gather in. In a way, it was even appropriate, since research about dragons was precisely what Rose wanted to do.

She picked up her son, who protested vigorously about having to leave his dirt, and placed him in the wagon.

"Are you sure they'll want small children there?" Mr. Miller asked when Rose voiced her plan for their relocation.

Rose paused. Fire-breathing infants would probably not be considered the ideal patrons of the Research Library, no.

"We can ask Mr. Teedle to lend us his office," she decided. "Or some other private room. I'm sure he would be happy to oblige."

"Oh, yes, he's a nice man," Mr. Miller said, nodding. "I asked him what to do when Cukie has nightmares, and he told me about what worked with his daughters."

"Does Cucumber have nocturnal terrors, too?" Rose asked with avid interest. "Violet, the blue dragon, does."

"All the dragons do, don't they?" Mr. Miller said, picking up his daughter, who thrashed, trying to escape back to the ground. "They all remember losing their original parents."

Rose was silent. Her son did not suffer from bad dreams. He was a pretty sound sleeper. It had not occurred to her that that was one way in which she and Henry were blessed. And Virgil, of course, because not suffering from panic on a regular basis like Violet did was certainly a privilege for him.

"Do Rosie and Plum suffer from nightmares, too?" she asked, as the two commenced walking down the sidewalk.

The crowd, more's the pity, surged after them. A few unwanted gawkers and bystanders took the hint and wandered away, but most continued to stroll after, giggling as Virgil tried to roll over backwards inside the wagon, a feat he had never accomplished even in less limited space, and then made commentary on how it would be easier if his tail didn't keep getting in the way.

The crowd seemed greatly amused by this, and there were many giggles at his persistence as he attempted to do it again.

"Rosie, yes," Mr. Miller said. "Plum, sometimes. Not so often. Plum has other issues Dr. McGrath has to help with. Poor kid; she thinks he might have something similar to diabetes. He's not a very healthy dragon."

Rose was startled. "Is Dr. McGrath ... a woman?"

She'd heard of female doctors, but she had never actually met one.

Mr. Miller laughed. "I said the same thing when I met her! She told me she's one of the first ... what ... five female veterinarians in the country? Anyway, she specializes in small animals rather than horses, unlike most veterinarians, so she's pretty much the local expert on dragons these days."

Rose felt a stab of intense envy. Imagine living in the same city as a woman like that! What conversations she could have with such a remarkable person!

Cucumber suddenly hissed and stabbed her father in the arm with her claw.

"Ouch!" he shouted. "Cukie!"

Cucumber was bored! Cucumber wanted to get down and play some more! Cucumber wanted to get down, or she would claw her father again!

Mr. Miller quickly moved to dump her in the wagon.

"No! Wait—" Rose cried.

GREEN! GREEN GREEN GREEN GREEN!

Two infant dragons scrambled for the edges of the wagon, trying desperately to climb out. Cucumber bashed her head against the sides in fruitless attempts. Virgil actually succeeded, tumbling headlong over the side. Rose barely caught him in time to protect his cranium from crashing into the pavement.

"Virgil!" Rose said in exasperation. Her young son figuring out how to escape his wagon at a moment's notice was not a milestone she had eagerly anticipated.

Virgil looked up at her with pitiful eyes. But *green.*

Rose sighed and put a hand to her forehead.

"Cukie, let's get out of their wagon now," Mr. Miller cajoled, reaching for his daughter.

The female dragon swiped at her father's fingers.

No! She wanted to stay here! This was an interesting place!

"I see she is in the mood to be disobliging," Rose said dryly.

"I'm sorry," Mr. Miller sighed, adjusting his hat wearily. It was a rather worn fedora that had small holes and loose threads all over. Rose rather suspected it had been clawed by his daughter. "She gets in moods like this."

"I am familiar with the dangers of a petulant child when one does not have scales to protect oneself from their claws," Rose assured him. "Why don't I carry Virgil, and you pull the wagon? Your daughter can use it for now."

"Sorry," Mr. Miller apologized again, reaching out and taking the handle from her. "I'd refuse, but ..."

"But sometimes one must choose one's battles," Rose said. "I understand. I even concur, in this instance."

Mr. Miller started walking again, and Rose continued at his pace. They were moving more briskly now that he was the one pulling the heavy wagon, rather than her.

Cucumber let out an exultant monologue about how she had gotten the box that moved and now it was hers and now it would be hers forever.

"No, it will *not!*" Mr. Miller snapped.

The crowd tittered.

Rose waited for her son to protest, but Virgil was blithely ignoring the other dragon and all the commentary she was making about how his wagon was now her own possession. He seemed totally absorbed with shredding a crumbling brown leaf that must have blown up to him.

"You can use it for now," Mr. Miller growled, "but you cannot keep it. It belongs to the other dragon."

No, there was no other dragon. It was all Cucumber's.

"He's RIGHT THERE!" Mr. Miller shouted, pointing at Virgil in Rose's arms.

Cucumber was ignoring what her father was pointing at.

Several people near the front of the crowd doubled over and howled.

"Cucumber," her father said through clenched teeth, "you cannot pretend another person doesn't exist just because you find them inconvenient."

Cucumber didn't know what her father was talking about. Cucumber was ignoring the memories her father wanted her to look at. Yes, Cucumber was ignoring them.

She poked her claws into the side of the wagon. There was a piece she could shred off here! Look, it shredded into lots of little bitty slivers! She could shred more of it!

"If you do that again, you're getting out of the wagon," Rose informed her.

The little girl dragon immediately went still. The mean lady meant it. The mean lady thought the moving box was all hers. It wasn't hers. It was Cucumber's.

"It's not, but never mind. It can be yours for right now," Rose said, shaking her head. Virgil was still not complaining. He seemed greatly amused by his leaf, his tail twitching and his back legs mercifully still as he kept examining the brown thing.

Cucumber felt vindicated! This was her box! She had won it! It was hers! She would breathe her name into it!

"No!" Mr. Miller yelped, diving forward to grab his daughter as she reared back to breathe a tongue of flame.

The quiet son in Rose's arms looked down, seeing that the object of dispute was now vacated. Virgil wanted to be in his wagon now. Could he be in his wagon?

But Rose barely registered that. Her mind was humming with a flurry of frenzied activity.

"Breathe her *name?*" she burst out.

Chapter 7: Veracity

"Yes, Cukie does that a lot," Mr. Miller said wearily. "She wants to breathe her name into everything. I wish she'd stop it."

"But ... but ..." Rose gaped at him. "Does that mean dragons have a *written language?* There's been no sign of that from Virgil's memories!"

Whether or not *Deinonychus antirrhopus* had had a written language was one of the greatest mysteries of paleontology. If the answer was now at hand, to ascertain the fact of it was of paramount urgency. It was thought that they reasonably could have had one, as there were stones scorched by dragon fire with scorchings that seemed oddly precise, yet irregular. If that was a writing system ... if dragons had a way of writing ...

If Cucumber could *read* it ...

Rose felt dizzy at the implications. The knowledge that could be gained by gathering as many as possible of those stones and asking a baby dragon to interpret!

"I don't know," Mr. Miller said. "I assumed she made it up. She knows my wife and I are always writing things."

"What if she didn't?!" Rose exclaimed. "Do you understand what that could mean?!"

"That dragons are intelligent. We know that."

Rose gaped at him. How could he not comprehend the implications?

"It could mean that there are *written records!* Lost knowledge that wasn't just stored in an oral tradition! It might be possible to *translate it!*"

The thought of written records that predated the dawn of humanity ... the idea of forgotten history that could be easily uncovered just by asking one who knew how to read it ... the very concept made Rose's knees feel weak.

Yes, newly hatched infants were not ambassadors, and not intended to be emissaries of their species. They had not been sent by design, nor filled specifically with knowledge to act as time capsules for their species. Yet, despite all odds, here they were, awake and alive. And if they could be a key ...

"Oh. Yes." Mr. Miller did not seem to grasp how milieu-shattering this revelation could be. "That would be nice."

"*Nice!*" Rose could scarcely keep her voice at reasonable levels. "Don't you understand the magnitude of how important that could be?!"

Cucumber shoved her head under her father's armpit, squirming tighter against him. She was scared of the mean lady. The mean lady was very scary.

Rose took a deep breath, trying to force herself to calm down. Her heart was racing.

Virgil butted his head against her chest. Could he go in his wagon now? He wanted to go in his wagon. He was behaving.

Her arms were shaking as she moved to put him where he wanted to be. Her mind was whirling. If dragons had a written language, why did Virgil not know about it? Why did none of his memories from his mother contain her breathing fire upon a rock to write something? She had been a studious academic in nature, just like Rose. Surely she would have recorded things in much the same way. So why was there no indication that she had done so?

Of course, there was the possibility that she was simply misunderstanding.

"C-Cucumber," Rose stammered, stumbling over the word. "Can you write your name so that I can see what it looks like?"

"I'm not sure that's the best idea," Mr. Miller said.

Cucumber would breathe her name! Cucumber wanted to breathe her name! Cucumber liked doing it!

"On what?" Mr. Miller demanded. "Not the wagon!"

Cucumber's father was showing memories of something that didn't exist.

"You were claiming ownership of it *one minute ago!*"

Cucumber didn't know what he was talking about. There was a green male in that moving box now, so it didn't exist.

"AHA!"

The crowd guffawed.

Maybe those nosy intruders could make themselves useful. Rose spun around to face them.

"Do you see a rock?" she demanded. "Something rather large, that she could breathe her name on?"

"Here's one!" somebody called from the back.

The crowd moved to let a teenage boy jostle his way through. In his hand he held a loose brick.

It was probably meant to belong to some sidewalk somewhere, but never mind that. This was too important to worry about where it had come from.

"Breathe fire on this," Rose said, drawing next to Mr. Miller and his daughter.

Cucumber reared back her head.

"Your hand!" Mr. Miller exclaimed.

Rose scarcely dropped the brick in time to escape the blast of fire that came from the dragon's mouth. Sweat beaded on the back of her neck as she realized how close she had come to being badly injured.

"Here, Cukie. Breathe your name on the rock from the ground," Mr. Miller said, setting the girl dragon down.

Seeming obliging now, for a change, the little dragon rolled over to the brick and reared her head back.

Fire roared from her mouth, in several different colors simultaneously. Rose watched in awe. She had never seen Virgil do such a thing.

Then the little girl dragon rolled back over to her father and informed him that she wanted up. Up. Up. Up now.

He picked her up. She amused herself by flicking her claw upwards and seizing his hat.

Rose stared at the rock, not daring to touch it because it was doubtless still hot. There was a symbol on there of two wiggly lines, one crisscrossing the other. It did not look like a C, nor like an oblong-shaped fruit.

"What does this mean, Cucumber?" she asked, pointing to it, her heart pounding so loudly that could hear the roar in her ears. "What does this symbol mean?"

The lady was so stupid. It was Cucumber's name.

"Yes, but *how* is it your name?" Rose demanded. "Is it the fruit you were named after? Some sort of English writing, like your parents?"

Stupid! The small female dragon seemed downright scornful. Cucumber's name was Cucumber's name! Cucumber's parents had given her that name, and it was Cucumber's name!

"See?" Mr. Miller said. "That's all she ever says about it."

"*Which* parents?" Rose pursued. "Was it your human parents or your dragon parents?"

Cucumber's *parent* parents! Cucumber was getting really angry!

"*Which* parents are your parent parents?"

The parents that were Cucumber's parents!

"Which ones?"

The parents that were *parents!*

"Which ones taught you to write?"

Cucumber exploded with fury. She would show her! She would show this mean lady!

Memory roared over Rose, a cascade of irresistibility, overlaid with a torrent of frustration and fury that she was fairly sure hadn't been present originally.

She was swimming around in her liquid, comfortably. Her parents moved close, so she could feel their presence.

She was greeting her parents. They were greeting her back.

Her father showed her a picture. This was her name. She would use it to mark things hers after she hatched. They had chosen it just for her. Could she show it to them back?

She showed it to them wrong, the picture.

No, no. She must get it exactly right. This was important, because her brother's name was similar. When it was time to breathe fire, she would do it this way, and that way ...

The memory started to fade. Rose came back to herself gradually, so stunned by the memory that at first she could not remember that she had human arms and no tail that she could swish behind her while swimming through the egg.

Rose breathed in raggedly. Her arms were shaking.

That was a true memory. I cannot doubt its veracity.

As if to confirm this, Cucumber's father's eyes were wide, and he was pulling a notebook and pen from his pocket.

Then the symbol she burns isn't the name of a fruit. It's the name her birth parents originally gave her. Perhaps all of their names were visual, rather than auditory.

But how ... how ... how had Virgil's memories never given her any hint of this? His mother had been highly educated. So if there had been writing, surely she of all people ...

Virgil rolled around in the wagon and poked his head up over the side. The female dragon who he wasn't thinking about and who also didn't exist had weird memories. She was making them up. Dragon parents didn't have names. Nobody had names except for human parents and their babies and also nobody could breathe fire that way. That was silly.

Rose turned around and stared at her son with an open mouth. *What ...?*

How could his memories contradict hers so thoroughly?

CHAPTER 8: VARIANCE

Her first thought was, *Maybe they come from different cultures.* But no, that didn't make sense. The two had been found in the same cave, in the same area.

Her second thought was, *Maybe they come from different classes.* But that didn't make sense either. Virgil's mother, at least, had been educated.

So how could their memories of dragon society have such an irreconcilable variance? She sensed her son's sincerity, and she did not doubt the other dragon's veracity either. But how?

Why would one family have abilities that another did not, names when another did not, perhaps even a written language when another did not?

Unless ...

Rose felt a little dizzy.

She, of all people, should have grasped the implications of this right away. Their two families had not been separated by distance. They had been separated by time.

Deinonychus antirrhopus had lived on Earth for millions of years. Over a span of millions of years, a species could grow and change. A culture certainly would.

Her son had come from a earlier time than Mr. Miller's daughter.

In fact ... her son was evidently a significantly less evolved *Deinonychus* than Mr. Miller's daughter, because she had an ability to control her fire-breathing that he did not.

How much? How much time had separated the two?

Rose's mind flew to Violet. Violet, who remembered the extinction event. The child who lived in the zoo might be the most evolved *Deinonychus* now alive today. Could she control her fire? Had she had a name?

It was almost impossible to be sure. Rose wanted to weep with frustration. Violet's memories of her life before the zoo were so corrupted by this point that they were worthless for anything but the entertainment of the masses.

Had anyone written down the earliest memories the little blue dragon had shared? She profoundly hoped that somebody had been wiser than her.

There will be other dragons, Rose reminded herself, but it was no consolation. The loss of one unique treasure trove of history could not be ameliorated by the discovery of another.

Why had she never realized the magnitude of importance of that which was casually degrading? Why, why, why, why, why?!

All the same ...

Rose slowed her breathing, forcing herself to calm down. All the same, she could be very grateful that she had met these two today.

Cucumber's father was scribbling hastily in his notebook, evidently desperate to capture every detail before they faded from his recollection.

Seeming to find this dull and unremarkable, the green baby girl at his feet was playing with a brown leaf, sucking it in against her mouth and then blowing it out again. At one point, a small spark escaped her nostrils, but it mercifully did not land on the leaf.

The wagon lurched as Virgil dove for the side. That was Virgil's game! The-dragon-that-didn't-exist couldn't play Virgil's game! Virgil wanted to play with that, too!

The crowd roared with laughter at her son's subsequent attempt to fling himself over the side of the wagon, his horrified yowl as he realized that if he landed below he would land on the green girl, and then his vehement complaining about how dragons who didn't exist shouldn't be playing with his leaves and toys and wagons. It wasn't fair!

Cucumber kept on playing with one leaf and then another, seemingly oblivious to the whole tantrum.

At last, Mr. Miller let out a long sigh as he completed his task and replaced the notebook in his pocket.

"That was a new memory," he said.

"I gathered," Rose nodded.

Mr. Miller's forehead creased with hurt as he stared down at his daughter, who pounced at a wind-blown leaf with claws extended. "She's never even given us the slightest *hint* of that memory before. Why wouldn't she tell us?"

"Maybe she didn't remember it until now," Rose said. "It might have been been one of her earliest memories. It might have been one that was already fuzzy by the time she started to hibernate. Sometimes ..."

She hesitated, because she could not think of a way to phrase this that didn't make her look bad.

"Sometimes," she said at last, "when I have had ... ah ... disagreements with my younger sisters, an argument has brought certain details back into sharp clarity that had been previously forgotten, such as who had stolen whom's best winter stockings six months previously."

She did not add that the culprit in that case had been her.

Mr. Miller looked intrigued. "You mean, becoming upset prodded her into remembering something old she had almost forgotten?"

"Most likely," Rose said. She added wryly, "Not that that would be a reasonable approach to apply deliberately. Unless, of course, it could be employed by someone who knew how to do it in such a way that would not inappropriately upset the subject of study ..."

The idea was intriguing! *Could* the strategy be used in some appropriate way? Rose's eyes brightened as she considered the possibilities.

The man laughed out loud. "You're a strange woman, Mrs. Wainscott."

Rose stared at him, startled. Chagrin flooded her, and she lowered her face. "Am I?"

"Oh, I don't mean that in any bad way," Mr. Miller said hastily. "I'm sure you're a great mother."

"Am I?" Rose said quietly. That was not something she felt sure about at all.

"Ah ..." Mr. Miller bit his lower lip. He suddenly seemed to realize that he had wandered into a dangerous subject. His eyes flicked back and forth, perhaps hoping for a conversational aid from the crowd.

But the crowd was of no help to him. There were howls of deafening laughter as Cucumber blew a leaf up into the air, it landed on Virgil's face, and the baby boy let out a furious tirade about how the wind had blown the leaf up into his face, and the wind had stolen his wagon, and the wind was really mean, and—oh, hey, now he had a leaf!

"I think anyone can be a good parent," Mr. Miller said quickly. "You just have to find a way to use your own strengths for your children's benefit."

Rose gave him a look of polite disbelief. She did not think her own strengths translated at all to being a good parent. That was why she felt so inadequate at it.

"It's true! I'll give you an example," the man said, stumbling over his words in his haste to correct his accidental faux pas. "You're good at ... uh ..."

"Paleontology," Rose said dryly. She failed to see how that had any relevance to nurturing living beings.

"There you go!" the man said with relief. "You know all about dragons! That has to translate to being very good at taking care of him, right?"

"I am not a nurse," Rose said, with some annoyance.

"I didn't say you *were*. But ... correct me if I'm wrong, but isn't that the field with people who dig up fossils? Like the ones who found Cukie's egg?"

"Yes," Rose said.

"I've been told that takes a lot of patience. And a lot of being careful about every tiny detail. Is that the case?"

"Yes. It is a highly methodical discipline."

"Well, don't you think that patience and being very careful are strengths that can be useful in parenting?"

Rose stared at him.

And stared at him.

She had never been particularly patient with Virgil. And she had never thought her detail-oriented mindset to be an advantage when dealing with him, because it led to such frustration when she could not control the actions of a living being, and that being's actions all too often resulted in a chaos she had to clean.

She had been measuring herself by the standards that she believed all mothers had to measure up to, and she had been failing abominably. But perhaps there was more than one adequate template.

Had she ... had she perhaps ... taken the wrong approach with Virgil from the very beginning?

Chapter 9: Virgil

She had made herself a promise all those months ago. A promise to never look upon Virgil as a subject of study. A promise to separate him from her love of fossils and remnants of antiquity, and to see him only as a child who needed loving.

Had she been wrong?

Had she miscalculated?

Virgil's birth mother, the dragon whom Rose so closely resembled, had not particularly wanted to have a child. She'd accepted the surprise grudgingly, and had continued to be rather grumpy at the egg's repeated interruptions. She had not exactly been Rose's idea of an ideal parent.

And yet, she was the mother Virgil had wanted.

That was why Virgil had chosen Rose.

For the exact same reasons that she felt so inadequate.

Rose drew in a deep, shaky breath. If Virgil had wanted her for that very mindset ... *should* she be treating him in a manner that was affectionless and calculating?

She felt like she was dangling over a precipice. It was like the universe held its breath, waiting for her to decide.

Was it better to give Virgil what he had wanted?

Or was that different from what he *needed*?

Rose let out a long, deep sigh.

It would be so much easier to give up on trying to nurture the boy ... and she had a fantastic excuse to do so. But she could not make herself believe that surrendering to what was easiest for her would be to his benefit.

Infants were not always wise. Even if he had chosen her for her weaknesses, that didn't mean she ought to wallow in them.

Still ... there might be a grain of truth in the man's words. In her determination to shield Virgil from her weaknesses, perhaps she had been withholding her strengths from him, too.

Rose laughed wryly, overcome with realization.

On the day they'd first met, Virgil had shown her memories of rejecting many parents. Many, many, many, many parents. Because they were not exactly like the ones he remembered, and he wouldn't take new parents unless they were exactly like his old ones. And why had he never found an exact equivalent until Rose?

Because someone like the two of them would not have gone looking for a child to adopt in the first place.

Rose shook her head, still laughing at the irony of her son's absurdity. No wonder he was so old, compared to Cucumber. Perhaps he was one of the oldest *Deinonychus antirrhopus* eggs that would hatch. He had been waiting for a very long time to find a mother who didn't want him. Because only a mother who didn't want him could possibly do.

She had to laugh, because otherwise she would start to cry, and if she started to cry, she wouldn't stop. Why had Virgil put her in this impossible situation? Choosing her precisely because she was the wrong person?

"... Mrs. Wainscott?" Mr. Miller asked, looking concerned.

Rose quickly shook herself, realizing she was surrounded by people. Fortunately, the crowd seemed thoroughly absorbed in watching and laughing at the antics of the babies, and the babies were so absorbed in goofing off to entertain the eager crowd that they were paying no attention to their parents. She had not expected to be grateful for the raucous mob, but ...

Silently, Rose observed the infants that the crowd found so amusing.

Virgil was now whacking his tail at leaves that "the wind" blew up at him, chattering eagerly about how whacking his tail at leaves was fun. Cucumber, meanwhile, was blowing leaves up at the wagon, commenting at how funny it was that "the wind" kept sending them flying in strange directions.

It seemed the two of them had found a way to play together after all, still without acknowledging the other's existence.

A slight smile curled on her lips. Her son was certainly strange, and the boy could be entertaining.

And with that faint amusement came a sense of peace that surprised her. It was not what she would have expected at this moment, yet it was there.

Perhaps ...

Perhaps it didn't matter that she was so unqualified to be the best sort of parent. Any mother Virgil would have chosen would have been exactly like her.

Perhaps it didn't matter that she had messed up so many things.

Perhaps the only thing that mattered was that he had chosen *her,* and she could choose to get better.

"Mrs. Wainscott?" Mr. Miller ventured again.

Rose tried to ignore the stab of irritation at his intrusion into her thoughts. He had helped her realize several things today, after all.

She drew in a deep breath. "I am fine, Mr. Miller. It was simply ... something I had not considered. Thank you for the insight. I will think upon it further."

"Oh, good." He looked relieved.

The rest of the visit with Cucumber and her father remained uneventful, with Mr. Miller carefully avoiding any subjects that resembled the one that had made her emotional, and Rose succeeding in extracting no new memories from either dragon, despite her repeated and fruitless attempts to interest them in being interviewed instead of playing with "the wind."

Eventually, after an hour had passed without their moving any farther down the sidewalk, Mr. Miller remarked on the time and they made their farewells, to the groaning disappointment of the crowd around them. It was not comprised of all of the same people who had been there at the beginning, but it had swelled to more than five times the original size, nonetheless.

As she turned towards the apartment to go back home, shivering as a brisk breeze picked up, Virgil complained vehemently from in his wagon. He was cold and he wanted to play more with the wind and now the wind was all gone.

Rose snorted, brushing the strands of hair out of her mouth that a puff of chill air had blown in there.

Also he was hungry. Virgil was hungry! Virgil wanted to eat chicken, chicken, chicken, all by itself!

"For crying out loud, Virgil," she said in exasperation, wanting to kick herself for forgetting that playing out in the cold would make him hungrier than playing indoors or staying under a warm blanket. "You can wait till dinner."

Virgil wanted chickennnnnnnnnn!

"You weren't so hungry while you were playing with that green girl dragon," Rose said acerbically.

Virgil didn't know what his mother was talking about. Green girl dragons didn't exist. He had been playing with the wind.

"You were playing with a green girl dragon, and you know it."

No! Virgil had not been! Virgil's mother was being mean!

"Virgil's mother does not approve of self-deception," Rose retorted, glancing back at the wagon as she walked briskly forward. "Virgil's mother thinks that he can play with whoever he wants, but it's ridiculous to pretend he didn't."

Virgil had been playing with THE WIND!

"Honestly!" Rose said, shaking her head at the memory of the two dragons' fear of one another. Interesting as it had been at first, the situation had quickly devolved into sheer absurdity. "Can you imagine what would happen if humans acted that way?"

Humans *did* act that way!

"No, we do not."

Yes, they did!

"No, we don't."

Yes, they did! Virgil's mother acted that way about Ophelia's parents! That was why Virgil never got to play with Ophelia!

Rose froze.

Anyway, Virgil hadn't been playing with a green girl dragon. He had been playing with the wind.

Rose closed her eyes and touched her forehead with her free hand. She stood still, holding the wagon handle with her other. *It isn't just their color. It's also that they're so polite that if I made some terrible faux pas, they wouldn't tell me. I don't know the rules of propriety, and if I made mistakes ...*

And THE WIND was fun, and THE WIND had blown the leaves around, and Virgil had been playing with THE WIND ...

"All right, Virgil!" Rose shouted, spinning around to glare at her son. "I get the message! I'll ask for the Lawrences' phone number when we get home, and I'll call them! Are you happy?"

Virgil stared up at her from the wagon. No, he wasn't happy. He was hungry. Playing with the wind had made him hungry. Could he have chicken, chicken, chicken, all by itself? Also, he hadn't been playing with a green girl dragon. Green girl dragons didn't exist.

Chapter 10: Vitamins

When Henry walked in the door, he stopped abruptly and held his nose.

"What is that smell?!" he cried.

"Liver," Rose said, coming out of the kitchen. Her hands were covered in red juice from chopping up chicken livers. She hadn't yet washed them.

"Why are you cooking liver?! I hate liver!"

"It's for Virgil," Rose said. "Advice from the Lawrences. Mrs. Lawrence said that organ meat is usually cheaper, and it tends to contain more vitamins."

"There's a reason why it's cheaper! It's disgusting!"

"You don't have to eat it," Rose said. "But it's nutritious for him, and it might be the solution to our budgetary problems."

Henry held his nose. "Could you at least not *cook* it?"

Virgil rolled out of the kitchen and into the living room, a blackened lump dangling from one side of his mouth.

Rose began, "I didn't—"

Hello! Virgil was saying hello to his father! He had made up a fun game of singe-the-prey because somebody—that was, somebody-that-didn't-exist—had shown him her memory of her parents doing it! Prey tasted much better when he breathed fire on it! He was going to do this all the time from now on!

"We've given you cooked meat before, Virgil," Rose said.

But *this* food tasted *much* better when it was black all over, and Virgil could do it all by himself, and that was much more fun! Yummy, yummy, yummy, yummy!

Henry looked woebegone. "So I get to smell charcoal, as well as liver, every day from now on?"

"How about I take him outside to eat the rest of his meal?" Rose said, picking up their son with her messy hands. "He can eat outside whenever he's hungry."

"No ..." Henry sighed heavily, releasing the death grip on his nose. "I've gotten used to the smell of his diapers. I can get used to this."

Rose quirked a smile. "You're a brave man."

"You'd better believe it," Henry said, shaking his head. He walked over and reached out for the happy baby, who eagerly lunged into his arms. "Have you been good for your mother's birthday?"

Rose started. She had nearly forgotten that was today.

Yes! Virgil had been very good! He had gotten to try new food that he liked way better, and his mother hadn't made him eat eggs, and he'd played with the wind, and there hadn't been a dragon that didn't exist —

"Say what?" Henry asked, looking perplexed.

Virgil's tail swung back and forth as he explained that they had gone to the zoo to play with a dragon, only it wasn't a zoo and it wasn't a dragon, it was GREEN GREEN GREEN, but then it had been fine, and there was no such thing as a girl, and anyway it was the wind he had been playing with ...

Henry looked at his wife in absolute bafflement.

Rose bit back a laugh. "It's a long and ridiculous story."

Two days later, on the morning of Valentine's Day, they walked to Rose's parents' house and delivered Virgil to spend the day there.

"Hello, Rose! Hello, Henry!" Rose's mother said, opening the front door to welcome them in. "Hello, Virgil!"

Their son poked his head out of the top of Henry's coat. He had been nestled in there for warmth the whole trip.

Hello! Virgil was saying hello to his grandmother!

"Would you like to help us make Valentines, Virgil?" Rose's mother asked, taking the little dragon from Henry.

Virgil didn't know what Valentines were.

"They're usually heart-shaped —" Henry began.

Virgil LIKED hearts! Virgil's mother had bought him hearts! Hearts were really yummy! Yum yum yum yum!

"Noooot quite the same," Henry said.

Rose wandered to the living room table, where she saw a scattering of paper and printed cards. As Sara leaned over Louise's shoulder to watch what she was writing, a burst of mischievous giggles broke forth from both of them.

"What exactly are you doing?" Rose asked suspiciously.

"Nothing," her two younger sisters chorused.

Given that both of them were in high school, she judged them to have just enough experience to get into a lot of trouble, and not nearly enough good sense to stay out of it. Rose stalked over and plucked the printed card from Louise's hands.

"Hey!" Louise complained.

Rose scanned the card. It seemed like typical, sentimental fare. She couldn't see any especial reason for her sisters' high amusement. "Is Harrison the name of a boy in your school?"

Louise giggled. "Nooooo."

"Is he someone at church?"

Sara snickered. "Nooooo."

"Who is it, then?"

The two girls guffawed.

Rose dropped the card on the table. "Not Harrison Jones!"

Her sisters howled with laughter.

Harrison Jones was the father of Violet, the dragon who lived in the zoo. He was a rough man, single, and fond of drink. Despite the fact that alcohol was illegal.

"You find him attractive?" Rose asked in mystification.

"No!" Louise giggled. "But if he *thinks* I do, maybe he'll marry me and then Violet can be my pet dragon!"

"LOUISE!" Rose shouted. "That is appalling on so many levels, I can't even count!"

Her sisters laughed so hard that they struggled to breathe.

"Try *not* to be preposterously rude to Mr. Jones," Rose scolded. "He has enough troubles in his life already."

That just made them laugh harder.

"Shall we go now?" Henry asked, following Rose into the living room.

"Certainly," she said, giving her sisters one last disapproving glare as she returned to the entrance with her husband. They were still tittering as she gave her mother a hug and promised to come back by dinnertime.

She and Henry exited the building, crunching out into the relative quiet of the sidewalk, flakes slowly drifting around them and filling in the grey churning in the streets by car tires and horse hooves.

"Where's the big Valentine surprise?" Henry asked eagerly.

"We'll be there soon," Rose said. "Be patient."

And I hope it is a present he'll like, she added silently.

Chapter 11: Value

"The museum?" Henry asked as she turned to enter its doors and beckoned for Henry to follow. "What are we doing here?"

"We're here for Valentine's Day," Rose said. "Trust me."

Looking a little disappointed, Henry followed after her. The two went up floor after floor. At the top of the stairs, Henry started to head for the Hall of Saurischian Dragons, the place where they had met Virgil. But Rose stopped them.

"Not there," she said, pointing. "There."

"The Hall of Ornithischian Dragons?" he asked in confusion.

"We met Virgil in the Hall of Saurischian Dragons," she said. "But you were heading to the Hall of Ornithischian Dragons at the time. I used to spend equal amounts of time in both rooms. If it hadn't been for Virgil, we might very well have met that same day while you were sketching the wings of a *Stegosaurus.* We can think of it as our place."

For a heartbeat, Henry was silent.

Rose swallowed. *Does he not like ...?*

Henry smiled, at last. "I can see that," he said. "Well, then, let's go into our place."

They walked into the room hand in hand.

Together, they admired the fossils, taking their time and discussing every detail they saw. Henry had a remarkable eye, and described interesting details of shape and theories about dragon colors that she had not thought to consider before.

At last, they reached the end of the room.

"Well ..." Henry said, looking around.

"Wait," Rose told him, holding up her hand. "There's one more thing."

"One more thing?" he asked.

"Yes," she nodded. "I'll be right back."

She hurried out of the room and walked briskly down the hallway to Mr. Teedle's office. She had told him to expect her at around this time, and he had told her he would stay either on or near his office until he saw her.

Fortunately, when she knocked on his office, her oldest friend was sitting there, filling out a form.

"Hello, Miss Pal—Mrs. Wainscott," he said, smiling. "Do you want the present?"

"Yes," she nodded.

He reached behind his desk and picked up a box of sand. It was not very large, but because of all the sand filling it, it was heavy. "Can you manage on your own?"

"I'll manage," Rose said, taking it from him. "Thank you for holding it for me."

"You're very welcome. I hope he likes it."

It was heavier than she'd expected, but she managed to carry it down the hallway back to the Hall of Ornithischian Dragons, where Henry was waiting. From the back, she could see that he had pulled his sketchbook out of his pocket and was penciling the curve of a duck-billed dragon.

Rose set down the box, wanting to wait for him to be done with the *Anatotitan*. She tried to be quiet, but it made a rather loud *thump*.

Henry turned around. "Oh! You're back!"

He put the sketchbook away.

Rose swallowed. This was the important part. This was the part she had spent all of yesterday preparing.

"I ... I love paleontology," she said. "As a child, my fascination started from the concept of digging up buried treasure. So I thought ... I would share that with you. Your present's in here."

"In the sand?"

"Yes."

"I'm supposed to dig in the sand?"

"There's a brush in here somewhere," Rose said hastily. She ran her hands through the sand until she found it, and then pushed the sand back over the top.

Henry looked bemused. He took the brush from her and knelt down next to the box. Then he brushed the sand away, not nearly as carefully as he should have, but the contents were not fossils, so she wouldn't say so.

He found a drawstring cloth bag and carefully shook the sand off of it. Then he opened it. Inside was a notebook.

Looking puzzled, Henry opened the notebook to reveal pages of Rose's tiny, tidy handwriting. Grains of sand rolled down and fell into the box.

"I recently realized that we should be recording Virgil's memories," Rose said, as he flipped silently through the pages. "Because that will be of value. But then I realized that there's something even more important, and that's our memories of each other. So ... this is our story from the past year. Every detail I remember. Which is to say, not everything, but a lot. I'm fairly certain I got all the dates correct, for instance. I have a better memory for details than most. I thought maybe I should use the things I'm good at to benefit you."

Henry was saying nothing. He was just flipping through pages.

Rose felt a lump in her throat. Did he not like it? She was terribly worried. She hadn't spent much money on this. Suppose Henry thought she was being cheap?

Henry put his hand over an blank square of space she had left in a corner. "There are empty spots," he said.

"I thought you might want to draw pictures there."

Henry looked up. There were tears in his eyes.

"Thank you," he said. "It's a great Valentine's Day present."

Rose let out a deep breath. "Oh, good! I wasn't sure!"

Henry laughed.

"If you want to, we could make this a tradition," Rose said. "Every Valentine's Day, we come here and we share the past year's memories we've made together. Not our memories of Virgil, just ... us."

"I'd like that," Henry said, holding the notebook tight across his chest. "I'd like that a lot."

"We could do the same thing for Virgil's birthday, too," Rose went on quickly. "I could write things down, and you could draw the way things look in his memories —"

"Shhh." Henry put his finger on Rose's lips. "No Virgil right now. Just ... us."

Author Note

Recording one's family stories is very important. Everything else pales in comparison, except for having the experiences that form those stories in the first place.

Perhaps it's not surprising that my idea of a romantic Valentine's Day present is a book.

ABOUT THE AUTHOR

EMILY MARTHA SORENSEN writes fantasy and science fiction books with realistic paths to a happy ending. She considers all her books clean, with zero swearing and not much violence, but the romance between married couples can be PG-13.

She likes clever characters with unique personalities who charge straight through her plot and spend it spinning wildly off the rails. (Those brats.)

She likes magic systems with strict rules and intriguing limitations.

She likes romance after the happily ever after. That's where the relationship begins!

She likes plot twists that will make your jaw drop.

She likes hope and fun and humor.

She likes darkness that exists only to help characters grow towards greater light.

She likes—

Wait, where did those uncooperative protagonists put the plot *this* time? They just ran off with it, cackling maniacally!

Well, she hopes they'll leave you grinning.

You can find her books at http://www.emilymarthasorensen.com.

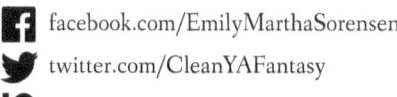

facebook.com/EmilyMarthaSorensen

twitter.com/CleanYAFantasy

patreon.com/emilymarthasorensen

ADDITIONAL COPYRIGHT INFORMATION

- "Weredodo Movie Night" originally appeared in this collection.
- "Weredodo Sleuth" originally appeared as a chapbook in March 2019.
- "Weredodo Stage Magician" originally appeared in this collection.
- "What Is Real, What Is True" originally appeared in this collection.

www.ingramcontent.com/pod-product-compliance
Lightning Source LLC
Chambersburg PA
CBHW050137120726
47903CB00002B/388